A novella by Alice Nunn appeared in *Mirrors*, an anthology published by Women's Redress Press in 1989.

Her first full-length novel was *Illicit Passage* published by Women's Redress Press in 1992. Illicit Passage was short-listed for the 1994 Tiptree Award in America.

In 1999 *Stella's Stripes* was published by Fagus Tasmanian Press.

Thanks to Rosalie for her suggestions and help with West Indian dialogue.

Many thanks to Kath who read the first draft and to Ros and Salty for comments and corrections on the final draft. Thanks to Gordon from Workhorse Design Group for help with the cover.

Alice Nunn

SAIL ON

Published by Fagus Tasmanian Press
fagus.com.au

All of the characters in the novel are fictional and any resemblance to any person living in the West Indies in 1969 is coincidental and unintended.

Chapter 1

Sail about a little and see the watery part of the world

It happened in the dead of night. A body plummeted downward and embedded itself in a late model Hillman Hunter parked on a concrete driveway. Glass smashed, organs ruptured, blood disgorged, shrapnel filled the air, bits flew into garden beds and fanned out across the parking bay, ricocheting off plant pots and palm fronds. Then the car, which had bounced like something woken from sleep under the shock of the impact, gradually settled back into stationary immobility. For a few more moments there was seeping and distending but then all activity ceased and the night returned to peace.

Now here's a strange thing. Nobody heard it. Why was that? An hour or so earlier the whole neighbourhood had been woken by someone screaming - everywhere lights had been switched on and curtains twitched. But the screaming stopped as abruptly as it had started and after people had muttered domestically for a while and there was nothing further to disturb them but the usual background hum of tropical frogs and insects, everyone went back to sleep. Not a single one of them registered the smash of body on car.

What would it have sounded like? Loud I would have thought - a cannon-roar of metal and a cymbal-clash of glass - very loud in fact. So loud that it <u>should</u> have set every Doberman in the district barking because after all the force of it destroyed the car. But as I said, nobody heard it. Very strange.

I remember that night. Even through a fog of alcohol it was a memorable night. It was a night of storms. At one point I was drenched to the skin in a strenuous tropical downpour when everything was flickering light and water. So the question logically arises, was there thunder? I don't actually remember. But I think there must have been, although at the time the body fell I would have been in bed and dead to the world (if that's not a tactless thing to say in the circumstances). But I would assume there probably was thunder: it's the only explanation that makes sense. The body falls, the lightning flashes and there is a sound like a thunderclap. Case solved.

It was all so long ago. I was 17, some other person, a total stranger. I am going to tell you the story of this stranger and it starts some weeks before the night when the man died. I never knew the dead man and yet his fall from the cliff had an impact on my life as it did on the lives of many others. Sometimes I wake in the throes of a nightmare, remembering the terror and all the ramifications that spread and engrossed so many people after that night. But at the time the story started, the man was still alive and still ignorant of his fate. Who knows what he was doing on the evening I arrived on the island. Perhaps he was at an evening class. Or maybe he was home reading a very long book from the public library.

They say - those who have come back from the dead - that your whole life flashes in front of you. But is that the bit you've already lived or is it the bit you would have lived if you weren't just then in the process of dying? Maybe the nearly dead, as they sink into the abyss, see all of the future they never had and realise they're never going to finish re-upholstering that chair or find out what happened to Ahab and the great white whale. Is it regret they feel or is it relief? Life can be a dull affair.

But coming back to my story. The best place to start is probably the dawn of the day after I first arrived. It's still dark and I haven't a clue where I am except that the dull gleam to my left tells me I'm beside water. The path ahead is wispy like a scrawl of smoke and I think I, she, this stranger, yes this land ancestor from 35 years ago, is sobbing. Or is that just the roosters breaking day, croaking and crying out?

She is not alone, even though it is barely dawn. There is a man standing there too but at that point she hasn't seen him. He's an old man newly risen from his bed and is idly scratching himself beside the lagoon. He's old enough to know about the weight of lives past and the flimsiness of lives future and sometimes here on the verges of dawn he hears a whispering siren calling him - a waterbeast blowing its breath very quietly like a sob. He hears the sob, very very quiet. There it goes again - grief croaking like a wadded cough. He turns his head to look along the track and sees through the gloom of night a figure in a light coloured dress walking towards him.

A paleness is starting to make solid shapes on the face of the water. There is an oyster-shelled luminescence like a swipe of soft jelly and things are starting to flap. Panic is rising, something urgent, something has to be done – yes, the roosters can see the white shape forming and greet it with beating cries and sharp lamentations and all the hope and terror that announces the start of another day.

I can now see with a biographer's eye that this whole story is what one would call an adventure, the kind of exciting action yarn you love until you get landed in the middle of one in reality. I can tell you quite definitively that by the end I didn't want adventures any more - I don't like the real stuff at all. Even at that point, before I'd experienced heartbreak, shipwreck and murderous assault, I was a lot less sure that I wanted to be a foot-loose free-falling heroine subject to the whims of fate. In fact, I was longing already for a nice safe bed in a safe house with some safe people. Let's face it, all those seductive propositions such as -"What could be more romantic! Out all night under the stars, in the soft warm air of the Caribbean" - well they're rubbish. It hadn't been soft and it hadn't been warm and no-one had told me that it would feel so bad.

But to continue. This young girl comes forward in the grey fog, on the verges of dawn, sob. And worst of all the light is now increasing at tropical breakneck speed, whishing and hissing up like a venetian blind until almost instantly she finds she is visible and she can see the man ahead of her on the path and she knows he can also see her. So she has to pull herself together and concentrate on making a dignified passage to wherever it is that she will end up going.

There she is, a heroine despite herself, whose first act of heroics is to stick an uncertain smile on her wobbling face as she goes to pass the old man. Well done so far, but oh horror, with an awful sinking feeling she realises the man is going to speak. His chin goes up in the air and he seems be gesturing back in the direction she has come, "Whaa-aaahm?" The way the sound emerges indicates that it is probably a question but it conveys no meaning to her whatsoever.

"What?" she says. "Sorry?" Trying to be polite but her brain is stuffed with noisy dry straw, barely functioning.

The man then turns and points to a rowboat which is pulled up on the mud. He jerks his thumb in the direction of the bay, talking at the same time. Now she understands some of what he is saying - he is offering to row her somewhere.

"How much?" she asks.

"20 cents" she thinks he says and she repeats it. Yes, she has heard it right. 20 cents local currency, that is just over a shilling on her reckoning. She instantly decides, yes, let him row her somewhere, anywhere, it doesn't matter so long as it is far away and somewhere else. Not that she can necessarily afford even such a small amount. How much money has she got? She thinks she has $14. About £4.

While she stands awkwardly on the shore worrying about her finances, the old man pushes the boat out until it is mid-calf deep and then gestures to her. Dumbly she takes off her sandals and feels her way through surprisingly cold water and slimy feeling mud and climbs in. The man gives the boat a big push outwards and scrambles to his seat in the middle. Then, getting settled, he takes up the oars and starts to pull.

What a strange cargo she makes, that young girl perching there in her leafy foreign dress like some exotic fruit, being rowed across the yellowing water by a man sitting in front of her who she can't quite look at because it doesn't seem polite to look at a man who is working for such a small sum as 20 cents. He pulls smoothly and strongly despite his age and they skim across the lagoon as she sits with foggy eyes trying to peer ahead past his working black arms, wondering what she is coming to.

What can I tell you about this young girl? Not a great deal. Her name is Lynnette, not a name I care for but most people call her Lynn. I am not aware of her having a thought in her head at that time, I can't remember any. She chose George Harrison as her favourite Beatle for no particular reason except that everyone had to choose one. She had no other opinions. So I present to you a completely blank human being and apologise in advance to those who are embarrassed by the stupidities of others, but what can I say? In her defence, she was very young and never had an adventure before, or met a monster.

She met Ed at the Port Sophia yacht club where Mrs Walpole, her mother's second cousin, had taken her to have tea with a retired Rear Admiral. Mrs Walpole said, in her precise loud diction, that one got a Better Class of Person at the yacht club. Meaning, I suppose, that it was expensive to park a boat in such a place and that therefore only the crème de la crème would be found in its hallowed club rooms. Unfortunately Mrs Walpole made this remark before meeting Ed and Mrs Walpole thereafter formed the opinion that in fact Ed was not a Better Class of Person. But he seemed to be bosom pals with her Rear Admiral and he had a boat and he was at the club and all of this made it hard for Mrs Walpole to establish reasons why Lynn should not go for a little sail with him.

Experiences in Port Sophia had been carefully selected up until then. Mrs Walpole was a widow whose husband had had major business interests in the West Indies and she continued to live there even though Teddy had been dead for some years. She was rich and middle-aged and the others of her set were also rich and elderly. And white. Or should that be White? I can't remember now whether we gave it a capital W or not.

Lynn learned from Mrs Walpole that there was a precise array of racial characteristics under the category of Coloured (which definitely had a capital C). Coloured ran the gamut from the very dark to the not dark at-all-at-all, because it included everyone who was not officially and certifiably European. At the top there were the light-skinned who would probably be bank clerks and shop assistants, even managers. It would probably be OK to meet and shake hands with that sort of person. Since Independence they had, in Mrs Walpole's words, been Coming Through into quite high positions. It was now politic to mix civilly at functions with the upper portion of this group.

Then there was the medium class of skin colour. Not so dark, not so light. These were domestic servants, taxi drivers, and so on. Below them were the very dark. Black shiny-skinned people with flat noses - Mrs Walpole indicated with a downward gesture of her lips that these were beyond the pale. In her view, anyone who was that dark belonged to the criminal classes and she would never, ever, have left Lynn alone with such a person.

Lynn found Mrs Walpole's strictures on all this irksome. However I wouldn't want anyone to think that this sense of irritation meant that Lynn had precociously acquired some advanced racial consciousness. No, she just wanted to dance.

Mrs Walpole took her to cabarets to watch entertainers walk on red-hot glass and limbo under impossibly low poles. After the show was over and while Mrs Walpole was still finishing her drink and chatting, possibly to Mrs Sunderland her especial friend, or to Mr Miller a rather gallant old ex-planter, Lynn would see exotic creatures in shining flamboyant clothes take to the floor and dance. It seemed to her that the passing parade in Port Sophia brought together a fascinating mix - a shuffling together of African Negro, East Indian, Chinese and swarthy Spanish-Americans with a good splash of European, which resulted in a patchwork of blacks, browns, tans, sandy-coloureds and skins pale like double cream. She thought some of them beautiful. And they all swayed together with a vibrant sensuousness that astonished Lynn who had been taught to carefully walk the floor in an arranged pattern touching in only the most formal way. And now she wanted to dance, it was as simple as that. "I wish someone would dance with me." It was a wistful thought and I suppose a dangerous one because she meant, "I wish someone would dance with me like that." But her partners were usually Mr Miller or some other old friend of Mrs Walpole, never the other sort of person, never the sort of person who danced ecstatically to a different edge of the rhythm.

Mrs Walpole would leave shortly after the dancing started unless it was at the Country Club, because otherwise, "You never know who you're getting in a place like this." She would lead the way firmly towards the exit and Lynn would follow dolefully, hemmed in by the protective curtain of Mrs Walpole's crisp wide-skirted print frocks and her cries of, "Keep up Lynnette." At other times too she would bob behind as Mrs Walpole strode with supreme unconscious self-possession through the down-town throng, carefully bestowing her favours - a smile and a wave to her Eurasian hairdresser, a nod of recognition and maybe a word to her husband's ex–accounts clerk and others of that ilk, and as for the rest not even a second glance.

That was going to be Lynn's downfall, giving a second glance.

Mrs Walpole lived in a large walled-in Spanish-style house behind high iron gates. Thick trees provided a constant lattice of shade; a fan thumped rhythmically on the ceiling all day - but still it seemed as if a fug of heat inhabited the house among the heavy drapes and furnishings. Mrs Walpole never gave in to the heat though. Her rigid starched dresses were always worn over stockings as if she still inhabited the temperate climate of England and to Lynn's astonishment she sometimes even rounded off her ensemble with a light jacket or cardigan. Two Coloureds, women at the paler end of the middle spectrum called Nellie and Billie, came in each day to do the housework and cooking. Most of the morning was taken up with Mrs Walpole vigorously engaged in telling Billie what to clean and Nellie what to cook.

One such morning shortly after Lynn arrived, when she felt she could no longer bear it in the house, she announced that she would go out and walk in the big park nearby. Mrs Walpole wouldn't hear of it. Go out? On your own! A world of danger for the young white girl it was intimated - unimaginable frightening experiences beyond the safe front door. So Lynn stayed in and read worthy novels tunnelled by silverfish or wrote ungrateful letters, We never DO anything.

Of course they did do things but not things that Lynn wanted to do. Every day they went out to lunch, or they had people in to lunch and if there was no social event of that kind they would go to the Hilton Hotel or the Country Club or somewhere similar. These were places where the right people went and where behaviour had to be always correct. To walk through the rain from the Hilton's swimming pool to the public phone in the reception area it was necessary to wear a towel over one's bikini, no matter that the towel got wet. That was the kind of life it was.

Mrs Walpole was kind enough but here's the irony - at that time Lynn longed and longed for adventure. She longed to meet people her own age, she longed for something more than a life with careful rules and set observations. Which is why she called Ed and said, "I'd love to come for a sail."

He said, "We'll see you at eleven o'clock on Friday morning."

She never thought, it never entered her head to ask, "Exactly who do you mean by 'we'?" She imagined he meant the royal we, the social we, we the in-crowd, the lolling laughing burst of voices that you would get when you went sailing with someone as popular as Ed. But if she had known then what I know now, would she have stopped and drawn back? How can I tell, with a girl who is so very young and so very very stupid. Sometimes such people will plunge in regardless and leave posterity to pick up the pieces.

The rowboat emerges from the lagoon into a greater bay beyond. It is full daylight and any minute the sun will appear from behind the eastern mountain and she can now see what she'd sailed past in the dark the previous night. The bay they enter curves in a big 'U' like a breakfast coffee cup with the lagoon as the handle at one side. Dead centre in the curve of the bay is quite a sizeable town stretching up the hill. "What's the name of that?" she indicates.

"Fort Jahn," says the man in his broad accent and laughs with cracked breath as if he is amazed at her ignorance. Or maybe he is just happy. Happy because they are nearly there. It becomes obvious as he pulls with one oar that he isn't ferrying her into the town but is heading just around the point where the lagoon enters the bay, towards a colourful tribe of boats that congregate together. She can already hear the gentle hollow thumping noise they make, as if even in the calm water of early morning the hulls are straining to be together. Above decks their spreaders are like a mad party waving bunting and below they are sighing and creaking and making bumping washy comfortable noises to each other.

The old man ships his oars cheerfully and they glide up to a landing. They have arrived. Yes, but where am I? But she can't say that in case it makes him laugh even more. She gives him 20 cents and climbs stiffly and clumsily up a ladder onto the pier. She thinks it must be the yacht club, a sort of provincial version because it doesn't look anything like the one in Port Sophia. It's a little down at heel, there is a slightly rakish lean to the posts and a distinct unevenness to the slatted piers and board walks.

There had been talk the previous evening about not having enough money for a berth - with accusing looks at her, what with the other costs of the trip! So she wonders if she is allowed to go in and she quakes as she can't bear any more unpleasantness. But the man in the boat is still there and she can't tell him he's made a mistake and she really meant for him to row her to town, so there is nothing for it but to walk purposefully forward as if she knows where she's going.

Then she realises she does know where she's going, the moment she sees it - a brick building with a door labelled Ladies. She plunges in, into its sour tropical smell of fetid matter and feels such relief - any lavatory however rancid would have been a source of joy and this is quite clean despite its bad-drain background smell.

It is wonderful, even though her bowels are not so bad now, to be on land, to sit at ease and give in to their aching insistence without any fear and with no-one to hide from. And there are leaves of crisp toilet paper there to be used with no feeling that she is taking what is someone else's.

In the same block are showers. There is a notice inviting users to put money in a meter for hot water but there are no warnings like at the Port Sophia yacht club - These Facilities for Members Only. So nothing to lose, she thinks. If someone objects, well she'll be clean already if she's quick. And then, what can they do? She finds a half-used cake of soap in one of the cubicles and stands under the cold water - so far so good - and she washes her hair with the soap and then because the coast is still clear she washes her underclothes and her only dress while she is at it and puts on her bikini. She has no towel - it never entered her head to travel with a towel.

The sun has cleared the mountain and is now falling directly on to the eastern wall of the shower block and she goes dripping into its hot yellow light and hopes that no-one will tell her off for being in just her bikini. She sits drying her hair, with her clothes discreetly hung out on a railing. No one speaks to her, no one tells her to go away. Gradually she relaxes. She sits with her head on her knees, clutching her ankles and looking down at the slightly greasy movement of sea beneath the pier, as she contemplates fate and the disastrous ends of things.

"This is Ursula," said Ed. Ursula had white blonde hair and an accent, Danish did she say, or Dutch?

Things didn't happen in quite the way Lynn expected because instead of being ready to set off straight away it seemed that there was shopping to do. Ursula said the two of them would go to the supermarket and at the time she found the notion quite exciting, another new experience. They took a route-taxi to a low metal and concrete shed which was so frigidly air-conditioned that going inside was shock-cold on the skin. Then down row after row she followed Ursula, who pushed a trolley and kept up a constant explanation of "We'll need some of that and we'll need some of this" while Lynn just blinked and stared.

As I said, this was a new experience and Lynn had never been in a supermarket before. You find that surprising? Well, it wasn't that she was particularly sheltered from the realities of food shopping but it was still only the late Sixties and most food shops that she was familiar with had counters and scales that weighed things and vans which delivered. However, even though she knew nothing about supermarket shopping it did look to her to be a huge trolley load, which seemed to indicate that there were going to be lots of people. At least half a dozen, probably more, although Ed's boat wasn't really all that big. She was quite happy to squash up however and if it was going to be a madcap party it wasn't likely that anyone would get much sleep anyway.

Eventually the process of food gathering appeared to have finished and they drew near a bench where people were putting their purchases - clearly this was where you paid. She helped Ursula get all the things out of the trolley. What a mound, it seemed to go on for ever. As the operator of the cash register started busily ringing things up, Lynn saw a raft of postcards on a stand nearby. She went over to look: yes here were pictures of exotic islands, the kind of islands she hoped they would be going to. Paradise at last. She was rifling through them when she became aware that Ursula was looking over at her. She must be ready to go, thought Lynn. The checkout assistant handed Ursula a long piece of paper. "It comes to $400," said Ursula showing her the bill.

"Wow," said Lynn, "that's a lot." Ursula had bought such quantities of food and expensive stuff too; Lynn couldn't help noticing the price of some of the steak and being astonished. She had been into butchers in London and she doubted that any of her own family would buy such expensive steak except for a special occasion. The postcards however were cheap, cheaper than normal, and on impulse she went back and got a couple. When she returned to the check-out area, Ursula had completed her transaction and wasn't looking at her but down into her handbag where she was busily stowing her chequebook and receipt with a rather red and angry look to her face.

Lynn paid for her postcards and they took a regular taxi back with the bags and bags of groceries. Ursula, who had chatted to her on the way to the supermarket, was now silent but Lynn didn't think much of it. She was excited, anticipating that now they would be going at last. But when they got back to the boat none of the other people had yet arrived and Ed had disappeared. Lynn sat around while the groceries were being sorted and stowed. Ursula seemed a very particular and careful housewife because when Lynn offered to help she got a rather curt refusal. Time passed and the life of the yacht club went on around them. It was well after lunch and Lynn was quite hungry. As she felt strangely unwanted on board, she decided to walk up to the bar - she knew they served light snacks there - and she was looking rather forlornly at the menu, which was more expensive than she had expected, when one of the stewards passed. “Are you the girl who is taking Ed’s boat for a trip?” he asked. “Well, we are all very pleased about that around here,” he said passing on. He was just being pleasant. She didn’t think any more about it and a moment later Ed himself appeared.

“Are we ready to go,’ he bellowed.

“I’m not sure,” she said. She was thinking of Ursula methodically stacking provisions for all the people who rudely hadn’t yet shown up.

“Well let’s just have a quick one to celebrate.” She wasn’t sure exactly why they were celebrating but before she could ask, Ed introduced her to a gin and tonic which was the source of her ruin. She wasn’t used to drinking anything stronger than cider or occasionally wine but she felt she couldn’t say no; it would look like she wasn’t prepared to enjoy herself to the maximum. So she accepted and said, “Just like at a party.” Because she knew that such things were drunk at her mother’s cocktail parties. Yes, a little party, a funny sort of party when they got back to the boat though, where one of the partygoers was looking angry and the other laughing in a merry and uninhibited way and where the rest of the guests had still not arrived even though it was some hours after the time that Ed had nominated.

She had always assumed that there would be others and initially she had been quite relieved at finding Ursula as she certainly never looked on Ed’s invitation as being a personal thing, just him and her, because in any event he was old. Not old like Mrs Walpole but at least old in comparison to herself. Older, an older man but interesting, alive, entertaining, having a huge number of stories that were constantly keeping the habitués of the yacht club in stitches. A man of the world, of the sea, because the skin around his eyes was deeply furrowed from gazing out into the glare and his lips were deeply cracked from salt and sun. He had a jolly jaunty manner and always seemed to exist in a noisy jolly group, which is why Lynn had been expecting a lively trip where everyone would laugh and shout “Ahoy!” a lot and have a good time. Reality however was so completely different.

Sailing has never been about having a good time and I don't know where it got that undeserved reputation. From a mode of transport much given to shipwreck and extreme discomfort, it has somehow metamorphosed into a benign recreation where participants are supposed to get some deep abiding joy from the activity. However Lynn discovered early on the reality of sailing – it's about throwing up and being wet and clinging to a fragile construction of lurching wood.

Though actually the throwing up might not be the sailing - that might have been the gin. Ed insisted, despite Ursula's lowering looks, on them both having another and it tasted oily and unpleasant. Maybe it was that which set her off. Poor Lynn, her first alcoholic vomit and oh so many other memories to embarrass her.

But now she is sitting against the shower block wall and after a while the heat of the sun and the soothing sound of the water evaporate the cloud created by these contemplations. It is hard to believe in a totally bad world when the morning sun is determined to pin the skin down in a pool of pleasure. From under a hedge of damp hair she eventually starts to look around with interest. Now she is used to the comings and goings she decides it is nothing like the yacht club at Port Sophia. More and more people are out and about and there doesn't appear to be anyone checking on them or enforcing a dress code. The whole place is turning into a hive of purposeful activity. On the boats, buckets of sea water are being pulled up and thrown about; young men in nothing but shorts dance up and down and women in short sarongs and bikini tops go here and there with purpose. Everyone has slender limbs like bronzed rope, knotted and muscled and strong. Already the boards of the jetty are hot and the bare-foot padding has turned into a sort of fast jerky shuffle. Two young men stop near her; they both wear long beige shorts and nothing else. "What are you doing?" asks one.

"I'm going to get some breakfast then we're off."

"Good idea. I'll come too."

She watches them head behind a brick wall screened by bougainvillea. Her hair has nearly dried - everything dries quickly now that the sun is full up in the sky. She gathers her underclothes into her shoulder bag, puts her dress back on and follows after the young men. She no longer expects to be sprung upon and thrown out - it somehow doesn't seem that sort of place.

Through an arched gateway she finds herself on the threshold of a large open space filled with tables and chairs. About half the area is roofed and the rest lies under a lattice of dappled shade from two purple flowering trees. Beyond is the edge of the water and wide views towards the main town. There is a lively hum of voices and a clinking and tapping and scraping of plates and glasses and cups from throughout the area.

She isn't able to see a vacant seat anywhere at the edge where she can sit down by herself and be inconspicuous. There are several seats at the bar still vacant and she chooses one as far out of the way as possible. It is time to make plans. What am I going to do?

What indeed, when her stomach has formed a mind of its own. Where's my breakfast - where's my big fried breakfast with eggs and mushrooms and tomato? This is the very same stomach that has spent the last few days throwing everything up - but now it's all forgotten and hunger is begging her to buy the very biggest plate of food the restaurant has to offer. But she can't do anything about such cravings because at last count she only had $14.

It had been her mother's idea for her to come out to the West Indies. Since she left school there had been an ongoing dialogue about what she was going to 'Do' – her future seemed to loom large with everyone except herself. Her father's household had one set of ideas, her mother's household another. She tried to establish her own competency by signing up as a temp with an agency but her parents were agreed at least on one thing - she wasn't going to be allowed to waste her life doing dead-end clerical jobs. She herself had no idea what she wanted to do with her future except live an interesting life and be happy – an ambition that didn't seem to convert into any career that was being thrust before her. In the end her mother decided she would go to finishing school in Switzerland next September.

It wasn't clear to her how the offer from Mrs Walpole had come about - Lynn supposed her mother had written and asked her. Her mother had married young and had become footloose and fancy free for the first time in her late thirties. No doubt a rudderless teenager was an encumbrance to her desire to make up for lost time and so Lynn was parcelled up and sent off to the West Indies.

Her mother paid the airfare because her father would never put in for anything that was her mother's idea. It is the cheapest non-transferable flight available - and she is booked to go back on Friday. Which means she has to get back to Port Sophia in a few days time and she hasn't a clue in the world how she is going to manage that - except through the humiliation of ringing Mrs Walpole and suffering a bout of Told-You-Sos and I-knew-right-from-the-start-about-Ed. She hates the thought of it.

And then when she gets back to England it will start all over again, such a galling end to the adventure. She set off on the voyage so keen, so excited, with some of the postcards half-written: Here I am on a yacht, sailing through the islands! Yes she'd planned to surprise everyone, managing something so enviable on her own: Here I am among tropical reefs trailing my fingers in a blue meadow of water, sipping sensuously on untried fruit, dancing to the suggestive beat of the Caribbean. But instead it is all going to end in failure. The hapless cast-away, got led astray and had to be rescued, and the moral of the story is how essential it is for her to go to finishing school - it will give her a bit of sophistication, stop her always trusting people.

Never Trust People is the lesson she is going to learn in finishing school apparently. That is the lesson she needs in order to become adult - so that she can then travel through life in a hardboiled and suspicious way, knowing that all and sundry will try to take advantage of her. It has never entered Lynn's head up until then that anyone would want to trick or deceive her - but this was based on the reasonable premise that she owned nothing worth being cheated out of. If only people would ask, if only people were straightforward, then trust would not be the dangerous thing that it is made out to be.

Her mother told her not to trust her father. Her father told her not to trust her aunts. Her aunts told her not to trust men in general and especially not her mother's new boyfriend.

The only thing they all agreed on was that her grandmother was NOT a role model to be used where trust was concerned. The fact that Grandma had lived a long and happy life while trusting the whole world was one of those quirks of chance and fate that could not be either explained or repeated. During her life they had all muttered over it. She'll end up dead, or worse, they said. Why, she even gives them money, she's just asking for it - they'll get her one night you'll see. She's never had any sense. She trusts everyone.

Lynn remembers her grandmother fondly, how she used to trot around the homestead in outback Queensland, her baggy old skirt hanging over her big behind. She would come into where the station hands were sitting at table with a loud, "Hello me dears" and look round beaming. "Everyone got everything they need?"

"Yes thanks Mrs T," they would all chorus.

"And here's someone new," she'd say. Producing him like a present. A new face. As if it was something to give thanks for - a stranger among them.

The newcomers could be unshaven young city guys or blank eyed hippies or travellers from foreign lands - all sorts and colours.

"Just passing through. Oh isn't it lovely, life's big adventure," she'd boom. Because she believed that everyone should keep on going to the very edge of an exciting world while they still possibly could. She was old and wise and knew how you lost your freedom in the blink of an eye - how the mechanics of making a living tied you to the earth, how the happy end to fairy stories meant babies crying all night and romance tidied away into a box and diary entries recording nothing more than survival.

Grandma did trust everyone and behind her back her loyal station hands made sure that she never had occasion to become disillusioned. She really believed in youth but she was ignorant of the hard-edged ferrety street-wise sort. She saw each wanderer as a young innocent, tentatively spreading his or her tender wings while hitchhiking the exhilarating roads of life - and that is why they would always be brought home for a comfortable bed and a nourishing hot meal at Grandma's house. Grandma's greatest pleasure was to sail the seas beneath these faltering Icaruses and bring them safely into shore, patch their wings, restore their confidence and send them off again with the message, "The world is a wonderful place, don't believe anyone who tries to tell you any different."

But her children had never imbibed that message with their mother's milk, quite the opposite. Lynn's mother believed she knew everything there was to know about trust gone wrong. "The world is a wicked place," she'd say, "and you must be so careful." People were out there just licking their lips and waiting to eat young people alive. So when Lynn had been sent out into such a world, great care had been exercised. She was seen onto the plane and met off the plane and accompanied here and there. But despite all that planning and care she is now cast away on this island and all because no-one had imagined that she could possibly need any money.

When she said goodbye to her father he had given her ten pounds as if handing over immense riches. Her mother gave her nothing except lots of good advice. She herself had about twenty pounds in her post office account and everyone had thought that would be plenty - more than enough. However it had proved over the course of the last few weeks to be woefully inadequate because while Mrs Walpole was happy to pay for pleasures that she enjoyed herself, she wasn't prepared to subsidise more exciting experiences. Thus, although Lynn was always longing to break free, she really had no way of doing so. In the end, when she finally managed to glue her wings to her back and take off, all she took with her was a large cloth shoulder bag containing her bikini, a few bits of makeup, her toothbrush and her favourite hairbrush with the long thin metal handle. And her purse, with all the money she had left in the world, eighteen dollars.

She puts her purse on the bar in front of her, the better to contemplate her misfortunes. It was a pretty thing once but is now somewhat stained and grubby. Anything made of cloth in the tropics seems to gather an accretion of sweat like a brown tidemark. But close up the pattern of leaves and birds is still visible, a restful symmetry at odds with her surroundings. Activity is swirling frenetically, with people coming and going and noise billowing through the restaurant in waves. Eventually she sees the young West Indian bartender coming down the bar towards her. He apologizes for the delay, "We're flat out this morning. What can I get you?"

Lynn considers the difference between what she would like and what she can afford. "Do you have just bread and butter?" she asks tentatively.

"Certainly do. What to drink?"

"Well just water, do you have cool water?"

"Water!" cries the barman. "We have water alright, though I never saw a person actually drinking it around here. These fellows only recognise it when they're sailing on it."

Another young man sitting further down laughs. "Come on Arthur," he says. "Rum and water, whisky and water, and what about all that water they put in the cat's piss beer."

"Let me tell you, Matey my man," says the barman, "that beer is connoisseur's beer. I hear they drink that beer in bars around New York."

"I know those bars," says the young man. "They tie you up in leather thongs and whip you and hang you upside down and humiliate you no end and then in the final act of kinkiness they give you this glass of yellow stuff to drink!"

Lynn laughs with the others, though she isn't quite sure why the joke is funny, probably because it is nonsensical. The barman goes and puts his head through a hatch. "Ah lord," he says coming back to the young man he called Matey, "this place! The season's now in full swing but he's not putting on extra staff. And the owner came in from Barbados today. On a charter day. And must have Rick go through the books with him."

"Where's Rae?" asks the young yachtie.

"Where's Rae? Ha! Where would you be if you're not being paid? In bed I guess."

"Tough life. Well got to go. Charterers coming aboard any moment, bless their grievance-laden little hearts. Apparently we've drawn the short straw this time. Skip reckons it's going to be a month of hell, so wish me luck."

A number of people are now getting up purposefully, calling goodbyes, plans to meet at such and such a place - exotic islands like on the postcards Lynn bought but hasn't sent. She sits there and drifts, having no place in this scene. She thinks she will just sit and let the air play about her skin from a pleasant breeze coming off the bay. She will just sit and swing her legs a little, almost as if she hasn't a care in the world. She will let the cool of the air float like oil on her irises and smoothly through her nose like a silken skein. Sit here till kingdom come or some other possibility arises.

She'd never been on a sailing boat in her life so how could she know you were supposed to be sick on a particular side of the boat. Well of course if someone had pointed it out she would have realised that it would blow back on deck. And no-one had told her about the toilet thing, the head. How was she supposed to know you had to do things to those levers or else all sorts of horrible things happened? She'd never drunk gin before and she'd never been to sea before, what did they expect?

That was the trouble, they seemed to be expecting something, or at least Ursula was. At one point she heard a strange conversation, rather like a row, going on below in the galley with Ed's voice low and under control but Ursula's boiling with emotion.

"What arrangement did you come to with her?"

Mumble mumble.

"Ed, what arrangement? I've bought all this food - with a cheque Ed."

Mumble mumble.

That was the snippet. She didn't understand it - how could an invitation be suddenly an arrangement? And what did she mean about the food? Such a huge amount of provisions couldn't possibly have been just because of her. Because it was just her. To her surprise, and possibly by then alarm, no-one else had turned up for the trip. Perhaps the other people couldn't come at the last moment. But by the time Ed suddenly cast off she was feeling unwell and it was too late to ask.

She threw up most of that night and for the rest of the time at sea felt wretched. She was so glad when they arrived at last on dry land where her misery might be at an end. And by the time they arrived there were real rows, warfare on board in which the cheque for the food, the cost of berths at the marina and the arrangement all got mixed together. She heard with alarm Ursula say, in response to something Ed had mumbled, "We're not going back, how can we go back, didn't you listen to what I was saying about the food?" But when she thought about it further she realised Ursula must have been talking about something else because how could they not go back to Port Sophia? Mrs Walpole was expecting her back on Tuesday. This is what Ed had said - this is what he had said to Mrs Walpole with his merry smile, "Don't you worry, we'll be back on Tuesday. Or Wednesday, depending on the weather, the winds." He'd waved his arms, encompassing the elements. And Mrs Walpole had made him promise to send a message if they were not to be back on Tuesday.

Lynn had expected they would sail away on Friday morning and be somewhere by that night or the next day - that was what she had expected from talking to Ed. And then they would just cruise around for a few days and come back. Instead they hadn't left until evening and sailed for days, was it? What day is it now? She can't remember. Monday - she is sure it's Monday. It had seemed as if they would never stop. By Sunday she had actually started feeling as if she was being kidnapped but what was the point of that. Ed had finally asked her and she had told him quite plainly: no, she had no money at all. Then Ed said that they were going to stop at St Claire, pointing to the island they were sailing towards. They dropped anchor in a deserted bay and Lynn looked about her and thought maybe the trip was going to be alright after all. Ed went below to make her a sandwich and Lynn was preparing to become convivial but then Ursula started shouting at Ed and when he came up with the sandwich it was clearly in defiance of some edict of Ursula's. Lynn sat there with it in her hand feeling awkward. After that Ed folded his arms and went to sleep while Ursula banged about below deck cleaning and occasionally coming up to shake things aggressively over the side. Something about the situation made Lynn feel nauseous again and she put the sandwich away in her bag.

Suddenly towards evening Ed woke with a flurry and immediately pulled up the anchor. They departed from the bay as the sun was setting. Lynn had no idea why they were sailing along the coast in the dark. Eventually, quite late, they saw lights in a bay. "Perfect," said Ed looking at the starry sky. "Still an hour, we'll do it easy." They slipped through the water like a ghost, shapes loomed and dissolved. A single small sail was all they used as they glided away from the lights into intense blackness at the periphery. Then Ed ran down the sail and Ursula paddled at the water with a pole. Lynn, who was rather short-sighted and didn't see well at night, could at last make out that they had come alongside some sort of jetty.

"Here we are at last, and here comes the moon, right on cue," said Ed while Ursula put down the pole with a bang and stomped away below deck. "Dry land at last. Good isn't it? Come down the road and have a drink to celebrate."

Lynn did feel that to walk on to the land was a cause for celebration, or maybe to walk off the boat was what she was celebrating. To get away from all the turmoil. She felt empty as a drum and so weak she could barely move. Ed however led her along, chatting away, just the two of them. She thought that probably Ursula had stayed behind to cook an evening meal. Lynn realised suddenly that the emptiness she felt was in fact hunger. She thought of eating the sandwich but considered it might look odd with dinner in the offing, plus she wasn't sure if she could manage it in a lady-like way - she feared that she would wolf at it ravenously like a beast. She certainly didn't want to do anything else wretched or humiliating so she left it where it lay, as heavy as lead in her bag, calling to her.

They walked for some way in the dark and then came to a rough tavern that quite frightened Lynn. "Oh it's alright," said Ed. "I've been here before. They're good sorts."

They didn't look like good sorts to Lynn. Drunk men stared red eyed at them out of slack faces and the man at the bar was hostile and curt with Ed. She wanted to leave but Ed seemed quite at ease and ordered her a rum and coke and one for himself and then another and another. "Look at these rings on the bar," he joked. "Know what these are? Yes, moonshine rum I expect, that's what we're doing to our stomachs. Boot-leg rum, yep. Drink up, another over here!" he called. Raw rum from a glass flagon teamed with cola that tasted like warm syrup. "If you ask me it's the cola that leaves the ring, this stuff will corrode metal. Did you know that these coca-cola type drinks have got drugs in them? Yes, some chemist told me that, they've got drugs in them," Ed gulped back his drink notwithstanding. Four to her two, but it seemed to have no effect on him although she was by then feeling dizzy and unfocussed. "They make it out the back I wouldn't wonder. Our stomachs are tough to put up with this stuff. Yes tough," he said looking at his watch. "Now you see, things are like this. Well you see how things are with Ursula. Women you see. It's that time of month you know, not a good time, and she gets some crazy ideas in her head. Anyway you see how things are and she insists that you go. I don't know where she gets these ideas from, she's crazy at times. Hard to understand aren't they, foreigners! Especially when they get excitable. Anyway the situation is, she doesn't want you on board, she doesn't want you going back there and, well, what can I do, women you see."

He rambled on and at some point Lynn went outside and was sick. This time it was not the involuntary letting go that had dogged her on the way over. No, this was some shocked throwing away of an unwanted gift - two rum and cokes from a man who had invited her for a little sail and was now abandoning her. Cast adrift.

When she went back into the tavern he had gone. The men leered at her with stained and broken teeth. She looked about bewildered and then in fright, and went towards the door but her way was blocked by the hard-faced barman. "Now," growled the man, his mouth surly, and he said something she couldn't make sense of.

"What?" She looked at him even more bewildered.

"Three dollar," said the man, she recognised that much.

"What?" she gasped again, uncomprehending.

"Yes," he said. "Three dollar."

It made no sense to her at all. "Three dollars for what?"

"For whaaat!" his voice went up at the end as if in indignation and his hands spread to indicate the bar and all its sorry stains. His voice strained to explain the matter but her brain seemed to have ceased to function.

"But Ed," she indicated the table where they had been and the chair he had sat in, in a helpless sort of pantomime.

The man raised his mouth with a noise as if he was spitting backward into himself. He hooked his thumb out of the main door and whatever the words were it was perfectly clear that the meaning indicated deep contempt for Ed who, as far as she could make out, had cheated him previously. The upshot of it all was a threat that she wasn't leaving till she had paid $3.

Her brain wouldn't tick over, the enormity of the betrayal would not sink in. Ed had gone. Run away while she was being sick and left her to pay for drinks that he had invited her to and forced on her even though she didn't want them. She got out the money for the man in a daze - she no longer had any rational connection with the world; money was just one of the things she no longer had. She was too scared to look as the men crowded around her listening and watching - she bolted for the door. But out in the dark it seemed that other figures lurched and clutched towards her. She cried out and ran. She was terrified. Everything was dark and muttering, every shadow billowed with menace. The moon came out from behind a cloud and she could see the track that they'd come along. She stumbled through the dark until she was nearly back at the jetty. She stood cornered like an animal; her fear of what was behind her was almost greater than her revulsion of what was in front on that loathsome boat. However when her breath and heart calmed, she found she could hear nothing - just a whisper of leaves and the lap of water.

The jetty was a rambling disintegrating collection of rotten wood that went out quite a long way and had an L-bend to it, at the end of which the yacht was moored. On the landward entrance were several thick posts which appeared to have once had some purpose before time and decay had set in. Lynn sat down between them, where she wasn't visible from the boat and was also screened to some extent from the land. Eventually she remembered the sandwich and tried to eat it, because shouldn't it comfort her now she was retched free of everything else? Shouldn't feeding the body, even if it is only a cheese sandwich roughly formed and reluctantly given, fortify a person against absolute despair? If only it didn't taste like ashes. If only it was not hard in her throat like unwanted sobs.

Time passed and the lights on the boat went out and the moon went in behind clouds and she somehow drooped down onto the rotting boards and went to sleep like a bird fallen down from the sky, crippled and abandoned.

The young West Indian bartender comes up with a plate on which is a buttered roll. He puts down a pitcher of water and a glass. "There now," he says. "No chance of you overeating and turning into Mama

Cass. If you only saw the amount that some fellows here eat. Why, it's a source of amazement they can still fit in their clothes. And here's some marmalade. That's fifty cents."

She opens her little purse and pays him. She now counts the rest. $12! So little, how is there so little? The postcards. The drinks. She is sure she had $14 left, but now it appears..... only $12. She starts to eat the roll but her hunger has receded with this new onset of worry. Less than three pounds in the world. And not a soul to help her!

Her mother has instructed her that the world is always willing to help those who are rich. The reason she has to go to finishing school is because then she will know how to act as if she is rich. Thereafter when small cash flow problems arise, there will always be someone happy to help her out. Those who aren't lucky enough to be born beautiful have to learn to act this way if they want to survive. Lynn gathers from these strictures that in her natural unfinished state, being neither beautiful nor rich, she is of no interest to the world and no one will care whether she eats or starves.

The fact is though that children, after they reach a certain age, should take no further notice of anything their parents tell them. Parental advice about the world and the future stopped being useful about the time they replaced steam engines. It was all right back when girls were only supposed to be decorative or had very limited career choices. But by the 1960s everything was changing at the speed of light. Girls were doing all sorts of jobs their parents had never even heard of. Making money their parents couldn't dream of. So what was the point of pretending to be rich when a girl might luck out as a TV producer or a computer programmer or some other new opportunity and actually GET rich?

And another thing. Even if Lynn didn't have the luck to be ravishingly beautiful, she wasn't ignored. People seemed to like her. I can't remember exactly what she looked like back then, those old photos from the 1960s are all so fuzzy and faded. But from what I've been told, she had bouncy blonde hair and a bouncy happy disposition. She was short and round with a snub nose, all ordinary and normal, but when the two young men had been joking earlier she had laughed and her mouth had curved infectiously into a semicircular slit of merriment. The effect this had on those who saw it showed that her mother was quite quite wrong and that the world embraces with enthusiasm pleasant looking girls with merry smiles who are neither rich nor beautiful. Certainly Matey had left with feelings of regret that he was bound for a four week cruise with a retired couple in their seventies while here in port was this little blonde girl, newly arrived and knowing a witty saying when she heard one.

The drifting away of people continues. They shout out messages and farewells. Everybody is going away with things to do and people to be involved with and Lynn is not part of it. She feels depressed. Her spirits sink and everything in her body is pulled downwards, like a paper boat that has got soggy and is giving way. Her chewing gets slower and slower. What on earth is she going to do?

"Now," says the barman leaning on the bar and looking at her half finished roll, "that's the best roll you're going to get round here you know."

She obediently picks it up again. "Everybody's going," she says. "Is there something on, so early?"

"Monday here is charter-day. The rich white tourists, they fly out Saturday and the next lot reach here Monday."

"How do they get things ready in time? With everything closed on Sunday?"

He laughs cheerfully, "Closed! Not round here. Not during the season."

"Is this the season then?" she says.

"November to May," he says. "Then most of the boats go back to the Mediterranean. Before the hurricane season."

"So there are no hurricanes now?"

"Oh yes. Sometimes a hurricane comes along. But it's not the hurricane season. That's the difference. You just reach here?" he asks.

She nods.

"Off a boat?"

"Chucked off a boat."

"Really! That sounds like a story that needs telling." He leans on the bar expectantly. She looks at him properly for the first time. He has a friendly breezy manner that would have affronted Mrs Walpole. Mrs Walpole demanded deference for her money and it is clear that this young barman, whom Matey referred to as Arthur, is not the sort to defer. He is probably a year or two older than herself. His skin is a light sandy colour, his short hair is dark and wavy, his teeth are white and even. He looks nice. She feels herself responding to him.

"It's too depressing to tell."

"Well start by telling me your name."

"Lynn," she says. "Lynnette," she corrects, "that's my given name."

"Linnet," he says. "They're song birds, right. The goldfinch, greenfinch, purplefinch, scarlet rosefinch. They're all linnets. Didn't some poet write an ode to them?" He sees a customer and disappears.

"It's Lynnette not linnet," she says but softly so no-one will hear her. Scarlet rosefinch. She has strayed into a still life of jacaranda and bougainvillea and for a moment or two she allows the magic colour of words to flush through her mind. Cinnabar, crimson, flame-flowering trees red like strawberries, and flesh, the caramel of soft wet sand or a nutmeg custard.

The barman comes back after ringing up the till and leans his arms on the bar again. "It starts 'Poor captive bird', but I can't remember any more of it. Keats or maybe Shelley."

"Poetry," she breathes admiringly.

"Oh only from school," he says quickly. "Everyone does poetry in school."

"When we arrived in England everyone was talking about poetry, as if it was important. I thought it must be something English, something to do with the weather."

"Where are you from then?"

"Australia."

"Right. There's a couple of Aussies round here. Don't go much on poetry in Australia?"

"Not as far as I know."

"Well I learned something out of a text book to pass an exam. And look," indicating around him, "look where it got me." She smiles her big smile. "There," he says, "that's better. Now tell me the story."

"Oh," she says reluctantly because it is going to be bad enough making humiliating phone calls to Mrs Walpole without also making pathetic disclosures to all and sundry. But he is looking at her, waiting for her to begin, so she tells him what happened.

"Sharks!" is his only comment.

"What?"

"Happens quite a lot. Pretending they're charter boats. But charter companies are picky and these boats are not up to scratch - not the sort of boat a company round here is going to use."

"He said something about chartering but I didn't know what it meant."

"Then he invites you on board for a little trip?"

"Yes."

"Then you agree and he acts as if you're chartering the boat, expecting you to pay the bills."

"Is that what it was? I didn't understand. If he'd said straight out I'd have told him I had no money."

"No money at all?"

"Hardly any. I've only got $14, no 12."

"A classic tale, another English book we did in school. The heroine is lured away from her friends to some castle because the man thinks she has plenty of money, then he sends her home quicksmart when he finds out she don't. Who was that by? I'm so well read it's ridiculous." He laughs. "So what are you going to do now?"

"I'll have to ring this lady I have been staying with. I don't know what will happen. I don't even know if I have enough money for a hotel tonight."

"You want to stay in a hotel? Immigration are going to take some interest in you if you're not on a boat. What did you tell them when you came in?"

"We never….." And then she remembers. "Oh God he's still got my passport! I gave it to him that first evening - he said he'd keep them altogether for when we got back. But we never….. there was no Immigration….."

"As I thought. Came in in the dark so the authorities have no record, probably bounced a cheque or two by the sound of it. Put you off when they discover you're no use to them and on their way again at first light. You're lucky they didn't make you get off in some deserted bay and walk."

"So what will happen to me without a passport?" She has this new horror to engage her now.

"Don't you worry, we'll find you a boat to stay on. They don't bother with you when you're on a boat. Only when you come off a boat do they want your passport. Hang on, there's Lucas, the very man. I'll tell him the story and he can go and check if the boat's still there. But I am betting they'll be gone already."

She sits there and gnaws her fingers. The barman is talking to another West Indian who she suddenly realises with a leap of dismay is a police officer. The officer turns and goes over to the pay phone at the end of the bar. She thinks, "Next he will come over and arrest me for not having a passport and it will all get in the papers. I'll be a criminal on top of everything else." Her heart has now slipped down, down, to rock bottom and she thinks, I will just sit here until the depths close over me and all sound is blotted out. Yes she will sit passportless in a far-off land, pursued by Immigration officials and police, and all alone. Pitifully alone. Cast off like the cream-petalled flowers browning among pebbles in the sun.

As she is withdrawing into an envelope of silent worry, the fabric is suddenly split open by a booming voice. A bleached-haired older man bustles into the bar. "Morning," he calls at various people in a powerful voice. A chorus of replies from various tables call back, "Boss, I know I'm up early when I see you about to turn in!" And, "Hey what's this I hear about last night?" and many other raucous remarks that make the man grimace and grin and push away their voices with his hand. He comes over the bar, "Oh Jesus, Arthur, give me an orange juice, I feel bad."

The barman laughs, "Now whose fault would that be Boss?"

"Oh don't," he says. "Libby's quarrelled with me again and gone off God knows where and then Charles, bloody Charles, remember him saying he'd had it with me after the last trip! Well he woke me up half an hour ago and says he's got me four charterers for the day, they'll be round at nine-thirty. What am I going to do?" he moans. "I've got to get provisions and oh god Arthur you've got to take the day off and come and help me," he wheedles.

"Can't do it Boss," says Arthur. "The owner's come over just now and is going through the books with Rick. I'm all on my own here apart from Jake and Cookie. I can't."

"There must be someone, you know everyone, there must be someone who could come and help. Oh Lucas, you here! Could you run down to young Jim's on that motorcycle, an urgent police matter, and tell him he's got to stop fixing that frigging boat and come and do some proper work for a day."

"No, I have an actual urgent police matter. Send Michael," says the young police officer putting down the phone and striding smartly out of the bar.

"Michael!" the man says in despair. "I looked for Michael. He's not there. He'll be out at the airport or delivering new chums around the hotels. Arthur Arthur, I can't do it all on my own, not with the head I've got. It'll be hell enough as it is with four loud Americans wanting the world and getting snappy when the ocean won't deliver. I can't stand any more of that whining - the lack of fish and the beer's not cold enough - and there all on my own. And then if we happen to catch something they're crowing they did the whole thing themselves and wanting to toast the sodding fish in champagne from now until the middle of next week and have their pictures taken with it, with the boat, with me and I'm not up to it. Arthur, oh Arthur, surely you can find someone to come and stand behind this counter and hand things to people. What kind of skill does that take compared with the skill in keeping four Yanks with money happy for eight hours?"

The barman laughs, "You're such a man for getting into situations. I never saw such a man."

"Well what about Charles dumping me in it. He is the end. He tells me he's got nothing and then suddenly he's round at crack of dawn with no warning. And he knows Libby isn't here."

"Boss, if he gave you two week's notice you'd still not be ready. Mr Unreliable he calls you."

"I knew he called me names behind my back!"

"No he's saying it to your face but you're usually too busy mixing your next cocktail to notice. Listen Boss, how are you going to make a business chartering here unless you hold back on the duty-free. You're meant to be drinking that at sea you know."

"Don't give me a lecture Arthur, help me for god's sake. I've got to get over to the shop and get provisions. I need someone. Please go and talk to Rick, I'm sure he'd let you come."

"He can't Boss, he's got his own boss with him and it would look like there's some problem here - a thing the owner don't like in Rick, you know how it is. But I'll ask around, so you go and get your shopping now. If I find someone I'll send them."

The man downs his orange juice with a gulp and leaves with loud lamentations to all.

Arthur comes up the bar and leans his elbow next to Lynn again. "I talked to Lucas, the police who was just here. He is going over to look now but if I know that sort, they'll be gone. There's plenty of cowboys around, defrauding people and that. Anyway don't worry about it, we'll find you a boat to get on so Immigration won't be bothering about you."

"Thanks," says Lynn gratefully.

"In the meantime," he says, "I think I have just the job of work for you."

"Not that man who just came in?"

"Exactly."

"But I was sick on the boat coming here."

"Sea-sick?"

"I don't know. They gave me a drink I never had before. I think it upset my stomach."

"Well, take a chance. Boss's boat is a different kettle of fish and you won't be going far out in big seas."

"But wouldn't I have to cook?"

"Yes and serve drinks."

"I've never done anything like that before."

"Dead easy. I'll show you the ropes. Now. Ever mixed drinks before?"

"No," she says in alarm. "Well, I've poured out ciders for people."

"Cider," says Arthur looking alarmed in his turn. "How old are you then?"

"18," she says. "Nearly."

"Oh well, that's old enough. Look, these yanks are not sophisticated sorts. They drink whisky and the women drink gin. But the only problem you might have is that someone has dared them to have a planter's punch and after that, that's all they want. So the thing is, when they get on board, ask them if they'd like a daiquiri. Maybe they've drunk a daiquiri before, maybe not, but they're a sight easier to make than planter's punch. Now here we are, this is how we make them in the islands." Over the next hour he shows her how to mix and serve drinks in between dashing here and there for his own customers. "White rum, limes and fine white sugar, three two one, that's the proportions. You make up a bucket before you sail and then all you have to do is strain it through ice in the cocktail shaker. So juice the limes, add in the rum and sugar ... see. OK then you have ice in the shaker here and you run it through like this and then you cut a bit of twist, see, that's just for decoration. That's basic. If they want planters you'll have to steer the boat while Boss does it. Now for food, that's very simple too. There's nothing to it. Boss'll get them lobster, he always gets lobster and salad stuffs. Now he'll probably forget to buy any made-up dressing so I'll show you how to make it. Three parts olive oil, one part vinegar, bit of Dijon mustard, little bit of horseradish sauce if he has it, few grains of sugar, herbs and you shake it all up and there you are. Now the lobster is dead easy. It'll be cooked already. Boss don't bother himself with live ones so cut the tails up into slices, then you melt butter in a pan so its runny, add paprika and lime juice to it and toss the lobster just a minute so it's warm. Then you just serve it with french bread and the salad. The rest of what you do is hand out drinks and peanuts and so on - these guys just want to fish."

"Oh," she says at the end. He looks at her with his expectant grin. "He's so nice," she thinks.

The young are so shallow and changeable. Only a short while ago she was contemplating the cold ruin of humiliation, deportation and death and suddenly the misery has receded to about zero and she is instead contemplating the warming thought of someone being nice to her, helping her, a nice-looking young man with a nice smile.

"I don't want to let anyone down though," she says. "What if I'm terrible and they hate me?"

His grin broadens, "That would not be possible," he says.

It is a day of arrivals on St Claire. Planes drone over Fort John and taxis and hotel buses zip inland to and from the small airport. Leather mixes with vinyl luggage and there is the occasional rucksack. Parties arrive neatly laundered with a taxi driver obediently carrying their suitcases. Money is slipped from white hands into black. Everyone is settling in. Around the bay, boats are being admired, crews are taking stock, last minute hitches are being fixed.

Where Lynn ended up is the marina. There is actually a yacht club as well but the marina is far and away the busier and probably the more profitable. The yacht club is situated on the next point of land, between the marina and Fort John. It has a beautiful old clubhouse built of stone, tables spread with starched white tablecloths and waiters discreetly attired in tails and bow ties. It seems to have barely stumbled into the twentieth century. It has been a bastion of colonial power in the past - at one time it was the only place where white people would socialise. But in keeping itself select it somehow missed a change in the times and as a result the marina was built and is now the place where over 90 per cent of the yachts visiting St Claire will berth. 'Cheap but cheerful' when applied to the marina somehow misses the point. Most of the yachties wouldn't even dream of berthing at the yacht club. In the minds of many young people, the yacht club is moribund - a place where you are forced to dress in too many clothes and disport yourself with a sobriety and taste completely at odds with everyone's idea of a good time.

After Independence the yacht club had tried to hang on to its exclusivity; to remain a place where the rich and white could still come to relax among their own kind. This led to some agitation at the time and it reluctantly changed its rules and invited a few select West Indians like the Premier to join, as honorary whites. The general membership believed that this was as far as you could go otherwise you would be swamped with undesirables and the yacht club was quite right in believing that the Premier did not wish to sip cocktails with the riff raff any more than anyone else.

The yacht club has many geographical advantages over the marina. It has flat land behind it that allows space for a slip yard for repairs but more importantly, its jetties give access to deeper water and as a result it has become over time the docking place for the huge ocean-going toys of the very rich. Such boats as frequent the yacht club do not usually have the need or desire to take fare-paying passengers. As a result, on this Monday morning it is lacking the hustle and bustle of the marina and people are coming and going with calm deliberation.

The Evangelica had slipped into port at first light and is anchored now a short way out from its berthing jetty. It is flying its quarantine flag, waiting for Immigration and Customs to come and clear it while its passengers work their way through an elegant four-course breakfast. Anthony Hamilton is the only one who is getting off; his leather valises are stacked near the boarding ladder. He is a slim young man dressed with negligent stylishness in a white suit. He has collar-length dark blonde hair and the look of someone dissolute but fashionable, careless but rich.

He toys languidly with a neat triangle of toast. "So the problem is," he is saying confidentially, "that once my father finds out that I have a house he's sure to want to stay there."

The recipient of this communication is a shortish sharp-featured man who is also trying to play some role in colonial whites but by no means as successfully as his companion. "I can't see why anyone would want to stay there. Tell him there's going to be endless noise and so on."

"Wouldn't bother him. He sleeps like a log through anything."

"Are you going to stay there yourself? I thought the whole thing was purely commercial."

"It is. Though I probably will stay there. To keep an eye on things. That's the problem. Because I'm there, he'll insist on being invited."

"Don't tell him you're staying there. Come to an arrangement with the Beach Hotel. Use that as a mailing address. How's he to know you don't sleep there?"

"Oh yes. Good idea, I'll go and see the manager. Yes I think an arrangement might work." He muses and is about, it seems, to finally dispose of the toast when he throws it on his plate laughing and indicates a group approaching in a runabout. "Oh Lord," he drawls, "look what's coming." He pushes his plate away and dabs at his mouth with a fine linen napkin. "I know that one with the big head. He's so like a gorilla, he might have left the jungle yesterday!"

The man sitting next to him shifts slightly and slides his eyes sideways at a coloured crewman who is collecting dishes. "Really Tony," he murmurs when the servant has withdrawn. "You're going to get yourself into trouble saying things like that out loud."

"Why, who's to hear?" says Anthony negligently.

His companion shrugs rather impatiently. "I just wish you wouldn't say such things in front of my crew, that's all. It makes them sulk."

"Sulk. Well let them sulk. Turn 'em off if it bothers you - plenty more where they came from."

The owner turns rather cold eyes on Anthony. "It's not that easy any more, as you'll realise if you're going to do business in this place. Things have changed and it behoves us all to at least conform to what's required."

"On the surface."

"Of course, on the surface."

"I shall be as nice as pie to coons in uniform. Nothing will beat me for conformity, you watch." He waits with a smug look of compliance on his face.

The interview with the Immigration officials does not, however, go as planned. Bad things start happening to Anthony Hamilton's day at the point where the official asks him his address on the island.

"My address will probably be the Beach Hotel. But I have leased a place nearby. To tell you the truth I don't remember the exact location. Christopher Morrison, the estate agent, has been organising it for me."

Up until this point the Immigration official has been treating him with a dry lack of enthusiasm barely on the right side of politeness. However to this response he allows one broad eyebrow to go up and something like a small smile to appear on his mouth for an instant. His face, however, returns to schooled indifference, a coolness as detached as that of Hamilton himself.

"Well that could be an unfortunate thing. Just as well you're staying at the Beach Hotel."

"Why's that?" Hamilton asks sharply.

"Mr Morrison is a criminal wanted for frauds of various sorts. It would appear the general public that have trusted Mr Morrison with money have been made fools of. I hope you yourself have not been so unlucky." The voice of the Immigration official at this point has a slightly malicious tinge to it.

Hamilton sits very still for a while. "I see," he eventually says in an expressionless voice. "And where would Mr Morrison be now?"

"That is for him to know and us to find out," replies the official and stamps Hamilton's passport. They leave and Hamilton lifts his coffee cup slowly to his lips.

"Trouble?" queries his friend.

Hamilton doesn't speak for a while. "Not with the house. Hardly worth worrying about. But I did give Morrison some money for certain, well, disbursements shall I say."

"I thought you said he was trustworthy."

"Yes, I thought he was. Or I wouldn't have left him in charge. Anyway who else could I deal with?"

"Surely there's more than one agent dealing with real estate?"

"There are others no doubt, but Morrison was the only white one. It seems you can't trust anyone these days."

Hamilton comes ashore with an ugly cast to his face. Dale Frankland sees it but without concern. He doesn't like Hamilton, he doesn't want to have anything to do with him, but this is business and can't be helped.

"Mr Hamilton," he says lifting his hat politely.

Hamilton barely bothers to look at him.

"I represent the owner of 16 Louisiana Street," Dale says as Hamilton brushes curtly passed, "now that Mr Morrison is no longer operating here. The owner has some concerns."

"Well he needn't have, it's none of his business," Hamilton says sourly, looking back with a sideways flip of his hand.

Dale however continues doggedly. “Then he would kindly request that you fulfil the requirements of the contract and pay him the four week’s rent owing.”

Hamilton’s sour look becomes savage. “I paid Morrison. The owner loses, not me.”

“Easy to verify,” Dale says soothingly. “The number of the cheque would settle the matter.”

“In cash.”

“Ah. You have a receipt then no doubt.” Dale’s posture is still polite but Hamilton has already turned on his heels and is heading out to the front of the yacht club. “The owner will be seeking.....” Hamilton is out of earshot and the rest of it hangs in the air. The owner will be seeking any excuse to evict him now he has heard rumours about the business Hamilton is engaged in.

Dale isn’t sure he wants to represent the owner - in fact he’s sure he doesn’t. There will be endless aggravation associated with anything to do with Hamilton. He sighs and is contemplating what his own plan of action should be when he is interrupted by an exclamation behind him: “Dale, the very man.”

“Ah young Jim. Up and about so early. Why it’s barely nine o’clock.”

“Yes it is pretty early,” Jim agrees without irony. “So I am out chasing the worm. Have you found me what I’m after, a nice little cabin up the coast somewhere where I can work on the boat, somewhere with a jetty. You know, cheap, very cheap.”

“Yes I’ve found you something cheap, very cheap. But why would you want to cut yourself off from your friends, way out of town, when they love you here?

“They love me, yes and charge me for that love. I can’t afford such affection.”

“I would have thought you being a lordship and all, you would have the best of everything and all for free.”

“Pigs might fly,” says Jim. “So where is this house? Can you take me there?”

“No I have things to attend to right now.”

“To do with Anthony Hamilton? I can’t believe that sleaze is back.”

“I can take you out at midday for an inspection.”

“Inspection! No, I’ll just take it if you say it’s alright. Tell me where it is and I’ll sail the boat up straight away.”

"You young people, you're so reckless. Always leaping into things. You'll come to grief."

Boss's boat is called Sweet Marie and looks to Lynn like a skyscraper. It rises from deck level in balcony after balcony of glass, metal and whatnots and from its lower deck it thrusts whiskers backwards, like a bristling fort, like a gun boat poised for speed and pursuit. She almost takes fright but she can't let Arthur down, not now he's spent so much time telling her things. She takes off her sandals and steps gingerly on to the deck. "Um hello," she quavers. She climbs over into a sort of depression in the deck padded with seats and looks down a hatch from where frantic sounds are coming. "Hello."

Boss stops picking madly at ice in the ice-chest and looks up startled. "Jesus," he says.

"Sorry," she says. "Arthur sent me."

Boss throws down the icepick and leaps up the stairs in one bound and grabs her like he has discovered a long lost sister. He pumps her hand, "Wonderful, wonderful."

"I haven't done this before," she waves her hand to indicate Boss's boat. "Arthur kept saying I'd be alright but you mustn't expect too much," she trails off.

Boss has meantime been murmuring "Wonderful, wonderful" at her every word. "Yes you'll be wonderful, come down," and leads her down the stairs. "Here's the galley. I've got everything" - he breaths deeply – "I think," and does a sign of some sort in the air in the rough direction of his chest. "What do you think you'll do first?" he asks looking at her, as if this is the test.

"Well I suppose I could make up a batch of daiquiris for when they arrive and then I'll organise snacks and things later."

"Wonderful wonderful WONDERFUL," he slaps his forehead and waves his arms around. "Arthur I love you. I love you too," he says turning to her. "I love you passionately, and after this is over I'll marry you. What's your name by the way?"

"Lynn."

"Lynn, sweet Lynn, Vera Lynn it's all yours." He dances up the stairs. "I have to get the fishing gear in order." He turns, "You know anything about fishing?"

"No, I told Arthur....."

"Doesn't matter," he waves magnanimously, "doesn't matter. Soon pick it up." He is gone.

She stows her bag and looks around. Her head still feels empty as if some of the search-out-in-a-logical-manner part of the brain is in receivership. But on the up-side she thinks, well, it doesn't matter anyway - nobody can possibly expect I will make anything but a huge mess of it. All her life people have been expecting her to make a mess of things and here is her big chance to prove them right. She'll be sick, she'll do everything wrong, they'll all hate her.

The alcohol is easy to discover and by a wonder the first bottle her hand finds is white rum. "What else is in here?" she wonders. "Pray god they don't want something complicated, I'll never find it." The ice chest holds beer and champagne. "Well that's OK, so long as I don't have to take the top off the champagne." Somehow she acquaints herself with the insides of all the cupboards - she finds the sugar and a juicer and she finds the limes and all she is missing is the cocktail shaker. Never mind, she finds a plastic ice bucket and pours the bottle of rum into it and adds what she thinks is the right amount of sugar and then sets to, pushing the halves of lime on to the plastic juicer, turning and pushing the greenish liquid from the shells. She cuts up twist from the rind of the limes. If only she could find the shaker. In the ice chest she realises the ice still sits in blocks and starts chipping what Boss has left. He suddenly appears in the opening. "They're coming!" he says in a voice of agony.

"Where's the cocktail….?" but he is gone. She keeps chipping and far off she hears voices with loud exclamations and laughter and a muted roll of sandshoes hitting the deck and bodies descending into the padded seats around the cockpit. A face appears at the top of the companionway, "Hi." It is a middle-aged face, balding with a red sunburnt forehead. "I'm Joe, what are you doing down there?"

Lynn smiles up at him. She hasn't met any Americans before but doesn't mind his intrusive loudness or his demands to be immediately on terms of known-from-birth intimacy. She stops picking ice and comes up to the hatch so she can shake hands. "Lynn," she says. "I'm making ice for all the cocktails you'll be drinking. Only I can't find the cocktail shaker."

"Hahaha," says Joe pleased. "Boss, the little lady down here is darned if she can find the cocktail shaker."

There is a split second pause and a gale of laughter and Joe passes down to her a cocktail shaker. "How did you do that?" she exclaims.

"Easy," he says. "We held the Boss upside down till it fell out."

"Hey Joe get out of the way, who you got down there?"

"Clear off buddy," says Joe. "I saw her first."

She shakes hands with Mel and Pat and Don, all of whom are dressed for the day in Hawaiian shirts, Bermuda shorts and white sandshoes. They are all old, older than Boss which makes them very old in Lynn's view.

"I'm here to minister to your every whim," she says. She has heard her mother say this to elderly males and it always seems to go down well. "I've been whipping up some daiquiris for you."

"Well," says Joe looking rueful, "to tell you the truth I think I'd rather have a coffee. This was only a spur of the minute thing so breakfast was a bit hectic."

Four coffees. The faces withdraw to enter conference with Boss and she looks nervously around. So far she has managed to get by without admitting to the charterers that she doesn't have a clue what she is doing. How much longer is she going to keep up the pretence? Coffee, for heaven's sake! That means heating water. She looks helplessly at the stove. That means - but first things first. She opens the cupboards and finds coffee in an airtight tin. No instant. Oh well. So there has to be a coffee pot. Here is the coffeepot. Well look, this has to be no more complicated than filling this jigger with coffee and the pot with water, see how we go. The stove. It looms and she puts her hand on it - to her astonishment it moves. She took no interest in Ed's stove so she has no way of knowing whether stoves naturally move on boats or whether this one just happens to be loose. By looking at all the other fittings, which despite Boss's unkempt appearance are in sparkling condition, she imagines that the stove is meant to be like that for reasons of a technical nature which need not concern her. So all she has to do now is light it. Fortunately at that moment Boss put his head down and says, "We're ready for off."

"The stove," she says urgently.

"Oh sorry," he hurtles down headlong, "of course. This tap here at the back, you switch it forward when it's in use and then put it back when it's not. Then you just use it like a normal gas stove." With that he is gone.

She finds matches and lights the stove and puts on the coffee pot as the sound of the engines starts to throb. Oh god what happens if….. She holds the pot steady as the boat parts from the jetty. All is well. Now what? She doesn't feel like going up on deck yet, she can hear the charterers in loud laughter and reminiscences. On impulse she decides to make bacon sandwiches. There's a packet of bacon in the ice chest and she finds a frying pan and puts rashers in to sizzle. The minutes fly by as she finds tomatoes to slice and bread and gets out butter to soften. After ten minutes she has the bacon cooling and the coffee is ready. She climbs a couple of stairs and looks out on deck. She is surprised at the speed with which they are travelling - in the galley all she had been aware of was a deep throbbing gurgle and an occasional lurch. "Now," she says, "what are the milk and sugar orders for this coffee?" Black, black all black. "My, you're all easy," she says.

"Yes," shouts Joe, "we're all easy, we're anybody's."

Guffaw.

As she is collecting cups from a cupboard, she finds a tray. She puts the coffee and sandwiches on it and carefully starts to negotiate the stairs. Joe leaps forward, "Here let me. Hey sandwiches too." "Well if you hadn't time for a proper breakfast….."

"Bacon sandwiches. Great idea. I could eat these all on my own." No way! Ah boy, strong black coffee. Wow this is strong.

"Oh dear, too strong?"

No no this fills a spot. Absolutely, this is my strength, not like that hotel coffee, weak as cat's piss. Hey language, not in front of the lady. Sorry!

She goes up the stairs to the next level, up into the skipper's lair, "Would you like some coffee?" she asks.

Boss makes a grimace, "Well I don't usually drink it for pleasure. I feel if I do it may lose its unhappy magic properties of sobering a man up. But on the other hand, after last night maybe it would be a good idea."

She brings him up a cup and he then disconcertingly gets out of his seat holding the wheel with one hand, "Here."

"What!"

"Just hold her course. See that mark on the compass? Hold her there while I get up in the crow's nest and have a bit of a scan."

It was hot in the galley and she has taken off her dress and is in her bikini. Not only is she now exposed to the absolute danger of steering a huge powerful boat that she has no control over but after the first five minutes of terror she is aware of the sun pounding down on her not-particularly-acclimatised skin. "Oh come down Boss," she murmurs within herself, too frightened to say it aloud, as she clings for all she is worth to the wheel and to the spot on the compass.

"Starboard," calls Boss waving with one arm and she turns the wheel in the direction of his arm. "Not so far, yes keep her on that." A new point, she clings there thinking, I'm burning up, everything is melting down.

Joe appears at here side, "He must have seen something. Can you see anything?"

"No nothing." She is squinting now into the bright immensity of sea.

"Ah well," Joe turns to look admiringly at her, "I see you can handle a boat."

She laughs. "Nothing to it," she lies. "Here, take it for a minute. Hold the wheel and keep on that mark there, see. I've got to pop down and get my dress. I don't want to get sunburned."

She slips back down into the galley and buttons on her dress. "Hey what the….." Mel is complaining as she comes up again. "Hey Joe, how did you get that job? Look at that, how did he get to be Skip just like that?"

"Well," says Joe looking at her, "you've just got to know the right people, hey little lady?"

The other three men are standing round grinning, "You watch him," says one, "he's a devil with women. Yes I can tell you a thing or two….."

"Now now," says Joe, "don't get into that. She's no older than my daughter so watch your stories you guys."

"She should be wearing shades," says Don. "Hey Mel, you must have brought some spares." Mel passes up a pair of sunglasses.

"Oh these are great," she says surprised. The relief of putting them on is in fact enormous.

"Polaroid," says Mel proudly. "That's what I'm in, that's my line."

Pat says, "And I do suncreams, Ambre Solaire, a very good seller. Here," he passes up a bottle.

"Thanks," she says and immediately rubs it on her shoulders which have started to sting after only ten minutes in the cauldron of the cockpit.

"She should be wearing a hat," says Don. "None of us do hats, we need to get into hats. We just bought these at the hotel, aren't they awful? Now there's a guy down at the beach bar who makes hats out of palm leaves, right there on the sand, but our wives….."

Aah aah! Not that word. We agreed not to use that word.

"Yes, I mean nameless people of the female gender told us they would blow off on a boat so we all lined up at the hotel shop and bought these. We need hats like Boss has got, yes we could make those a goer."

Everybody looks up at Boss and from behind her broad comfy eyeware she sees him in his captain's hat scanning the seas. "Oh Joe," she suddenly exclaims, "you're off the mark."

Get away from there Joe, failed your licence, ha ha ha. Now we'll never find any fish.

But Joe readjusts the wheel and they all stand there swaying as the big boat cuts through the waves with a slight roll and scoop. "Amazing." thinks Lynn to herself. "I haven't felt sick for even a minute."

"OK," says Boss eventually descending. "There are seagulls out there, maybe a shoal and where there's a shoal of little fish there are bigger fish following behind. Let's hope there are really big fish, a nice black marlin, what do you say boys?"

"I say let's up and at 'em," says Mel.

"Yes," they all say. Now, who's going first?

There are two seats at the end of the boat, wide important-looking seats and the four charterers go down to group around them in discussion. "OK," says Boss coming back to Lynn, "once I start putting the bait over keep an eye on me. When I put out my hand go that way, if I wave my hand like this go further round, if I put my hand up and down go slower."

"Slower?" she says looking at the panel.

"Oh yes, here are your throttles see, slower. Right, and if my hand goes up like this, faster, see. OK." He takes the wheel and she clings to the side of the wallowing boat as he brings it round into waves where seagulls swoop and cry. He hands her the wheel, "Keep her like that." She struggles with the now difficult boat which is caught up in cross waves.

She hears Boss call, what did that mean, she slows. He shouts again, wrong, that means faster and she moves it cautiously up the range wishing every minute that he would come back or someone would save her. She looks ahead concentrating on the spray and curling waves; her dress is blowing out behind her and she feels like a doomed Boadicea of the seas unable to contain the advance of the hordes. Time goes by and eventually Boss is back by her side. "Lovely," he says. "Take a break."

"You didn't drink your coffee!" she says. "Do you want something else?"

He looks over his head, "Is the sun over the yardarm yet?" He shouts to Mel, "Hey is that sun over the yardarm yet, do you imagine?"

Mel looks at his watch. "Half eleven," he says. "Must be near."

Lynn gets the idea. "What'll it be?"

"What did you do with the daiquiris?" asks Boss.

"Put them in the ice box to cool."

"I'll have one of those but listen, add water or something to mine. I know it's a terrible thing to do to alcohol but while I'm running the boat I've got to keep the intake down, doctor's orders. But these guys, look, they can drink all they care for and then more. Hey, you hear that you guys? Those who aren't fishing are drinking and vice versa, that's the rules on this boat."

Aye aye cap'n.

She skuds about the boat busy and surprised at how organised she is - she serves them drinks and then prepares lunch, then more drinks, peanuts go round, then more drinks. All of this seems both purposive and yet purposeless to her; it keeps her busy but the rest of the boat seems to be gradually sinking into lethargy. Until about 4 o' clock when they catch a fish. A big one. It leaps from the waves in lilac iridescence, like a watery dancer in a shining dress - pirouetting away on the sea-surface towards the horizon in swirling light and a cascade of colour.

Joe has it and the rest gather to cheer him on. For well over an hour Joe fights the fish, reeling up and letting out, reeling up and letting out, until it seems he must drown in sweat and exhaustion. Boss is watching intently and jockeying the boat to follow where the fish is breaking. "If he lands it," Boss tells Lynn, "Christ it's a big one! and it could still get away, then….." He is going to instruct her further it seems on what could happen in the final critical moments when suddenly he hands her the wheel and darts to the back of the boat.

The fish, a giant marlin, leaps in now tired arcs from the water, but no threshing fear that it feels is anything like the fear that nearly overwhelms Lynn at the possibility of doing something wrong and losing this catch for the men. Somehow in the blur that marks the end of the day the fish is landed, hauled thrashing aboard by a winch and everyone collapses back on the cushions.

"Now what do I do?" wonders Lynn, who is still at the wheel. The sun is a huge orange disk descending down into the sea but to the east she can see a couple of boats heading for a point of land. It must be over there, the port, she concludes narrowing her eyes to squint and as no-one tells her anything else she heads in that direction, now putting up the speed and waiting for Boss to come and do it properly. Time goes by and he doesn't move, but she can see now an opening and a line of buildings on the beach. Suddenly Boss shouts up, "Hey Vera, Vera Lynn, what do you think you're doing?" Is it the wrong place, is this wrong, how does she know where she is supposed to be going?

"The flag, the flag!" he cries and leaps up near her to open a box from which he takes two flags - one of a fish and one of a bottle of champagne. He runs them up the flag pole. "Go and get the champagne," he says taking over.

She goes down into the galley and pulls a bottle out of the ice box and takes off the silver wrapping and the metal cage. She finds glasses. She looks at the bottle. They make loud bangs and she suddenly has no desire to find out how you take the top off. She looks up through the hatch. "Mel," she says to the man nearest her, "can you take the top off?" and hands up the bottle. Immediately there is a pop and she rushes up the stairs with glasses and nearly falls, Aah. Everyone leaps to hold her upright and Mel pours the bubbling froth into the outstretched glasses. "Six glasses," says Mel, "we need six, where's yours?" She goes back down and gets another and has it filled with the yellow liquid. "Well here's to your fish," she says.

"Gentlemen, the fish," says Boss and the others simultaneously and they all drink. It is the first time since sitting at the bar in the cool of the early day that Lynn has come to a full stop. The bubbling liquid seems to swirl straight around her head and she suddenly loses all desire to do anything else.

"That's right!" says Joe, "time you sat down for a minute."

The lights at the Beach Hotel are starting to twink as they glide past in the nearing dark and by the time they get through the heads and tie up at the jetty, the brief twilight is over and the night is as thick as an old blue duffle coat. Generators throb around the marina and the boardwalks are lit in an uncertain faint glow.

"The fish'll be safe enough here overnight," says Boss. "Come back tomorrow early and we'll weigh and measure it and have some photos taken."

"Well, you'll come down the Beach for a drink with us, both of you," says Mel.

"Sure thing," says Boss.

"I'll come later," says Lynn not moving. "I've got to clean up."

"No no leave that."

"It won't take long," she says and holds her point through several urgent arguments. She is too tired to do anything and she feels sticky and salt laden and she has no clothes to go to a hotel, better to prevaricate. The charterers climb off the boat. "Oh your sunglasses," she suddenly remembers.

"No no, they're yours."

"Oh thanks!" She is surprised and pleased and gives him a big smile.

"It's my pleasure!" They're all gone and she lies down for a minute, just a minute, to recuperate and immediately falls asleep.

Some considerable time later she hears someone come aboard and thinks it is Boss returning. She hears sounds in the galley and then a voice from the jetty and someone replies, but it isn't Boss. She opens her eyes, she suddenly thinks, "What's the time, oh my goodness it must be the middle of the night!"

To her surprise it is Arthur moving about in the galley. He comes up the steps and closes off a light. "Hi," he says sitting opposite her. "How'd you go then?"

"It was fine. I'm so tired."

"I've got somewhere for you to stay. You can't stay here."

"Can't I?"

"You wouldn't want to. Boss'll be back soon from wherever he's drinking and then all sorts will stop by. You heard one just now. Lights on in his galley and it's a sign for all the world to come on board. They call this the Last Port of Crawl. And no-one sleeps while they're drinking either, they'll have you up and joining in. Now I know a couple with a boat over on the other jetty who have flown back to the States for a while and I'm sure they would be happy for you to caretake it for them while they're gone, save me having to keep an eye on it. So let's go, make your escape while you can."

"What time is it?" she asks as he helps her on to the jetty.

"One in the morning."

"I've been asleep since seven! I was going to clear up."

"I had a look and there's not much to do. Boss can do it himself tomorrow, I don't think he has a charter."

She is rather unsteady on the uneven boards and he puts out his hand and takes her arm and guides her. For some reason she can't define she suddenly feels absurdly happy. They stop beside a largish sail boat, much bigger than Ed's.

"Here," he says. "It's called the Golden Dawn. Go down the back cabin, that'll be easiest. See you in the morning."

"Thanks," she says and creeps over the rail on to the deck and feels her way down to a bunk. Before she goes back to sleep however, she knows with every fibre of her being what she is going to do tomorrow. She can see the words she is going to put on the telegram forms, one to Mrs Walpole, one to her mother. "Not returning, working St Claire, will write. Lynnette."

Chapter 2

At sea in unfathomable waters

There is another woman sending messages home but these are not lettered and spaced and formulated. Rae is floating deep in a Nautilus capsule, water crashing in her ears. She too has been having adventures and meeting monsters. Above her the air swelters with hot orange light but a groaning mass keeps pulling her down into grey-green toneless regions where great unseen shapes loom like nightmares. Like many adventurers, she is drifting.

Eventually she is dragged up in the wake of slashing propellers, barely missing being gouged again. The ceiling fans go crump crump, thump thump, crump crump, like the sound of blood, an internal pounding. She lies there with her eyes shut, letting her veins throb.

In the course of time ordinary things impinge - the raucous cry of birds, a distant voice and then plop BANG something lands on the roof. Bloody hell!

She opens her eyes to find a sheet over her face. She breathes out, onto cotton the colour of bean-water and smelling stale like old farts. Uggh! She throws it violently off and, Oh Christ! She moans aloud as the light hits her eyes. Then she moans again as she looks around her. Here I am trussed on an onion bed in a sea of squalor. I'm always cleaning things but they always get dirty again - she is answering her accuser who sits disapprovingly in the shadows looking remarkably like her mother. Oh get away, get away, you stupid old woman, I hate this. She curls herself into a ball on the side of the bed, I hate this bloody place, I never wanted to come here.

Which isn't true because in the first place this is Paradise, remember? And when Rick had said, "I've been offered a job in the West Indies, managing a bar," she had danced around their Ladbroke Grove flat banging her fists into the cushions on the settee howling, "Hooray Hooray."

Her mother's reaction had of course been exemplary. "What would you want to go to a place like that for? Living among all those darkies and so hot and with fungal growths. You can't be too careful, I've read about it in the Readers Digest and what about keeping up your standards when you're surrounded by all that? And the food, yes the nigger food, the things they've touched, how will you bear to eat anything?" Her mother, the one with the standards, who wore shiny cotton dresses with detachable pads under her armpits, and who was determined to stick to her like glue and interpose herself on all occasions. Get away you awful old woman! Nothing should be allowed to spoil this voyage to an exotic scented island where the cold milk-junket-smell of nutmeg and the warm apple-pudding taste of cinnamon and the flitches and fragments of piled up spice all fought for supremacy. And all around, look, look, a sea closed in by coral and a land twined with lush scented flowers. "Oh please," she had said back then, dabbling her finger on the map, sticky with the need for nectar, "Please let me go there!"

And now she is here. Everything she has ever wanted. And the taste of vomit in the edges of her mouth.

If only she could remember the events of the last couple of days. Yesterday she remembers only wretched desperate lurches to the lavatory and the fight with Rick. And the night before that a collage of vague images and then nothing. It isn't the first time she can't remember getting home, waking up with a rueful laugh, "Oh my god, drunk again!" This time is different however. It's different because Rick, who has always complained before about having to carry her home and her less than charming habit of lying in bed and being sick straight up in the air, this time Rick didn't bring her home. That was the fight.

She'd gone missing and she can't remember how she got home, nothing. Not a thing. Not then, not now. It's awful. How could Rick have allowed it to happen? It appears he doesn't care enough about her to keep her in view any more. It's a horrible thing to have no memory, she could have done anything! A hundred ugly scenes from bars she has worked in float across her mind. People who were drunk and made fools of themselves, threw up or took a leak in public or divested themselves of their clothes or threw things around or got in ugly brawls or sang off key – there is no end to the possibilities of humiliation.

She gets up unsteadily to go to the bathroom. As she pushes the door open an outsize cockroach emerges from somewhere near her foot. She dives for the toilet brush, throws it and misses. Shit. The woman in the shadows gasps in outrage, Really Raelene!

It's over thirty years ago and it's hard to remember how much things have changed, but I really remember the first time I heard a woman say "Shit". The shock, the low commonness of it. That's a word we never use now, 'common', because we're all pretty common these days. I sit in my car screaming Fuck fuck fuck at the traffic lights, shit bugger bum, though I don't say cunt - yes there are still some taboos.

Even Rae is shocked at herself. Yes, she never used to say "shit". Yes mother, I'm becoming coarse and common. Who knows how coarse and common? On an island this small, it's only a matter of time before someone says, "I saw you the other night, doing such and such. Hawhawhaw."

And the worst part, what makes her even madder, is that it was one of the few nights when she and Rick had gone out together, one of the very few. Because most nights it's just the Frangipani and work, work, work - she is there every night because she can't afford to go anywhere else. Resentful images flicker, she works at the bar to help Rick but gets no payment. Why should I work for nothing? I want money, I want to swan off during the day with friends and lie in sun lounges under shady umbrellas and have nice lunches and a few drinks in the evening somewhere other than the bloody bar. Then there wouldn't be a problem with Her Drinking. How dare Rick! It was her night out so of course she had a few.

She goes back into the bedroom. Look at that bed, just look at it! How can you live in such a pigsty? She ignores the giant mother succubus and lies back down. The thing is, Rick knows something. When they had the fight last night, she can't even remember much about that either but she does remember him saying about her acting like a tart and bringing herself and him into disrepute. What did he mean by that? Is it just not knowing where she went? No, she's sure he knows something more. And how can she defend herself if she can't remember. Sometimes it seems on the point of coming back to her. Strange houses with thick murmuring walls, what did I hear? Just voices, but I heard voices. Don't listen to them, they like to party. Did I say that? No, someone else. Who was it? Dozing, she drifts.

Something clatters on the roof again plop BANG. Damn! She scrabbles and eventually gets herself upright and takes a long time trying to focus. She goes to stand in front of the mirror, to confront her reflection and feel less ghostlike. Her face stares vacantly back at her. She has put on a bit of weight, her hips are a little heavier, her breasts larger. Yes she is becoming droopy, look, blossoming backwards into buttocks like stuffed sacks filled by this, she grabs it in a sudden fury with herself and everything around her, this flab. It's not having anything to do and all this drinking, and the face - you're disgusting, you're absolutely disgusting. But she isn't that bad. Not like Rick, he's getting fat, positively gross.

She wishes she had a friend. Now the season is in full swing everyone keeps going away and Libby has somehow drifted away too. Having nothing to do is dull. All she seems to do is clean the bloody house. She's always cleaning the floor and washing the sheets and the rest of the time she's working in the bar. It's because she doesn't any money, how can she do anything else if she doesn't have any money. Bloody Rick, he's the problem. If it wasn't for him, I could be having a wonderful time. Well here we go, girding herself up. Are you watching? She rips off the sheets and pillowslips, slaps madly into the laundry and throws them into the twin tub. And in goes the soap, turn the dial to wash away the impress of nasty bodies, to wash off the stale smells and erase it all. And while she's at it she grabs a mop and bucket and starts flailing at the floor, why is it always so dirty? Hair and skin flakes and gobbets picked from nostrils and stale crumbs. No wonder there are cockroaches. I hate them - and there's one there in the laundry! She smashes at its escaping black shell with the mop and misses. "Shit," she says again.

She gives up cleaning and goes and has a shower. Look at this spastic trickle of water, it's because we're at the end of the road, we should have had the other house - Rick chose the wrong bloody house. Everything has turned out wrong.

She droops back into the bedroom and listlessly takes a sarong out of the drawer and tucks each side across her breasts in a practised motion. She catches sight of herself in the mirror again, this time a south sea maiden. Mmmm, the spirits rise and she cavorts sinuously in front of the mirror for a minute and then rushes at her heavy wet hair, there's another grey one - no - well, there'd better not be! Someone once said she looked like something from a painting by Gaugin. He would have painted her hair in great hanks as it falls now, thick and wavy. What it needs is a big lollopy flower and she goes out under the white flower tree and - can you believe it? All the flowers within reach are brown around the edges. God! The sound explodes from her throat. Now she has to go and get a chair which she bangs under the tree and climbs onto until she finds one. As she hangs there, she hears a voice call, "Rae, is that you up that tree or is it a jumbie?"

Haha! She sticks the flower behind her ear and without any thought flounces next door onto Arthur's terrace.

So the line is crossed and her mother gasps in horror. And there are all her mother's Chichester cronies gasping too, all those printed matrons playing tennis with ooofs and aaahs now reduced to widemouthed silence. They always knew how it would be. They long ago murmured into their lime and barley waters, "How will a person know how to behave? Let's hope there's a better class of people out there to show her the way, what with all those black people." And the query they whispered persistently, "What will you do when those darkies get fresh?" Negroes. Not marginally acceptable darkies like Indians who look almost clean when they bother to dress properly, but all those black men with wide nostrils and their skins soaking light like blotting paper and their broad mouths saying, "Tickets please." Having to live among them all, what sort of impertinence would you have to put up with? With them acting like equals in a country that is no longer British, there is bound to be a certain coarsening.

Yes here she is, coarse and heedless, on Arthur's terrace. Arthur who works for us in the bar you know. Her mother would think it is perfectly alright to communicate with a servant, to give him some instruction of some sort. Quite right mother, I am going to instruct him to entertain me. That is the command she is going to give, so that she can forget what a horrid time she has been having recently and he can stop lying all relaxed and drowsy in his hammock and wake up and tell her some things.

"You alright now?" asks Arthur. "I heard you weren't well yesterday."

"Yesterday," she says bitterly. "The night before that was the problem!"

"Well you're up now at least."

"I don't exactly have any choice. How can I sleep when everything makes such a bloody noise?" She looks down to the marina with all the chirping and chattering and carolling and drumming, the noise of generators and voices and bustle below. "And," she adds plaintively, "there are always things bouncing off the roof, coconuts and things."

"There is no coconut tree within 50 yards of your house."

"It sounds like coconuts. Those awful people up the road must be throwing them."

"It's only avocadoes from that tree overhanging. See, they're dropping down. You should pick them up and eat them."

"What, those slimy green things? No fear. I hate them!" Urgh, snot-coloured and oily. Having tropical fruit at your beck and call is one thing - actually having to eat them is another. She sits down in a cane chair and stretches out her legs. "Everyone is away on their stupid boats, everybody is out with charterers." She sighs, no-one to go to the beach with. She hates being alone. "And there are cockroaches in our house," she continues. "Huge ones, football teams of them running all over the place." She shakes with disgust.

"Spray," murmurs Arthur.

"Spray," she exclaims looking upwards to heaven. "I've given them spray. I've stood there spraying till I'm about asphyxiated. Do you have cockroaches like that? I bet you don't, it's just our house. I knew Rick should have chosen this house." She sighs again and fiddles with her hair discontentedly. Arthur isn't joining in with her concerns, possibly Arthur being a West Indian doesn't mind cockroaches. They would be used to them, used to the climate too - they don't get heat rash, they don't get bitten to death by mosquitoes. No, they just lie around brown like left-over sugar crystals quite prepared to sink, distilled and rum-like, into tropical lethargy. Brown bodies. Something keeps catching at her memory - here she is thinking about the night before last again. Useless reconstructions. "Arthur, have you ever forgotten what you did the night before - woken up the next day and looked back and it's one long blank?"

"No I never have, because I never took much of a liking to alcohol myself."

"But everybody drinks." When Arthur says nothing, she adds, "Well everyone I know drinks."

So she can't have a drinking problem, not if everyone drinks. Where's the problem? What about Boss, night after night? It's the social scene. Arthur probably doesn't have a social scene, he seems to spend all his spare time in his hammock. She's never seen him wrestle with problems like having no friends to go to the beach with.

No - the clicking of needles from her mother who has grimly followed her and is now over in the corner - they just lie in the shade and when they feel like breakfast go and pick up an old avocado off the ground. They just live day to day without a care in the world, what with the whites here to tell them what to do and provide them with civilisation. If it weren't for us….. Someone said that recently, who was it?

And what a load of rubbish. The fact is, she should have had this house and she should have had that hammock and she should be lying there like Arthur with half-closed eyes looking down at what's going on in the marina. "Rick won't get a hammock for our veranda. I'd go and get one myself but he doesn't give me any money."

"Maybe if you ask him nicely."

"Rick is in a bad mood."

"Is he? I hadn't noticed. Why?" Arthur looks at her surprised.

You're not going to tell him about your private affairs! Her mother is leaping to attention outraged. Coloured people, servants! Good god what is she coming to? She comes to it without a second thought. "We had a big fight. But there's something else as well. Something to do with Ed Hamilton and money that's getting to him, but whatever it is he won't tell me. I bet you know. You know everything that happens down there."

"No, I don't know."

"He's very secretive. Especially about money. Arthur, I've got to get a job. It's all driving me mad. You've got to help me."

"Help you find a job?"

"I still can't get over you sending Boss some young girl to help him the other week, someone that nobody had heard of, with no experience when I could have done that - there'd be good tips in that too. Why didn't you come and get me?"

He sighs. "How could I come and get you? Rick was with Hamilton. Oh sorry, Mr Hamilton to you boy."

"There's Jake, he could have looked after things for five minutes."

"You know that wouldn't work. Especially when the owner is there. Anyway," Arthur adds, "Boss couldn't take you on account of Libby. I hid the kid on Tom's boat afterwards in case Libby went on a rampage when she found out."

Rae bites her lip and nods her head. Yes there is that. There is definitely no way she would want to stand between Libby and Libby's property.

But Arthur continues, “There’s a funny thing now. That kid is doing trip after trip with Boss and not a murmur.” He frowns. “I hope Libby isn’t getting into bad company.”

“I’ve seen her,” says Rae listlessly because Libby’s defection is a sore point. “At the Beach. With Hamilton’s son, is that what you mean by bad company? It’s what everyone else thinks. I don’t know why, no-one will explain it. He’s got rich friends, he dresses well. Big boats come here with beautiful people and he’s the only one who gets invited.” Arthur doesn’t respond. “And his bloody father’s still here. Why is that? Surely it doesn’t take two weeks to go through the books. There’s something else! You do know don’t you?”

“I hear that he and his son are engaged in some real estate deal that will surprise and delight us all.”

“Oh is that it? I thought it was more clandestine that that.”

“You don’t need to know what else young Hamilton gets up to, because what you don’t know can’t harm you.”

“I’ll ask Libby when I see her. She’ll know.”

“Yes, that’s what I’m worried about.”

But Rae isn’t really listening to him. “And then they say that he’s heading off again in a week or two, when that Havermore fellow with the big boat comes back and they’re going up the islands. How can he have a business and keep disappearing?”

“It could be the sort of business where the principal is better off elsewhere.”

“I don’t understand these things,” says Rae creasing her brow. “Who runs it then, when he’s gone?”

“He’ll get in some new sidekick. Someone with a criminal record no doubt.”

Something turns over in Rae’s brain. The Hamiltons had both been there the night before last, at the Beach Hotel. Rick had said that she was a trollop and a slut to be going off with ‘such a man.’ It can’t have been the elder Hamilton, he made her flesh creep, and as for Anthony Hamilton, surely it wasn’t him he was talking about? ‘Giving us all a bad name, bringing me and the bar into disrepute.’ What does that mean? The effort to remember is making her head hurt - she is trying to recall with all her might but some other part of her seems to be following along and putting up walls. She puts her head back to concentrate but instead falls into a sort of doze. Time passes and she is aware that Arthur has taken up a book.

“What are you reading?” she asks.

“I found it in Randall’s room.”

"If it's one of Randall's books I don't want to know about it. Fancy you reading things like that, I'm surprised at you."

"No, it's not like that, nothing indecent has happened. In fact nothing has happened at all. It's about some men in a boat, they just go sailing about."

She snorts disbelievingly and leans forward to discover the title. "Moby Dick!" she cries in surprise. "But that's a kid's book."

"Really," says Arthur surprised in his turn. "Are you sure? It's got one set of hard words in it for a children's book."

"It's about a white whale. I've never read it myself but I know they kill it. And there are lots of fights and people killed and adventures and stuff on the way."

"I'm glad to hear there's some big ending to it. All they've done so far is just sail and sail."

"You can't expect it to be too exciting, it's a classic. It's all got to be toned down, so as not to frighten the little ones. Fancy Randall having such a book!"

"He has a lot of books in there like this."

"Maybe I should read a book." Nothing could be more dreary than that she should be reduced to reading a book. She gets up though for something to do and wanders into the house. It is an exact replica of her own, a low modern bungalow in the shape of a 'T' with glass sliding doors from the roofed terrace opening into a living room which in turn leads into a kitchen/diner. At right angles there is a corridor, with the bathroom and laundry and two bedrooms, a double and a single. The corridor also has sliding doors out on to the terrace. The doors to both bedrooms are open. The larger bedroom reveals two single beds neatly made up with clothes carefully piled and everything in order. The single room could not have been more different. Coming in from the scented shade of the terrace Rae is nearly driven back by the smell of unwashed clothing and male odour. You're never going in there? exclaims her mother.

But he's a white man, surely that makes it acceptable?

Her mother is knitting things for execution and jerks the wool on its needles. Acceptable! When has it ever been acceptable for the races to live together in the same house, what kind of white man is that? He's the sort that contaminates.

Rae picks her way over the rubbish to the shelving unit that takes up one entire wall. On these shelves are quantities of magazines, films in blue metal canisters and crumpled books. She looks them over with distaste, she knows what subject matter they contain and it certainly isn't for these that she has ventured into this fetid lair. However on the bottom shelf, somewhat more tidily arranged than the cascade of material above, are a dozen or so books propped up against a sponge bag. Crime and Punishment, Lord of the Rings, Oliver Twist, two Agatha Christies, half a dozen spy thrillers, and to her surprise, a romance. She comes back out on to the terrace, "I can't believe it, he's got Georgette Heyer!"

"What's that?"

"Women's fiction." Arthur looks blank. "You know, where the heroine marries a duke. Romance. Lots of adventure and misunderstanding, then all they do at the end is kiss."

"Is there something wrong with that?"

"It's about stupid ninnies falling in love. It's pathetic."

"It still sounds better than all this sailing about for no reason. And what has made you so sour about love of a sudden? You were happy as could be with Rick on Saturday night."

That's true, she had been happy to be going out with Rick. All dressed up in her long frock with the red frill at the bottom, her bosoms clenched in the low-cut shiny satin, her hair up, make-up on, looking good. But then. She remembers something now about that night, it's coming back. When they got to the Beach, bloody Hamilton came over as if he was expecting to see them. Rick never said they were meeting him there. And then having to sit with him and watch him hatching some plan with Rick, when she should have been getting the attention. Her mind returns to the problem - where did she go after that and with whom? She worries at the few images she has. The same old blank. Coffee. That's what she needs. She wants coffee and she wants Arthur to go and make it for her. She puts the proposition to him.

"Coffee," says Arthur showing no sign of moving. "You know there's nothing in our kitchen."

Rae goes into the kitchen to look, "Oh you liar. You've got a jar of Maxwell House. Nearly full!"

"That so. That would be Lucas," Arthur murmurs drowsily. "Our Lucas is the house-proud one, he goes shopping for things like toilet rolls and soap and he's always sweeping and washing. I bet you won't find anything else though."

Rae doesn't want anything else. She makes herself a cup, black and strong, and wanders back out. She really wants the kind of coffee they have at the Beach, properly percolated - she'd kill for a coffee like that. But anything is better than nothing. Arthur has taken the book up again.

She stretches out a hand and picks up a magazine that is lying half under her chair, just to read anything. "Oh look at this awful thing," she says in disgust throwing it down again. "You'd better watch out, your Aunt Marion is bound to come over if it's your day off. I'm always amazed that she lets you live here with a sleazebucket like Randall, with all these magazines all over the place. Isn't she afraid that a delicate flower like Daphne might pick one up and lose her innocence?"

"They're not usually out here. His friends must have come round last night."

"What an ugly collection they are - do you think they're really his friends? I'm sure if I had friends half that ugly I'd never let people see me hanging out with them. They give me the creeps. Which reminds me, I wonder when Rick is coming up for lunch".

"He won't be coming home to lunch, he's down there on his own."

"Why, when's Lawrence coming in?"

"Lawrence is not coming in, Lawrence's services have been dispensed with. It appears we don't any longer require a third barman. According to Hamilton."

Now this is news with a vengeance! It goes without saying, cutting costs. Ed Hamilton is an animal. Fat-faced old bastard leering down the front of her dress, what a disgusting saggy-armed mole-covered red pimply-nosed hairy old goat he is, with his fat hands reaching out to paw her when Rick went to the toilet. Ugh! And what horrible attitudes he has, waving like a sultan and bellowing "Boy" just like the fat white retired tool-manufacturer from Detroit that he is. Whisps of words come away like cobwebs blurred by rum and sugarfroth, "Too friendly and they won't respect you, just the right distance….. Remember, these Coloureds have got their own government now but they don't amount to much in the real world. It's still us", he said it loudly so everyone could hear, "who are organising things, managing the bars, the hotels, the charter operations. Bringing the jobs, the investment. It's our money that is keeping these one-horse organisations going. If it wasn't for us they'd be paying for things in bananas," laughing immoderately at that and inviting Rick and her to join in. But she didn't laugh, even after three planters punches she wouldn't laugh at something that wasn't funny. All that lovely sweet syrup that swirled so magnificently focus-free - and what a waste when you had to sit with that pig Hamilton. And Rick, sucking up to him, he'd never been like that in England. Rick has changed. Yes, in England he would never have put up with things like this new development, getting rid of Lawrence - only Arthur to relieve him. The bloody bar will engross all his time now. They already have no personal life, no sex or hardly any, is it? She is trawling her memory again and she knows there is something pressing and large that she has to remember - she shuts her eyes and tries to revisit the evening again. Everything keeps slipping just out of reach.

She jerks back awake. "I remember something," she says. "At the Beach Hotel, the bloody Premier stopped at our table. And Rick, you know how Rick is with him, affable but not exactly inviting. Hamilton – listen - Hamilton said when he'd moved on, 'There's no call for that. Don't go encouraging them or they'll be coming into the bar." We just stared. Even though Rick doesn't really want him coming in the bar because of how he's carrying on with Libby. But just then the son appears and is all over the Premier like a rash, shaking his hand, slapping him on the shoulder. Well then the penny drops with Hamilton and he got really angry and said Rick should have invited him to sit down and have a drink! I don't know what the rules are in these games Hamilton plays. For instance, the Sergeant comes over and he's about as low as you can go in my opinion but Hamilton seems to think it's alright to encourage him, for reasons I don't understand. So I sit there being polite like the rest of them. And then," again something is catching at her memory, "he starts acting as if I like him. But you know, I don't like the Sergeant at all."

"No, but telling the Sergeant what you really think of him is not a good idea," murmurs Arthur. "He is a man best left to his illusions."

Thoughts of the Sergeant are very much in the mind of Constable Lucas Frankland as he guns his light motorcycle up the narrow hill between the marina and the lagoon. He is a young man and anger burned bright like fresh blood half an hour ago but the activity and lapse of time is already slowing and clotting it as he nears the house.

He has taken the long way round in order to calm down, following the back road through the hills behind Fort John and down past the old Protestant church. Sometimes when he goes that way, he stops and goes in to the graveyard there because it's quiet and shady and rarely visited – it contains the last remaining monuments to so many young and very young white men who came to St Claire for many reasons but died always the same tropical death. In the same desperate graves lie their named offspring aged 3 weeks or 10 months or 4 years. And their wives. The whole family dying in the cause of copra, bananas or Her Britannic Majesty's Royal Navy. But today he drives on down the winding picturesque streets until he emerges from the colonial heritage into the discordant untidy unpainted but vibrant present. Bright sun, dirt, discoloured concrete and rusty iron. But real, full of residents rather than tourists; everyone going about their business, going to the shops, going to lunch. The road to the marina is also the road to the ocean beaches and therefore carries a good deal of traffic so he has to keep his wits about him as the route taxis in particular are erratically driven, the drivers being more concerned to look for passengers than to bother themselves with the other traffic about. He turns in at the marina and fights his way up the rough gravel track to the house - it is barely more than a footpath, not wide enough for a car and covered with loose skidding stones that strain man and machine. All of this requires concentration so that by the time the puttering and exploding of his engine announces his arrival, he is considerably cooler in temper than he was. He parks his motorbike and clatters up the steps to the terrace with his peaked cap under his arm.

Rae thinks, I ought to go. Lucas always drives her mother into paroxysms of rage. It must be something to do with the taking-charge manner he has - a misdirected confidence that he counts in the scheme of things. On the other hand he always has the most interesting news. Somehow it seems necessary to put up with the mutterings in the corner in order to find out what is going on in the world. Therefore his first words keep her where she is. "I could kill that Sergeant," he says.

"We were just talking about him," she exclaims.

Lucas goes into the room he shares with Arthur and shuts the door. Rae says, "He's not going to start cleaning again is he? I shall go home."

"I'll come with you," says Arthur.

They both lie there without moving. Look at me! thinks Rae. I can't even work up the energy to get away. I'm trapped here until he tells me what the Sergeant's done now.

But he'll go back to work shortly and then everything will drift back into the disconcerting line of thought she has been pursuing. She actually feels she was getting somewhere before..... Again her mind drifts until Lucas emerges a few minutes later wearing just shorts. "You're going to wash the floor," groans Rae. "I knew you were." He looks at her and then glares and then starts to stamp about as if in pain. What! What's wrong with saying that?

Lucas swoops up to her and with wordless rage grabs the magazine that's lying under her chair.

"It's Randall, not me."

"I know it's that bloody Randall, he does this on purpose. He leaves this filth so everyone can see it. The whole island must know what a jackass we share a house with. I've told him, I've told him and told him to keep this stuff to himself." He strides over to Randall's room, throws the magazine in and slams the door. "How can I deal with the Sergeant when I hear on the criminal grapevine that all the pimps and sleazebags are up at Constable Frankland's place on any given night - he makes me a laughing stock."

"Well," says Arthur, "it was you who thought he would be OK, lift the tone of the place, have a white man move in."

"He's not that white," remarks Rae. "Being out in the sun all day."

Arthur says, "Well he's not white white white to look at but he's whiter than we are."

"I don't think he is. You hardly go out in the sun at all - I bet you're paler than he is. Though Lucas is not that white."

"Nor," says Lucas with dignity, "would I want to be. The coming thing is black. Black is what we want on these islands. White has had its day of being in charge and bossing everyone around - it's time to move on."

"Black!" says Arthur. "You're calling yourself black now?"

"Yes I thought that was a racial slur," says Rae. "Am I supposed to call you black? What happened to 'coloured'?"

"No black is what we are, black power, black is beautiful."

Rae laughs in outrage. Black is beautiful! What a stupid idea. Who would want to be black if they possibly could help it? All those West Indians in London using skin lightener and straightening their hair and having nose jobs, what a hoot. Black isn't beautiful at all! Who ever saw a black woman who was beautiful?

Arthur is also laughing, "Black, black. You're not black!" he cries pointing at Lucas. "Oh Lord, what an idea." He gets out of his hammock. "Look, come here. Come come. Put out your arm. Here Rae," he grabs all their arms and puts them alongside each other. "Now let's call a spade a spade."

"Hey, watch who you're calling that."

Haahaa, they all start to giggle and their arms shake together and shiver in a line. "Now", says Arthur, "keep still. Look, this arm is pinky brown, this arm is browny orange and this arm is browny brown. Where is there a black arm here? I don't see anything black."

"You've got no political consciousness," says Lucas withdrawing his arm with dignity and holding it with his other hand as if he sees in the thin slake of skin some glittering medal-like honour.

"Political consciousness!" says Arthur. "Now you've been told about using that word around here That word is not to be uttered or we'll take it and throw it into your room there and slam the door." Arthur gets back in his hammock laughing.

Rae wipes her eyes, oh my. But then watches disconsolately as Lucas fills his bucket. Now it will be all mopping and water flying - he always makes her feel so hot and desiccated like some bunch of a thing that can barely move, oppressed by heat and humidity, while he skips around in that grasshopper way of his. She gets out of her comfortable chair and lies on the concrete balustrade out of range. There he is, roaring around so that everyone in his orbit is inundated by piston firing energy, his absurd thin body all angles like a khaki-coloured locust with a locust's ravening hunger. "Well," she says ironically, "if they ever give promotions for clean floors you will be a sergeant yourself one day."

"Then there'll be peace," says Arthur, "instead of all this beating about with a mop." Lucas doesn't respond.

"Boss's boat is in today I see," Rae can see it now from her new vantage point. "This'll be the first time in days. You remember Charles saying he'd never use him again after all the other drunken disasters. Then he's suddenly in constant demand. That girl you got for him must be having a day off. All that money. She's probably out buying a hammock." She sighs.

"I saw them again this morning, in the dawn," says Lucas, his head down. "They had cine cameras and flash cameras and all sorts of cameras and they were all lining up for pictures. Next to some fish."

"And all thanks to Arthur for finding him that girl. Let's just hope Boss doesn't feel like making her a fixture."

"Now that should be interesting," says Lucas slowing down thoughtfully. "I don't know if the marina could cope with that amount of interest. I think we'd need a lot more police officers to attend to law and order."

"It seems that Libby is off being interested in someone else," murmurs Arthur.

"Now," says Lucas stopping and leaning on the mop, "that will create interest of another sort with Immigration if she's no longer living on Boss's boat."

Rae is surprised. "Yes but Immigration, they're hardly going to do anything when someone high up is involved."

"Don't you be so sure of that. A certain high and mighty person might think he can spread favours to all and sundry but Immigration can't be corrupted. They will take what decisions they see fit. And it is always muggins here who has to take the debris to the airport when they get deported, it's always me that has to take them over to Port Sophia and load them on a plane for home. I hate that, with them always weeping and wailing fit to burst."

"Well wouldn't you be howling too? If someone forced you to go back to England," says Rae.

"I would go back like a shot," says Lucas glumly. "I could further my education."

"You're stuffed full of education already. Why would you be wanting any more of that?" says Arthur.

"Yes, you always laugh at my diploma, but let me ask you where you think you're going with your life, without an education? It's a very useful thing, any sort of accountancy qualification. I would be very useful in a fraud investigation. In fact the Chief Constable himself has said that Constable Frankland would be a valuable man in a fraud investigation. The Chief Constable believes in improving the skills in the force."

"Ah Lucas, the Sergeant is not a man who would be letting you distinguish yourself in any way like that," says Arthur. Lucas promptly goes into a frenzy of floor washing as if to drown out such a suggestion but even Rae knows that Lucas has no hope of promotion under the current regime. His Sergeant and various of the Sergeant's rough and ill-favoured friends occasionally descend on the Frangipani and from their conversation she has gathered that Lucas is considered an effeminate freak who won't last the distance if ever the going gets rough. Knowing the Sergeant, Rae thinks the going could get rough at any time.

"Why do you stay at that station?" she says. "I'm sure you'd get on much better if you were in the main town, or another station. That Sergeant is bad news."

"He'll go too far," says Lucas. "One day he'll get caught out." He finishes his mopping with an energy that shows that in reality he is flaying skin and thrusts the mop back in the bucket with a bang.

"Thank god that's over," says Arthur.

"Poor Arthur," says Rae who has turned her head to look down the hill, "I fear you are about to have a new visitation. Aunt Marion has been shopping and is looking hot. Daphne is carrying all the parcels and is looking harassed. And I bet you have no cool drinks to offer them." She lies back down in the chair again. Life is always interesting on Arthur's terrace. Really they should have had this house, this is the house where everything happens.

The marina has been constructed below a narrow ridge, about a hundred yards long, that curves round into the lagoon and Arthur's house is on top of the hill with a view down over the boats and the Frangipanni. Rae and Rick's house is at right angles to Arthur's and looks out towards the mouth of the harbour and the Caribbean beyond. Apart from the track which Lucas has just driven up and which zigzags from side to side in a haphazard way, there is also a more direct stepped path to the marina up which Rae has seen Arthur's family advancing.

Aunt Marion is a large brown-skinned woman dressed in a calf-length maroon and yellow dress. A thin girl with severely plaited hair struggles in her wake, weighed down with packages. Rae sighs in advance. Nothing could now drag her away as she knows that some serious gossip is going to ensue but her regret is that she probably won't understand all of it. She isn't sure what happens because she and Arthur and Lucas have just been chatting away in standard English, but the moment Arthur's aunt arrives the talk will immediately sink into a sort of grammatical dyslexia. Words will surface which aren't in any dictionary, all sorts of damage will be done to verbs and participles, and vowels will suddenly become thick like plaster. Even Lucas, who most of the time has a disconcerting North London accent, will suddenly start peppering his vocabulary with outlandish words and constructions. But worst of all Aunt Marion will eventually take Arthur away and she will be left on her own with Rick not even coming up for lunch. She wants to lie on the beach in a long lounging deck chair with a cool fruit drink and have someone to talk to but where is she to find anyone to go with her?

"I wish I had a little car," she says aloud apropos of nothing. "I'd go and see if Jim is home. Has anyone seen his new house? You know if Rick got me a car I wouldn't mind working for nothing. He's such a tightwad. How much would a little car cost to hire, not much I bet. But I know it would be too much for him. Don't you think having a car would be good, Arthur? We could use it for the bar - I'd go into town and get supplies. Bloody Michael's never around when you want him."

"Rick's short-handed and could do with your help. Maybe it's a good time to ask," is all Arthur says.

A car. Oh if only she had a car - she could zip off anywhere. Just a little car and she would be free. The suggestion turns and turns like a cat and settles itself comfortably. "You could use it yourself," she says to Arthur, "think how useful it would be. You could put it to Rick too, how we need one," the idea pummels and claws urgently at her attention.

Meanwhile Arthur's aunt heaves herself up the last steps onto the veranda with the wheezing difficulty of the well fleshed. "Here, wet again, Lucas Frankland!" she puffs. "You always mopping this place, these tiles will wear down. And you Arthur, loaching again, you there like a king jajah doing nothing the whole day. Michael tell me that the manager is down there on his own, so I know you get the day off. It is midday already and I can't see you yet! I must come over myself. And Daphne too," she remarks as she sinks into a chair and fans herself.

"Well Tantie," Arthur says mildly, "yesterday I work from seven in the morning until well after one o'clock in the night and I start again at six this evening so I am resting. After I have rested in this hammock I am going to have a siesta on my bed. And then I might come out here and rest some more."

Aunt Marion clicks her tongue, "I hear Lawrence get fired. I wonder what happen, boy."

"The owner is a pig," says Rae. "The owner thinks Rick and Arthur and everyone should work longer hours for the same money."

"That's what you get working for the yankee dollar. But you can't lie down the whole day and expect to get paid well you know."

"I don't want to be well paid Tantie, I just want to be well rested."

"Boy, you too young for this, what rubbish. Young people don't sleep so the whole day. When you old you can get in a rocking chair and doze, no-one ain't going to care then. They no business with you. Now get out of that hammock and let me make you something nice to eat at home, where you come to make my fence."

He'll go, thinks Rae. No backbone. He doesn't want to go but he'll go anyway. He'll make exaggerated sobbing sounds but he always does what his family wants. Families, Rae thinks bitterly, they only come to criticize. What do you do all day? Look at this floor! Don't you iron your sheets then? And then when I get mad she goes away, I mean my mother, I'm talking about my mother, she goes away in hurt silence. Then I'm all alone. I wish Arthur wouldn't go, what am I going to do then? I'm not going down to the bar if Rick's still mad at me, why should I? I've got enough to cope with. I'd kill for a good cup of coffee though.

Arthur meanwhile is temporizing. "I can't go," says Arthur. "Look, Lucas come home to clean up and I can't leave him to do it alone."

Lucas lets out a laugh and puts his hands on his hips in mock indignation. "Don't put me in this now. He's just too idle Tantie. Have you ever seen him do anything, clean anything or go down to the store to get anything. You'd better give him something to do, yes, let him fix the fence for you."

"You could fix it," says Arthur. "You're good at that and then Tantie would cook you a nice pot of pelau. You ain't going to get that here."

"No, we never have a piece of food in this house. Every time I turn around they eat out everything no matter what I buy. But I have to go back to work. The Sergeant knows I'm off for the afternoon but he's taken it into his head to go and investigate a crime that's not even in our district. So I have to close the station and put up a sign saying, 'Closed'. That's crazy for a police station! But otherwise he's going to walk all over me."

"So what is the big crime?" asks Aunt Marion sitting up and looking interested.

"Common assault this morning and a set of screaming and shouting last night over in Louisaville. And don't talk about the neighbours, they're all putting in their piece. It has nothing to do with the Sergeant but still he has to go and investigate."

"Ahha," says Aunt Marion greedily. "Screaming and shouting. In Louisaville. But maybe they just arguing - sometimes these women scream and shout and it is just they like to argue. But you don't expect this from rich white people."

"First of all it is not coming from a house where the man is married. And second it isn't the type of moans and screams that you would want me to talk about in front of Daphne."

"Louisaville, well I live near there. I wonder where it is? Maybe someone I know." Aunt Marion is full of pleasant speculation, "Tell me where Lucas."

"Oh gosh Tantie," says Lucas in irritation. "This isn't any business of yours. You will know about it when the time comes." He eventually gives in. "It is Anthony Hamilton's house where the bacchanal happen."

"Really, the owner's son, the owner of the Frangipani, his son!" everyone is thrilled.

"I wonder when this happen boy? Last night and this morning? I am surprised no-one tell me yet."

"Yes," says Lucas seriously. "It surprises me too. I thought you'd know but Pa didn't have a chance to tell you yet perhaps."

"So who get beat up? The person living still?"

"He isn't dead - in fact he wants to throw Anthony Hamilton out bag and baggage."

"The man who own that house! I expect Dale was with him, he would know everything that goes on. And to think that he ain't even come by to tell me anything. Look, let me go home. Well Arthur, come with me now."

"No no you don't need me, you want to go and maco what's going on with the rich people. You won't even have time to see about your fence."

But his aunt is set on it, if her fence is ever to be done who must do it but her own flesh and blood, her nephew. "Arthur, come let we go now."

"Well I shall go to the Beach Hotel," says Rae, "and have a quiet cup of coffee away from such excitements. Sit and rest with my feet up. Quietly contemplate life and maybe have a snooze."

Arthur groans in envy.

Down by the road Aunt Marion is in a temper. "Where is that boy now!" she says. "He was just there and he's gone again. I am not going back for him. If I only hold that boy it will be trouble!"

Heat and white dust from the side of the road enfold them. Sweat trickles down the line of Rae's spine and she stands dreaming of a car. "If only I had a car I'd be there by now," she thinks. "I must get Arthur to help me persuade Rick, after all how much would one cost? We could hire one by the month. I reckon Rick gets heaps of money under the counter - he knows a thing or two about getting money on the sly from a set-up like the Frangipani and he never spends it on anything, we never go anywhere, the other night was the first time we've been out in a month. And he hardly gives me anything for housekeeping so he must have it stashed away somewhere." Rae becomes irritable as she considers her domestic situation. "He's changed. He's gone really secretive, he never used to be like this about money." For a moment she feels a twinge of conscience, a feeling that she might be part of the problem and really she ought to brave his anger over whatever happened the other night and go to the bar and help. But now she is here there is also a strong feeling of discontent starting to crystallise again in the waves of heat coming off the glaring white road. "He never tells me anything. He used to tell me things, why doesn't he tell me anything any more?" But anyway damn Rick, damn him, she will get her own job and make her own money, she won't put up with this. In future there'll be no more waiting on the side of the road for old beaten-up taxis bobbing on broken springs. There must be jobs making scads of money, other people seem to find them.

Meanwhile Aunt Marion is fanning herself impatiently, "Where's that wretch gone?"

A car pulls up with the word Taxi emblazoned on it, "Where you going," says the driver to Rae, ignoring the others. "You going to the Beach? Two dollars US."

"Get lost," says Rae waving him away impatiently. Almost immediately a battered older car peeps them and stops. Rae gets in. There is room for one more.

Aunt Marion orders Daphne in too, saying she will wait another two minutes and then if he doesn't come..... Her body language hints at family violence.

"The cheek of that guy," says Rae to the car in general indicating the taxi in front. "Does he think I'm stupid or what! Do I look like a rich fat stupid American who would pay two dollars US to go to the Beach Hotel?"

"They'll try it on," says the front seat passenger turning round. He is a handsome well-groomed islander, stocky with square fingers and a square gold ring. He seems shimmeringly familiar. “Good morning Mrs Elliot,” he says to Rae who feels some deep shock at his somehow knowing her. “And Daphne too,” he says when she says nothing. “How you going girl?”

Daphne lets out an inaudible breathless squeak.

Rae sits bolt upright. Daphne is sitting with nearly the same rigidity.

“You get home alright the other night?” he turns back to Rae smiling his almost perfect white smile.

“Ah,” is all she can get out, every other word being now scrambled. For a moment she panics, from the familiarity of the question it implies….. Well clearly he knows something, that she had been drunk otherwise why ask if she got home. And there is another layer of familiarity, as if he could possibly tell the others in the car something. What? She doesn’t know. But instead he turns to her companion.

“And Daphne, how’s the family?”

Daphne just puts her mouth into a rictus and says nothing. Like prey in the orbit of a snake, Rae realises that he is turning back to address her again. She feels hypnotised.

“Of course you could have forgotten my name, Mrs Elliot. Max de Troy. You know my brother, Sergeant de Troy.” He puts out his hand over the seat towards her. She shakes it with reluctance, she is aware that her own mouth might have formed into an ape-like gibber of fear. She can’t explain, but she is sure it has something to do with her lost evening. She tries to compose herself, she must change the subject otherwise who knows what he might say about the other night.

“We were just talking of your brother,” she manages to say in what she hopes is an off-hand manner. “I believe he is out this way investigating a crime.”

“A crime is how one person might look at it. Another person could look at it as self-defence, or exercising his just rights. Matters of business involving business documents. Everyone should be allowed to run their own affairs. These are small things, tying up police time in petty matters. Everyone adding to the story and making a meal of it. The neighbours and them, talking about moans and cries coming from the house when clearly it is that cesspool up at the Fort, all the folks up there using it like a brothel.” He waves his hand dismissively. “These are all stories put round by malicious persons, trying to ruin a young man’s reputation.”

Rae doesn't understand what he is saying but the casual way he dismisses the case against Anthony Hamilton brings the recollection, just forming, of the two of them the other night, together at the table.

"And what is bringing you out this way?" her new acquaintance continues.

"Just going to the Beach Hotel," again she is reluctant, although where she gets out is not something that can be hidden; he will see where she alights.

"Yes I am going there also. I hear the food is good." He taps the back of his seat as he looks back at her. "Perhaps you will be my guest, so that we can become re-acquainted."

She feels frozen under his gaze, his implied understanding. Anyone, such as her mother, might think that Something Is Going On. But for some reason, instead of becoming severe and distant she finds herself contemplating the hot wash of desire through her body. Where did that come from, the relaxing of muscles and the seepage of liquid? Coarse, she thinks, look at me. On heat in a taxi with a man I know I should have nothing to do with.

Daphne stands drooping beside a rutted unmade road, in a patch of shade. The main road to the ocean beaches has a veneer of modernity with stretches of tarmacadam that almost pass muster, but once off that it is as if the second half of the twentieth century has disappeared. Unrecognisable shreds and patches, vague squidgy things, litter the roadside and there are bad smells, the way things smell when death turns the undergrowth putrid or when drains are the work of a half-hearted municipality.

A few minutes later Aunt Marion emerges from another route taxi on the main road and comes over to stand with her daughter. She is flapping a fan, showing that she is disturbed. "Just so he met this white girl and he bringing her to make a fence with him. We all couldn't fit in the taxi so he….." A car turns into this secondary road and hoots and Marion waves it down. They get in and the beaten-up old car toils up the dusty pot-holed track. They lurch uphill banging against each other and the other passengers and all the way Marion exclaims, "Can you imagine, this little white girl no bigger than a stick in a little dainty dress, coming here and making a fence with him. I don't know what this boy is thinking in his head. He might have asked Rae you know but she a little bit too prim and proper to come in a house like ours. This is too much for me!" She shifts round in the available space, uneasily recounting this amazing fact over and over, that a white girl is coming to her house and who has ever heard the like.

The gradient eases and they are now running parallel to the sea below. Small cabins line the road and the taxi slows and stops near a group of ramshackle shops. Aunt Marion is distracted by more pressing concerns. "You wait here for them, I am going to go and check out some things."

Beside the shops Daphne again stands drooping, looking unattached, as if someone has dumped her there like a sack awaiting an owner.

Ten minutes later Arthur and Lynn emerge from another route taxi. "This is my cousin Daphne," says Arthur.

"Hello," says Lynn shaking her hand with happy enthusiasm.

Daphne says resignedly, "Ma's in the shop gathering gossip."

Arthur says, "Well let's not wait now."

As soon as they've gone a few steps from the shop and are out of range, Daphne says, "Rae and I got in a taxi and guess who was there? Max!"

Arthur stops, his expression goes blank. "You tell Tantie?"

"No." Daphne snuffles like a frightened rabbit in its lair.

Arthur says nothing and walks on. His manner of walking is not now the crisp movements of a barman with a range of tasks to accomplish. He is indolent, slumped. He idles down the road, his loose sandals splay sideways in the dust channelling the white fume behind him.

The development that caused so much amazement to Marion came about because Arthur had been wandering resignedly like this after his aunt's broad back when he heard a cooee from the direction of the jetty and Lynn bounced forward with a huge beaming smile, waving her arms and dancing. Words could barely express her pleasure at seeing him, or in the morning generally. The enormous largesse of all the charterers (in American dollars too!) and then Boss paying her on top of that, all the days of work she'd had making her by now the richest person in the whole marina and all thanks to him.

"The man at the bar said it was your morning off and I understood from him that you were in a hammock somewhere, having a lovely lazy time."

"Well you can tell him when you see him that my aunt came and got me out of my hammock and now I have to go and make a fence for her. That will make him feel better."

She looked at his wry mouth. "Don't you think you'll like putting up a fence?"

"I don't think anyone would enjoy such a thing, would they?"

"I used to love it. I used to help with the fencing on my grandmother's cattle station. She had a big property in Australia."

"So you're not a city girl?"

"I never lived in a city until we went to London."

"And you used to love fencing. I see," he says slowly. "And what exactly are you doing right at the moment?"

"Well I was going to go out and see something of the island. I don't know if there are buses, you'd be the person to know. You see, isn't it lucky I saw you just now!"

Was it luck? Who knows. Sometimes fate takes a hand and we start voyages that seem to have been intended from the very beginning. Looking back, I can't imagine a past that didn't include Arthur inviting Lynn to his aunt's house and Lynn enthusiastically accepting.

They are now on fairly level land just below the rim of the hill. It is thickly covered with backyard vegetation. Corrugated iron roofs, red with rust, poke through the screen of mango, coconut palms, nutmeg, governor's plums and other species of fruit and spice trees that seem to have found a little oasis up here. Arthur leads the way along a sandy track, past houses where old women potter among vegetables and chickens peck bare earth underneath banana palms, punctuating their browsings with gentle exclamations of 'What is this that I see look look look and who is this walking down our street look look look.'

After a dozen or so houses the road turns a corner and starts running up hill. Soon Arthur turns through an opening into dense shade where a cracked path of stone leads them through a mass of entwined flowering shrubs and fruit trees. The house is almost hidden behind all the foliage, yet despite years of neglect it is evident that it has once been a house of some solidity and affluence. Lynn glimpses what looks like a huge old gate post topped with some sort of sculptured griffon among the thick tangle of bamboo, palm and the broad boles and foliage of other trees. "Where does she want the fence?" she asks Arthur puzzled. But he just smiles as he puts his hand through the letterbox of a rather fine but warped door and hooks up a key. He turns it in the lock then gives the door a sharp bang with his shoulder and hip to force an opening to the domain within.

Chapter 3

These eyes are windows, and this body of mine is the house

I wonder what sort of dreams people have, who have never sailed away from home. They must be so safe and comforting. I can't imagine that they ever wander endlessly through strange rooms looking for connections, pulled on from corridor to corridor, past the packed layers of flotsam which have drifted out of vast oceans and ended up stuffed on shelves and in cupboards and at the back of drawers.

But there is a guilty pleasure in opening hidden doors and finding that rollcall of objects: a white plastic raincoat, a bakelite lamp, that row of untidy books. These are the sweet dreams of strange and welcoming rooms. If only they were not interspersed with dangerous dark caves, creaking chests and the dull red jewellery of nightmare.

Aunt Marion's house, surrounded by its jungle fecundity, is a warren of unknown rooms the day Lynn crosses over the unfenced boundary. Arthur stands holding open the door. His aunt, who has raised him from a child, frowns on friendships across racial lines. She believes that Coloured should stay with Coloured, Indian should associate with Indian, White should stick to White. "That way no one is getting hurt."

But I've said before, children should ignore all such advice from parental figures. Each generation should listen politely and pretend to agree. Tell the wrinklies what they want to hear. This leaves the young free to dissolve the existing lines of prejudice and incomprehension and replace them with new forms of misunderstanding and intolerance – and so the world moves on.

The irony is, of course, that the young will be old themselves one day. As I am. Then we have to listen to our own children making soothing remarks about where they are going, who they are seeing, and what they are doing. The lies they tell us!

Up until the point that Arthur opens the door for Lynn, he has maintained a sort of status quo with his aunt by not telling her anything in particular. Since starting work at the Frangipani he's got to know many young men of his own age who happen to be white. He's joined in on the wisecracking and horseplay, unleashed some high spirits by kicking a ball about on a nearby piece of wasteland and then gradually he's found himself being invited onto their boats, included in group outings, regularly spending his day off surrounded by lethargic figures settling in on his terrace for a bout of idle chatter.

But now here is a complication, well two really. First of all, this is not one of his male yachtie friends. His aunt knows about them of course – her habit of turning up on his days off has made the acquaintanceship inevitable. She disapproves in theory but he thinks that she also rather likes some of them. He has no idea what she is going to think about this latest friend because this is a girl, a young and pretty one. And secondly, this isn't his house at the marina; this is a private realm where none of his other friends have yet been. He is opening the door and who knows where it may lead.

There is a wide uncarpeted wooden hallway. To the right a door opens onto a show bedroom with all Tantie's best things: an antique bed that she inherited from her grandmother, a carved wardrobe, an incongruously modern dressing table. The bed is covered very neatly in a white lacy coverlet with large worked pink flowers and all the other surfaces are covered in worked lacy runners. The walls are bare wood like the hall and are hung with a number of prints mainly of flowers but a couple are English scenes with watermills and horses.

There are other doors off the hall but they are shut, most of the rooms at this end of the house are empty. His aunt has lived in this house only a short time and all the furniture from her previous tiny cottage barely fill two rooms. However she has attempted to replicate the clutter of her old home by arranging small ornaments on the walls of the hall; a framed biblical quotation, a plate inscribed 'Barbados', carvings of ibis, and coloured prints and straw-workings and tinselly items forming a frieze of cheerful colour. One room off the hallway has a door slightly ajar and that room is crowded with clothes hanging on hooks and orange boxes upended and stuffed with shoes. She needs more wardrobes, Arthur notes. He knows the wardrobes in the best bedroom are empty in case the room is ever required as a guest room and all the clothes that used to be in them are out gathering moths and silverfish. He sighs; he must mention it to his sister when she arrives in a day or two.

The door at the end of the hall leads into a large living room. The living room floorboards are covered with a few brightly-coloured worked rag rugs which are spread out in an attempt to give a feeling of plenty when in fact they only make dots of colour and tend to enlarge the room. The furniture consists of an old day-bed piled with red and yellow pillows, a carved antique side board and a beautiful mahogany piano, all of which came with the house because, Arthur suspects, they would crumble apart from termites if they were ever moved. These three pieces of furniture are the only things in the whole room. The side board is covered with souvenirs, dolls of many countries and gaudy pottery and the piano is thick with family photos. There is also a huge straggling cactus which has burst out of late into florets of bright orange. But the room has an abandoned air as if it is rarely used. The walls have been wallpapered at some stage in a floral design predominantly of pink roses, but the plank boards of the wall are visible through the paper either in outline or where the paper has worn through. There are slat windows all down the side through which one can see thick vegetation and to the front are a pair of impressive decorated doors looking as if they are waiting to be thrown open (in fact they are so warped that this is impossible). Despite all the windows, the room is dark with a closed-in, heavy feel. Two long strips of flypaper are plastered with flies but the uncaptured still noiselessly circle.

Off to the left, through a door and down a short corridor past a large pantry is the kitchen, a scullery and steps down to the under part of the house. The kitchen is exactly as Aunt Marion's previous kitchen had been - a cacophony of colour. Plastic fruit and flowers of unnatural yellows and reds are bunched among plastic mottoes and improbably-coloured luminescent doilies. Brightly-coloured cafe curtains dangle over the windows. Glasses with purple and green stripes sit arranged on a shelf along with a large yellow-daisy jug. On the wall beside a green enamel gas stove is pinned last year's calendar. '1968' it says in huge glittering letters, a gift from the

Federation Chamber of Industry and Commerce. It is still stuck in August with a photograph of a young girl laden with bright red flowers the colour of sauce bottles.

Reds, oranges, lime greens and purples are the predominant colours of the kitchen - swirling like boiled lollies around a aqua laminex table and several metal and vinyl kitchen chairs mainly of aqua and silver but some of a very brave speckled pink.

Lynn wanders here and there examining things. "It's like the old sugar plantation houses we lived in in Australia."

Arthur raises his eyebrows. "That's interesting," he says. "I heard that the original owner made money from sugar. But not here, they tried to grow sugar on the island but it wasn't economical, so they went back to copra and bananas."

He opens the door to the veranda and leads the way out. He is unprepared for Lynn's cries of delight when she follows him. To tell the truth, he has never thought about his aunt's house except to feel pleased that she settled on one at last. He knows how difficult it was for her to move out of the tiny cabin that she had lived in for so long and how she resisted anything lavish. He suspects she chose this house because no-one could possibly be intimidated by its crumbling antiquity. And yet here is the kid genuinely charmed by it, clapping her hands and exclaiming with pleasure, when under the precepts currently in fashion everyone is supposed to look down on the unpainted, the unplastered, the un-new and the inconvenient.

The veranda is magnificent in its own way. Or rather it is magnificently useable and homely. It is as wide as the whole house and over 20 feet deep, supported by the posts of great trees plucked somewhere from the surrounding jungle and worked not by the hiss of modern machinery but by the toil and hand of man. The corners of these great slabs of trunk have been shaped and carved and although there is nothing figurative about them, they look like great limbs holding fragile humans in their palms. Above, a roof gives shade and below and entwining the whole is the garden. Clearly no-one would want to spend any time in the interior of the house when the veranda is all one would ever need for cool air and protection from the sun and rain. In addition, it looks out on an uninterrupted sweep of sea, with further bays and inlets to the west and, far off, more islands. There is almost nothing to be seen of the beach hotels or suburbs below because in front, where the land falls away, the edge is curtained in huge flame trees and coconut palms and a lushness of ripe flowers among luxuriant foliage so that the eye travels outwards over a profusion of rich colour to blue blue horizons. Meanwhile the breeze sweeps gently over and cools the viewer who sinks into a cane planter's chair, stretches at full length and goes to sleep, as Arthur promptly does.

Steps lead down one side and Lynn wanders down them. A door is open and she can see into a large room under the veranda which is in danger of being invaded by an onslaught of flowering creepers. Great bundles of white perfumed droplets hang along the outside and spill into the cool interior. The room is lined with the same bare boards as upstairs on three sides but on the outer side there is a wall of windows, the slats of which have stood open so long that the flowers of the creeper now live between them. Net curtains hang in bunches and move gently in the breeze like ladies rearranging their lace. There are two beds and clothes hang here and there. Lynn imagines that Arthur's relatives have sensibly rejected the upper floor and have made their bedroom in this cool and joyous room perfumed by its intruding flower-lanterns. It looks out onto a chaos of garden crowded with tropical flowers so lush that their scented presence crushes in on all sides.

A new construction to one side is in fact a modern bathroom, quite recently completed by the look of it because busy tendrils are only just beginning to make their way up the outside of the shower bay. One day it too will be engulfed in flowers like everything else. Sleep among flowers, rise up and wash among flowers; the wind chimes gently clang eight bells and women gather blossoms to wear in their hair and sit gracefully on cushions doing peaceful things.

Lynn walks towards the bottom of the garden, past old stone statuary now competing with jungle regrowth. At the bottom, near where the land suddenly starts to fall steeply and turns into a cliff, she finds tumbled stones like a wall.

On returning to the house, Lynn finds Arthur dozing on the veranda and sits down in one of the cane chairs. Daphne has been watching Lynn closely through the drip of bead curtaining that keeps flies from the kitchen. Daphne is 15 and much under her mother's thumb and has been told many times that any relationship between White and Coloured is against the law of nature and someone will get hurt. She therefore is at a loss what to do about her cousin and this girl because she is sure that if anything happens before her mother arrives to take it in hand, it will be her who will get the blame.

But nothing has happened. Arthur, her admired cousin, has gone off to sleep and the girl is back and is just sitting in a chair. "Arthur," Daphne asks shyly, going out, "would you like me to make you a drink?"

He rouses himself slightly and agrees.

"Is it the bit where the stones are," asks Lynn, "where your aunt wants a fence?"

Arthur yawns. He says, "You see any fence materials down there?"

"No. Just lots of stones. Does your aunt want it made out of stone? I don't know anything about stone."

Arthur mutters something in his throat. Daphne sighs, now Arthur will get angry. Ma is always going on about him making the fence but she never will organise anything, as if it can be made out of the air or the trees or the rocks. She goes into the kitchen and squeezes limes and adds the sugar and the water and takes some ice out of the refrigerator. She takes down the glasses with the coloured patterns and fills them with the juice and takes them out on to the veranda. Lynn sips it, "Oh this is nice," and smiles.

Daphne thinks, she has a way of smiling at you that makes you glad to do things for her.

At this moment Aunt Marion comes puffing in. "How's the crime going, Tantie?" asks Arthur languidly.

Lynn sits up, "Crime. What crime?"

"Well I don't know if that is a crime. Girl!" she shrieks at Daphne, "what you doing all this time, the rice ain't on yet? Oh lord," she says flopping into a large rocking chair, "that man Mustaffa, that man can talk! He hears any and everything about this investigation; who handling it, who thinking what, who thinking something else and all this time people coming and going, he packaging rice and tea. What a man, talking talking talking!" Daphne is standing at the door indecisively. "Daphne Daphne, what you standing there for?"

Daphne says, "There is..... in our taxi. There is....."

"What? What is the matter with you Daphne?"

"Max," says Arthur cutting in. "She get in a taxi with Max."

Aunt Marion draws in, changes colour and starts to breathe in a distressed way, "Lord have mercy," and puts her hand to her ample front.

"He is speaking to Mrs Elliot as if he knows her," pursues Daphne, "though she didn't seem to know him. He is talking about the crime as if he has information about it, being the Sergeant's brother….." She stops and twists her skirt nervously.

"Come, say what you have to say or we be here all day!"

"He tells her that it is people up at the Fort making the noise and there is no crime at Mr Hamilton's house, just something made up by the neighbours."

"Made up! Yes, he would know about making up crimes. That man is the very devil, he should never be allowed to walk the streets with decent folk. He's evil. What they think they're doing letting the man come back here! Well they have corruption everywhere. What a government. We elect men that don't even have a good plan to keep criminals out." She waves her hand at the world to drive such unpleasant thoughts away and enters into some forceful explanations with Daphne about the cooking of lunch. "Well well," she continues, "this life ain't easy, trouble could meet you any time. And that Sergeant de Troy poking his nose in people's business and you know, he's not wanted. And don't talk about when the person is White. All that getting covered up, you mark my words. People up at the Fort, have you heard any rubbish like this in your life?"

"What's the Fort?" asks Lynn.

"It's just along there," says Aunt Marion. "And his house is down there, way down there," she says pointing with her finger towards the edge of greenery.

"Does it have soldiers, making the noise?"

Arthur laughs. "Very probably. No, it's a ruin, an old fort from way back."

"Really! Could I go and look, is it far?" asks Lynn

"Well come with me now," says Aunt Marion lumbering to her feet "Let us go and look. I can tell you there's no way you can make a mistake, people up there….. Daphne, check the rice."

"Oh Ma!" wails Daphne. "Let me come too," her face crumples at the thought of being left behind.

"Well who's looking at it if you come?"

"Don't worry Tantie, I'll look after it," says Arthur good-humouredly.

"What - and come back for burned rice! You'll sleep and make a mess of all my pans, you might catch the house afire."

"I'll run back ma, as soon as I look," insists Daphne. And with that Aunt Marion is finally content.

They go back out onto the road which climbs, as Lynn can now see, to an overgrown untidy area some distance ahead. Rough grass grows over stones and for a while approaching it Lynn thinks it must be a graveyard. Progress towards it is slow as Aunt Marion is not only a slow walker but also a fast talker and as a result of the greetings and explanations entered into en route, many of her neighbours decide to accompany them. The group soon swells to over a dozen, composed of women, children and a few old men who walk even slower than Aunt Marion. When they get there, Lynn sees there is a notice of some sort, rather rusty and rather scratched, but after puzzling over it for a short time she is able to make out that what they are looking at is an old gun emplacement, where cannons protected the harbour approach in colonial times. "Wow," she exclaims, "I'm surprised they don't do it up for the tourists!"

"No because the government would have to spend money on it, get it tidy and mend the road and they won't do it because no money in the back pocket for them. So they just letting it gather rubbish," says a sharp old woman with a clenched mouth.

Yes, if they clean it up and the tourists come, we could sell our bananas and mangoes and eggs and maybe some trinkets here, we could have a little stall, drinks, yes cola and them - they all grumble. If the government would do something but no that is beyond them, all feathering their own nests.

Aunt Marion leads the way, picking a path over creepers and through thickets of coarse grass and Lynn can see that there are substantial stone foundations but it has all now virtually disappeared under regrowth. Eventually Aunt Marion stops. She is standing on a stone platform that is nearly clear of creepers and is fairly well covered with bottles and debris, indicating frequent use of the site for picnics and parties and other entertainments.

"Well look at it for yourself, you can see everything now," says Aunt Marion. They are on the western side of the heads and the platform has a 180 degree view of the sea. To the east, the cannons would have had a clear shot at any ship entering the harbour of Fort John. But it is not to the east that Aunt Marion is looking. Directly below is a steep cliff on which nothing grows except creepers, descending on its northerly slope to the sculptured gardens of Louisaville, the houses of the well-to-do, some of them having swimming pools and some of them having tennis courts and all of them having large grounds running down the hill to the ocean.

"Which is the house?" her neighbours all clamour.

"I know it well, I went to look over it with Sheila when she was here that time. There, it is the one with the swimming pool." So so! So it is, just below them, you can almost throw a rock into the garden. It has an orange-tiled roof and is surrounded by a tiled terrace with a bright blue pool, the tiled area extending out to a low white wall.

"Well," says Aunt Marion dramatically, "you want to tell me that the neighbour there" (pointing down to one of the houses on the right) "hear sexual moaning and groaning coming from that house" (jabbing below), "and it is now said that it come from up here! You think it coming from up in the air or is it coming from across the road? The Sergeant think people stupid or what?"

"Ah ya yie," says the old woman looking down at the slab at her feet, "people been here. Boy, look at this disgusting thing they have left."

Everybody sucks in their breath and looks around them "The government should clean up all the place, disgusting," and they speculate on likelihoods, names are surmised and local scandals simmer to the surface and sink again.

"No sign of the police," says someone returning to the subject of the offending house.

"No, they go be home for their meal by now," says another and as she says it Aunt Marion remembers. "DAPHNE!" she shrieks and Daphne jumps and hurtles off like a startled rabbit. "Oh my, that rice is burned girl, I should not have let her come." Aunt Marion fans herself and starts back in the direction of her house. Lynn follows reluctantly with the rest. There is a strong temptation to stand staring at the spot below, unwilling to leave a possible vantage point for action, mystery and intrigue.

Aunt Marion is now flowing at quite a good pace. Lynn follows with the sharp old woman who says, "That is a young American man apparently, who living down there. I hear he owns the bar in the marina."

"Oh really!" says Lynn.

"Yes, I hear he one bad john, always making baccanal. My grandson working in a bar and he seeing….."

"What, what's that?" says Aunt Marion who is well ahead but seems to have acute hearing and has now stopped dead.

"That young American man getting drunk and getting in all sort of fights. And all sort of things going on with young girls and them. And he got one set of friends he liming with that should all be in the calaboose, especially his new pal….." The old lady appears to recollect something and changes tack. "All busting a lash on anyone at all, down in them bars."

"Well I can tell you in Arthur's bar that would never happen. Arthur wouldn't put up with that nonsense," says Marion, and then asks indignantly why it is that such people should be allowed in the country, as if the lack of manners among the locals isn't enough.

"Well they let them stay no doubt because there something in it for someone," says the old woman.

"Rick wouldn't allow Anthony Hamilton to act like that in his bar, even if the man is the owner's son. And Arthur wouldn't stay working in a place where that happening."

"My grandson working at the Harbour View and saw that young Hamilton fellow having words with a yank sailor and there is plenty military police there and he busted one of them in the eye when they trying to break it up. The regular police come in but nothing is done."

No nothing is ever done, they all agree sucking in their breath, that Sergeant never does anything.

When Lynn re-enters Aunt Marion's house, it is to a smell of warm rice and spices and the bustle of Daphne frying things. Aunt Marion has now joined Daphne in the general activity and Lynn slips past her onto the veranda wondering what she should do. She certainly hasn't been invited for lunch, she hasn't even done anything to justify being given any.

Arthur is peacefully asleep still in his planter's chair. "It's a wonder he woke up to save my rice," says Marion who follows her with a handful of cutlery and other implements. At that moment she is made aware by a rustle of paper on the other side that someone else is there. "Dale!" says Marion. "You here?"

"Yes I'm the saviour," says a man of about Marion's age who is reclining to read the newspaper. "He would still be sleeping even if the house catch on fire."

Arthur moves and opens his eyes sleepily, "I had it all under control, Tantie."

"Ha," laughs the man.

"Well boy you had better get busy and set the table, lazy good-for-nothing. This young lady called….."

"Lynn," Arthur supplies, getting up and taking the knives and forks from his aunt.

"She has just arrived on our island. This is my brother Dale."

"Dale comes to collect the rent," Arthur says to Lynn. "And my neighbour Rae thought we must owe him a lot because there's always one set of shouting when he comes around. She didn't realise at first we're all related."

Dale, who is a big man like his sister, lets out a yelp of laughter and leans back in his chair, puts his hands on his stomach and starts to shake. "Well that Lucas owes me something, I'm his dad, hee hee hee. But maybe Rae is hoping you all get chucked out. She likes your house better than hers, though I don't know why. Boy that Rae always wants what she can't have. She'll get in trouble that girl."

Lynn turns to Arthur, "Lucas. Is that the policeman, he's your cousin?"

"I'm related to half the island, either by blood or marriage. Tantie's late husband's brother's eldest son is just married to the niece by marriage of the Premier."

"Yes," sniffs Marion, "but don't you go pretending to her that the Premier is someone special. You can't pull the wool over my eyes about that man, I know he's no better than he should be."

"Oh, you've heard," says Arthur.

"What?" says Marion sharply but Arthur has become busy setting the table.

"Why," says Lynn innocently, "is there some scandal about him?"

"Scandal!" cries Marion. "That man is one long no-good scandal. Trouble is that man's middle name! Everything I hear about him….. You're too young to understand. But when next I see him I will give him a piece of my mind. It just a big pretence at the wedding, playing nice to me."

"Then afterwards it's all downhill," says Arthur with a laugh. "Yes a top politician's bad behaviour only gets a distant mention in this way because of his position. Everyone else's affairs will be laid before you during lunch as most everyone else in the family is of no account, isn't that right Tantie?"

Dale starts to laugh even harder but Marion looks rather offended and goes off into the kitchen. "Oh," sighs Dale, folding his hands on his substantial stomach, "you have to laugh. So what's he doing this time? Not another married woman?"

Arthur looks round towards the kitchen and lowers his voice cautiously, "Well not married exactly."

"That white woman he was dancing with at the Beach, and no doubt she belongs to one of them yachties….."

"Umm. Well she'd probably tell you she doesn't belong to anyone."

"Well if she's a free agent well and good, but I know, because I've seen them, that there is an arsenal of firearms down among those yachts. I went down to talk about a house with one skipper and he is at work in his engine room and what did I see strapped to his engine room wall but two firearms, a rifle and a shotgun. And he's not the only one. So this woman don't belong to anyone but the someone she don't belong to will hear about it and get his gun and go shoot our Premier and what a glorious scandal that is going to be. Oh boy, a man hasn't lived in vain if he provides a bit of entertainment for his loyal subjects. I'll keep voting for the man so long as he's going to die in bed with some elegant white lady and the sheets stained with his heart's blood and the Sergeant running in and out and yelping because oh goosh he's going have to go and ask serious questions of a white man that may lead to that white man being hung by the neck until dead. Heeheehee."

"Yes but what if he shoots the woman," says Arthur, "that wouldn't be funny. It's alright for the Premier to be a figure of fun, I don't mind that - I don't like the man. But the woman is a different matter."

"Yes, it's possible," says Dale. "When some men go mad, they spray bullets all over the place - they don't have the control to shoot one and leave one."

"Shoot who, what shooting?" says Marion coming out. "Is there another crime?"

"We were contemplating our esteemed relative's funeral. I'm looking forward to it keenly, however sordid it may turn out in the end. But who else do you think will come to it? He makes us a laughing stock around the islands so I wonder if the other Premiers will attend. England will have to send someone no doubt. Is it a junior fellow or will they send someone all dignified to show us how it ought to be done?"

"That's to be seen but you were talking of something else, what bacchanal you were talking of? I missed that one. Anyway, you ready for the lunch?"

"Lunch," murmurs Arthur who is setting places at a beautiful old carved table that looks as if it has been right in that spot since the veranda was built. "Lunch! it's nearly time for dinner let alone lunch."

Marion comes out with a tray piled with food. "Arthur, bring out some chairs from inside. Right," she puts plates of steaming food down on the table. "Now little miss," she's forgotten Lynn's name again, "you sit here and Dale you take that one."

Talk, after grace is said, is mainly Dale giving a description of what he knows about the fracas in Louisaville, which isn't much more than they know already but Marion must exclaim and go over it with great relish. Lynn's own relish is reserved for the food she is eating. "Yum" she says when finished. "That was so good. What was it?"

"Chicken pelau."

"That's the nicest meal I've had since I came to the West Indies."

"What about that friend of your mother's you were telling me about in Port Sophia," says Arthur. "Didn't you have nice Caribbean dishes there?"

"Nothing like this, it was more like English food."

"People in England don't go much on rice, they mostly eat it as pudding," says Dale.

Aunt Marion meanwhile is beaming, highly gratified at Lynn's compliment, "Plenty more," she says. Lynn regretfully refuses.

After a while, when the main topic has been worn out, Arthur says ruminatively. "Lucas thinks he's going to be the next sergeant when the current one does his dash."

Dale laughs again and then looks angry, "That Lucas, he gives me the pip. He gets these impossible dreams, as if he only has to act like something out of a book and he'll get promoted."

"At least he goes by the book. I doubt the Sergeant has never even read one."

"Life's not that simple," Dale grumbles into his second helping of chicken and rice. "There's a whole set of other factors."

Some time later Arthur looks over at Dale's watch and is making preliminary sounds about leaving. Just then, Daphne who is in the kitchen, calls out that a car has just pulled up outside. "Who's that?" wonders Marion rising in surprise. Then she clicks her tongue. "If it's Mary-Jane with that man….. You take this little miss and go right now," she says to Arthur. "Otherwise who knows what she will be exposing her to."

The front door dislodges without even a knock and heels click on the hall floor.

"It's probably bloody Erica, come in a taxi," mutters Arthur.

But suddenly there is a burst of greeting and acclamation and everyone rushes forward. Lynn is left to stare in wonder. In overheated closely-inhabited metropolises like London, such sights might occasionally occur. But here - castaway on this island far from the world of fashion, image and style - what she sees is all the more remarkable.

Stepping out onto the homely worn boards of the veranda is a most beautiful woman. She has a creamy pale-golden complexion and a cascade of black frizzled hair that is partly pulled up and partly all art and curls down her back. She is dressed in an exquisitely tailored tank top of pale pink and a white mini skirt - clothes that look newly minted from the pages of Vogue - and she is balanced on impossibly elegant red sling-back stiletto shoes. She leans back at their clamour and laughs with perfect teeth before bestowing kisses on each in turn.

When the general bustle and outcry has died down, Arthur introduces her. "Lynn, this is my sister Sheila, Sheila this is Lynn."

Sheila extends a languid and perfectly manicured hand that is cool and soft to the touch.

"Come eat something, girl," says Marion "You come in time, before this boy eat all the food."

"She doesn't eat," says Arthur. "Do you Sheil?"

"Of course I do," says Sheila playfully hitting him. "But not in the middle of the afternoon. I'd love some cold water, Tantie."

"Sheila is a top model," Arthur says to Lynn, "so she is pure as driven snow in what she eats. Lynn just had her first proper home-cooked island meal," he says to Sheila.

"Really!"

Sheila turns her eyes on Lynn and Lynn can't help herself. "Your eyes are green," she just blurts it out.

"Green, green are they?" cries Arthur and turns his sister's face with his hand but she shuts her eyes and smiles. "They were mauve last time."

"How do you do that?" asks Lynn in amazement.

"They're only contact lenses," says Sheila.

"But with your colouring, I mean black hair, aren't your eyes brown like Arthur's? Can you change the colour to green?"

"My eyes are actually pale blue. Yes I know it's odd, but we're such a mongrel breed - my grandfather was Scottish."

"They love her in New York, Paris, Rome," says Arthur. "She makes more pots of money than you'd believe possible and yet here she is sitting at the table, almost like an ordinary mortal, aren't you Sis?"

"Oh you," she says nudging him affectionately. "Don't you complain. You know I keep offering to fly you up but you'd rather laze in a hammock down here. I'm amazed to see you upright. Every other time I come you're lying about dead to the world."

"Are you really a model?" asks Lynn.

"Yes, she gets to strut up and down with virtually nothing on," says Dale.

"What do you mean nothing on? Look I'm fully clothed and this is what people wear. Look at Lynn, she's just in a little dress too."

Lynn looks down and cries in alarm, "Oh this isn't anything like your clothes! Anyway, I only came to help Arthur with the fence."

Sheila puts her head back and laughs a trilling pink-mouthed laugh, then puts her arm around her brother's neck. "You are finally going to make Tantie a fence!"

He grimaces. "Well if Tantie would bother to get in some wood and some nails and some building materials, I would make her one. But it's too late now," he says. "I've got to be back at work soon. But I came prepared for it, if Tantie hadn't got herself distracted." Then he adds, "Now you're here, you could help," and he grips the top of her arm with his thumb and index finger. "There'd be a bit of muscle in here, after all the lifting and carrying of heavy things you do."

"What heavy things?"

"Your wallet for a start," and Sheila bursts out laughing again.

"But what do you have to do as a model?" Lynn asks, genuinely interested in this glimpse of a faraway life, thrilled that fame and glamour should be here at the same table - the elegance of expensive perfume mixing with the flowerheads. "Do you just walk up and down, is that all you do?"

"Not at all," says Sheila unwrapping herself from her brother. "It's very hard work. I can't sit around like Arthur with the clock ticking and the months and years rolling on because in a few years it will all be over for me. I'm 22 and if I can squeeze out another five or six years I'll be really lucky. So I take everything they offer me, as much as I can fit in. Photographic, cat walk, anything. I spend half my time travelling. And there's really no such thing as a free day because if I don't have any work then I'm still up early to go swimming and ride horseback and there's my dance classes and my acting classes and my voice coach - I have to fit all those in when I don't have an assignment. There'll be time enough to lie back in a hammock when the wrinkles come. Then I can wallow like a seal on the sand and get fat and blubbery and order servants around in a cracked old voice, hahaha." They all join in the laugh as they all know it can never come to that.

"And will you be looking at any more houses this time," says Dale, "because there's been a couple of things come on the market since you were last down and there's a land deal that is getting everyone excited."

"Oh yes and what's the land?"

"A big parcel round at Arrow Bay."

"The swamp!"

"Why would she put herself to any trouble buying that nasty place?" says Marion.

"For development," says Dale. "Untouched virgin land."

"Untouched alright because of the swamp fever and all sorts of other bad things!"

"You spray it," says Dale. "There's sprays for all that now. You just spray the area."

"But what would she want to buy down in that area for," says Marion, "when they have so many other nice places around town? Now listen Sheila, you know that place we went to see in down there in Louisaville that time, the one up under the hill? Well….." and Marion is off in her knock-em-down tone with the whole story of recent events. And she finishes with her voice lowered on all the possibilities of suspicion and guilt.

Sheila laughs, looking round at them all. "Who says this is sleepy hollow when all this is happening, and this very day too. And what else is news? Who's died, who's married, who's cuckold, who's divorced?"

There is a slight pause while Marion leans back to consider what Sheila needs to know and into this small space Arthur says quietly, "Max is in town."

"He was in my taxi," says Daphne in a squeak.

This news seems to shut everyone up with uncomfortable constraint and Lynn wonders what the story is.

Sheila says nothing to Arthur's comment but turns to Dale, "Have you got a cigarette?"

"You shouldn't smoke," he says, "not if you want to keep that skin. Look, you're getting little lines round the eyes already."

"I know," she says gazing dreamily out at the view. "It's my one little vice, but if you haven't got any….."

"I'll run up the shop for you," Daphne says breathless. "I will. It would only take a minute."

"Give her some money," says Marion to Dale, finding her voice again.

"No no," says Sheila and looks at her thin gold watch. "I've got a car waiting outside." She laughs. "I said I'd only be ten minutes and look….." she points at the dial. "I just came to tell you I'm here, I'm staying at the Beach."

"You know you can stay here, you know I would love to have you here, the room is all set up for you any time you come. It's no trouble at all," says Marion.

"Thanks Tantie," she says getting up and giving her a hug, "but I'm working. There's flocks of people down there waiting to pull at my hair and check my makeup. I'll only be here for three days and it's going to be really hectic but I'm coming back in a week and I'll have more time and I'll come up and stay then. Now listen, I'm going to make a break for lunch in my schedule. We'll all have lunch one day, when my gorgeous brother gets the time off. Not till Thursday! What slave drivers they are, well that's fine, Thursday lunch it is. We should just about have finished by then."

She completes a round of kisses and stands ready to go.

"You could give Lynn and me a lift if you like," says Arthur. "I have to be back at work."

She smiles her acquiescence and leads the way with her sinuous walk, balanced on her tall heels. Lynn gives thanks for her lunch. "We never even got to look at your fence," she says regretfully.

"Some other time," says Marion beaming at her.

The car outside is a mini-moke. "What what what!" cries Arthur like one of the neighbourhood chickens. "Now I always thought that someone as important as you would have an important car." But Sheila is engaged in waving back over his shoulder.

Once out of sight Sheila turns to her brother and says, "Why did you tell me that back then? You know how it upsets everyone. You could have told me quietly in the car or some other time."

"Sorry," says Arthur "but as far as I knew you were settling in for the afternoon and I had to get going. What if you'd seen him in the street and found out that I knew and didn't tell you?" He puts his arm around his sister. "He'll want to avoid you about as much as you want to avoid him. I'll pass the word through Lucas to his brother."

She leans her head against his briefly, and then moves away. "He did me a good turn anyway, got me out of this place. Yes, thanks to that man….." The car jerks and grumbles through the potholes and she turns her mind back to present things, exclaiming, "Look at these roads! What important expensive car are you going to drive around here without getting it ruined? This is the kind of car for these roads."

"Yes it is!" says Arthur suddenly struck. "This is the sort of car we need." He leans forward. "How much does one of these cost?" he asks the driver but the man raises his hands as in, Don't ask me, I'm just the driver.

Arthur gives up and puts his arm through his sister's and squeezes it affectionately, "You always look so good. And what are you here to do?"

"Tomorrow at first light they're getting me out under a palm tree in next season's Paris evening wear. Then I think a spread on Mary Quant swimsuits."

"Are they topless?" asks Arthur.

"Will you be scandalised?"

"No nothing you do scandalises me, but I'm just bemused. Why wear anything at all?"

"And then we do one day of the film. I've got to come back to do the rest because the schedule couldn't fit in more."

"You're in a film now!"

"We're going to do it all over the world. I play a model who travels a lot and this man keeps on leaping on planes and following after me. The planes are always Pan-Am because they're putting up the money. All I have to do is look alluring. They've got some actor I've never heard of from some American TV program….."

"You're a film star!"

"No, I'm a model. I think I'm supposed to be an enigma who's being pursued by some guy with an obsession. All I do is sit around in cafes and bars and sail yachts and walk on beaches and ride horses at sunset. It's one of those travelogues. If you're stupid, you too can follow a figment of your imagination about the world and waste your life for no reason."

Rae gets back to the bar after an eventful few hours at the Beach. She thinks she is in a good mood but she is in actual fact slightly belligerent, having had a couple of drinks and a rather surreal and occasionally uncomfortable lunch. When she walked into the Beach Hotel at mid-day the first person she saw was Libby, so she immediately went over to her table, only to find that Max had followed her and that Libby appeared to know him quite well. The Premier appeared, Hamilton senior floated in and out along with various other people and all was going rather well until, after a couple of drinks when she was feeling relaxed and happy, Max started whispering insinuatingly in her ear, something that she didn't understand, something that quite honestly she didn't want to know. She abruptly said she had to go and relieve Rick and it was in fact a relief to depart. So here she is ready to relieve Rick and what does she get for her trouble? Recriminations and abuse, that's what.

Rick is saying, "Where have you been? Oh god you're drunk again," in a set teeth-grinding voice, low and venomous.

"Oh don't start. I am not drunk! I've had a drink or two with Libby," and when he continues she says, "Two drinks. That's all, what is this, the Spanish inquisition? I've been having a lovely time and….."

"And what about me?"

"Well what about you?"

"You said you were going to come and help."

"What? When? No I didn't, I never said….."

"You said, never mind what the owner does, he's a bastard. You said, I'll help if you're going to be on your own all day."

"I never said….. I didn't even know about Lawrence until Arthur....."

"You said, I'll be down to help at lunch, you said, you can count on me."

"When did I say that? Last night, I was throwing up last night, how can you….? I was sick as a dog last night. Why didn't you tell me this morning?"

"I did tell you this morning. I said I'm going now, are you coming down at lunch and you said, Yes."

“I never….. I never, I don’t remember speaking to you, I thought we weren’t speaking, no.”

“You said yes, I'll bring you down some rice salad, you said you’d make me a rice salad.”

“I said rice salad? I never said rice salad. You don’t even like rice salad.”

He continues, “I've been here all day without a chance to stock up. You know I can’t rely on Jake and now Arthur’s here the stores are all shut.”

He breathes out through his nose looking at her and she says, vaguely fiddling with her hair, “I don’t remember a thing - the last two days are a blur. I had to go to the Beach to get some proper coffee - I’m alright now. You see if we had proper coffee here I would have come down. If I had a proper position here…..” her voice goes up as she enters old territory, “if I was on the payroll with my own wage…..” So there it is again, an atmosphere sharp as broken bottles, stabbing at the chest in a knife-hail of sentences. Blood flows beneath the surface, in the side-face, in the blotched neck, blood in the hot lids of soured eyes.

Rick’s head is moving from side to side in disgust. They have been over and over this. She continues, “Or you could buy a car, hire a care then. I’d drive and get you stuff, I don’t mind that, but having to work….. It’s the principle. I should get paid. Why do you put up with it then? If you can’t manage. Why don’t you confront him?”

These are the knifing words, because they go straight in and he can’t answer. He does have an answer but he can’t tell her and Rae can’t see how she’s driving the explanations away. Every day getting further away as the knife goes deeper in.

Arthur sighs as he enters; here he is starting on a seven hour shift and the place is a mess and they are just standing there bickering. There are glasses uncollected, tables unwiped. The casual busboy Clive is behind the bar serving drinks because Rick is in such a temper. Tut tut, maybe Rick will end up paying everyone busboy wages and expecting them to serve. Not his problem, he himself wouldn’t work for that sort of wage but if others want to, their look out. He starts to collect up glasses. Yes, let Hamilton pay barman’s wages to the man who clears the tables. That’s the way to save money!

“Hey Arthur!” It is Boss breezing in with Libby. “Arthur, my favourite son, did you hear about our continuing run of luck? Man what a day we had yesterday, the sweetest mother, and big - you should have seen it. I credit all this luck to you my son, for being a good fairy."

Arthur grins but looks uneasily at Libby. She has sat down at their usual table and is gazing off to one side with the curved lips of seeming complacency, so it seems everything must be alright, which itself is unsettling. But maybe she wasn't paying attention - because Rae has now sat down next to her and is pouring out her troubles.

"Good start," he murmurs to Rick when the manager comes back behind the bar, "Boss is drinking champagne before he's barely in the door."

"Nice for you," says Rick. "If he keeps going you should make a bit. I'll be off early if you don't mind. It's been a long day. I'll be back to close up." He looks worn and grumpy. He should stand up to that old shark, Arthur thinks. Instead he's working 12 hour shifts without relief because the owner wants to milk the place for all it's worth. But surely old Hamilton can see that while he's interfering, the bar just isn't working as it should. Not Rick's fault, no-one can blame Rick.

The bar hums; it is after six and the light is on the point of falling over the edge into twilight. The sun is behind the mountains and the evening clouds are bright rolling oilslicks of green and orange that give the sky a slippery fabric look, sequinned with jewelled drops of light, the whole roll sliding off and down the back of the dark land mass. Rick has put on his new Janis Joplin record, her harsh voice seems to meld with the savage tropical colour. But the bar needs organising, Clive to gather glasses, to tidy up, and the floor swept before the big rush commences in earnest.

As he is settling all this, a tall young man comes to a halt behind his companion on their way towards the bar. "Do you know," he says as if struck by an apocalyptic vision, his clear-skinned experience-free face luminous with an insight he has to share, "do you know, I think you and I are going to be friends for a very long time."

His companion turns and looks at him and then looks at Arthur. "A new chum," he says. "Arthur meet Oscar."

"So Jim my man," says Arthur, "how is this new house turning out? It's certainly turning you into a stranger round here."

"Transport isn't that easy I've found. Damn route taxis hardly come past at all."

"Yes well there's a rumour that when you get out that far you're surrounded by wild animals and jungle creepers. And what's more, they have strange religions out there with wild men dancing around sacrificing chickens."

"Poppycock dear chap, we are the epitome of civilization. Why hardly a hop step and a jump from the Exhibition ground, right in the very hub of it all. Isn't that so Oscar?"

"Well, I hope you're filling your time profitably," says Arthur.

"Certainly," says Jim. "I'm turning serious. I've become a wage slave."

"Have you!" says Arthur. "I could have used you for a bit of that a week or so ago but Lucas wouldn't go and get you out of bed so I had to find someone else."

Jim spreads his hands with exaggerated unconcern, "The Fates had something else in mind for me Arthur. Big. Very big. What do you want to drink, Oscar?"

"A lemonade," says the young man. "This is a really cool environment here. This is a very special place, I can feel it." He is carrying a big hippy Nepalese-type handbag which dangles from a long string. His gentle moonface is surveying the bar like an acolyte at a temple.

Arthur pours out a lemonade and gets Jim his usual rum and coke. "Oscar has come down for the Island Fair," says Jim and for a moment Arthur's mind goes blank. The words mean something, he's certainly heard them before, but it takes a few seconds for the context to click into place.

"That has started already?" he says surprised.

"Certainly it has," says Jim carefully. "How remiss you are Arthur. It started more than a week ago. But of course Oscar got here early so as to set up his booth and get ready, before the rush started."

"Ah," says Arthur thoughtfully. "And what rush was that?"

Jim concentrates on his drink. But Oscar is a man who likes to communicate. He is from California and Arthur can see he is about to start on a spiel that includes peace and love and the effectual qualities of some very special merchandise he has to offer. Arthur cuts him short. Custom is lining up at the bar and it is the evening sprint to fill up after a hard day in the sun – the yachties need quick service if they are not to start snarling and tearing flesh with their teeth. So Arthur flits like a swallow behind the bar, taking orders for food, pouring drinks, leaping for money and sending out cascades of change. Betty is working tonight. She is quick and efficient, he likes that. He doesn't like having to dive into the kitchen - it is bad news in there and he is fastidious about his clothes. And Clive is working well too, the three of them easily keep pace. He pities poor Rick, on with Jake who doesn't yet know the ropes and is occasionally clumsy - and with Cookie too, who is quick but slatternly. Everything goes well and by 9.30 the rush is over. Now there is just the smattering of drinkers and the very occasional food order. He leans on the bar and relaxes.

He sees that Lynn has joined Boss and his friends. As he watches, she catches his eye and smiles at him. It shakes him. It is that smile, he is helpless. He has to start fighting that feeling. Oh-oh, now she is up and bouncing over to the bar.

"Hello Songbird," he says, trying not to grin too broadly.

"I think I should come and talk to you for a bit." She drops her voice. "Libby's there! Everyone's been telling me to look out. You got me into this remember so you have to protect me." And she gives him a conspiratorial look.

"Yes, quite right," says Arthur. At that moment Jim comes up to the bar. "Jim, this is Lynn, have you met Lynn? She's been working on Boss's boat."

"Ravished," says Jim gallantly bowing and formally kissing her hand.

"Watch him," says Boss appearing at their side. "He's a lord. Women's heads get turned, having their hands kissed by lords."

"What are you a lord of?" asks Lynn.

Jim is shaking his head and trying to answer but Boss is shouting "Lord of all Manor of drinking. Arthur, more champagne. We have to celebrate but let the kid open it, she needs the practice. She's always putting on this helpless act and getting the charterers to do it and as they're all bloody hopeless themselves half the bubbly goes over the deck, we never get any in the glasses."

"Yes," she says, "I'm scared of opening them, in case the top hits something or explodes in my hand you know."

Arthur laughs, "It's easy. You hold it like this," he takes her hand under his. 'Twist the bottle this way and the cork this way and don't grimace. No no look at it, it's not going to bite you. Twist - POP – voila! There, just keep practicing and it won't gush either, you were shaking it."

"I was shaking fullstop," she says and laughs, relieved.

The glasses are filled and the noise level goes up as Boss fights, without much difficulty, for supremacy. "To Arthur, for finding the kid" he shouts and they all lift their glasses. Boss has knocked a good bit back. “Here’s to all these bloody charters and Charles has more. More and Yet More,” he bellows. “Old Charles is getting soft, was a time when he wouldn’t give us any, just because of a few stuff ups. Here’s to Charles. And here’s to good times everyone, and to another bloody big fish, to a fish. Oh and here’s to the kid, our lucky talisman, to the Songbird.”

Arthur slides a glance anxiously at Libby. She would certainly have heard this time. She appears unconcerned as she stubs out a cigarette but it’s hard to say, those lines could be smoker’s lines or little angry lines. Let’s hope she is otherwise engaged as he suspects and can count the dollar signs, because she could make the kid’s life a misery if she wanted.

Jim has the same thought. “She’s very young.”

“Well grandpa, hark at you, she’s nearly eighteen.”

“I mean young to be setting up against Libby. Mincemeat. And she’ll blame you, both of them will. Well all the more for others. I shall make my move when the opposition has been properly annihilated.”

“Not like you. I was thinking you would be in like Flynn straight away!”

“No no, not among friends. Finders keepers old chap. Till the final reckoning.”

Arthur says nothing but his heart sinks. This will never do. If people are thinking that..... It will rebound against the kid. He must become more….. He mustn’t go inviting her here and there. He’s got to be stronger in the future and not go giving in to that smile. For her sake.

Boss is a generous man especially when times are good and now times are very good. He orders and his friends drink four more bottles of champagne. “Well,” thinks Arthur, “Rick’ll be pleased.” Rick has a separate book-keeping system for fine wines and champagnes - the owner knows nothing of the celebratory bottles that are consumed on the premises, nor of the good mark-up that Rick scores. Arthur always gets a cut on these deals, cash, which is good because he needs to buy a new shirt. His sister is so particular. If he turns up for lunch on Thursday looking shabby she is quite capable of..... almost anything.

Lynn comes over again and leans companionably on the bar. “Gosh I’m squiffy,” she says. “Can you give me some plain water. I’m going to have to go to bed, I can’t keep up the pace. Charters are so tiring because you have to smile so much and be so nice and then we keep catching fish and if we get in late they want us to go drinking with them and then I have to get up in the dawn to have photos taken. They want to have pictures of me with the fish. Have you ever had your picture taken with a fish? I don't know quite how I'm supposed to look. I think it's a bit improper to be there smiling and smiling beside some poor thing that is dead and is going to be eaten and if you stand up close they smell really fishy and dead which is awful especially first thing in the morning. But then the charterers are all so nice, they give me such generous tips and sometimes they give me other things like sunglasses and hats - one group sent me a hat all the way from America. I'm so happy I got the job," she looks at him with one of the smiles that he is trying to steel himself against. He mustn't make too much of it. People are grateful and mean nothing more by it and it doesn't do to add them unaccountably to your dreams. He must keep it just cool and professional. I am the barman, you are a white girl from a different country. "Anyway I'm going back to the boat now," she says and waves her hand back at him as she weaves off, nightynight.

"Take care," he murmurs.

Whatever his own part in it, he is pleased that Boss is getting his act together. If things work out he ought to get through the season with enough diesel to get him north at the end of May, if only he stays with it. All those charters he wrecked when Libby served a few too many cocktails and he lost it, or when he and Libby had a no-holes-barred fight in the middle of the trip. This time, hopefully.....

Libby is the problem and he realises that for the whole of the evening he has been on alert, ready to rush in and protect the kid. He has to stop thinking like that. The kid is getting to him.

Boss and his party move off eventually, rambunctious and noisy. He can hear their progress. He starts to put things in order for the night. About five minutes before closing time Rae comes in looking fed up. "I can't believe they keep doing this," she says.

"What?"

"Libby and Boss. They've just had another big fight. I could hear it up at the house. Rick can't be bothered, he sent me down to close up."

"Oh, what now?"

"Libby has smashed a bottle on the marina boardwalk and stormed off. There's glass everywhere. People will be cutting their feet again and Boss will get a warning again - and another clean-up bill."

Karlo, Boss's best buddy, slopes wearily back into the bar. "Give us a night cap, can't go home just yet, the night is young. Yes, everyone's been chucked off. Boss says he wants to be left on his own to drink himself to death."

"Poor Boss."

"No bugger him, drunks are no fun."

"Mmm," agrees Arthur.

"Drinking is God's gift to man," continues Karlo in his comfortable slurred way. "After all, if God didn't believe in alcohol why did he invent it? Water into wine. Yes God is right into the odd little drinkie. You go to church and front up to be purified and they give you wine, quite right. But drinking to topple yourself, that is a crime. A waste. If you can't remember the good things you had the night before you should leave it to those that can. Cheers."

Karlo continues with his chatter while Arthur is busy tidying under the bar. He is surprised to see Rae suddenly mutter under her breath and head into the kitchen. What on earth would she want to go in there for, he wonders.

"Oh bloody hell," mutters Karlo pausing in his monologue, "It's that bloody Sergeant. The people you have to drink with nowadays." Arthur looks up without interest. He doesn't care for the Sergeant but he certainly doesn't need to scurry off into the kitchen. What he sees though made him stiffen and then stand slowly and grimly. The Sergeant is not alone.

Sergeant de Troy comes over to the bar with his usual swagger. The Sergeant is a big man, at least 6 feet tall and well built, almost fat. He has a straight-legged way of walking, shoulders slightly forward like a bull advancing, and his expression is one of 'Stop me if you can'. When he comes to rest, he stands on the back of his feet with his legs apart and pulls his wallet out of his back pocket while swaying to and fro. It is an intimidating stance. "Lawrence not on tonight?" he says surprised.

"Lawrence has been put off," says Arthur expressionless, his arms folded.

"Ahh," says the Sergeant giving a questioning look, to which Arthur does not respond. "Well no doubt Rick knows his business. Yes, there are some rascals working around here alright. I hear a great number of stories. Often a discreet word though is all that is required. Rick could have talked to me."

"What," cries Karlo outraged, banging his drink and looking from Arthur to the Sergeant. "I heard that Lawrence was put off because the owner was cutting costs. What are you implying Sergeant?"

The Sergeant bristles slightly. "I'm implying nothing."

"Yes you were, you were implying that Lawrence had been dishonest. You'd better have a care. Lawrence will be taking you to court for stains on his character."

"I'm sure Lawrence will do nothing so stupid," says the Sergeant coldly.

"You're not above the law you know," says Karlo waving his index finger at him.

"And neither are you. I hope you remember that when you next come to renew your permit."

"Don't you threaten me. I'll have you know the Chief Constable is a particular friend of mine."

The Sergeant sneers. "Of course he is. He's a white man. But he's retiring soon and you will all have an islander to deal with after that."

"Well," says Karlo sliding off his stool, "he will not retire until he has sorted out the likes of you!" He drains his glass and stalks off.

The Sergeant shrugs and leans casually on the bar watching him go. "You have some trouble-makers in this bar I see. But my brother and myself are here for a quiet little drink I notice that such people do not venture in when a police officer is here."

"The bar is closed now," says Arthur.

For a few seconds the Sergeant does not seem to take this in, then looks at him, stands up and glares; his breath coming hard through his nose as he taps one leg with his wallet. "Closed, when has it ever been closed, Rick never turns us away here. Where is Rick? What am I talking to you for?"

Arthur says quietly, "You are talking to me because I am in charge when Rick is not here. I shall always be happy to serve <u>you</u> Sergeant de Troy, when we are open. However, that is not the case with regard to your brother. Especially," he adds, "now my sister is in town, with all her entourage and bodyguards." He is speaking while looking directly and unflinchingly at the Sergeant. Rae, who is peering out through a slit in the door, is relieved to see the Sergeant's demeanour alter subtly during this speech, his shoulders lower, his eyes drop to his watch.

"Ah well," he says turning to go, "if you're closed you're closed. I think we will go on down to the Blue Lagoon."

Rae waits until they have gone and then walks out behind the bar again. “What was all that about?” she asks.

“Could ask the same of you.”

“I can’t stand the Sergeant,’ she replies airily and unconvincingly even to her own ears.

“I’ve never seen you go into the kitchen for any reason before,” says Arthur, “not even for the Sergeant.”

Rae for a moment battles with a self-protective instinct not to tell anything, though the stupid thing is that there isn’t really anything to tell. “I met his brother Max today, he was just being friendly I suppose, but when he came in just now I had this overwhelming urge to get out of sight.” She looks at him curiously, “You obviously don’t like him. The brother.”

“No I don’t. And if I were you I’d follow your instinct when it comes to Max de Troy.”

As she helps him close up the bar, Rae is thinking, “But it’s my instincts which are the problem. I feel this almost helpless attraction, like a rabbit held in a headlight. There’s this unknown fear mixed with fascination. I wish my mother would shout louder or I’ll be off again to the Beach tomorrow. And where will it end?”

Chapter 4

Much running backwards and forwards among the crew

It is with a feeling of luxurious wellbeing that Lynn flutters her eyelids in the early day, with the dawn about to break and the light seeping across the sky. It's hard to remember the feeling she had waking up on her very first day on the island where the whole world had formed itself into one terrifying hostile entity. Now she gladly opens her eyes to watch the streaks of yellow and green above her which are just the swelling of an exciting sun below the horizon, for what indeed is there to fear? Already she has more than US $200 in her bank account and money to burn in her purse as well. A fortune. She snuggles happily in a sheet on one of the deck's padded bench seats which makes a lovely bed out in the open. She has been lying under the stars, under the moon, under a brilliant black sky that lulled her to sleep and now she wakes to a world that is perfect, where it doesn't matter about tomorrow because today will be just wonderful.

She has done how many charters with Boss? Already the days tumble into one another. Ten she thinks, or is it more? And on all of them they have hooked a fish even though they haven't always landed them. Boss has suddenly got a reputation for being lucky. He sights the shoals that the other game-fishing boats somehow miss. On all of his trips there is the adrenalin of coming close to the goal and if on some occasions the fish escapes, Boss has instructed her that it is no-one's fault and so far it doesn't seem to have been hers. Either the charterers were awkward or the fish escaped through sheer size - leaping in an arc towards the boat in all its silver flashing majesty, breaking the line and gone. Never mind, it is a life well lived and the charterers are generous money-wise, some more, some less, but all of them expressing enjoyment which makes Lynn happy. She dozes again and the boat rocks in a companionable way. Soon the sun will come up over Hope Mountain. Such a rosy romantic name, she thinks, except of course it is named after an early governor. But whatever the derivation, it gives her pleasure to think of the sun rising from the midst of Hope. Soon it will be striking the deck and later the tarpaulin that is draped over the rolled mainsail for shade. Warming up, time to rise and shine. She sits up and drums her toes on the deck for the pleasure of feeling the wood grain through her rapidly hardening footskin. She is just folding her sheet neatly when Boss appears.

"Hi Boss," she says surprised. "You're up early."

"Charter." He gargles his words roughly from a numb-looking mouth and slumps on to the bench opposite.

"Oh," says Lynn. He hadn't said anything to her. This is a surprise but she doesn't mind last-minute additions. "I didn't know we had a charter today."

"No, Charles came to the boat last night. Damn stupid of him, it's all his fault. Libby was lying down on the bed, she's got her period and she was as cranky as can be. Bloody hell why didn't he check if she was there first?" He holds his head in his hands. "So he's saying this and that about these bloody people and Libby just appears while he's in the middle of it and says she'll come out and do the cooking. And Charles said 'No way!' - said it straight to her face in the baldest way. If only he'd toned it down a bit, been diplomatic but no he must dot the 'i's as well and say he'd give the charter elsewhere if she's involved after all the others that….. Well not all of those were her fault but there's some truth in it and I thought the whole thing was settled. But when he's gone she says, 'Who is he to be telling us who will or won't go out on our boat?' And we had a few drinks and she got me worked up and I thought, 'She's right! Who is he to lay down the law on a fellow's boat?' But when I woke up this morning I saw in the clearest way that we'll be sunk if I take the charter and Libby comes. Charles is a man of his word and I need these charters - I like to live like this, all this money, this is what makes being here such fun. But what are we going to do? Libby's still there, on the boat. I'll have to cancel, we'll have to cancel, you've got to go and explain it all to Charles. She'll sink the boat or something, she'll..... Well she can be violent. Songbird, you're going to have to go and tell Charles."

The responsibility is big like a black cloud. "Alright," says Lynn. "If you like."

"But what do you think about it all Songbird? No-one will tell me anything. Tell me honestly."

"I don't think Charles will be very happy. In fact I don't think he will be very pleased at all and just when you were getting such a good reputation."

"Yes, yes, I know about that. But Libby, she was alright before, never said a word. I thought she was happy about it all and now she's back hanging about on the boat - she hasn't stayed on it for weeks and then yesterday she's back, actually on the boat living there with her clothes and whatnot. But she could go off for the day, go to the beach with Rae, no need for her to be around like this..... Why all of a sudden?"

Now this is an unchartered sea with the sudden howl of wind and wild white tops to waves. She doesn't know what to say and frowns to concentrate. "I don't know why Boss. Maybe she was missing living on the boat."

"No no," he moves impatiently, "it's nothing like that. With Libby everything is always calculated. There must have been a shift lately. I thought I knew what was going on, but now I think I was wrong. Have you heard anything?"

"No" she says. "I don't know anything. Maybe you should ask her."

"Is that what you think? Do you really think so?"

Lynn feels desperately unprepared to answer such questions and he is here in front of her, his eyes fixed on her, urging her. It is his urging that makes her answer, though she would rather not admit her ignorance. "Boss I don't really understand about other people's lives. I don't understand why people who are always shouting and fighting and being angry stay together, and people who seem to never have a cross word suddenly walk away from each other as if there's a wide ocean between them, as if they've never even been married. That's all I know."

He is silent then he lowers his eyes. "She's been very good to me," he mutters.

"Well I can't tell you anything else. I think I'm too young..... Or something....." She is embarrassed. People do talk but all she knows is that Libby is leading some sort of dangerous double life that requires everyone to drop their voices conspiratorially, though what the conspiracy is she has no idea. In the end she says, "I think you should go and tell Charles yourself and ask him. I think Charles is the sort of man who can answer questions like that. I think he would know a lot about what's going on."

"Yes but I don't want to know from Charles. He's a cruel man. He frightens me the way he sits there with all the power to make us rich or make us poor." Boss is dragging at his hair with his hand.

"Boss, if you start cancelling like this, on the very day you're due to go out, he won't give you any more charters anyway," says Lynn stating what she thinks is the obvious.

"I know that too Songbird and I need the money for the diesel to get me north at the end of the season. If not this one, then ones in the future. Oh god," he groans, "what am I going to do?"

"We'll go down to Charles together. I'll explain and then we'll see what he says." She puts on her sensible voice while saying this, the voice she's heard her mother use when serving up unpalatable facts, and she gets up purposefully as the main reason for such a voice is to give impetus to action.

"No, I don't know….." he groans indecisively. "I don't know how I'll get past the boat. Libby'll be looking out. If she sees us together heading over there, who knows what she'll do?" Boss's boat is now moored at the beginning of the same jetty as the Golden Dawn and he peers in that direction with a trapped look on his face - an animal at the end of a branch watching a python insidiously advance.

Lynn drums one foot on the deck again, but not with the sensuous glad-to-be-alive feeling that had come with the first flush of waking up. Now it is to fill in time while she thinks. Drum drum, the deck is getting hot, time is passing, her eyes search for clues. "What about the little boat there?" she suggests, looking at the rubber dinghy tied up behind with its outboard motor, the same little boat that so many of the yachts drag behind them.

Boss jerks upright. "The tender! Yes, Songbird you're a genius," he says ecstatically with a surge of energy. Yes, yes, into the tender with Boss fumbling with the rope and pushing off. "I hope it's got fuel," as he pulls the line with a jerk, pulls twice, pulls a third time and the little engine roars. "You beauty!" He guides the rubber boat away from the side of the Golden Dawn and, quickly curving out into the harbour, he doubles back and comes to rest near the marina gates. He ties it up to the jetty there. "Now," he whispers, "we'll have to go from here like Indians on our stomachs," and he proceeds to do just this, slithering along and then bolting through the gates. She laughs, then follows a lot less like an Indian and a lot more like a jumping frog.

Charles Hook is the manager of W.I. Charters Inc. and Lynn is aware that many of the yachties, at least those that rely on him for their livelihood, are rather afraid of him. He is a dour hard-faced man in his thirties, his face reminding her of a chisel - oblong, squared off and rather featureless. His hair has shrunk back from the blade and clusters at the edges like wood shavings. He has a way of looking down at you from a great height like a giraffe with opened cloud-squinting eyes and mouth pursed in a treetop-munching moue.

I am here to be judged, she thinks, by a person in authority, and I will be made smaller because I am so very unimportant. Older women of her acquaintance would have just walked straight up to him and gone tap tap tap at him with their sharpened red fingernails - how do they get that sort of confidence? If only she could act like that then people wouldn't look at her with a patient benevolence that puts her on a par with old people, small children and idiots. Other women seem to have an extra layer that protects them from fear of failure - it is a kind of courage or insensitivity that sends them into battle with a confidence of victory that Lynn doesn't have. Nevertheless, she has promised to be the spokeswoman and so she must do her best for Boss - who absolves himself by strolling in behind her and casually taking up a sailing magazine off a table as if he is another customer and will hang around until Charles has dealt with the person ahead of him.

"It's about Boss's charter," says Lynn holding her hands in front nervously and looking round at her employer.

Charles's eyes flicker from her to Boss who is turning the pages of the magazine as if seriously looking for something. He says in Boss's direction, "I would never have told you about the charter if I'd known that Libby was on the boat in ear shot. I might have known that the temptation to be a spectacle would be too much for her but I won't have any more scenes like we've had in the past, not if you're working for me Boss. I would have told her before but I was never put on the spot….." He trails off and looks away. Libby is too much for him too, with her mass of vibrant red hair and her beautifully designed vivid print bikinis. "I've been tempted to withdraw the charter and give it elsewhere," he looks down at a pile of paper and starts sorting it. "As it happens," he looks up once more and fixes Boss with a baleful stare, "I'm in a hole. There's too many of them to go on the Liberty. These people think they can snap their fingers the day before and tell me they're bringing an extra four passengers. Boss, these are the sort of people who create their own incidents without Libby getting in on the act! I don't want stuff ups. They're important people, they could do a lot for the industry down here." He is sorting papers rapidly as he talks, casting his eyes down and putting piles to one side when he finishes, and as he seems engaged in activity Lynn doesn't immediately feel any need to continue an explanation. Charles finishes with his papers and looks up, "I'm sure you'll be alright," he says to Lynn. "After all, what can she do? She's got a reputation for violence but if they get the police in one more time I know for a fact they'll have her on the next plane out and if she doesn't know that already Boss, you ought to tell her." He grabs a piece of paper, leaps up and goes over to the board and pins it on. When he comes back, Lynn is in the same position still looking at him not quite knowing where to take it next. Charles clutches his side hair. "Listen if you're afraid….. I'm sorry - it was an honest mistake, I had no idea she would be on the boat. She's not been there for weeks which is probably something that has got to be known by Immigration….."

"Is that why she's back?" bursts out Boss. "Is that what it is?"

For a moment no-one speaks. This time Charles looks at them. He is clearly now waiting and Lynn steels herself to break the band of tension. "Libby won't let Boss take the boat out with me," she says. There it is, as bald as can be. "She says either she goes or it doesn't go at all." Charles stares. It is the best she can do and Boss is now hunched over an article on spinnakers. "I don't know why it is," she shrugs her shoulders and wrinkles her forehead. "She's not jealous is she, do you think? Of me?" her voice goes up because the suggestion strikes her as ludicrous. Boss is old, well not old but over twice her age.

"Jealous of you?" says Charles in a flat tone looking at her.

"Well yes. Why is she suddenly acting funny? After all the charters I've done."

Charles's expression has changed gradually to one of gravity that verges on outrage. "No, I doubt if she's jealous of you," he says with a snarl of laughter as if he too finds the suggestion ludicrous. "Damn bloody damn."

What?" she says puzzled.

"The pair of you," says Charles, but it seems he is glaring at Boss. "I can't believe it," he scrabbles at the frizzy hair above his ears.

"Boss doesn't seem to know what's going on with Libby."

Boss, having dropped the magazine, is staring out of the window. He sighs. Charles sits down, swivels around and rubs both his hands over his head and sighs in turn. He then gets up and savagely sharpens a pencil saying with rising irritation, "Don't expect me to blow any whistles. I won't. For one because it's not my business, and number two because I can't see how it will do any good, and lastly for the good of the marina, I don't want a scandal. Now if you will excuse me Boss, you have wasted my time long enough, I am going to have to look for someone else." Just at this point the phone rings. He throws down the pencil violently and plunges back at his desk. 'What,' he screams, immediately afterwards adopting a completely judicious and calm tone, 'Ah-ha,' he says several times, 'Right, OK.'

Lynn thinks they had better leave but to her surprise Charles mysteriously holds up his hand to stop them. Lynn wonders if he has thought of something else, something bleak and final perhaps. Meanwhile Charles is saying into the phone, "You realise you'll forfeit your deposit, the owner has gone to some expense….. OK, no that's fine. No no, ring me, we'll fix you up when you're ready." He puts the phone down and breathes out. He sits on his desk and looks at Boss for a while. "They've cancelled. You're a very lucky man. If I had brought in Douglas it would have cost me more than the charter was worth and you can be sure I wouldn't have used you again, ever." Yes luck has shone and Charles puts his hand in the drawer and pulls out some American banknotes. "Here is your share of the deposit, though god knows why I should give you anything." Then he turns and goes to a large board where various boats are chalked in and wipes out an entry. "Oh," he says to Lynn, "I see Tom and Yvonne are due back any tick of the clock. They've got a charter in a week or so, I'm holding it for them. Tell them to come straight in and see me when they get here."

Once out of the office, Boss is a different man. The difficulty has been removed and with it goes all trace of his former anxiety and he starts to dance with his hand on his stomach and the other over his head clutching the money Der-der-der-da-da-da-der-dum, he congas in the direction of the bar. "Come on kid, some of this is yours, let's celebrate." Dada-dada-da-dum. "Arthur, we're here for a champagne breakfast. Hello hello Jim lad, you in early too! You don't have any mystical types selling hippie trinkets with you do you? Well come and join us then. Look, we just got twenty dollars US for doing absolutely sod all, isn't that right kid. Do you know the kid? Songbird this is Jim, Jim this is um….."

"We've met. My name's Lynn," she says.

"Yes," says Boss. "Now let's see, how about scrambled eggs and bacon and pancakes, toast anyone yes let's drink a toast."

"Orange juice for me," says Lynn.

"Coffee," says Jim.

"Right. And champagne, no I insist, how often do you get out of a horrible mess and get given twenty US into the bargain. And come and drink with us Arthur, oh well, this is a sad place, they don't have enough staff on. There was a time when old Arthur here or Rick or whoever was behind the bar would come and drink with their customers, which as I see it is sound commercial sense. After all if the barman drinks with you, you keep coming back don't you, much nicer drinking among friends. Yes I know it's only 7.30 in the morning. Now Jim lad, where have you been, I haven't seen you for ages. The last time you were in company with a rather odd young man who tried to sell me some piece of cheap tat I forget what, and I mean I would have bought it too only Libby took a dislike to him. He didn't seem a very jolly type, wouldn't drink. One should never buy stuff off people who won't drink, there's something wrong with them, they have a rather sad attitude to life I always think. Tell us the story, Jim."

Jim brushes back the hank of sun-bleached hair that keeps falling over one temple. He has another hank haphazardly constrained in a pigtail behind. He is somewhat more exotically dressed than the first time Lynn met him and this morning he wears a red bandanna around his forehead, a large loop of gold in one ear and a black leather thong round his neck hung with sharks' teeth. He wears no shirt but has on a black waistcoat embroidered in scarlet silk and a pair of washed-out red jeans. He looks like a pirate, Lynn decides, but one of those that you'd find in Boy's Own Annual, who wash their clothes and clean their teeth before they set out pirating.

"I'm here at this ungodly hour because there was supposed to be stuff arriving on the early plane but it hasn't come so I might as well stay here till midday, see if it comes in then. You see I've got a job out at the Island Fair," he explains to Boss. "Oscar the tee-total hippy is paying me to help at his stand. And paying me commission too."

"Island Fair, what's that?" says Boss. "What, oh yes, yes I remember, it's burst upon us from nowhere and will put us on the map. People are flying in by the plane-load from all over, the papers say it's an 'outstanding success' and all thanks to whatisname, our wonderful elected Premier who is out there pumping flesh and all that, which is nice as it keeps him from hanging around me. I don't know why it is but I don't like the fellow so the more time he spends with his electorate out at wherever it is...."

"Well you're wrong on all counts," says Jim. "First if the evidence of the first two weeks is any guide it's a dismal failure. I don't believe the Premier has shown his face since the opening and you watch, he will shortly start blaming everyone else. And far from a swelling mob of eager spectators there are only a few locals from town, some chamber of commerce types and business people from the islands and a few tourists."

"Oh well poor old Oscar, coming down here with a pure heart and such unbounded optimism in his fellow men."

"Don't waste your prayers on Oscar, he will do very well. Yes in fact he is a man who will be a millionaire before he's thirty, a really rich hippy. Scary. You must come soon and check it out."

"I think we should. We will secure Arthur as he's a man his aunt reliably informs me is always wasting his days off. And Lynn here would love to come too wouldn't you?"

"Yes I love fairs. Are there dodgems and things."

"Ah," says Jim. "No you are confusing the sort of fair where you have fun with the sort of Fair that has a capital F. No-one has fun at our sort of Fair, it is strictly business. We are going to make lots of money. Or rather Oscar is."

"With that cheap tat he was showing me!"

"Certainly. They all costs a few dollars US wholesale or less but they can be inscribed with lurid messages such as Present from Barbados, or Antigua or wherever -tourists love to take stuff like that home with them. Since we started we've turned over five hundred US in retail every day, that's just retail, not trade. As for trade, last week a man who is setting up a gift shop in a new hotel on some little island wandered in and when he'd looked around, he said he'd have a thousand of this and a thousand of that. If there were more like him you would be seeing before you a wealthy man. It sure beats deckhand work. By the time we finish, I should have made enough to fix up my engine and maybe even get a new sail."

"Well done my son," says Boss admiringly. "I see I am in the wrong business. And I never thought of you as an entrepreneur before."

"I'm not," says Jim, "I'm hopeless at it. I can't add up for nuts, I have to write everything down and do it long hand or else I get into a hopeless muddle. I only just sort of somehow get through without making an idiot of myself. Whereas Oscar just goes Ommmm! and then does it in his head and adds riders like, They're 38 cents each or 25 cents per hundred but if you're wanting it in thousands I'd let you have them at two hundred and something, which is a so-and-so percent discount and if you're looking at bigger numbers then we negotiate, everything's negotiable man. You know, peace brother."

"Wow. So how long does it go for?" asks Lynn.

"Another two weeks but Oscar won't last the distance. He didn't calculate on the retail demand and the trade has more or less gone through already. He had my whole house full of boxes to start with but now we're down to one corner of the lounge room. But you know, we're the star attraction. He has the pavilion set up like a Carnival float, and he's got live bands and singers and between whiles he plays Caribbean music on a really big music system, Mighty Sparrow and so on."

"We definitely need to plan an expedition out to this luminous event," says Boss. "It would be a sad reflection on us all if we allowed such a major happening to pass us by. Ah breakfast. Arthur my friend, what time do you get off here?"

"I get five hours off over lunch but I am otherwise engaged," says Arthur.

"And tomorrow, no, well how about Saturday?"

"About 4. Why?"

"Have you been to the Island Fair? No, I can see by your expression that you haven't. Well we are going to go. You must gird yourself up for an outing. And tell all our friends that the Frangipani is organising an excursion, no excuses will be accepted, even humorously feeble ones. At four o'clock it is ordained that all good men shall come here to form a party and we will set forth together to discover whatever there is to see. Now Songbird, how about opening the champagne? This is going to be a very good day, I can just feel it."

They have breakfast which lasts a couple of hours and Boss drinks most of the champagne, after which he decides he might like to go and lie down for a bit. "But what about the dinghy, we have to take that back Boss," says Lynn.

"Later," says Boss in his lordly way and wanders off.

"Oh," sighs Lynn.

"What's up?" says Jim. "Can I help?"

"We brought the little boat round so Libby wouldn't see us and it's at the end of the jetty near the gates but I don't know how to drive it and I don't want to leave it there."

"I'll give you a lesson in a mo, if you like," says Jim who is engaged in rolling a thin cigarette. "They're as easy as pie to work."

"Thank you," she says gratefully.

"Whereto Songbird?" says Arthur as they depart.

She goes up to the bar and leans both arms on it to pull herself up a bit taller, "Boss took the rubber boat from the Golden Dawn and now he's gone off so Jim's going to help me take it back." She watches his face carefully in case there is any disapproval of this plan.

Her scrutiny makes Arthur want to express himself in some physical way such as throwing a book of matches, or hitting her on the head with a bread stick, but there is nothing within reach. In the end he just says, "So how long can you stare at me without laughing?"

She immediately crinkles up in a giggle. "No but is it alright about the boat?" she says leaning forward and dropping her voice. "I've only really just met Jim and maybe he doesn't know any more than I do."

"Oh you can trust him," he says. "There's not much he doesn't know about boats." For once he regrets the confinement of his work, that he can't just drop everything and go and help her himself.

"Now," says Jim when the two of them are sitting in the dinghy, "it's dead easy. You steer with this, here's the throttle, and this is the starter lead. So give the lead a good smooth pull. Harder, no don't jerk it, there," the engine roars to life. "Now, we're sitting here tied up. The next step is to undo the line." Lynn dutifully fumbles with the rope and undoes it. "Good, now we're floating free." He gives the jetty a push. "And now our prow is pointing towards the open water. The main thing with these is that although they're made of rubber, yacht owners are still not enthusiastic about you running into their valuable vessels so we'll keep the speed down in port to prevent untoward mishaps. So open the throttle," the boat starts to move forward under its own power, "now turn the tiller to the left."

Left? Left? She turns it haphazardly and nearly goes into the jetty. She quickly turns it the other way. "Well missed," says Jim. "You'll soon get the idea. We'll go for a little spin so that you can practice steering. Head up the line of this jetty and make for the harbour entrance." They chug out of the marina and across towards the yacht club. "We'll go round this dirty big millionaire's yacht that just came in, look at it, so big it won't even fit into a berth at the yacht club. It's obscene, isn't it, that people have got so much money. I wonder if Oscar will have a boat like this one day."

"I think it looks fantastic," says Lynn.

"Do you! Do you want to go on board?"

"Why, do you know them?"

"No of course not, but I've heard they're having a cocktail party on Saturday night. We'll go and gatecrash."

"Oh we couldn't do that," she says in terror.

"Yes we can, so long as we arrive on a boat, how are they going to kick us off? Don't hold back, these are only nouveau riche you know, newspaper magnates or some low trade like that. The more people who turn up to their parties, the bigger the crush, the more they like it."

"But I've got nothing to wear."

"Well then go nude and say it's the latest thing from Mary Quant. It's settled, we're going."

They complete their circuit and approach the Golden Dawn, "Now throttle right down and come in sideways so I can grab hold of the railing and tie up. Slower." They approach cautiously. "Shut it off," and Jim leaps over the side of the Dawn holding the rope and goes to the rear of the boat but as he does so he turns and cries, "Tom my old fruit, you're back!"

A head has appeared at the companionway and a voice calls out, "Ah-hah, caught you red-handed," and a man with a beard leaps up on deck. "Ah lad, you don't know how glad I am to see your beautiful golden hair waving in the sunshine again."

"Ooh sailor," pipes Jim giving him a playful punch. "Give us a kiss, I didn't know you cared." They wrestle, laughing. "Oops hang on," says Jim, "there's someone I have to introduce you to. Come aboard Lynn," and he comes back to the rail to give her a hand.

"Sorry," she says, "I'm not very good at this leaping from place to place yet."

"Tom this is Lynn. Arthur got her to caretake for you while you were away."

"Oh I'm very obliged to you," says Tom throwing himself down on to one of the cushioned seats. He is a youngish man, in his late twenties, of middle height and with fine dark sprouting hair and whiskers.

"So where's Yvonne, how was your trip, how was the wedding? She didn't stand you up did she?" says Jim in a jocular teasing voice.

"No, I stood her up," says Tom.

"What!" says Jim and looks at him. "You're not serious. Show us your ring finger. Bare! Oh my god, what have you been doing?"

"It's a long story and I'm tired," says Tom.

"And you want us to leave you alone with our curiosity unsatisfied and go round and spread malicious rumours until you feel strong enough to tell everyone the real story."

"No, you're right, I'll tell you what happened but I think I have to have a cup of coffee first. Hang on, I'll put the kettle on."

"I'll make it," offers Lynn and goes below.

"Hey," says Jim. "What the hell? I thought you'd be coming back in the pink, barely able to speak for smiling and here you are and where is Yvonne?"

Tom rubs his forehead and eyes. "Well you know Yvonne went on an earlier flight so she could get there and have fittings and all that, organise things. And I was to follow on later. Well, I met this woman, we were sitting together on the plane and got chatting. She'd been here on holiday and guess what? - she was going to Chicago too. Then there was a delay when the plane landed at Miami and I got completely out of it, I can't remember what happened….. Because we'd already had quite a lot to drink from the on-board bar and then we had quite a few in Miami and by the time we got to Chicago I was paralytic. I'd missed my onward connection so she offered me a bed, and - well I don't know how but when I came round I'd been there nearly two days locked in a carnal embrace and still going strong. I mean the only thing that put a stop to it was the fact that she had to go to back to work. Then I came to my senses and thought, what am I going to say to Yvonne? But I cobbled something together about problems down here etcetera, as if I'd set off later, then the usual problems with the phones, couldn't ring, thought I'd get there before a telegram, missed a connection rhubarb rhubarb….. And Yvonne swallowed it! Amazing really, but she was too preoccupied to get into her usual ferreting and I thought I was safe. But then a few days later this other woman turned up, I don't know how she got the address, maybe I scrawled it into her address book when I was drunk….. It was awful Jim, awful, there was the biggest scene. I know now how it must have felt going in a tumbril to the guillotine when I saw the Chicago woman coming up the path to the house. Why are you laughing, it wasn't funny, this has been the worst few weeks of my life."

"Tom," says Jim eventually, stretched full length and looking up into the canvas awning, "there is no hope for you. You are a lost man."

"But the thing is," says Tom ruefully, "I actually wanted to get married in the end. I admit that I was a bit lukewarm talking about it down here, I had my reputation to think of. But I was actually ready, I would have gone through with it and I don't know why Yvonne had to make such a fuss, just because the other woman is there weeping and carrying on. I'm saying over and over, 'Yvonne, between the two of you, I am choosing you. It's you I want to marry'."

Lynn brings out cups of coffee and the boat rocks and they all lie there dreamily looking up into nothing and then Jim says, "This other woman….."

"What about her?"

"What was her name?" Silence. Jim looks sideways and then starts to laugh face down on the cushions. "Ah Jeez," he says propping up his head with his elbow and taking a sip of coffee, "He doesn't even know her name," and he laughs again. And then Tom laughs and groans and says he could cry and Lynn smiles at both of them and the time drifts by.

"Oh," says Lynn, "Boss and I had an interview with Charles this morning and as we were leaving he said he'd got a charter for you in a week or so if you want it."

"Glory be," says Tom. "We spent all our money and time doing up this boat so we could charter it after we were married. This was going to be our first few careless years before the urge to nest build. God damn and blast." He gets up and starts to wander the deck. "You see this bit, she varnished this. Lovely bit of varnishing, you can hardly see a brush stroke. And see the mainsail, there's a bit of the mainsail," he starts searching for it "round one of the eyelets that tore and she mended it, she was terrific at stuff like that. And in the main cabin," he goes down the companionway and his voice floats back, "she made all these curtains for the bunks, she sat right here at the table and sewed them." He stands in silence for a while then climbs into one of the bunks groaning and pulls a pillow over his head.

Jim and Lynn quietly leave.

"It's terribly sad," says Lynn once she's out of earshot.

"It's exactly what one would expect from him," says Jim without emotion. "Yvonne must have had rocks in her head to even let him out of her sight. She would never have made such a mistake down here."

"So it's all Yvonne's fault!"

Jim lets out a laugh, "Only for wanting to marry a man like Tom. They were perfectly happy living together but then she got the idea that she would like to be married in a church all in white. The shock to poor Tom's system….. you can't imagine. I expect this liaison with the other woman was all a subconscious rebellion against the idea of the whole thing. Now of course he's probably torn it because Yvonne can hardly crawl back down here, not when he's humiliated her in front of her whole family. I think he actually does love her, married or not."

"Well now you've explained it, it still seems terribly sad."

"Don't give in to pitying him, that's what he wants, he'll lap it up. When he misbehaves we must act with brutal indifference otherwise he'll get to thinking he's cute. So we must all laugh unmercifully at him, and the more he sighs and groans and weeps the funnier we must find it. OK?"

When they reach the end of the jetty Lynn says she thinks she will go into town and Jim wanders back into the Frangipani. "How d'you go?" says Arthur.

"Have you noticed how women can't tell right from left? Left, I'll say and she turns the tiller but it seems to be completely arbitrary which way."

"Sheila has a big bloodstone ring, great heavy thing, which she wore for her driving lessons. She used to look at her hands when the instructor said right, that was the hand with the ring on. And the hand without the ring - that was left."

"That's an idea! Next time I'm in town I'll buy her a ring from Woolworths."

"Careful how you give it to her, you might end up married like Tom," says Arthur jocularly.

"Not married like Tom you mean," says Jim.

"Now what?" cries Arthur, and Jim tells him the whole story.

"Oh my God," says Arthur wiping his eyes, "Tom certainly knows how to make life interesting for everyone." They stand shaking their heads and laughing. Then Arthur straightens. "Here's trouble," he murmurs under his breath.

Anthony Hamilton has walked in. He is dressed in a carefully cut safari suit and flashes of gold flicker at the edges, a gold watch and gold ring, a gold chain round his neck.. He ignores the other people in the Frangipani.

"The famous Hamilton junior. I saw him coming off some huge rich-man's toy down at the yacht club a while ago," murmurs Jim when the man has seated himself at a table some distance from the bar.

"You have been out of circulation recently. The son of our esteemed owner had barely been back a fortnight when there were police on his doorstep."

"Oh excellent, a man like that needs to keep up his quotient of scandal. Ah and talking of scandal, how do you feel about us gatecrashing this cocktail party on the Beau Jeste?"

"That would not be a scandal, that would be invasion, riot, breach of the peace. You won't get away with that."

"Nonsense, my blood is up. But you're going to have to lend me some clothes."

"You're not really going to try it are you? The sort of people who have big boats like that only come ashore to go to the Beach. They're not yachties, they're not even normal people! Even you won't be able to carry this off."

"You want to bet?"

"Ten bucks."

"Local?"

"No American."

"My my, you are confident. But you're coming too. Don't think you can just put your money down and then hide round the back and snicker."

"Man, if you're taking me with you I bet you $20. No, a hundred. I'll strip you clean of every dollar you made at the Fair. Ha ha," he tosses a glass, "money for jam. I promise you, you will be humiliated."

"Persons of breeding such as myself never suffer humiliation. If we lose we withdraw in good order with a curl of the lip. Hey up, the Space Oddity is coming over."

Anthony Hamilton has been looking impatiently at his watch and now approaches the bar with disdainful hauteur. He keeps his eye on the entrance while saying with a distant authority, "You there. A person by the name of Max will shortly be coming here. Tell him that I couldn't wait any longer and he can meet me back at the house."

He then turns to go but Arthur says with calm precision, "If the man you are talking to me about is Max de Troy I won't be giving him any messages. He is not welcome here while I am running this bar and I certainly don't intend to speak to him at all."

Hamilton stands stock still with an expression on his face as if an unseen minion is readjusting the rod up his bum. For a moment all that moves is the flicker on his face. Then turning with a stiff legged fury, he walks back towards Arthur as if to better hear an almost unbelievable response. "I beg your pardon," he says in a high voice. He is now against the bar and looking at Arthur with a heightened colour and white lips. "When I give you an order I don't require any discussion about it."

"You can't give me an order because you don't employ me. Rick does," says Arthur.

This eminently obvious remark has the same effect on the young man as poking a scorpion. "Listen boy!" the man is lashing forward and foaming and can barely get his words out for rage, "when I tell you to do something you do it unless you want to be sacked."

"You can't sack me either," says Arthur with the same calm voice. Various yachtie identities have now drawn near the bar as Hamilton's voice has risen to such a pitch that everyone is aware of the altercation. "But if you have a problem you had better go and see Rick who is now having a well-deserved lie-in - he being somewhat grumpy and stressed of late. Perhaps you can persuade him to sack me but you'll have to find someone else to take over the bar. Or maybe," he indicates the till with the flip of one arm, "you intend to take it over yourself." He then puts both hands on the bar and waits expectantly.

"How dare you!" the man gasps stepping back sharply as if he is about to hurl himself across the bar in a fury and attack Arthur. Unfortunately he hasn't seen Karlo who has been drawn from a pleasant contemplation of odds for the Barbados Cup into a closer inspection of the fracas, as the idle are drawn towards bustling activity. In stepping back he steps on Karlo's foot which causes Karlo to grasp his arm and say, "Careful." Karlo is more than twice Hamilton's age but also twice his bulk and sports a broken nose from a rather lively youth, and the way he expresses this caution makes the young man aware of the attention the scene is creating. He stands there for a moment gasping in his breath in seething gulps before saying through gritted teeth, "I'll deal with you later," as he holds up a finger at Arthur and strides off, his face livid.

Before he is out of earshot, one of the yachties remarks ironically, "There'll be a heap of screaming and moaning when that happens but don't worry Arthur old son, we'll all rush to your rescue."

When Rick appears in the bar at the end of Arthur's shift, he certainly does appear grumpy and stressed. He shows no interest in the scandal of the previous hour except to say, "Bloody hell, Arthur, can't you stop making life more complicated than it is. Fortunately for you the owner is somewhat put out by his son and heir's involvement in scandal of late. Make sure you're back at 4 on the dot. I have to get in some more supplies, we're seriously down on some things."

Arthur leaves the bar and immediately heads for the centre of town and for a menswear boutique, the best one around. Rows of Hawaiian shirts line one side which he picks through nervously, wondering which will have Sheila's stamp of approval and which she will consider tacky. On the other side of the shop are tailored shirts. "If I got one of those I'd have to get some new trousers," he thinks. "If only I could find a nice casual shirt I could wear with my good jeans." He tries on a dozen shirts without being certain that any of them are right. As he dithers between a choice of two, he looks out of the window for inspiration and from the corner of his eye sees a face he recognises go by. He rushes for the door. "Hey Songbird," he calls. "Lynn. What are you doing?"

"I've been shopping," she says bouncing up to him. "Look. I've bought some shorts and a little dress and a shirt all for ten US dollars."

"Well come and help me," he says. "I have to go to lunch with my sister and if I don't turn up looking right she'll..... Well, I'll be in all sorts of trouble."

She follows him in and he shows her his choices, "What do you think?"

She feels the fabric. "But they're polyester," she murmurs.

"Is that bad?"

"I'm not sure, I think so. My mother is in the fashion industry, in a sort of way, and she hates polyester. She's into velvet and thick cottons and silks and satins, rich materials." She rummages along the rack. "Maybe rayon's alright." She turns to the boutique owner who is hovering anxiously now, "Haven't you got cotton or silk?"

"Well we have some lovely shirts in silk. Just reach here now. I've only just started unpacking them," and he brings out a tunic style shirt in pale blue.

"Now that's nice," says Lynn, "try it on. Hold your arms up, is it a little big?" She worries at the fit and he worries at the colour and eventually he is equipped with a green batik-patterned one. "They're awfully expensive," she murmurs but he doesn't care.

"If my sister likes me in it you won't believe what a saving it will be, whatever the price," he says. "Now let's get out of here. You going back to the boat?"

She nods. "Now I've got all these extra clothes, I'll feel much more confident, having a choice of things to wear. Isn't it fabulous having money? Just think, every time I go out with Boss, he gives me $50 local and on the first trip all the charterers gave me ten American dollars, each!" she squeaks. "It seemed like so much money I felt nervous carrying it around with me, so I started a bank account."

He laughs.

"Why is it funny?" she says. "Isn't it a lot?"

"Oh yes," he says, "that's more than a deckhand will make in a week, even adding the value of food and stuff on top. That's a very nice start and I'm glad they're all so generous. Sometimes the charterers give nothing, even if they catch a fish or have a wonderful cruise. The rich are sometimes very mean with their money. No I didn't laugh because of that. I've got my sister constantly in mind and she makes so much money that she wouldn't even think $50 US in her purse would be enough to go to the corner shop to buy matches. And to go shopping, real shopping, she'd have to have a sheaf of hundred dollar bills. And, well," he leans over and looks anxiously once more in his carrier bag, "if she doesn't like my shirt, if I turn up at her lunch and she thinks I'm looking shabby, she is capable of leaving all her other guests and rushing me into town to buy something else."

"Wow!" says Lynn. "Is she so very particular?"

"Oh yes," he says. "I'm very glad you were there to help. I don't know what she would have done if I'd turned up in polyester." Lynn giggles. "So your mother's in the fashion industry too?"

"Not fashion like your sister, but a kind of fashion. She does interior design. Everyone wants their houses to look a certain way. She works a lot with fabrics and they are always really expensive. She seems to be able to tell if it's cheap material. I know I wouldn't be allowed out if I was wearing nylon or something."

"Relatives can be hard to cope with," murmurs Arthur. "Let's not talk about our families any more."

"Sometimes I wonder what else I can talk about," she says. "I haven't done anything yet that's worth talking about. My family are the only people I really know. I envy people who've lived interesting lives, they have so much more to talk about. I thought I would have met interesting people in Port Sophia but my mother's cousin didn't seem to know any. You see, I'm boring you."

"No," he protests, "I was looking at my watch so as not to be late for the lunch. Why don't you come too?" It is out before he is even aware of saying it.

"With your sister? But I've only got these clothes!"

"It doesn't matter for you, she's not critical of anyone else. You see, she makes so much money she wants to shower me with it and my aunt as well, but what do we need down here? I have a fitted dinner jacket and some dress shoes but how often am I going to wear them? So don't worry about that. Show me what you bought." He looks in her parcels. She has bought a pair of white shorts, a little halter top and a T-shirt made of flour sacks.

"No - it's a dress."

"What?"

"It's a dress, not a T-shirt. There's a boutique down by the wharf that sells them. They're made of old hessian flour sacks."

"Well wear that," he says. "It's so different she probably won't even know what to say to it!"

"How much will the lunch cost though?" says Lynn. "Maybe I should go back to the bank."

"Oh no, she pays."
"But she hardly knows me."
"So? You're my guest."

Lynn is at the marina gate in her new dress at one o'clock. She can see Arthur coming down from his house in his new shirt and best jeans. She worries now that her floursack dress is too short. She has bought some sandals with big yellow flowers between the toes, but maybe they look cheap and outrageous. It certainly is a bit of a strain thinking about going to lunch with someone who wears only the best clothes. She can see that Arthur is also anxious but he gives her a grin when he comes up. He does have a lovely smile. She finds she doesn't care if his sister is disapproving, it is so nice to go somewhere with him.

"What do you think?" he says.

"You look great," she gives him a big encouraging smile.

"Hey Arthur," Michael's head comes out of his taxi, "I hardly recognise you, you all dress up looking so nice. Jump in, your sister don't want you to be late."

"My sister ordered a taxi, you see," he says. "She does this. She organises my life while she's here." They get in, "Now Michael, Michael, tell me now, how I'm looking?"

"Man, you cutting it in that shirt," says Michael happily.

"No but you know Sheila, what will she think?" he is leaning forward over the huge bulk of Michael's shoulder to look in the car mirror.

"You looking nice, man," Michael turns his head ignoring the oncoming traffic and winks at Lynn. "Ain't he looking nice?"

"Yes, he is," she says enthusiastically.

"Oh well," says Arthur. "We'll see."

"Don't worry," Lynn says. "She'll be so horrified that someone was dragged along to her lunch wearing flour sacks that she won't give your shirt a second glance."

He laughs. Then frowns. And sits back, and sits forward, and generally looks uncomfortable.

Lynn is not that comfortable herself. Sitting down she realises how very short her dress is. However she is wearing her bikini underneath, because then if she is thrown out by Sheila in disgust, she can always go to the beach. "What do you think your sister will wear? I expect it will be amazing."

“Yes, probably something floor-length, see-through and topless.”

“Topless!” Lynn exclaims.

“Just joking. She’ll be on her best behaviour with my aunts and uncles and cousins there.”

Sheila is wearing a crimson minidress of clinging crepe that makes everyone else in the room look orphaned and ragged. She sees them come in. “Brother,” she calls and Arthur comes through from the back.

“Oui papa,” cries Aunt Marion, “what you in style! That a nice new shirt man. Oh that a nice shirt.”

Sheila puts her hands on his shoulders to give him a kiss and then looks at the shirt. “Yes,” she says, “quite nice.” Arthur breathes easier, that is at least a pass mark. And lest she be given time to be more critical, he turns and says, “I saw Lynn in town so I invited her too.”

Sheila looks arrested. “Oh my goodness, where did you get that?” bursts from her lips and Arthur thinks “Oh no, she can’t be going to do one of her ‘Who is Responsible For This’ routines, treating the kid like family,” and he nerves himself to save her.

Lynn says, “I just bought it today, they make them here…..” and the rest is lost in Sheila’s urgent, “Where where where? Simon, over here Simon! Simon we must have some of these,” she is holding the kid by the cloth of the dress and examining it with ravenous attention. “This is wonderful, I love it! Simon go down right now and buy as many as you can find. We’ll have everyone in the background of the shot wearing them.” She beams at Lynn. “And it looks so nice on you. Sometimes I want to be small so I can wear something like this. Now has everyone got their drinks? Arthur, get something for Lynn. We’re going in, I have to be working this afternoon so…..” She is leading the way to a screened off section of the restaurant with a long table.

“I think we passed,” says Arthur.

“Yes,” breathes Lynn. “Fancy someone as beautiful as your sister wanting to be little like me.”

“Models play at wanting to be someone else. Sometimes they do it so well they turn into actresses.”

Arthur gets her a planters punch. “You can relax now, but I have to work at 4 so I’m just having a beer.”

Sheila has reserved a seat for Arthur beside herself and Lynn is fitted in further down the table next to Dale and opposite Lucas, who is off-duty and whom she doesn't at first recognise. Large menus in dark green leather are propped in front of everyone and from behind hers Sheila leans towards Arthur. "So is this something special you've got with your little friend over there?" she murmurs.

This calls for frank and full confession. "No, I only met her a couple of weeks ago," and he tells Sheila the circumstances. "I've ended up feeling sort of responsible for her, until she finds her feet. Then I went down to choose a shirt and she just happened to be walking past with all her new things so I got her in to help me, knowing what a terror of a taskmaster you are. Then I just invited her to lunch on the spur of the moment." He certainly hadn't intended to invite her, for this very reason, being cross-examined. Somehow it has just happened again. No matter how much he thinks to caution himself, the kid will give him a smile and there will be his mouth in motion, inviting her. His sister continues to look at him with slightly raised eyebrows.

"Ah well," she says and goes back to her menu, "I'm just interested in the company you keep."

He feels somehow flustered again and can barely read what is in front of him. What does she mean by that? He's told her everything there is to it. Just because both of the times she's seen him in the last week it is with the kid in tow - it is purely by chance and he hasn't meant anything by it and he knows the kid knows that too. But he also knows exactly what is in his sister's mind, it is almost written in the glance, "Be careful, brother mine. If that little girl opens up her eyes and looks at you wide with admiration and gives you the big smile one more time you will be a goner. I have to find someone more suitable for my little brother, he needs a down home girl not some young white foreigner."

There are thirty at least at table. "Where's Uncle Henry and his Canadian lady friend?" exclaims Sheila having checked out the members of her extended family. "Didn't anyone invite them? I was sure one of you would have invited them."

"Ah well, they have a bit of a problem," says Dale. "I can't say for certain that they're still together."

"Oh that's sad," says Sheila. "I thought you told me he had at last met the love of his life. I thought everyone liked her too. So how did he mess it up this time?"

"It was a bit of a sad thing," says Dale. "One of those coincidences. I saw it all."

"Don't tell about Mary-Jane," says Marion.

"Mary-Jane!" says Sheila.

"Hear me Dale," says Marion but Dale seems oblivious.

"She's a nice woman, about Henry's age, no maybe a bit younger. I don't know exactly how old she is but she ain't today's story. Anyway Henry invited her to a big dance at the Beach the Saturday before last. The Merrymen were playing and it was $20 to get in and you needed a suit."

"No just a jacket," says Arthur. "Any old jacket. You should have seen some of the yachties who went, scruffs with jackets on five sizes too large! And that rule was supposed to keep the riff raff out!"

"Well it didn't," says Dale, "and that was the whole point. But Jennifer, that's the name of the lady, is good friends with her neighbours, our lovely cousins in Trafalgar Street that sadly are not here today….." A small rustle of mirth whispers round the table.

"Didn't I hear that this lady was from Ontario?" asks Sheila.

"That's right, and working with some religious mission and she's renting old Bart Baker's house. That's how she met Henry, through Dora and Thea. Dora introduced them and, well, Henry was quite a hit apparently. And really, I don't care what some people say, when you get to a certain age there's no colour difference - everyone is getting grey and looking the same if you ask me. So they were going out and getting on well. Except she's been sick with a stomach upset and kept having stomach cramps, throwing up and having to see the doctor. But Henry was good there with the visits the next day and the 'How are you's' and flowers and you could see he was coming on at last, and about time because next year he'll be fifty and there's no getting away from it, you do slow down when you get to that age and get a bit stuck for female company if you don't look lively. So everyone was saying, come on Henry pluck your courage up and we'll get you down that aisle at last. Well then comes the dance and Dora had Jennifer dress up in one of them long velour low-cut dresses she has and Henry is telling her and telling her how she is looking so good and looking so nice even though in Dora's words poor old Jennifer looks more like a corpse done up in undertaker's plush after weeks of throwing up everything she ate. No, but Henry finally got the message - that you don't tell a woman the truth, you tell her she is looking lovely. And I think maybe she did to him. So we are all at the dance and having a nice time and I'm pretty sure Henry was thinking about popping The Question. Then it happened. That man Bolton Presley is there….."

"Yes for sure," bursts out Marion, "and him only out of the calaboose a month."

"And the police come in, right into the middle with the Premier and all sorts of bigwigs there and arrest him and wouldn't you know it he's sitting in Henry's seat and is talking to Dora….."

"And she playing holier than thou and putting herself on some pedestal and she talking people bad all the time. She's there mixing with this criminal for all to see," says Marion with venom.

"Well he is related….." ventures someone.

"Only by marriage," says Marion. "Which amount to nothing with a man like that!"

"Apparently there had been a big robbery at the Industrial Works," continues Dale, "and there was a white female accomplice. And there is Jennifer sitting right next to him. She's a white woman so she must be the one. And they arrest her too."

"Arrest a white woman," says Marion. "Did you ever hear such a thing?"

"Henry had been queuing at the bar to get his lady a nice cocktail. Imagine! He comes back and the woman of his dreams is being marched out the door in handcuffs and. Dora is hysterical….."

"That was just because Jennifer have on her stupid dress," says Marion.

"And everyone calling on everyone else and calling on one and all to ring the Chief Constable, that it was the wrong woman. And poor Henry left holding a drink in each hand so he drinks them both and rushes down the police station to tell them his mind. Eventually after a couple of hours she is let out and Henry brings her back to the dance which has been going on with a swing for all that and there she is among us again. So everyone crowd round to console her on the bad way she was treated and she said, Oh no it wasn't that bad. She forgive them as her Christian duty. It seems they lock her in a cell while they interview Bolton Presley and her cellmates were a shock to start with, being highly rambunctious and apt to pick fights but then everything settles down when she explains her refusal to sit on the bench with them as being a fear of ruining Dora Powers' good dress and nothing personal. And it was then that she fell into a certain intimacy with her new companions on account of one of them being very well acquainted with Dora and in fact related to her. I name no names on the request of someone here present. Anyway, they were getting along just famously when a very smooth looking chap - this is how she told it - in a superior suit comes to the door of the cell and look through and then shouts for one of the police in a high fury and says, 'READ that description. Read that description of the woman,' batting with his hand at some report. 'Go on, read it out man.' And the man read this description, 'Blonde.' And then the chap screaming 'Is this woman blonde? No this woman has been blonde long time ago but this is an old woman with grey hair, grey not blonde and what else - READ it'. So the other man read, 'Age late-twenties to thirties.' And the first chap is screaming, 'Is this woman late-twenties? Is this woman in her thirties? Is this woman young at all at all? You arrest this woman because she alongside Presley but she is old old old, probably sixty! What are you thinking of, man?' And that is something Jennifer can't forgive them for. She is sitting at a table at the Beach Hotel with tears washing down her face saying, 'There was I thinking I was looking flirtatious and desirable and a real dish and all the time,' she wails, 'I was looking sixty.'

Well after expecting to hear dreadful stories from being locked up and abused, of course everyone starts to laugh. And Henry misses his chance again! He should have leaned in and told her how short-sighted the Chief Constable's assistant is, it is a well known fact and you know kiss kiss the man was only overstating the case to make the other man look stupid and no-one could possibly believe she is more than late-thirties and so on, with the arm around the shoulders giving hugs and kisses and rubbing up against her. But what did he do? He just laughs like the rest of them even though she is weeping fit to burst. What an ass he is, that man will die a lonely old bachelor you mark my words."

"And then Dora and Thea will get all his money," says Marion. "I expect the whole thing was cooked up by them in the first place."

"Well you're bitter against them because of all that history," says someone else, "and they're plenty mad from not being invited here today and everyday our Sheila rise like a star is a day they must rue their nasty tongues. But all the same, I feel sorry for that old fool Henry for missing his chance."

"But there is no chance, not with a white woman," says Marion. "Whatever Dale say, I feel different. You know my poor dead sister-in-law have a whole set of white relations and they treat her bad bad. They ever do anything for Arthur or Sheila? No, their nose too high in the air for that. So Henry and this woman could never work out. It is better to end this thing before it get into a serious love affair which would only cause more heart strain and pain for everyone."

Sheila smiles and nods and looks sideways at her brother. But the food is now arriving and he doesn't notice her expressive glance. Elegant entrees followed by lobster thermidors, fine cuts of scotch fillet, and whatever else they want.

Aunt Marion falls into despair over the knives and forks. "Why don't they put labels on them," she complains. "Why don't they tell people what these things are for. Which is for which, which is for fish?"

"It doesn't matter Tantie," says Sheila. "They're only bits of metal for getting food into your mouth without dropping it in your lap. You can eat it anyway you like, with your fingers if you like, look at me. And you Arthur, you, the one who says I never eat, what is this I am doing? Well, you take note."

"I see you. And next you'll be eating all that lettuce leaf there," he laughs. "How you going, kid?" he says looking up the table to Lynn.

"The food's lovely," she says, "I wish I was bigger and could fit more in. I'll never be a model," she says laughing to Sheila, "I like food too much."

"Well I like food too," says Sheila.

"But you must diet, to stay in shape?"

"No, I eat what I want generally. Except chocolates in case of pimples. I tell you what I hate doing is those chocolate commercials. I can't swallow the wretched stuff. I have to keep spitting it out after every bite so we can do the next take. And even so, I look at my chin a couple of days later and often I can see a blemish coming. But don't let me put you off having dessert."

"What'll we have?" says Arthur.

"Something outrageous," says Lynn. "What's this one? Island Dreams - chocolate mouse, orange sorbet and Grand Marnier sauce served in a pineapple."

"You'll never eat all that."

"But if I have it, I can hope to eat it and then even if I don't it will be a lovely attempt," she says.

"Now that's the right attitude to life," says Arthur dreamily.

"I must go back to my office now," says Dale. "Sheila, if you want to come and look at this land deal you'd better move quick - already it has people muscling in from all sides."

"Uncle, I have to fly back to the States tomorrow early early but I'm back down in a week for this stupid film. Will it wait till then? Everything is too hectic to be rescheduled."

"OK, but I can't promise it will still be there. It's a government thing and they've put it out to tender. Maybe I'll put in an offer from you anyway - you can always withdraw later."

"Whatever you think, uncle."

Pastel-suited figures are starting to swarm towards Sheila, who sits serene. A photographer thrusts a light meter at her face. "We could do some inside shots first," he remarks.

"As you like," says Sheila.

"Can I stay and watch?" asks Lynn.

"Sure," says Sheila. "Oh and Arthur, I've got something for you. Come out here."

It's nearly four o'clock when Arthur strolls towards the bar of the Frangipani. "My, you're looking very nice," says Rae. "How did the lunch go? I wish I could get to meet your sister. She looks so beautiful in those magazines, she makes me feel like a lump!" Rae says this with no sense of being contradictory. A few days before she had laughed at the idea of Black is Beautiful. But in her mind Arthur's sister is beautiful, and therefore she isn't black. That is as rational as it gets. Envy is the main emotion. Although she also thinks, I could scrub up pretty well myself if I had some decent clothes, with my hair done properly, if there was anyone here who did hair or who sold the right kind of makeup….. "It isn't fair. How did your sister get so perfect looking?"

"Luck," says Arthur after reflection. "Plus a determination to overcome adversity."

"What adversity!" Rae is scornful. "I can't believe anyone who looks like that would ever have any real adversity to contend with."

Arthur's expression becomes ironical. What would Rae know of adversity? She is a middle-class white woman who thinks her destiny is to be looked after by all around her. "Been helping Rick?" he asks to change the topic.

"Oh it's been very quiet, I might as well have gone to the Beach. I would have gone if there was anyone to go to with, but Libby is in such a foul temper there's no fun going with her." Her expression is disgruntled.

"Yes, the kid's stayed there. I would have liked to have stayed myself and lolled around if I hadn't been working. After a good lunch and a couple of drinks you feel like stretching out and taking it easy until the sun goes down."

"The kid, what's her name again? So she's along there at the Beach Hotel is she? Whereabouts, which side, near the Beach Bar?"

"In front, in one of the sun loungers."

"What, but they're just for guests! She'll get chucked off."

"No, Sheila's there. She liked some dress that the kid bought in town and she's been having her sip drinks in the background plus me and anyone else so long as they're wearing a floursack shirt. Look at this, I spent a fortune on it and what does she do right after lunch but get me into some old shirt made of hessian."

"Oh is she still there? I think I'll go and take a look. I'll even wear old flour sacks, I'll wear anything….." She suddenly laughs at herself - yes to be conspicuous - I know what you were going to say mother.

Arthur says, "Oh well take these and bring the kid back with you when you come. I don't know if she knows how to use the route taxis on her own."

"What are they?" says Rae.

"Car keys. You know what we were talking about on Monday, about Rick getting a car for the bar? Well I stupidly asked about a mini-moke that Sheila was being driven in. I should know by now to never, ever, mention I'm interested in anything while my sister's around."

"She's letting you use her car this afternoon, how great!"

"No, worse than that," he says. "She's gone and bought it."

"To use when she's down here."

"No, for me. She's bought a car for me. Why would I want a car?"

"Oh Arthur," Rae exclaims excitedly, "a car! And can I use it sometimes, can I?"

"I expect you will," he grins.

At nine o clock, five glorious hours later, Rae is dancing back along the wooden walkway to the bar singing Oh Lord Won't You Give Me, with Lynn's arm through hers and at that moment she doesn't want anything else in the world. Suddenly in one day she has a car and she has a friend to go to the beach with. What a wonderful life it is to be sure. Except..... "I could have been a model, we could have both been models," she stops and exclaims solemnly.

"We could still be," says Lynn.

"But we're not tall. We could have been models if our parents had made us taller. I blame them, a curse on all parents of short people. It's their fault."

"All their fault."

"Isn't it sad?" says Rae looking up at the stars. "We only have one life and if we're not tall it's as good as wasted."

"Because no-one will ever fuss over us. I don't suppose we'll ever have our own personal assistants will we?"

"Our own makeup artists....."

"Someone to look after our clothes....."

"A man from reception to be constantly bringing over little messages and saying things like, 'It's New York, they're holding. Can you ring Paris urgent.'"

"But I think we can still have a happy life without all that. I don't think I should mind being short as long as I can be happy," says Lynn.

"No," says Rae, "I refuse to be lulled. I'm going to hang out for being tall and I will settle for nothing less!"

Chapter 5

There is no folly of the beasts of the earth which is not infinitely outdone by the madness of men

It is Saturday and a number of excursions are taking place. By midday, out past the airport, a utility truck loaded with locals has arrived for a picnic on the shore beyond the runway. It parks in the shade of a derelict house. It is not a particularly pretty beach they have come to, the surrounds are flat, windswept and littered. However it has a few advantages over the more traditionally scenic beaches to the south. For a start, it is not much frequented, especially by tourists. And second, the coconut palms are on land belonging to the airport authority and generally there is no-one around to stop a person climbing up and getting young coconuts to drink. One of the men in the party is expert at this and he climbs the long trunks like a centipede doubling and extending his body. Shouts below indicate the preferred pods which he chops with his machete so they crash down like cannon balls. The green nuts are then slashed and the tops sliced off. It was hot on the truck driving up and they gulp at the nuts to quench their thirst. After a while, someone brings out a flagon of rum which is added to the contents of the nuts. There is a general sigh of contentment.

The women start opening the food on the back of the truck and soon plates are handed round. There is crisp roasted pork still warm from the oven, a dish of baked macaroni, some roasted vegetables and plantain, rice and salads. Without more ado everyone heaps their plates. One of the men makes a particularly good meal of it. He is fond of crackling and despite some muttering from his wife pretty well corners the market in it. When the meal is over, he leaps up and grabs a spade off the back of the truck and tells his wife to keep a look out – to sound the horn if she sees anyone coming. His wife chirrups at him, "At least let that meal settle! You eat like a horse and then you go digging in the heat of the day."

He ignores her and walks down the shore for some way to a small mound. Such mounds are another advantage of this particular beach. He is accompanied by an older man and all the children, who watch as he starts digging experimentally. Soon his companions grab bits of stick and rocks and start scratching around in the sand and dirt themselves. It is one of the children who first makes a find. It is a partly rounded coarse stone like half an egg, weighing a couple of pounds. On the flat side a face has been carved in deep but primitive score-marks. Eyes, a broad flat nose and an open mouth can be made out. There is a sad look to it, a face in full possession of its grief. On the other side, on the curved part, there are further carvings that are not representational, just dots and one long and two short strokes.

"I wonder what they mean?" The man examines the sculpture carefully.

"You say tourists will give money for such things!" says the other man in bemusement.

"They got them in museums," he says. "People will pay plenty for old things these days."

"I thought the government was stopping all this."

"They just looking for their share. My boss fix all that. He getting me good money for this kinda thing." He goes back to digging and they all follow suit.

It is a pleasant excursion, they have eaten a lot, they are drinking a lot, and on top of all that there is the possibility of making a few bucks. They are enjoying each other's company; they laugh, they say and do frivolous things and laugh some more. No cloud is on the horizon. There is no warning. How could anyone possibly know that in a few hours the man who is digging will be dead?

Back at the marina a lot of boats have come in from charters. After hectic work many of the crew now have time off and the word has gone out among them about an excursion. People are changing into their going-out clothes and sauntering into the Frangipani ready for gossip and entertainment. "So I hear Arthur nearly got the sack. Close call. I'll say! This bar wouldn't be the same without him, we'd all have to go and drink up at his house heheheh and then bloody Hamilton wouldn't make a cent of profit. And who is this Max fellow, never heard of him, must be a total ne'er-do-well if he's got anything to do with Hamilton junior. He's the brother of the Sergeant! Ha, as I thought - a man of very doubtful character. So what's the story Rick?"

Rick grunts tiredly. "I said, 'Sure, sack Arthur. Sack us all and let the bar run on its own'."

"But Hamilton senior did not accept your kind invitation," says Karlo. "A pity because then you would have been able to accompany us on our outing. I am sure you would have many worthy remarks to make on an event like this International World Fair, whence we are now repairing to gain instruction and elucidation."

Karlo has a loud and resonant voice, perfect for rounding up and motivating people. "So who's coming?" he booms, arms linked with Boss and Rae. "All ashore who's going ashore." A party of over a dozen wander down the road.

"You ready Arthur?" says Jim who has come along to be their guide.

"I'll go and have a shower, I won't be a minute," he says.

"This obsession with cleanliness, it's a habit you've picked up from the yanks," says Jim. "You're only going to get sweaty again."

"It's not just sweat," says Arthur. "It's grease and spilled food and splashes of alcohol and the smell that clings to you when you dive into our kitchen. Have you ever been in our kitchen?"

"Nor ever wanted to. OK. Only hurry or you'll miss the highlights." They are standing at the point where the way parts, the path up to Arthur's house and the path along to the main road where the route taxis run. As they are about to separate they hear a Yoohoo behind and see Lynn trotting towards them. Arthur feels a smile lighting up his face and fights to reduce it.

"I thought you were with Karlo and his mob!" he exclaims. "They've gone on down to get route taxis."

"I've been washing things and hanging them out. I'm having a bit of a crisis. I don't think I can stay on Tom's boat any more. He's so up and down and drinking so much. Sometimes he's glad to see me and then he gets drunk and I feel like I'm in the way or unwelcome. I think I can stay with Rae, she said something yesterday. I've just been getting organised and forgot the time. Have they really gone?"

"Only just," says Jim. "And we'd catch them up in no time in this spanking new car I've been hearing about, if only Arthur could be persuaded that he does not smell like rancid fat. You will have to give him a sniff," he seizes her by the arm and drags her up against Arthur's chest.

Sniff sniff sniff goes Lynn wrinkling her nose and Arthur, finding this process suddenly arousing, decides to give way which he does with a laugh saying, "Well you have to sit in the car with me so on your head be it. No," he says to Jim, "this was your idea, so you have to sit in the front next to me and get the whiffs."

Right. They pile in, Hey great car man! and drive out on to the main road where a few of the yachties who haven't yet managed to fit themselves into taxis are still standing. "All aboard" calls Jim. Lynn comes round to the front and sits on Jim's knee and puts her hand on Arthur's shoulder to steady herself and the others get in behind. Arthur drives trying to give his full concentration to the car, with everyone singing "We're all going to Strawberry Fair" at the top of their lungs.

Eventually after travelling some miles up the coast in great rowdiness and satisfaction, just at the point where the good beaches end and the hotels thin out, they come to a large area covered in the coarse short green vegetation that passes for grass in the tropics. On it a number of grey pavilions, like corrugated iron tents, stand dotted about and a huge near-empty gravel area signifies the parking lot. As they turn down the short road to this area they pass Karlo, Boss and company to whom they give a rousing round of off-colour verse and many hoots before they come to a gravelly sliding halt in the carpark.

"Well," says a policeman coming over with his cap under his arm, "I might have known it would be you."

"Lucas," cries Jim. "Listen everyone," he deposits Lynn on the ground and stands up on the minimoke fender to address the new arrivals. "Did you know that our very own Constable Frankland gave up a part in Z-Cars to come back to the islands? No, this is an absolute fact, I jest not. Tell the story Constable Frankland."

Lucas gives a cluck of disclaimer but under pressure concedes, "They wanted me to be the cleaner who finds a body. They were going to give me fifty quid but my dad had arranged my air ticket and I couldn't take it."

"You were going to be on Z-Cars! You were going to be famous and had to give it up to come here! That's tragic."

"Oh well," says Lucas flicking a particle of dust off his uniform. Then he straightens, "So Arthur, what are you bringing all this rowdyism to the Fair for?"

"Well what are you doing here yourself? This isn't in your patch," he rejoins.

"Solving a crime. The Chief Constable has chosen me to look into a certain matter."

"What, young Hamilton hasn't jumped on someone else's head, has he?" cries Karlo.

"No, nothing to do with him."

"I didn't know it was possible – a crime without Anthony Hamilton involved!"

They all move off with Lucas. "I heard that weasel is employing the Sergeant's brother. I hear the man has some sort of record," says Karlo.

"Is that right?" says Lucas coolly, though his eyes flick sideways at Arthur. Then he stops and looks at his notes, "Pavilion 5," he says looking around.

"Over there," Jim says and Lucas strides towards it with a serious and official look on his face.

"Let's go and check it out," says Boss. "I do love a good crime" and they all giggle and straggle after Lucas's departing back. "What time does the gate shut? At 6? Well I think we should get in some good hearty laughter before then."

The pavilion that Lucas enters is displaying local wares but afterwards no-one can quite remember exactly what. The space is divided into areas supposed to represent a house. One area is supposedly the bathroom with a basin and then a shelf of wares - cakes of stuff and aromatic herbs and texts in Chinese and small spiky branches interwoven with ribbons and berries. A small notice states, 'Please Do Not Handle'. In another area, clothes are hanging and different cakes of stuff are piled on a dressing table and scrolls of Chinese writing hang from mobiles. A similar notice, 'Please Do Not Handle', in red copperplate writing is taped to the bottom of the mirror. In the area meant to look like a kitchen, cakes of stuff are interwined and arranged around normal kitchen objects. Throughout the pavilion there are different coloured and textured herbal products made up into varying shapes and sizes and everywhere accompanied by Chinese writings on scrolls or wall hangings, some of which look old. In the centre of the pavilion is a table covered with pamphlets and a notice saying, 'Please Take'.

The reason Lucas has been called in is that some things have been stolen from the exhibition. The person in charge, an elderly Chinese man from Port Sophia called Gerald Lee, is there wringing his hands. He says, "There were a great bunch of people all pulling at things and picking them up and taking them apart and I seen a woman walking out of the tent with one of the good luck scrolls and I said, 'Hey no Missy Missy', but there was all the rest following right behind with whatever they were holding and not taking any notice of me - as if they need only talk to themselves." Lee tried to follow them but being old and lame and moving slowly, by the time he got out after them they were already down by the gate and he was waving at the guard when he saw a police officer nearby. "I saw a Sergeant right there but he would do nothing, nothing at all. He said it would look bad to arrest those people, they were white people, rich tourists. And then he started telling me it was all my own fault for not having valuable things locked up. He said what did I expect if I put them out where people could take them. And now what am I supposed to do?" says Lee. "The scrolls were lent for the exhibition, and who is to pay for the things that have been broken and taken away? These are expensive oils, these are very valuable items and what cooperation do I get from the police? It's a disgrace! I have complained to the Police Commissioner about the way I have been treated."

The smell in the hot fibreglass pavilion is indescribable and even though it seems to be keeping the flies at bay, the party soon gives up on the scene of the crime and everyone is glad to get outside. Phew-aww - there is a general exhalation. Karlo says the smell reminds him of a cross between gingerbread and an orgy at a hash party.

"A hash party?" says Lynn looking puzzled.

Arthur leans in towards her. "Ganja, heads of Indian Hemp," he says. "Sticks of hash, you smoke them."

"Oh," she says enlightenment dawning, "I thought he meant cornbeef hash. I didn't think it smelt like that, that's a completely different smell." He laughs but the crowd is moving off and he puts out his hand to take her with him and for a moment her hand rests in his, like a smooth silky object, like a satin pincushion which you might pick up momentarily but instantly put down with a blush in case anyone saw you with something so feminine and tactile. He lets his hand drop away in the most casual way he can as he moves off after the others but is alarmed a moment later when, emerging from some dream, she darts after him and to slow him down puts her hand back in his, and there it rests for a good two minutes as she questions him.

"So how do you smoke hash?" she asks.

"You can buy a stick at the corner store," he says. "They've usually got it behind the counter. It costs four dollars. Generally you mix it with tobacco in a spliff like a cigarette or you can smoke it in something like a hookah. I've never tried it, my aunt would kill me."

"And there are hash parties?" she persists.

"People sit around with their eyes red and their bodies numb and listen to music. Some people like it but it seems just a way of wasting time to me."

"And then they have orgies?"

"No, I don't think so. You have to be pretty lively for an orgy."

"So what happens at an orgy?"

He laughs and drops her hand, "Sex, Songbird, what do you think? Everyone having sex with everyone else, mindlessly coupling and not even knowing each other's name."

"I don't suppose your auntie lets you do that either," she says demurely and he laughs until the tears run down his cheeks and he has to mop his face with his handkerchief.

After they have visited some other pavilions and seen tractors and paeons of praise to the copra industry and the banana industry and some brave words about re-establishing the sugar industry and some other stuff, they repair to the refreshment tent and Rae says, "That Chinese guy was right about it being a disgrace. It's a disgrace when you lure people out to a god-awful place like this. Fancy calling it an Island Fair. What does a Fair mean to you? Education and inspiration and entertainment at the very least, but instead what have we here? Ugly pavilions full of ugly stuff and why would you want to come and see it when you don't have to? And as for the Scene of the Crime, who is going to come out here to see a pavilion full of lumps? With no explanation as to what it's all about."

"But there were pamphlets," says Lynn. "They could have taken the pamphlets."

Bits of paper folded up, cheaply printed in blotty ink, who would want to read those? No they agree, nothing to enjoy here, just another example of people making fools of themselves. Nothing to marvel at and covet, just hot pavilions miles apart in the middle of a hot field buzzing with flies. Flies everywhere landing on lips and eyes and trying to get into ears and noses and people walking to and fro in the heat trying to find something wonderful to engage their attention or at least somewhere cool and in the shade. No, that man with the lumps should be glad people have been breaking up his things. Someone has gone away with the taste and smell of his expensive oils, carrying his priceless parchment to use as a book mark. Well someone somewhere is getting some good out of it.

"I wonder if Lucas will make any arrests," says Jim. The others laugh. The crime of the century.

"Well," says Arthur, "he'll try. He has a very defined idea of right and wrong and if someone took something they shouldn't have, he'll try and get it back."

"Yes," says Karlo suddenly indignant. "What kind of protection do the islanders have if their own police won't do anything if there's a white person involved?"

"I wonder who that particular Sergeant could be?" says Boss ironically.

"Anyway, relax," says Jim. "I've shown you the bad and the ugly. Now get yourselves together and let's go and look at the good."

The sun is sinking low on the flies and the dust as they dawdle drearily through the endless fields of scratchy grass, but as they near Oscar's pavilion the sound of rambunctious road-march music suddenly propels them forward with rhythm and verve. Now this is cheerful, this is something to liven up to after the arid wasteland and here is pan skittering about like wayward wind chimes. Let us dance to this pan man, let us bump hips and fraternise. Ah what is this? A hat from the islands - I have to buy this, I have to buy these cork flamingo coasters and I have to have this T-shirt. How much is this T-shirt? There's hardly anything left in my size!

And now they are lively alright, dancing to huge speakers blaring reggae and steel bands.

"Hey Jim," shouts Oscar, "only one more week and I'm closing. I've signed two more exclusive deals and the whole of the Carribean is sewn up." Jim congratulates him. "But listen," Oscar continues. "When this record company heard I was going to close early they've offered to come in and sublet, make it a band showcase. I don't know why I haven't been charging them from the outset! We'll clear up the place next Friday and then on Saturday I've booked some live bands and we'll have a bit of a party. What do you say? I've got the distillery to give me a good price on rum and we'll mix up a couple of drums of punch, are you in that?"

Are we in that? Are we in that? You betcha. Manna from the boggy swamp, a party! Time to go now, the Fair is closing. Amazing that they close it down at night, you can't understand their thinking. Well there wouldn't be enough electricity down here. Is that right? They barely generate enough for Oscar to run his music and it's always blowing, imagine with lights.... I see, but where are we going to rock on to now?

The let-down of the whirring end, the choking to death in the middle of a track and silence. Out once more into twilight nothingness.

Jim stays for a while to help Oscar as the others wander off.

"Hang on for a bit," Arthur says to Lynn. "Jim wants me to wait for him and I'll give you a lift back when he's finished. Maybe I should go and have a word to Tom. But you're probably right - now would be a good time to hop off that boat. I'll try and get you a berth somewhere else. Staying with Rae is only going to be short term - you need to be on a boat. Immigration are nosing around everywhere these days."

Jim finishes and comes out. "Now," he says rubbing his hands, "let's get ready for this cocktail party."

"You're not really going ahead with that?" says Arthur astonished.

"Certainly," cries Jim. "We had a bet. And Lynn here is desperate to go."

"Not really," says Lynn. "Not if we get in trouble."

"No trouble. No trouble at all. We just need to go and get some clothes from somewhere. We should have invited Rae. She's the sort that would have a spare frock to fit Lynn here."

"Rae's gone to meet someone. There was a man out at the Beach Hotel who was very insistent she met him somewhere. I don't think she wanted to go but in the end she agreed. She didn't look very happy about it at all."

"I hope she's not getting into the same crowd as Libby. Big trouble," says Jim.

"Trouble indeed," says Arthur.

Lynn looks up and catches his expression. "What, is something the matter?"

But Arthur just says, "There's always something the matter on this island."

Aunt Marion is lying at full length in a cane chair on her veranda. Her shoes are off and her feet gently circle in the evening air. It's now too dark to read the magazine she has in her lap so she is peacefully watching the colour being chased from the sky and listening to the serious deepening of cicada-percussion, that strata of noise that fills the bottom half of consciousness in the evening. She is comfortable. Of course these cane chairs are old and she would have preferred perhaps some of those nice vinyl ones with the flap that comes out for your legs, something with a bit of a colour. But Sheila bought the house with furnishings and why buy new stuff if you don't have to? She gives her toes a bit of a turn the other way.

Who could have seen all this a few years ago! During the family's darkest hour. She remembers waiting for four hours at the Post Office to get through to Dale in England. She has a horror of telephones and that is one thing that even Sheila can't persuade her to get. A telephone can be a harbinger of bad news and she doesn't want one in the house. Now a telegram is what it looks like and you can prepare yourself for the worst but if you have a telephone who knows when it rings whether it is someone inviting you to a game of cards or someone telling you something terrible has happened.

She knows what a sacrifice it was, Dale coming back to the island. Especially when Cecily told him not to bother going back. But your brother is your brother and if you can't rely on him, who can you turn to? Cecily was a short-sighted sort of woman and you can be sure she has regretted it since. Getting in such a stew about Dale giving up his job and saying he would never find another one so good and look at Dale now, he is doing very well. They are all doing very well. Who would have believed that something with such a tragic beginning could end up in such a way. But the thing that gives Marion the most satisfaction is knowing that all the people, even those in her own family, who believed what that criminal was saying back then have all been proven wrong! They whispered and tightened their mouths, no smoke without fire, but now everyone can see what sort of man that Max de Troy is. That is vindication enough.

Yes the family is doing well. Arthur did well at school, all of his teachers telling him he should go on to University. Of course he can do better than just working in a bar but right now she is glad he doesn't want to go off overseas to study and especially now that he has a car. Boy, that is a valuable thing to have, a nephew with a car. There is no end of places..... She is thinking pleasurably of the following Saturday and the outing that is planned to look at this land. And the fact that Sheila is coming back and is going to stay right here in the house. Sheila, always thinking of little things to do for her. Apparently there is to be new furniture - cupboards and wardrobes. And Sheila thinking about her brother too, thinking they should all start finding Arthur a wife. Though in Marion's view there is plenty of time for that, a married nephew not being nearly so attentive as an unmarried one. Even Daphne, well Sheila must stop worrying herself about Daphne's 'career'. As if Daphne is ever going to have a career! Daphne has had quite enough schooling for a girl and she will stay home till she gets married, as did Marion herself, and there is certainly a lot to be taught to her here. The girl is still not cooking the rice as it should be.

Marion sighs and turns her mind to supper. The night sounds are acting as a soporific. She breathes deeply and her head sinks on her ample chest.

Then Daphne calls out, "Ma, it's Arthur. He's here in his new car. He's brought some friends."

Marion opens her eyes and grunts, what was that? What did Daphne say, she is always mumbling. She is now aware of the front door opening and laughter and voices approaching; someone has come and nothing done in the kitchen no doubt - people wanting a bite to eat and not a thing to be had. Arthur comes out followed by two other figures, "Hello Tantie, we've come to get into some clothes."

"Hello, hello..... put on the light, Arthur." She can't see.

It is that little white girl again and another..... Oh it is Jim. She likes Jim and immediately makes to get up. "Don't move Tantie, we're not stopping. We're going to gate-crash a party, we'll probably end up being thrown in the harbour. Or in jail. I expect you'll read about it in the paper tomorrow....."

"Now what, now listen here, don't you go taking any notice of this rascal Jim" she says. He is a lively young man and he makes her laugh, always coming into Arthur's house as if it is the most natural thing in the world and this little girl with them. She is a bubbly little thing, no airs and graces about her but here she is with Arthur again and as the thought strikes her, her maternal heart becomes speculative and cautious. Sheila is right, it is time Arthur got a regular girlfriend, a nice island girl.

"There any towels Tantie? We all have to take a shower."

"Daphne!"

In the end of course it is Daphne who helps them find everything, Daphne who helps them rummage through boxes of stuff while they take it in turns dashing in and out of the shower. It is she who finds Jim a set of tails "My god, where did you get these?"

"They belonged to one of my uncles. Ma, which of my uncles was the waiter?"

"He was no waiter, child," says Aunt Marion indignantly. "Your Uncle Matthew was a Maitre D, that's French for a manager. He had fourteen waiters under him and he used to meet the guests and talk to them. That's why his clothes were so nice, made of the best cloth if you please. Well maybe a bit worn now but you must remember how old it is. Don't borrow the man's clothes and end up in the harbour with it now!"

"Don't worry," says Jim laughing, "Arthur has no faith. With clothes like these," he picks the suit up and lays it across his other arm, "they will think they have royalty coming on board." Bow and scrape, bow and scrape, he dances away in his towel to try on his gladrags but stops. "Hang on, what are you going to wear Arthur?"

"I have a dinner suit. Sheila had it made for me when I was in New York on holiday. I have to find it, I haven't worn it since and I don't know….. Where is it, Daphne?" thump crumple through the boxes that need to be unpacked, through the piles littering one of the spare rooms, crumple, crumple. "Where the hell's it been put?"

"Well," says Jim, preening himself in front of the best bedroom mirror, "not bad. Is there a cummerbund?" he goes back into the other room where Arthur is putting on a frilled shirt, "Oh great shirt, better than this blasted starched dickie," and then for some time they both struggle with bow ties in front of the mirror.

"I still can't find the damn suit. What are you going to do for shoes?"

Shoes, oh no. What do you wear to a cocktail party on a boat? What a dilemma. Although they are nearly the same height and build, Arthur's feet are a full size smaller than Jim's and hysteria is starting to mount with Aunt Marion now scouring the various cupboards for her late husband's footwear. Into this Lynn bounces in a pink flounced minidress. "Dah-dum," she shrieks, "What do you think?" Well. What do they think? It is the sort of dress that a tall tanned statuesque woman might wear, staring insolently back over one shoulder, and look stunning. On Lynn's short paleish body it looks oddly benign like a nightie. “Out of the way, out of the way,” she cries, “I have to put on makeup. Damn, the light’s no brighter here either.”

Marion clucks her tongue, “I don’t know why you young people want all these bright lights to smudge this warpaint all over your faces. Sheila use the mirror in the kitchen.”

“Are you two ready?” cries Lynn as she dashes into the kitchen. “Arthur, you’re still in your underpants!”

“Daphne help me find that suit.”

“No shoes,” calls Jim, “help me find shoes.”

“Shoes, shoes,” echoes Lynn, “I can’t find any either. Sheila’s are far too big for me.” Again Daphne comes to the rescue and lends her some little pink strappy ones.

“What about Sheila’s shoes for Jim?” says Daphne. “She has some black ones…..” She goes and gets them while Jim started to prance and sway on his toes going, “Oooh” in a high voice, “I’ll look just gorgeous.”

The shoes that Daphne brings are patent flat shoes and they are so soft they just fit. “Hooray I’m ready.” He walks up and down. The shoes are just a little odd but fortunately the trousers being a bit long cover them and then again the jacket is just a little wide and the whole ensemble….. But then he catches sight of Lynn and laughs. With pale pink almost white lipstick and layers of blue and white eyeshadow and her short blonde hair backcombed up as much as she can manage, hands on hips cavorting in pink - she looks ludicrous and sweet at the same time. She bounds up to the mirror and they both laugh at each other.

“Arthur…..”

“I’ve found it,” he calls back muffled.

“What do you think?” asks Lynn.

“Never say die,” says Jim cheerfully. “I think we’ve scrubbed up as well as can be expected. Come on Arthur or we’ll be late. Mustn’t keep em waiting for their guests of honour. Let’s see you.”

Arthur emerges, a vision. His hair is brushed flat with the help of some hair oil and he is dressed in a fitted white tuxedo, his hand casually slung in one pocket. He is elegant, his dress shirt is quietly elegant, his bow tie is elegant, his black trousers are a perfect fit over his perfect shining shoes. Jim and Lynn give a gasp, followed by histrionic cries, “Oh Arthur you are so beautiful, look at you, LOOK at you! Here we are done up looking ridiculous and there you are looking so gorgeous, bags I walk in with you, can I be your friend, can I Arthur, can I?" They fall about, and Jim says, "Chances are rising. They'd never dare toss a man dressed like that in the drink. Are we off?"

"Hold on, hold on," says Aunt Marion genuinely charmed by the spectacle. "I have the camera, I just need a flash bulb" and time is good-humouredly lost looking for one but eventually the three pose proudly formal as Aunt Marion snaps them.

They roar down in the minimoke to the marina and pound up the jetty. "Tom Tom, are you in there, you old misery? Get up, we want to borrow you and your tender for a bit. Give us a lift over."

"Why don't we just go to the yacht club? They'll have Beau Jeste's tender there." says Arthur when Tom proves fractious.

"No," says Jim, "we'd never get anywhere without an invite. We have to be actually there on the spot with Tom disappearing over the horizon in his boat. Come on there Tom, shake a leg, you can't lie all day and all night moaning because you've stuffed up again. Your whole life will waste away at this rate."

Eventually Tom is roused from his bed of rum-soaked suffering by having Jim prise him up bodily and push him out into the pale light from the jetty where he falls to his knees on the deck. Looking up he sees Lynn. "Oh here's another beautiful creature," as he grabs her hand and kisses it. "Will you marry me?" he cries with tears rolling down his cheeks.

"No," says Jim patiently, "you can't marry Lynn, she's going to marry a handsome prince. Now come on, I'm sure you're still capable of driving the tender. I've seen you much worse than this and not think twice about it. Come on, come on," he says encouragingly.

They are in the tender trying not to get their feet wet with Jim driving and explaining things to Tom. "Now when we get to the boat I'm going to put this in neutral and we're all going to spring aboard. Then you have to take off. Don't hang around or all may be lost, understand?" Tom stares vacantly. "Well anyway," says Jim, "do as much as you can."

The boat where the cocktail party is taking place looms out of the harbour, bright with lights. The Beau Jeste is a beautiful boat, an old-fashioned traditional cruiser like a mini ocean liner. On the upper deck they can see the sinuous movement of couples dancing and around the edges there are elegant people in elegant dresses clinking glasses and talking brightly. Through the whole scene - insistently tempting everyone to move their feet, rotate their hips, sway their waists - is the sound of steel drums cal-lyp-so dumm dumdum dumdum.

The invaders fall silent as they approach. Angled down the side of the boat for easy access is a set of steps and Jim brings the boat hard round and cuts the engine so that they glide quickly sideways into position. He grabs a rail and pulls himself up on to the steps holding the webbing of the tender. The next minute Lynn finds herself being lifted almost bodily out and Arthur lightly follows. Jim immediately pushes the tender off leaving Tom slumped in the boat which now is drifting.

"Will he be alright?" asks Lynn but as they watch Tom grabs the tiller and opens the throttle. "Where's he going? He's heading out to sea?" She watches anxiously as the little boat's black outline putters into the soft reflective wash where the dark hills of the harbour part.

"Oh, don't worry about him," says Jim callously, turning away to give his mind to the trials and challenges ahead.

Challenge and risk are the new recreations of our super-safe sophisticated world. People are always pushing the boundaries, putting themselves in hazard, overcoming tremendous odds. Having said that, I'll go where crocodiles lurk, I'll swim with white pointers, I'll stroke snakes, I'll even stand in the same room as a spider - but some things are too much for me.

So when I describe Lynn's introduction to high society on this wretched boat, I have to psyche myself up before I can allow the recollection to trickle through my brain again. One day hopefully they will have a cure for memory and then experiences like this can be gratefully blotted out.

"Hello!" Jim greets a man in a uniform. "Sorry we're late, which way to the big chief?" Lynn marvels how a moment ago his speech was ordinary and chatty and is now loud, confident and public school. In the same split second, his bearing has suddenly become slow and dignified. He has his hands behind him, his shoulders back, head in the upright and commanding position above an expression of infinite disdain. Some of this confidence rubs off on her for a while as she is coming up the steps and is still behind his back and shielded. It is only when she arrives at the deck and is exposed to view that Lynn's heart sinks. They will resent it, they have every right to resent it. There they all are talking, laughing, strolling, all the beau monde of which she is definitely not a part. What had seemed such a giddy gay carefree thing to do a short time ago, now feels like a burglary. Everyone is looking at her. No-one has ever looked at her before as if she were a spectacle. They are not only looking at her but their eyebrows are raised. A woman at the top of the steps looks at her very much in the tone of 'Oh dear oh dear oh dear' - eyes travelling over the pretty pink dress. Oh deary deary me. Lynn manages to stop a little mew that she feels rising to her lips. She must bite her mouth and not let everyone down even though she is suddenly desperately embarrassed and doesn't know where to look or what to do. She knows the colour in her neck is blushing up under her chin like a tidemark. She must stand behind someone so that no-one notices. If only Arthur….. She wants to hang back for Arthur who is coming up the steps behind her; she wants to link arms with him so she won't have to face these people alone. How cool he looks. If only he would tell her the things she needs to know so that she doesn't make a fool of herself. If only he would stand with her apart while Jim carries on and wins or loses….. If she could just talk to Arthur then she wouldn't mind anything else. But worse things are starting to happen. The emergence of Arthur has escalated the astonishment in the glances that now read, "Oh my god, it's a native!" What before had been cold questioning stares – "Who are these ludicrously badly dressed people?" – have now become stares of outrage. Lynn, looking around, sees with a sinking heart that there are no other West Indian guests, not even the Premier which is a glaring omission. The Premier also has a very nice tuxedo and is invited to the white parties for form's sake. Maybe he was invited and couldn't come. No, the Premier would drop everything for a party like this.

The deck they have arrived on has a narrow walkway around it. The walkway to either side is however roped off and arrivals are channelled through double doors which open onto a large internal area with a bar along one side, from which waiters in short white waistcoats are rushing with trays. The room is quite full with people circulating freely, an aspect to the arrangement that Jim views with favour. All the easier to slip through unnoticed and make for his ultimate destination which is the next deck up, the outdoors deck where the band is hammering away on their drums in calypso rhythms. Jim's aim is to get as near to the noise as possible, thus making it more difficult for untoward questioning. He is therefore leading the way towards the stairs to this upper deck when he is stopped by a loud "Hello". If the band had not happened to cease at that juncture he would have ignored the call because it did not bode particularly well. But in the resulting silence he stops and swings round with aplomb to be confronted by a slim very tanned middle-aged man in a white dinner jacket cut rather shorter than Arthur's and with a pale blue open-neck shirt and mauve silk scarf around his neck. Oh dear, thinks Jim, not one of the casual dressers, the worst kind and not friendly either. It is a pity he isn't friendly. He does not respond at all to Jim's welcoming smile and there follows a rather ominous silence as the talk dies away and everyone's eyes are riveted on the scene.

"Do I know you?" the man says with blunt savagery. Clearly he is a man who has the habit of command. A fierce captain of his ship who will make interlopers walk the plank without a qualm and will be admired for it. Remember when those awful people came on board and brought an islander. You mean - oh my God! Yes, shudder - fancy bringing one of those on board and trying to pass him off as a guest, the effrontery of some people.

Meanwhile the question definitely requires an answer. "I doubt it," responds Jim distantly. "The Hon James Primrose, how do you do." He holds out his hand towards the man who ignores it. "And may I introduce….."

The man's face is hard. You can almost hear the frizz of scandal. And then he was actually going to introduce poor Adrian to some Coloured in an evening jacket that was too long. It must have belonged to someone else. You don't find people like that owning their own and you should have seen the man doing the introductions, dressed in some frightful waiter's outfit! I would have died rather than wear such a thing. What they were thinking of, I've no idea. Fancy imagining they could get away with it. With a man like Adrian!

Lynn feels as if a great silence is forming into which terrible holes will implode like the suction from whirlpools. Silent drowning deep underwater awaits her. The man has turned, looking for someone, the crew no doubt. "Ackroyd" he bellows. This is it, we're going to be chucked off. She feels the movement of the tumbrils under her, carried publicly towards the guillotines and the blood, the pounding blood, the jeering crowd and then the cut to awful headless silence.

But just as she is ready to sink, when death indeed seems the better option, some gorgeous creature, who has that minute come down the steps from the upper deck, detaches herself from the ruck and drifts in a chiffony haze over in their directions. "Arthur, is it really you? Arthur, it is you!" she cries and aims a kiss vaguely at either cheek. "Oh look at you, you look wonderful."

"Oh hello Blanche," Arthur says without enthusiasm. "Hello Florence," as another gorgeous creature advances squeaking towards him.

"Oh thank goodness someone thought to send you an invite," shrieks the first woman. "I would never have thought of it - I don't even know what island we're on. Where are we anyway? Is this where you live? Sheila's told us about it of course but….."

"Is she still here? No, of course, she said she couldn't come. Are these your friends? Oh," screams the second woman holding Lynn's dress, "they were going to make me wear this dress in Milan, me with my colouring, isn't it a fright. But Sheila carried it off, she always does, how I hate her. Now Arthur, who don't you know?" An older woman comes up, "Babs, you remember Sheila's brother."

"I certainly do, I wanted you for my menswear page. Now that jacket is stunning! Adrian, look at the line. You see how Giovanni cut it longer, so elegant. We must have a feature. Where's John gone….." The women grab Arthur between them and take him off talking non-stop towards an animated group that have descended the stairs and are now engaged in kissing him like some gigantic group rite. Arthur who in an instant is no longer Coloured, Arthur who is suddenly merely the right shade of tan. Sheila's brother. Not Sheila Harris! It's her brother, you can see the resemblance - isn't he stunning-looking? And the owner is addressing his minion indignantly, "Ackroyd, these people haven't got drinks, jump to it. Nice to have you aboard, what did you say your name was? Hon, that's an unusual name, I thought you must be foreign for a minute. Make yourself at home, stay to dinner, we're having….. Oh here's my wife. Anita these are friends of Sheila Harris's brother, her brother has just arrived."

A woman in a simple drop-dead-gorgeous white evening gown with a tanned body like oiled sandalwood, gives an exclamation and grabs her husband's arm. "Her brother, where is he?"

"Babs led him off to meet John."

"Oh no, you must….. Come on, introduce me or else….. You know Sheila hates that photographer! Do excuse us." Turning an exquisite all-over tanned back she hurries her husband away leaving the two of them standing there in the middle of an emptying deck.

The flow which has been channelled inwards like water towards a plughole is checked and people rock gently away again because they are not interesting, a man called Hon in a waiter's uniform and a girl in a dress that failed at the Italian collections.

"I can't believe we're here," says Lynn. "I'm still terrified in case someone finds out what shams we are. What a good job Arthur was with us and all those women knew him, or they would have thrown us off for sure and it would have been so horrible."

"Lord no, a slight problem arose due to the man not being au fait with polite society, but I had a few tricks up my sleeve, never fear."

It is some hours later and Lynn and Jim cling to a table of sculptured fruit. All around them voices spin stories of lives that Lynn can't even begin to imagine. Darling, haven't seen you since..... My ashram phase, oh I'm over all that now, yes yes the brown rice.... Colonically irrigated, but did the party go alright? Drug squad of course…. Then the curtains caught fire and Ben used Mummy's Ming vase to throw water on it….. She made me a ward of court. What, because of Simon? Oh, you do have all the luck.

"Everyone's so rich," says Lynn.

"Of course, that's the point. They didn't fly here just to go to a party. They flew here so they can tell people they came here for a party and everyone will know how rich they are in consequence."

"Are you rich?" asks Lynn.

"Lord no!" Jim looks as if she has tried out a dirty word on him.

"I just wondered about the Hon title. Does it mean something?"

"Oh no, nothing at all. Except my father's an earl but it doesn't come with anything much, it's all been eaten up in death duties. There's a hall in Norfolk that poor old Lionel gets lumbered with next. He's in the city trying to make his fortune so he can install central heating."

"But it must have history."

"Oh yes. Very ancient. Back to Richard the Second."

"Really, so what year was that?"

"Oh lorr, don't ask me history, I was no good at dates."

"Who came after Richard the Second?"

"It was all Henrys and Edwards back then. Until the George's started. Probably an Edward. None of the Edwards did anything but the moment they died everyone felt like a bit of a war to liven things up."

"Henry Eighth had a son called Edward didn't he?"

"An Edward followed by a Bloody Mary which reminds me, ahoy waiter…. Then after her there was peace till the next Edward."

"Queen Elizabeth was alright."

"Yes but your queens you see are usually alright. They all live forever and everyone has a good time. Elizabethan, all that culture and stuff. And then along comes Queen Anne and suddenly you've got furniture. You can relax when a queen's on the throne because you know she's going to be there for years and years and there's going to be a whole chapter on her, not whizzing on to the next thing like kings. Look at the present Queen Liz - I bet in twenty five years she'll still be hanging on."

"But some of the kings ruled for a bit, didn't they?"

"No, hardly any. No stamina for it. They either die or go mad. I say, are we going to do the whole of British history tonight?"

"We could do. Why not?"

"Because I'm drunk."

"Good. So now you're drunk we can go and dance."

"How does that follow?"

"One two three, one two three."

They slump on chairs giggling, contemplating the energy required to get upright. "Here's Arthur! Well my son you have been busy. No prising into your little enclave, you were surrounded closer than the President's bodyguard."

"Let's get out of here," says Arthur wearily.

"Oh, aren't we staying for dinner," says Jim leaning over to him and holding a bunch of large black grapes over his mouth.

Arthur turns his head and says somewhat bad-temperedly, "Because of you and your damn dare I have been fawned over and kissed by total strangers and displayed like a puppet you pull the strings to, everyone wanting a piece of the action. I have just escaped and if we don't go now I will be made to sign some piece of paper which will destroy my life and have me in New York in winter prancing about in stupid damn clothes, a dead man."

"A rich man," says Jim who has been placidly eating the grapes during this bitter outburst. "Beautiful people are the new royalty. That's all you need, a pretty face and to get yourself in Vogue."

"I don't want to be in Vogue, I don't want to be rich."

"You're amazing."

"I'm not amazing."

"You are amazing, you are morally amazing, most people want nothing other than to be rich."

"Why should I want to be rich? Sheila's rich, why should there be two of us rich? Every time I look round she's buying me something, a car, houses, who knows what next."

"She's bought you houses!"

Arthur looks quickly sideways at Lynn who is concentrating on sloppily peeling a pear and shushes him.

"Come on my son," insists Jim lowering his voice. "I knew she bought that house for your aunt but I thought you held her off on the block of apartments."

"Yes but then she went and bought those two houses behind the marina, mine and Rick's. But I won't have anything to do with them, Dale is managing them. Don't say anything," he whispers urgently. "Nobody's knows."

"Well," says Jim looking at him ruminatingly, "there you are. You're the one with the suit, you've got the car, you've got some desirable real estate and you've got all those long-legged gorgeous women. Arthur, I think I'm going to die with envy!"

"You're going to die of alcohol poisoning first," Arthur observes.

"No, I'm not rich enough to become a real alcoholic. But Arthur, all these joys of life, and what's stopping you having a great smile on your face? Why the glums when you've got everything a man could want? Everything," he waves his arms and looks at him affectionately. But Arthur turns down his mouth. Jim, he thinks, I'm Coloured. They'll pay me the money but they won't let their daughters marry me so how can I have everything? And then as if his friend has partly guessed his thoughts, Jim pulls himself upright.

"Lynn! Of course!" he grabs her by the hand. "I wouldn't let Tom have you because I was saving you up for something better and here he is." He pulls Lynn over towards Arthur and she comes giggling. He can smell the alcohol on her breath as she puts her arms around his neck and perches on his knee. He can smell the cheap scent of her makeup and the faded Guerlain on the dress and sweat and skin smells from her velvety arms.

"We must go," he says. "Come on," getting up and pulling her upright with him. "Jim."

"You old spoil sport, we could have been supping on the repast of millionaires and now you're dragging us away from all this lovely gaiety and fun."

"Most people are ashore already. Look, nearly everyone's gone."

"Oh bother, where are those stupid shoes? I can't find them! Arthur, will Sheila be very cross with me? And who do we have to say goodbye to?"

The owner is standing by the gangway saying goodbye to some elderly but elegant Americans. Jim manages to get himself upright enough to make a dignified obeisance before the man but somewhat diminishes this by nearly pitching headlong down the steps, oops. The main thanks, regards to such and such and regrets for leaving come from Arthur. He bears the full weight of the kid who merely smiles beatifically on all. Very nice party, lovely time, so nice to meet your wife, regards to Babs but have to leave. Sigh. They are finally down in the tender and Arthur husbands his charges against the side from whence any urge to be sick may be the more easily accommodated.

The kid shows no inclination to unlatch herself and now he urgently wants to take her home with him. He wants to take her home and take this ridiculous pink confection off her and wipe off the ridiculous caked makeup that is no doubt smearing his shirt and then when she is..... when she is..... Oh man, enough of that, think cold thoughts, think rejection and contempt and the loss of self-respect. Think of anything rather than the soft breasts that rub against him. He must do up the thicker cloth of his jacket, he must button himself in.

It is about a mile from the yacht club to the marina along the main road and it is a distance that Jim proposes to cover as noisily as possible. The Beach Boys are his weapon of choice. After a while he stops singing and says with satisfaction, "They'll never believe us, and won't Rae be sick. It's just the kind of thing she'd sell her soul for. She'll be so sick she'll never forgive us. But wait on, why are we repairing to a common-as-muck place such as the Frangipani? We should now be swanning it with the best, mingling with the exalted. What do you say? I think this is a night to go somewhere tophole where you can buy me a drink with all the money you now owe me from the bet."

Arthur stops. "I owe you! Ha! You would have been thrown overboard and left for the sharks. You never told me it was a magazine publisher who owned that boat - I would never have agreed if I'd known I might meet all those sort of people. Anyway you two are drunk enough, you ought to both go home to bed."

Lynn stops when Arthur stops. Everywhere is blurred, lights run together like watercolours in swirling outlines. She is quite happy to stand in the dark with Arthur while the two men decide, to feel Arthur's smooth coat against her side, to lean in against him looking up at the stars which never dim.

"Go home," exclaims Jim lurching dramatically, "no fear. Come on, what are we going to do now?" And Lynn certainly doesn't want to go home while the night is young and the sky is sparkly.

Where to though, and remember, the sky's the limit. The spoils of the evening however are unclear. "We have," Jim detaches some notes and standing unsteadily, holds up his hand, "ten dollars that we have to spend, ten dollars. Hey, how come you are always getting women draped over you? I want some." He goes to Lynn's other side and puts her arm round his shoulder. "Right," he says, "the Beach."

"Oh no man, somewhere else, not that place….." He can't bear it, not after meeting so many people who are staying there.

"OK," says Jim, "the Lotus House, we haven't been there for ages."

The Lotus House is an expensive guest house nearly ten miles out of town. It has an open air arbour bar hung with heavy white flowers and is reckoned to be the best bar for dallying on the island. They locate Arthur's car and set off cheerfully singing Get get get around, I get around. Round Round, I get around. "What we need to do," says Jim leaning forward from the back seat, "is run up a bra on the flagpole at the Island Fair. That might liven the place up a bit."

"And you just happen to have one on you?" says Arthur.

"No old son, but then I haven't had gorgeous girls rubbing themselves up and down me all night."

"Fat lot of good it would do you. They don't wear bras and most of them sleep with other girls."

"Really!" says Lynn. "I would have thought they'd make enough money to have a room to themselves."

Both men laugh and Jim leans forward and nuzzles her neck. "You are such an innocent."

"But I wouldn't be innocent if someone would tell me what you're talking about. Arthur you tell me," she says turning in her seat to him.

"Yes go on Arthur, go on," Jim nudged his shoulder, "tell her about women sleeping together," and Arthur tries to hit him and swerves, oh oh.

"Now you both look out, you're distracting me."

"Stop," suddenly calls Jim.

"What!"

"The sea."

"What sea?" says Arthur starting again.

"No, no, turn down here, we have to go for a swim."

Arthur sighs but then recollects that in light of the amount they've both drunk, a swim might sober them up before they go barging and giggling into the Lotus House. He turns down a dirt road to where the sea gleams below, and pulls up where the track meets the sand.

"Hooray," cries Jim leaping out and starting to tear his clothes off. In an instant he is naked and rushes at the water whooping, his pale bottom gleaming in the moonlight as he runs.

Lynn, inspired by this exhibition, pulls off her dress and runs to the water, then drops her underpants on the edge and runs in going Sploosh as she hits the water. Arthur soberly removes his clothes and follows in his underpants. "Oh Arthur," calls Jim out of the blackness, "don't be so modest." But Arthur thinks, It's OK for you, no-one will think twice, but for Lynn, she mustn't be known as the sort of girl who goes swimming naked with islanders, her naked, me naked, she'd get a reputation. He thinks of the descriptive words they'd use of her. Someone has to think of these things. He dives in cleanly.

"Lynn," calls Jim, "you just swim over there and get those underpants off him" and she giggles and starts to swim towards him. He swims easily away, the water is second nature to him, cool and resisting like the drag of silk across his body. He puts down his head in an Australian crawl and lazily powers out. When he stops he is astonished to find she has kept up with him. "Lord," he says surprised, "you're a good swimmer."

"Yes, I used to love swimming," she says floating there pale like a submerged sheet, her arms like gills moving slowly against the luminous water. He looks away.

"Used to. Why, don't you swim now?"

"I don't mean that. I meant, when I was in Australia it's what I loved to do all the time. I did all my life saving medallions. I would have liked to be a life guard above anything - except you can't as a woman. There are so many things you can't do as a woman, it's a shame. But anyway I'm probably too small." They are treading water side by side, "Isn't it lovely, I love the feel of the water, especially when I'm a bit tipsy."

"There's a storm coming," says Arthur. "Look at the clouds building up."

"YooHoo," calls Jim, "what are you two doing out there?"

"Damn." says Arthur aloud. Here he is doing what he was trying to prevent, looking at the sky with a naked white woman. He starts to swim back. He is immediately afterwards aware that she hadn't moved, he knows it without looking. He stops swimming. "Come on," he says, "that's a storm coming, we're going to get caught." Already he is sure that rain is falling on the further glassy hills.

"What's that?" she says. "Look, it's a sort of bright silver arch."

"It's a moonbow."

"I've never seen one before. And what do you find, at the end of a moonbow?"

"You find," he says, "a wet dinner jacket and a good talking to from your auntie."

Whoops, they swim rapidly back and Arthur runs up the beach to put up the tonneau cover on the minimoke. Lynn is suddenly shy. The clouds are covering the moon and she breathes her thanks but oh god, now she can't see where she's dropped her underpants. Ohhh, she is wasting valuable time, the moon might re-emerge at any moment. She finds them, her wet sandy feet feel them underfoot, and barely stopping to shake the sand out she bolts them on and rushes up the beach with her arms across her breasts and flings on the dress, whew.

Jim has his underpants on and is hopping with one leg in his trousers trying to get his other leg in when the rain hits, and he hops under the cover yipping like a dog. "Oh god," he says lying there on the back seat laughing, "you should feel it in here now. It's like having your bum rubbing on raw coral, full fathoms five, and the legs too. Oh I tell you I shall be scraped raw." He sits up and glares at Arthur, "How come you're so bloody elegant? Look at you!" Arthur has put his shirt back on and is tying his bow tie in the pale reflection from the driving mirror. "You'd swear from the way he's sitting that he doesn't have a particle of sand in his pants. Oh look," Jim dives his hand down and it emerges with something white. "Arthur's underpants! The very thing for the flagpole, come on chaps."

Arthur carefully manoeuvres the car up to the road through the tropical downpour, "God look at it" as a bolt of lightning irradiates the landscape like a strobe of neon light. And now, to the Fair.

Five minutes later they turn in to the car park where they were that afternoon. "It's all locked up," says Arthur.

"Can you drive over that grass? Go along a bit further, there's a hole in the fence. OK, here we are. And away we go."

"Not till….." but Jim is off at a run through a hole in the wire and disappears. "Jee-sus," says Arthur. "Those trousers will be ruined. Not that they are any good for anything but Tantie does hate to throw stuff away."

"Yes I know," says Lynn. "It's like putting left-overs in the fridge till they go off. All my English aunts do that. You're not allowed to throw things away till they're mouldy."

"And that dress," he says pointing at what she is wearing. "Sheila threw it in a waste bin but Tantie got it out and hung it in a plastic bag, even though till you came along there was no chance of anyone ever wearing it."

"Did Sheila really throw it out?" says Lynn. "Oh I think it's so pretty. But it seems," she says wistfully, "that no-one else does. I don't understand fashion."

He turns to look at her, for a moment moving nearer but then turns away to look out the front into the falling rain. "My sister loved your flower sack dress."

"I like your sister," she says inconsequentially.

"She's coming back next weekend."

"Oh really."

"Yes she wants to go and look at some land."

"I'm surprised she didn't stay for the party tonight."

"Paris tomorrow. Rome the day after. She only goes to parties if they're about work, someone important to meet. But I don't think she needs to meet anyone else important now, she can't take on anything more even if they offer it."

"What land is it she's looking at?"

"A beautiful swamp, full of scarlet ibis. They're going to spoil it no doubt like they spoil everything else." She is listening to what he has to say with an engrossed expression and he finds himself saying, "Do you want to come?"

"Ooh yes," she says.

Jim lurches back out of the murk. "God it was so dark I couldn't find the way for a bit and I just avoided a security guard, wasn't expecting it and suddenly he was shining a torch only a few yards from me. Didn't see me though. I just hope your auntie didn't sew your name in your underpants. Maybe you'd better drive out without your lights on."

Arthur starts the engine but instead of moving forward there is the ominous hum of wheels turning uselessly in wet grass.

"Bloody hell, we're not driving anywhere, we're stuck!"

"Oops," shrieks Lynn. "Now Lucas will find us at the scene of the crime."

"Relax," says Jim, "what are the handles for! We'll have to carry it."

Carry it, carry it, all dressed up in my dinner suit again and we're going to carry the bloody car bloody bloody, but you can take your dinner suit off, well of course I'm going to take it off, bloody hell now I don't have any jocks any more. Arthur strips down and then both of them stark naked and laughing crouch at either side of the car and grab hold of the handles. Lynn you steer and we'll drag it, good idea, switch it on Songbird and keep your foot gently on the accelerator, I can't drive, gently does it, not too much spin, I can't see, oh Christ I'm covered in mud, stop laughing, hahahah, woohoo yes she's free, help I can't drive, I can't see, I can't drive aaaaaagh.

"There you are you see, you can drive!"

Lynn gets out and flails at them both in the dark "You rotten sods, I could have been killed." They dodge away laughing, Ow ow ow, then Arthur catches her arms around her body from behind and holds her. "I could have wrecked your new car," she is nearly weeping but nearly laughing and his arms holding her are wet with rain water and she can feel the breath of his laughter escaping in gasps behind her. Oh lordy.

Get around, get around, I get around. Arthur and Jim put their clothes back on and soon after they arrive at the lighted car park of the Lotus House, look at us. Yes look at us, how we started out so fine, the clean clothes, the careful makeup, the well brushed hair, oh how we have become disarranged. But the Lotus House has lovely capacious bathrooms with tissues and hot water and everything needed to revive their ensembles. They emerge once more into the light of the foyer. Arthur still manages to look debonair even though his shirt is crumpled. Jim's trousers are muddy and his jacket is creased and his tie has got wet and hangs not so much in a bow as in a flowery droop. Lynn has removed most of her makeup though a ring of black smudge still surrounds the perimeter of her eyes like someone who has laughed or cried for too long. Look at us, how we have lived!

Right so we have ten dollars to fritter away, what should we drink? Rae drinks Black Russians. They're dangerous, you watch out for Rae and her Black Russians and her black anythings. Maybe we should buy a bottle of champers and not mix drinks. Or how about rum punches? I had one at the Beach, they're full of fruit like fruit salads, lovely.

The clientele of the Lotus House tends to be conventional, well-behaved, softly murmuring in shady nooks. Jim surveys the scene with contempt. "Look at all these people. Even though they're rich they're going to grow old being dull. I'd rather die than end up like this. I want to end up like Boss blowing myself out in loud long parties. Arthur if ever I start sitting round like a stuffed pudding, you must promise to shoot me."

"Sure thing. Certainly. In fact I'd do it now only you never keep still." Heeheehee, they wrestle. Shhhh. Who said that?

"Right," says Jim adjusting his cuffs. He strides with dignity over to the grand piano which is situated in the middle of the room. He rests one hand on the top and turns formally to right and left and then pulling out the stool he raises his tails in a quick practiced gesture and sits, parting the garment behind him. He raises his arms slowly and adjusts his cuffs again, stretches the fingers of one hand, the fingers of the other, and then clasps his hands together in concentration while he bows his head and sits for a moment in contemplation. Then he draws himself up on the stool, clenches and unclenches his hands and holds them high in readiness over the keys. Then breathing deeply, he plunges down. Da Da Da Da Da Da, Do do do do do do, Da Da Da Da Da Da. Da. Da-dum. Chopsticks. Lynn lets out a gale of merriment, play it maestro. Then she rushes over, making him move up on the stool with her hip. Now together, off they set again, drumming on the expensive piano with glee, laughing, with Arthur conducting, yes play it. The other patrons, women in shimmering backless dresses and men in silk shirts and ties look up from their dim liaisons, disapproving or amused. But the three of them don't care, they are held in their little pool of hilarity, cut off from the great world that surrounds them, blameless as youth and giddily happy.

When a woman in a short evening frock puts her eye to the gap in a Chinese screen and sees the source of the commotion, she realises she is not happy at all and hasn't been all evening. It is only when she sees these three familiar figures that she realises how impossible the whole thing has become. How did she get tied up like this in something so….. well sordid. Watching the three young people innocently having a good time together causes her to make up her mind. She turns to her companion, "I've no idea what I'm doing here. I can't imagine what possessed me to come out here with you. I'm leaving. You don't have to take me back, I'll go back with my friends over there."

Her companion reaches across to take her arm. "Don't be so hasty," he smiles lazily at her. "We make sweet music together you and I."

She throws off his arm, "No we don't," she says.

"Oh I think we do," he says without lessening his smile one iota. "I've got a souvenir, something you should see. I'm sure you'd find it no end of fun," reaching out his arm again for her.

"I don't know what you're talking about. I don't want any souvenir of anything to do with you, keep it for yourself," she says, not caring what it is, just wanting to get away from him.

"I'll bring it down to the bar and show you. And Rick, maybe he'd like to see it."

"Don't bother," says Rae getting up impatiently.

Rae comes round the screen towards the piano and Lynn, who sees her first, carols, "Rae! Yoohoo! What a night we've had, you should have come," and starts to tell her about it but is suddenly aware that Arthur's whole demeanour has changed. He is looking at that man she saw earlier at the Beach Hotel and who is standing behind Rae. The man is well dressed and negligently smoking a cigarette and apparently at ease although the expression on his face is somewhat of a mask, a careful smile that defies categorising. Rae turns to look where Arthur's wooden gaze is leading and makes a noise of annoyance in her throat and is obviously about to say something quickly with temper when the man raises his hand in salute to her and carries on out the door.

"I can't get rid of him," says Rae angrily. "He's so bloody persistent! You're right, Arthur, he's a creep," she shakes herself as she says it. "I was so glad to see you all here, you've no idea. Now tell me what I've missed."

Jim gives a little trill with his right hand on the piano in the upper register and affecting a Noel Coward voice starts on a story that somehow mixes drunk Toms with elegant models and ends up with wet underpants in a way that makes no sense at all but Rae laughs at the sheer nonsense of it.

"I'm going to stick with you guys in future," she declares. "Whatever you've been up to, at least you've been having fun."

Maybe it was fun. Certainly it was memorable. All these years later I remember that chaotic night as the real starting point - the first time I was drunk, the first time I saw a moonbow, the first time inchoate thoughts started to gel into self-knowledge. On that night, it was clear even to an innocent ignoramus that a point of no return was about to be reached after which everything would get out of control. And yet I went right ahead and crossed the line anyway.

Chapter 6

Vague flitting ideas of the general peril

Getting a charter yacht ready for a voyage in 1969 was not the huge production of previous centuries. Even up to the end of the 19th century, boats had to carry the whole world with them – everything they needed for repairs and victualling. To forget the mustard pot meant months if not years of doing without.

Of course today it is not necessary to measure anything with precision because nowhere in the world is more than 24 hours from the nearest K-Mart. Whatever other advances have happened in the 20th century, nothing can beat the rise and rise of shopping. However over thirty years ago, it wasn't quite that easy. Crews had to look at the possibility of spending up to two weeks or more without access to certain necessities.

Sunday is not a day of rest at the marina. Boats which off-loaded charterers the day before are working frantically to get ship-shape before a new lot arrives on Monday. Cleaning, laundering, provisioning, grog. At first light people are scurrying here and there.

There is also a certain tension in the air because it's impossible to know with charterers. Everyone goes around muttering, "I think I'm prepared but you never know with charterers." The average charterer is by nature fickle. The very process of chartering is a mysterious act of perversity. A yachtsman dreams of a newer and more up-to-date boat but that is not necessarily what the punters seem to want. After running their eyes over the glossy prospectus produced by W. I. Charters Inc., a surprising number of charterers will knowingly choose old boats with acres of antique brass; brass which is constantly needing attention - wearing out the crew with constant rubbing. This bloody-mindedness is astonishing to those who have laid out the money on low-maintenance fibreglass and stainless steel. Also it would seem to a logical person that if a boat has gone up the islands with one charter, this would be the most convenient boat to charter back down the islands, but no! The charterer has no logic at all. Boats that have come into port on Saturday are even now sailing flat out to get to somewhere else, while other boats are pulling every stop to reach St. Claire by Monday morning. Stress and anxiety are the result of this anarchic unpredictability.

It is a stress that passes from person to person like a contagion and the staff at the Frangipani are no exception. It is a busy day and both Rick and Arthur have been there from first light and neither of them are well-rested.

Rick is suffering from a combination of long running indigestion and an accumulating sense of unease. He left the bar very late the previous night because for some reason the regulars clung to the place as if they could not contemplate the joys of being comatose. Boss was depressed by his domestic circumstances, Karlo was depressed by his lack of domestic circumstances, and a number of boat owners had simpler sorrows, in that they had no charter for the coming week. Rick crawled heavily up the hill about two in the morning and then found that the bed was empty. He wandered the house and his stomach burned. Gossip seethes in the close-knit world of yachting. The very nature of the business means that the skippers and their crews move in a smallish world, spending long periods of relative isolation and the result is that once the shore ropes are tied and everyone can relax for a while, one and all turn their mind to gossip. Everything and everyone is fodder for their speculation. Rick is aware that Rae is out and about, hints and innuendos are the roads by which the information arrives. But he always thought she would be discreet. Good god, if she wants forbidden fruit take it, but don't broadcast it. And don't take it with that bloody Max shitpile who is a dangerous man, a man to stay well clear of, a man with a murky and disreputable past from what he has heard. It wouldn't do, he was going to have it out with her and there was no point leaving it till the morning because she would pretend all innocence or all ignorance again, too drunk or whatever. No, this couldn't go on, the reputation he has built up couldn't be put in jeopardy now. He needs things to go along smoothly, with these Hamilton deadshits thinking he is willingly going to work himself to death out of loyalty or stupidity. The last thing he needs is a woman who has turned into a wild card: the whole pack could tumble and fall and he could end up going home with nothing. No way is he leaving with nothing, not after all of this.

But in the end it seems it hadn't been anything he was imagining. She came home with Arthur and that kid who worked for Boss, all of them dressed up for some party or other that Jim had organised and the kid so drunk and giggly she could hardly stand. Arthur said that the kid couldn't stay on the Golden Dawn any more as Tom had started asking her to marry him so she went to bed in their spare room and Rae crashed fully dressed and at last he got a few hours' sleep.

If only she'd say where she was going instead of disappearing like that, not a word. Or had she? Maybe she had told him. Sometimes she told him when he was doing two things at once and he didn't remember but then she'd say, I told you at such and such a time and Boss or whoever was there, and he could remember vaguely the outline of it all but not the solidity of the actual words. He needs to go to the doctor again, just keeping going is hard enough on so little sleep and he isn't eating properly - Dr Woodrow will read him the riot act again but what can he do? Rae gets angry when she cooks him a meal and then he can't get away. So he's given up on that, regular meals, regular everything.

So here he is without much sleep and here is bloody Hamilton coming in at this hour, his old-man's bulk moving through the tables towards him. Rick is not pleased to see Hamilton but he's astonished and furious to find that Hamilton intends that he drop everything he is doing so that they can have a meeting. On a Sunday morning! Rick staves him off for half an hour until the worst of the breakfast rush is over and then trying to keep a grip on his feelings he leaves Arthur to tend the bar on his own. He leads the way into his office and sits down heavily among a mess of papers and overflow of cartons. Hamilton as usual insists that the door be shut even though it is so warped that this can only be achieved with great difficulty.

Hamilton had told him several weeks before that he was putting up the bar and marina as collateral in a really big deal. Several others were putting in, big money he said. We're talking really big money, so Rick, the bar needs to be looking good on paper. Better than it is now. So there'll be some changes. And no-one needs to know about this Rick, you understand. The deal hasn't gone through yet, it's all in a delicate phase at the moment and what we don't need are people talking out of turn. So button the lip, as they say. We are looking at big finance here, not the local banks There'll be executives in suits coming in on this one. And these men know what they're doing so it has to look really good.

It is part of the process of looking good that sees Rick in his office with the door closed, cooped up in this mildewed hole while outside poor Arthur is trying to cope with the morning rush. Hamilton has stayed on at St Claire in order to keep an eye on the figures and the last confrontation with Rick had been unpleasant. On that occasion he'd said, "You're not pushing it, I said double the figures. These aren't anything like what I was expecting."

Rick had opened his hands and gestured towards his invoices, "I can't sell what I don't have. You said these people would know what they're doing so they'd smell a rat straight away. If you want to make, then you've got to spend!"

"Get whatever you want."

"Yes but what's the point of saying that if there's no money to buy it with! People here need money up front. No-one runs on big credit on this island; it's not like Europe or the States. They want the money for the last lot before they give you the next lot. You want me to buy up big, I'll buy up big - I'll get in cases of top shelf stuff and champagne. But I need a great big healthy bank account first."

"What is it, the Dark Ages here?"

"It's just a small island. You want to turn a little business into a big business - well it can be done. But you've got to throw money about like water."

"Well if that's the only way you can do business….." Hamilton had grumbled. "But listen," he'd burst out, "I'm not sure you're giving me the full picture anyway. Where's all the champagne? I don't see these figures showing many champagne sales. My son says that people are always drinking champagne but I don't see any reflection of that in here," he'd tapped a book significantly. "He tells me you're running some sort of racket for yourself."

"Your son wouldn't know what happens in here. He hasn't been in since that run in with Arthur but now he sends in that dodgy fellow he's got working for him and the moment Max arrives any desire of my regular patrons to celebrate seems to vanish and they all leave to go elsewhere. Except when Arthur's working: he won't let him in the door so those nights we have a better run. But what can I do; I don't have a quarrel with him and he works for your son."

That was what he had said back then and Hamilton had made it clear at the time that he didn't believe this statement and that he was watching Rick. However a few days later he had said "So there's something wrong with this Max fellow is there? I thought when he came on board….. But my son said he's the Sergeant's brother."

"Well the Sergeant's pretty dodgy too."

"They seem pretty solidly set up all the same, the two of them," remarked Hamilton.

"Yes the Sergeant would have a bit put by for his retirement fund. He gets plenty of sweeteners from certain quarters."

"Why! Are you paying him?"

"No, not me. Never needed to. But if I started doing anything dodgy myself I would certainly be giving the Sergeant a cut. If someone offered me some bottles of French champagne at a very cheap price no questions asked, then the next time the Sergeant was in I would be sure to let him have a bottle for himself."

The owner straightened out the cover of one of his account books. "So he's on the take. That's useful to know."

"He's a cunning sort of man. I can guarantee that all his money will be well laundered and sparkling clean," said Rick.

On this particular Sunday, having dragged Rick away from what he should be doing, Hamilton seems uncharacteristically slow in getting to the point. He asks how things are going, how Arthur is going. Rick feels himself becoming impatient and says, "You were going to come up with some cash so that we could start to expand the figures but I haven't seen any yet. And as for Arthur, he's overworked as we all are. We need more staff, especially if we're going to justify the kind of figures you're talking about."

Hamilton doesn't seem to be listening. He scratches at his bristly chin and moves uneasily around in his chair. "So what's my son mixed up in?" he asks abruptly.

Rick regards him with astonishment. He has been called away from a busy bar to talk about family matters! He suppresses his irritation and answers with a certain wariness, "He doesn't broadcast to the world what his business is. I wouldn't like to say."

"He doesn't like the way this bar is run."

"You mean, he doesn't like Arthur." Rick doesn't elaborate. Hamilton had raised it after the incident but Rick had made clear that he wouldn't sack Arthur. Putting off Lawrence as part of some public relations exercise with a bank is one thing. Lawrence had never been particularly serious about his duties. But putting off Arthur who was both efficient and popular would leave Rick virtually on his own, 18 hours a day. Rick made it plain that if Arthur was sacked, then Rick would have to be sacked too. So that's where it had been left. At that time Rick had formed the impression that Hamilton was both contemptuous of his son and also perversely rather afraid of him.

Hamilton sighs and shuffles some more. "He's gone up the islands."

"Really," says Rick wondering why Hamilton is telling him this and what possible interest he thinks Rick would have in the movements of his son.

"This morning. Or last night. Didn't say a word to me and I only saw him yesterday." Hamilton is looking uneasy. "He told me last week he'd changed his mind about going on the Evangelista, that he was staying here to help with this deal - I understood he'd got in touch with Havermore and told him so."

The heat and lack of air in the office is telling on Rick's nerves and temper but Hamilton is sitting there as if there is some significance to be drawn from all of this and it is something that Rick too should be concerned about. He remembers Hamilton, after the police investigation involving his son, saying, "It's all completely trivial but the main thing is, it won't have any effect on the deal fortunately, because I'm the person they have to negotiate with, it's all just in my name. Of course in reality it's a consortium, I could never do it all on my own, quite beyond my resources. But even though Anthony is buying in, that's just an internal thing. So whatever happens, if he gets charged with some nuisance, keeping his neighbours awake at night or whatever, it's not going to affect the wider picture. Though it's unfortunate, the timing. The whole thing is still at a delicate stage. The last thing I need is to be connected in any way to a scandal."

Rick had smiled ironically at the time. There was always going to be scandal when Anthony Hamilton was involved. But here is Hamilton in a much less confident frame of mind, gnawing at his finger nails and contemplating his son's defection.

"I don't know what he's playing at," continues Hamilton. "I thought….. There were things he was going to do when the bank people came over, entertaining them. That sort of thing always helps.

But instead….." Hamilton is sitting there with an envelope in his hands looking at it helplessly. "He just wrote me a note. Saying he'd decided to go with Havermore after all but that he's still keen on being counted in on the deal. He's left me a bank draft for a big sum. And just up and left that business of his. It must be lucrative too, to be able to hand over such a large sum in ready money." He has taken out a slip of paper and is tapping his knee with it.

Rick says nothing. He is interested now, but not in Hamilton's son. If Hamilton can be persuaded to plough the bank draft into the business….. A large sum. This sounds like what he's been waiting for.

"The thing is," says Hamilton, "he's gone off leaving all this money and then adds a rider."

Rick waits. He has no idea what is coming.

"Anthony thinks that progress could be made with the bar's figures if Max came here. To help."

Rick stares; for a full few seconds he doesn't take in what Hamilton is trying to tell him. And then he laughs. It isn't even a forced laugh. Well OK, he has had some subterranean plans for making his fortune but the moment Hamilton speaks he realises that he is quite ready to go, to be bought out, he has had enough. His trip home will be paid for and whatever else he can screw out of Hamilton in lieu of his contract, well that will all be a bonus. He is pretty sure he can scare Hamilton into a very nice pay-off, after all he knows a lot of what has been going on and he can sink the deal. But the sheer ludicrousness of what is being proposed hits him.

He wipes his eyes. "Up to you, you're the boss. You'd better make me an offer, I'll go quietly. I'm not staying here if Max….. Ha ha ha," he can't forebear bursting out again. "That shitpile Max coming to work here! Oh my, wait till I tell the troops! They'll bust a gut running for the exit. Hahaha."

"No," says Hamilton alarmed. "Don't tell anyone. I'm just telling you what my son suggests. I thought he would be leaving Max in charge of his own affairs. I don't see who else is going to be looking after them while he's gone. For god's sake don't go telling people that Max….. This is my business and I'm in charge. It was just his suggestion. God." He wipes the sweat off his brow and eyes and shifts, groaning slightly and holding his side before continuing somewhat tangentially. "The other day I went to see that white doctor, Dr Briony, over in Louisaville. The man should be struck off. Hasn't a clue. His brain is so rum-soaked….. I told him what the doctors in the States said and it was as if he didn't understand the words. Recommended bi-carb of soda and a couple of aspirin! Well if he was any good would he be practising in a place like this? I had no choice, I had to go and see that other man Dr Woodrow yesterday; either that or go back to the States to see a decent doctor. Other white people go and see Woodrow. I asked around and the general opinion is that he's good. As a doctor. Impertinent as a man, as they all are, these Coloureds who get above their station. He told me a lot of things I didn't want to know and then he poured some stuff into me. Maybe he knows what he's doing because it did give me some relief. He said I'd be dead in five years unless I pulled my socks up. And then he said he'd heard a rumour I was mixed up with Max de Troy and if that was the case he'd have to revise his estimate of my life expectancy downwards. Good day to you, as cool as anything. As if he didn't care any more for my business than anyone else's, the cheek of the man. But it's sort of been working on me ever since. I realised I didn't know what Anthony was up to or what he employed Max for. If it was a club he couldn't just go off and shut it down could he? People have paid for membership. You must know what goes on, people must have talked."

Rick is evasive. "People talk but I don't have time to hear them. Was a time when I would sit down with my customers and have a good chinwag but how can I do that now? Arthur and I are always flat out just doing what needs to be done. No, I'm no wiser than you are. You'll have to go and talk to some of the idlers here. Karlo. Or Boss. They know everything that goes on."

Of course Rick is not telling the truth, he knows perfectly well what Anthony Hamilton is up to but he is pretty sure that so does Hamilton, or most of it anyway, and just wants it confirmed. But why should Rick do anything for Hamilton, with these working conditions - at least no one will blame him for anything, if anything happens.

He watches the piece of paper that Hamilton is fiddling with until eventually Hamilton turns back to the matter in hand. "This is the draft connected with the business deal he left me. As you can see, it's for a very considerable amount. I've taken on board what you told me the other day. You can use this, buy up big as you said. In the meantime, I'm going back to Barbados tomorrow and I'm going to see a man there who knows about accounts. Give me a couple of those invoices to take as examples. I'll see what he can come up with in terms of bookwork."

He hands the draft to Rick and Rick stares at the amount on it. "You want me to move all this through the business?" he asks, almost in a whisper.

"Do what you think is necessary." He hands over to Rick a thick deposit book for the main bank account. "Just make sure it all ends up in there. Now you'd better get back to work, the bar seems to be pretty full for once." He gets up and leaves.

But Rick sits in the office for a long time and thinks about things.

As he gets up to go, he tosses the deposit book towards a metal tray on his desk. The leaves of the book separate and a thin cheque book slides out of it, mainly stubs. He picks it up. Now here are some interesting payments to some interesting people, he thinks. And a couple of unused cheques at the back; Hamilton clearly hasn't meant to leave it with the deposit book. Rick tosses it back towards the tray but it slips off the edge and falls into a half empty carton of Angustura Bitters on the floor. After staring after it for a minute, Rick leaves it where it is.

When he emerges from the office, it is to the first little ripples of scandal that are spreading in waves around the Frangipani and its neighbourhood.

Rae drags a chair out onto the veranda. Despite her well-crafted collapse last night she hadn't been particularly drunk; she had merely wanted to avoid a too detailed discussion of the night with Rick. Better he just got a general impression. Having Arthur and Lynn as alibis was both provident and important - she had been sailing near the wind meeting Max like that. The end of it has left a sour taste in her mouth; some thing he had wanted to give her, with that set smile, almost menacing now she comes to look back. And what had he said about Rick? Surely he isn't going to go to Rick and say that they met for dinner. With a man built like Rick and with Rick's temper it would be a madman who'd go and present such facts to his face. Thank god she kept back from the actual brink, she doesn't know now what she saw in him. She has to admit her own behaviour….. In view of those veiled and then more explicit invitations…..

Something is gnawing at her now, god the man gives me the creeps, I hope I never see him again. She feels an unease about it all that she can't dispel. One reason is that her mother has stopped speaking to her altogether. Clearly she has wandered so far outside the pale that there is nothing now to be said.

She sighs and wishes Lynn would get up so she can at least talk to someone, anyone. I've no-one to talk to, no-one talks to me anymore - she is becoming sorry for herself. Eventually the spluttering of a motor cycle advancing up the hill below her intrudes into her discontented reverie. "Lucas," she thinks. "Come to swab the deck." She tries to work up a correct attitude to her neighbour, one of slightly patronising amusement at the misuse of all that energy. He thinks he's something now the Chief Constable has given him a task but I know from what Max has said….. She stops. Bloody hell what is she doing believing anything that creep told her? She gets up and strides next door.

"Ho Lucas!" She is surprised to find that Lucas has not yet got into his deck swabbing shorts but is in fact engaged in firmly combing his hair in front of a mirror propped up on the kitchen table. He has around him articles of toilet - a battery-operated shaver, a bottle of aftershave, brylcream, various implements for manicure.

"So how goes the crime of the century?" she asks negligently.

He gives her a look of astonishment. "So news has travelled this far already! Well I knew they would never keep a lid on it."

"Keep a lid on stealing cakes of soap, no I don't suppose they will."

"Oh that. I am just going to see the Chief Constable about that particular matter. And the other act of vandalism that has occurred out there."

"So what vandalism is that?"

"Someone has run a pair of men's smalls up the flagpole."

Rae laughs. "That's not vandalism, that's a political comment."

"Well you may laugh at it all. Other countries have put on trade fairs and they have been the talk of the world. We are only a little island. Some people take it very seriously."

"Deary me," says Rae. "If you are going to be so serious yourself then I shall go away again. So it is the vandalising of the flag pole you are trying to keep the wraps on is it?"

"No it is not, though that sort of mindless prank ought to be publicised. But I hear all the press are out at Louisaville and that will chase it off the front page. Not that I am trying to keep the wraps on anything. It is not in our district and none of our concern." He has finished with his hair and is adjusting his shaver.

Rae is puzzled. "Louisaville. Why are they out there?" But Lucas is now applying his shaver to his already smooth chin. Rae goes out and flings herself into Arthur's hammock and waits for him to stop. Eventually he seems satisfied with his facial appearance.

"Why Louisaville?" she calls. "Not Anthony Hamilton again!"

"Who else? And him skipped the island when there is a body to be explained."

Rae's mouth drops and she comes out of the hammock in a hurry. "A body? Someone dead. Where? When? How?"

"It's too early to tell. A suicide. Or misadventure. Or maybe something worse." He is spreading aftershave on his hands preparatory to larding his cheeks.

"Not a murder, I do love a good murder! Anyone we know?"

"No I'm sure you wouldn't know such a man. But it is a man with a wife and child so not something to glory in."

Rae doesn't take the slightest notice of this censure. She is now feeling a powerhouse of energy, repository of such great news. "So where did it occur and how?"

"I don't know any more than that. The Sergeant must go there of course even though it's nothing to do with us. And here I am, as a result, having to close the station, bringing the force into disrepute yet again."

"But you must know who's dead."

Lucas clucks his lips as he now turns to concentrate on his nails but then says, "Well you will know soon enough because the gardener is telling all and sundry. It is young Hamilton's servant who lies dead."

"What - not Max!" cries Rae. "Why, I only saw him last night." Lucas looks up and she immediately adds, "At the Lotus House. Jim and Lynn and Arthur were there." Safety in numbers.

Lucas says, "No, it is not Max, no such luck. It is the indoor servant who lies dead."

"And Anthony Hamilton suddenly gone?"

"A very suspicious circumstance I would say. As well as the screaming. But then they say there is always screaming. Moaning. Cries. The neighbours are always complaining and no-one doing a thing because there are some big players and some big money about. But no doubt the Sergeant will bring the whole thing around and absolve everyone as usual. It will be a sad day for law and order when our Chief Constable retires and there is no-one to keep such things in check." The latter remarks he says mainly to himself, turning back to the mirror. He is now satisfied and looks at himself from all angles. He looks at his watch and leaps up, "I must not keep the great man waiting." And ignoring all Rae's demands for more information he bowls away on his bike to meet the Chief Constable.

Rae is not a person to keep such astounding news to herself. A murder. How delightful! She goes to get dressed. Of course it was bound to happen. Whatever it is that goes on up at Anthony Hamilton's house….. I can't make out what it is….. I think it's some sort of gaming house, that sort of thing. And everyone's involved, the list of suspects could include the premier and everyone. The whole thing will be hushed up, Lucas is right. Still, make hay while the sun shines. How pleased Karlo will be, he hates Anthony Hamilton. And old Hamilton, serves him right. Just the sort of son he should have.

Rae winds her way down the steps into the precincts of the marina. And there he is, look, bloody Ed Hamilton. Coming through the bar larger than life and looking as if nothing has happened. No doubt he'll think it hardly worth mentioning, only an islander, nothing to get agitated about.

"Oh you here Ed!" she cries. "I've just heard the news, how awful for your son! Just too gruesome. And possibly murder they say. He must be pretty cut up about it all. Especially if he found the body….. Oh no, I remember the gardener found it. But then maybe it wasn't murder after all, maybe it was suicide, the man may have gone mad, that would explain the screaming. Still what an awful thing to happen! And just after the police were up there only a week or so ago about all that other screaming."

Hamilton stands stock still and stares at her. Rae notices that he has gone a dull red colour under his tan. He doesn't know! Or maybe he's angry at her bringing it out in the middle of the Frangipani where everyone can hear. She burbles on, "Yes all the fuss the other week over a bit of screaming, and now the police are over there a second time. And the press too I hear but they would be, turning everything into scandal, aren't the press just awful! And there's something about a murder that seems to hang around even the innocent, tangling everyone up. Hopefully they will find it was just an accident." She waits for him to respond but instead he draws in a deep breath and then strides away without a word. "Well that went down rather well," she murmurs.

At 10 o'clock precisely Constable Frankland presents himself at Headquarters. Here, among the other branches, the CID have their home - a nerve centre crouched around a couple of telephones, coordinating the major crimes division. The Chief Constable's office is at the top of the building.

"Come in Constable Frankland," says the Chief Constable. "At ease. Take a seat. You have a report for me? Ah yes."

Lucas perches rather stiffly on the edge of a modern metal chair in front of a large ugly Swedish desk while the Chief Constable takes the pages that he hands over and sits reading them. Eventually he looks up. "Thank you. You have responded very promptly."

Lucas changes position slightly, says nothing and waits.

The Chief Constable is an Englishman in his fifties. He is red faced, grizzle-haired and overweight. He is a great stickler for the law and once handcuffed a politician and marched him in front of a magistrate for offering a bribe. He is respected and feared in the police force but he is retiring shortly and the local newspaper is speculating loudly that his job would, and should, go to a West Indian. He now slowly turns the two pages of Lucas's report with his thick pink fingers.

"Yes. I'm very impressed."

Lucas stirs and holds his breath. From what he has heard, the Chief is known to lull the unsuspecting with introductory remarks and then unravel for them their incompetency and inefficiency with a quiet and savage intensity that can reduce a strong man to tears.

"You named names."

Lucas blinks.

"Few police officers in my experience will name names of other police officers. It's not surprising of course, they are all protecting each other's back. You interviewed the police sergeant Mr Lee talked to and wrote down his exact words. Including the suppositions of this officer as to your mother's current occupation and unflattering remarks about your own character. It would appear that this officer considers himself an arbiter of the law and will enforce it as he sees fit. He has decided in his discretion not to prosecute a crime." He puts down the report and turns to look out of the window through which can be seen the hot blue sky waving small clouds above the harbour. For some minutes he taps with his fingers on his desk while Lucas sits petrified. Was it wrong of him to have put all that in? He's never been asked to write such a report before. Don't you put everything in a report? He waits despondently, he has no way of knowing how to go about such an investigation, a private investigation for the Chief's eyes only as it was expressed to him. So of course he put in everything. It seems it is not the thing to do. Meanwhile the silence continues oppressively and Lucas watches the fingers as they tap rhythmically on the table.

The Chief eventually sighs and starts speaking as if to himself. "Of course I thought things would change after Independence," he wipes his brow slowly, "otherwise what was the point. The islanders would run it their way, have the reins in their hands, make their own mistakes. And of course there would be something in it for them, job opportunities, new confidence. And if you look at Port Sophia that's what happened. There's been an enormous release of vitality there, new businesses starting, old businesses expanding. And the government bringing in laws on squatter's rights, very popular with the poor. All of that engenders enthusiasm; people get involved, the rule of law isn't something that just concerns the police, it includes everyone. So why isn't it happening here? Why is everything here sinking into corruption and apathy? Poor Mr Lee. It seems that because he was upset and thinking only of his scrolls he missed out on the courtesies required when dealing with a police officer and failed to mention the price that he would be willing to pay to get his property back. This is not stated in so many words of course by your brother officer, who expressed instead some prejudices about the Chinese race." The Chief leans back wearily in his chair and folds his stubby fingers together. "Now people look at the time before Independence as the golden age when such things didn't happen. But no-one seems to have the energy to do anything about it. And as a result you get a general disrespect for the law and that's going to lead on to bigger and bigger problems. Once people lose respect for individual politicians and individual policemen they eventually lose respect for their political and legal institutions. What's to stop them taking up arms if that seems to be the only way to achieve change? Then if they need a new Chief Constable they just shoot the old one. And if they want a new government they just have a revolution. It all starts because the poor get no protection from the police, either in their person or in their property and it eventually reaches a point where they have nothing to lose." The Chief sighs gloomily and then turns in his chair to face Lucas. "I've heard already about your discreet approaches to the Beach Hotel and how Mr Lee's scroll was forthcoming almost immediately with apologies from the persons concerned. He has thanked me profusely and I am happy that it didn't cost him a cent and he can go home believing that the attitude of the police officer in question was an aberration. But what about the people who are living here? How are we to regain their trust, Constable Frankland?"

Lucas sits to attention. It seems that rather than being reprimanded he is to be commended. He isn't totally sure about that. But in any case here is the Chief Constable talking to him as if he has something to contribute, here he is being privy to the thought processes of the island's most powerful law-enforcement officer.

"I am going to be retiring soon and do you know what is going to happen then?" the Chief continues. It is almost certainly a rhetorical question but Lucas is rather wound up and feels that if he can say anything he should do so.

"Yes sir, the Premier will offer the position to Sergeant de Troy." He can see straight away that he has said the wrong thing. The Chief bristles and goes red from his neck upwards, his teeth clench and his breathing becomes heavy. Lucas keeps very still. He knows his chances are not very good under a future dispensation but he is hoping to at least preserve his tenure under the present one.

"Yes," says the Chief after a while when the mottled purple colour in his cheeks and neck subsides. "I am aware that the Premier will offer the job to the highest bidder. What do you think Sergeant de Troy has to offer in this position, that's what I'd like to know?"

Again the comment is probably in the nature of a rhetorical question but again Lucas feels compelled to answer. "Sergeant de Troy knows the seedy nature of the Premier's extra-curricular activities and is prepared not to broadcast the news, at a price."

The Chief Constable lowers his head, as if praying. "Yes, I can believe the Premier would think the Sergeant a very good choice on those grounds." There is silence for a while and then the Chief Constable looked directly at Lucas. "However, I will not be retiring until after the next election. I live in hope that a new Parliament will bring men of integrity and vision on to the scene but if that is not the case then….." he taps the desk and looks grim. "Constable Frankland, I still have a few tricks up my sleeve and if I was staying you would be a rising man. I can't imagine though that your talents will be at all valued under the reign of a Chief Constable De Troy."

"Oh I know that, sir," mutters Lucas hollowly.

"As you may know, when St Claire signed the articles of Federation with the other islands, we entered into a joint policy with regard to Immigration and Excise. The Act that passed through the various Parliaments for that purpose is an interesting Act and one which perhaps the members of Parliament here did not examine in regard to its policing with the rigour they are wont to bring to matters dealing with money and land and anything where handouts may be forthcoming. One thing that they perhaps failed to notice is that an Immigration Officer is not under the control of this Parliament here as you and I are but under the Federation's control through its Congress. A big difference and one that our Premier has suddenly of late become aware of. Fortunately or unfortunately depending who you are, there is not going to be time to change the Act before the next election." The Chief rubs his hands briefly during a pause. "Constable Frankland, I would like you to become an Immigration Officer. I have discussed this with the Head of Immigration in Port Sophia and he is going to appoint you as a temporary officer in an undercover capacity in addition to your current duties. It is unnecessary for other people in the police force to know of this. It may mean, no it will almost certainly mean, that after my departure and if the current government is re-elected, this move will not do you any good in your career in the police force here and you may wish to turn it down, it's up to you."

"I would accept of course, sir," says Lucas after he gets over his astonishment. "I would like to be useful while I can."

"Good. Secondly I would also like to have you help investigate the death that occurred in Louisaville late last night or this morning. This would normally be a legitimate exercise of your powers as an Immigration Officer as young Mr Hamilton is an American and has taken up residence on the island, although I believe he has suddenly departed elsewhere. I think you should be looking at whether Mr Anthony Hamilton is a suitable person to have residency here. However as I said, I do not want your new status generally known so I have come to an arrangement with Dr Woodrow the coroner. I want to appoint you publicly as the coroner's assistant. What do you say to that?"

Lucas sitting even more rigidly to attention says "Thank you very much sir. I should be glad to work with Dr Woodrow."

"Yes he's a good man but the job of assistant has been advertised before and had no takers." Lucas knows this, and knows why. It is the least pleasant part of police work, dealing with newly deceased. And dealing with the not-so-newly deceased is even worse. The Chief Constable continues, "You can tell everyone that I offered it to you, as if it were a reward for your work in solving this other crime. They will all think you have been taken for a ride and laugh behind your back. No matter. Usually it would only require you to get positive identification and find out the cause of death. In this case we know who the young man is - the cause of death has been investigated by the police and has been found, according to them, to be suicide. I don't know if it was suicide, that is for the coroner to decide but your job will be to get extra information to help the coroner make up his mind. Anything you can find out about the man and about Hamilton."

"Yes sir."

"It will mean a lot of extra work. On top of your police duties."

"I would like to do it sir."

"Good. You had better go and see Dr Woodrow." He hesitates. "I want you to understand, if you haven't already, that all of this means that you will almost certainly lose your job as a police officer when I retire, if the succession is as you suggest."

"I shall probably return to England in that eventuality, sir."

The Chief Constable frowns. "You won't get into the police force there," he says sceptically.

"No, but I have been offered acting work in the past. Occasionally black men are required for small parts in TV dramas and I seem to have a comic look to me that is attractive to television producers."

"It's a pity, if bit parts are all you have to look forward to in England. I hope things will change and that it will be possible for you to stay here. I think one day you could play a starring role."

The trouble with news is that it's like a drug - after the feel-good hit you are on that downward slope waiting for the next fix. The Frangipani is getting desperate. Karlo sets up a command headquarters at a table near the bar. Karlo doesn't talk about his past at all but it is well known, from the kind of gossip that spreads thick and clings like peanut butter, that he was once someone in charge of something in Africa, before the British pulled out and, so the word went, he narrowly escaped with his life. Mum's the word, tap the nose, the inference being that Karlo has done desperate deeds but no-one really knows what. He is therefore the obvious choice for the role of private detective in a murder drama.

Once every word and sentence that Rae gleaned from Lucas has been examined, once Ed Hamilton's demeanour has been closely discussed, there is nothing more to feed the ravening maws of excited yachties. All morning people are leaping back from whatever urgent task has compelled them to be absent shrieking, "Any news? No?" On they go, between victualling and burnishing and scrubbing and fuelling the cry is constant, "Any news?"

Karlo decides after mid-day that it is time to get pro-active. Clearly the news is not going to come to them, it is essential that they go to the news. A frontal attack on Anthony Hamilton's house? Ah great idea, a person in disguise with a press badge, is that what they have? Do they have press badges, what do they look like, if I knew what they looked like I could….. But hang on, that Max fellow will be there and he knows us all. Rae aren't you a buddy of his, why don't you…..

Rae's expression clearly indicates that this suggestion is out of order.

Better idea. Better idea. Aunt Marion. Yes, Arthur's aunt. She will know everything there is to know. "Arthur you must contact your aunt."

"No need. She knows I get off at 2 for a few hours and she will be arriving at my house the moment my head hits the pillow."

"Pillow, you can't nap! This is serious stuff here. The man's appalling, remember how he wanted to sack you. Surely you want to make sure he's arrested, tried and hanged for this dastardly crime."

"Well you can all come up to my house. I'll snooze in the hammock and she will have someone to talk to."

Settled.

Just as Arthur predicts, Aunt Marion arrives at the marina shortly after Arthur goes off for his break and finds to her surprise that there are numerous hands to help her carry her shopping up the hill. Eager friends help her into the most comfortable chair. She fans herself and catches her breath, the slope is always a problem for someone of her bulk but nevertheless it is all worth it to have such an attentive audience. She settles back and starts to exclaim at Mustaffa running out of crackers and such like, such a run he's had on them he says, but if you ask her he has turned his mind too much to gossip of late and not enough to the running of his business. But then of course he is related by marriage to the uncle, the 'uncle of the deceased'.

And the police saying it's most likely suicide. Well, cries Marion, I ask you, does a young man like that jump off a terrace? And she knows that terrace, she has stood on that terrace. There is a great steep drop below straight down maybe twenty or thirty feet to the neighbour's car parking. And only that low wall..... She said to Sheila, she'd want a big fence if she lived there, she wouldn't feel safe. She wouldn't like living near such a steep drop, it is bad enough at her house with a great cliff below but she never can get anyone to put a fence up for her. She looks round accusingly at Arthur who is now pleasantly asleep but before she can follow up on this line of grievance someone hands her a large cool cola and puts some little things to eat on the table, all brought up from the Frangipani for the better ingestion of some solid news at last.

Marion takes a luxurious pull at the drink and slides her feet out of her shoes - this is all very pleasant, she is enjoying herself. She tells them the story so far. The fellow in the house below Hamilton's is some rich fellow with a couple of fancy cars and the dead man landed plumb on top of one, dented the whole roof in and not discovered by the man himself but by the gardener and just as well. If you are a rich man with a nice car you wouldn't want to be eating breakfast beforehand. And him ringing the police all the time complaining and complaining about Hamilton and nothing being done and now there he is with his car ruined.

As for the dead man rest in peace, his name is Selwyn Panday. In Aunt Marion's view Mustaffa is such a tower of information, the police should pay him to solve their crimes. Mustaffa knows all about everything. Apparently the boy is Indian from a very respectable family and then took up with a coloured woman - mixed marriages are never a good idea. And it is a bit of a wonder young Mr Hamilton's employing him at all as he is thought a bit of a bad lot by his relatives - apparently there is some suspicion attached to him regarding a break-in at his uncle's hardware store. But then it seems young Mr Hamilton is not such an ideal employer himself. Mustaffa knows all about that too and it all sounds pretty fishy what goes on down there. Hamilton had another man working for him that was known in like manner to the police and this man went around complaining he was beaten up when he objected to certain things. But the police did nothing. Even though there were bruises all over him. That police station at Louisaville, they are as bad out there as Sergeant de Troy. They are all the same unless you give them money, only that's no reflection on her nephew Lucas, that's only what Mustaffa is telling her.

So as for Selwyn, it was thought a great piece of luck that he got the position with Mr Hamilton, in a good big house like that, in such a nice area. His mother was very relieved to see him settled so. She's a very respectable woman, her second husband manages that big chicken farm out beyond Cape Cloud. So Selwyn had a good upbringing alright, good schools, all that. But then he took up with his father, his real father, a man who drinks, a very low type with any number of women apparently. And that brought Selwyn into bad company. And now there he is, dead with a wife and child, well not a wife exactly but they do say the child is his. But there was violence at that house of Hamilton's on a regular basis. Marion lowers her voice and everyone leans in to hear. Screaming, she whispers. For ten minutes by the clock. And the neighbour he is not a man to put up with it. He rang the police on the very night. The very night! If they had gone round, well who knows what would have happened. But nothing was done. And now today there he is. Dead. Head first into that car and goodness knows how much the man paid for such a vehicle, they don't come cheap and quite undriveable now, not that you'd want to in any case. Splattered from end to end according to the gardener. No, not a pretty sight. It was the gardener found him and of course he told it all to Mary-Jane or so she says, she is full of it. Marion becomes distracted from the main story to worry how Mary-Jane came to know the gardener, that woman is a disgrace. Fancy coming round this morning bold as brass to boast of all the gory details. And she is there still drinking and supping and eating her out of house and home and all the neighbours in there too. Marion becomes suddenly purposeful, "Arthur, you must drive me home. I come only because she going over and over these things and not a bite to eat in the house for any that come late. Arthur you hear me!"

However Arthur is not required to do anything immediately as there are so many questions, so many exclamations, such an engrossed flurry of interest especially when Marion describes the morning reconnoitre. The assembled yachties learn that the scene of the crime is just below her house and you can see it from the fort, oh yes much coming and going, knots of reporters trying to see and none of them with the sense to come up there. Yes the best view in the district and she was there early too, after Mary-Jane burst in at first light to tell them all. Daphne was sent back for chairs as her legs are not built for standing so long so she was very comfortable and she saw Sergeant de Troy arrive and many others who you wouldn't think would have any business being there including some Very Important Persons though she can't swear to that. Daphne has better eyesight than her but she tends to get excited and exaggerate things. In Aunt Marion's view there is enough misinformation being spread about by those newspaper people. Of course she couldn't see where the body was, that was down the side of the cliff but she saw people making calculations, measuring things. There seemed to be a lot of science in it all. Then Dr Woodrow arrived and they all stopped what they were doing while he had a look. He's the coroner you know and an islander: they passed over that white chap down the road and no-one is surprised. She wouldn't go and see Briony even if she only had a common cold. Such stories you hear of medical incompetence but her family have been going to Dr Woodrow since he first set up his nameplate, about eight years ago now. Yes he is a very good doctor. If there is anything behind it all he will nose it out. He won't have a bar of people like Sergeant de Troy trying to hush things up. Dr Woodrow would have it all out in the open and a fine lively trial they would have once he has the whole thing investigated and look here is Lucas and, "Lucas," her voice goes up a notch, "you are not to start mopping the floor with all this company here."

Lucas has just been visiting Dr Woodrow. An autopsy was about to be done by a pathologist from Port Sophia who had come in on the noon plane and Lucas found the doctor reading the paper work associated with the case. It was clear from the start that Dr Woodrow was not particularly impressed by the police investigations and had no intention of bringing in a verdict of suicide until a full investigation had been done. The doctor spent some time with Lucas on the sort of information he would need if any satisfactory conclusions were to be reached in the case.

Dr Woodrow's surgery was not far from the centre of town. As Lucas knew that most of the work would have to be done at home and kept out of the way of prying eyes, he went afterwards to a shop that sold office equipment. His pay being slender, he walked through the part at the front where new things gleamed, to the back area where everything smelled of typewriter oil. A suave young man offered him a small second-hand safe at a very reasonable price, delivery included. Lucas agreed and asked about typewriters. He had in mind a battered old Remington like the one they had at the station. The salesman however indicated that they had recently acquired an almost new portable in very good condition. It came with a hard grey case, new ribbon, why didn't he try it? He looked at the price and almost didn't, but the moment he put his hands to the keys he knew clickety clickety clickety he had to have it.

He now arrives at his house carrying the typewriter under one arm and a ream of paper under the other and he could not have chosen a more public moment to appear.

"Look at you, carrying all those things on that motor bike, you will have an accident. What have you got there?"

"The Chief Constable offered me the post of assistant to the coroner." He says it proudly, he isn't playacting, he is genuinely delighted to be doing the job even if no-one else wanted it.

His aunt is immediately enraptured, "On this case at the Hamilton's?"

"Among others," says Lucas.

Marion claps her hands in delight. "Oh my, Lucas, you are a coming man and now you will know as much as anyone on the island!"

"Yes Tantie, and what I know I am bound not to tell."

"We will read your face for clues," cries Karlo. "If you look grave we will know young Hamilton is likely to get off, if you look happy we will know you are building a case against him and if you look ecstatic we will know that that Max fellow is going to the gallows as well."

Yes there is a great deal to talk of still but Aunt Marion has become conscious of the time that has elapsed and feels a renewed urgency to go back and see what Mary-Jane is up to, especially as she now has a fresh snippet of information. She determinedly prises herself from her chair and shakes her nephew from his peaceful sleep.

Arthur yawns and stretches. "Four o'clock," he remarks looking at his watch. "I'll drive you home Tantie and then go down and relieve Rick so he can have a snooze before the evening rush." Two hours have gone by most restfully and he is feeling pleased and he thinks, Anthony Hamilton has done me a favour which would grieve him amazingly as I have had two hours of uninterrupted sleep because of him. Lord if it wasn't for him Tantie would have remembered the party and I would have had to describe in detail everything we did last night but now, let off scot free. No-one could care less about all the tiresome people we met or all the stupid things we did now there is something more recent and interesting.

Aunt Marion is disappointed that he has to go back to work straight away, she was wanting him to help Daphne hand round the finger foods but her discontent is wiped away by a very general wish on the part of those present to go to the fort and see for themselves what is taking place below. Arthur's car and Michael's taxi are soon full and Aunt Marion is almost overcome with the responsibility of it all. She will herself show them the way, she will naturally point out to them what things of interest there are to be seen, she will have Daphne struggle up from the house with lemonade for all of them. This will be her finest hour.

Chapter 7

Seeking honey in the crotch of a hollow tree

We are much given to herding together when young - milling around in small spaces with a lot of noisy people our own age. In this way, the world can be explored without too much effort or originality. When the mapping has been done, however, the horde of high energy acquaintanceship can become burdensome. What we really need is a friend.

Now Rae is happy. She has found a friend. Look mother, a girlfriend and good-tempered too, willing to do anything and go anywhere. Not like Libby. What sort of pal is constantly yanking out her compact to stare at her face before saying, "Have to be going, I have the most important engagement." What could possibly be more important than going to the beach and hanging out with your pals?

Libby - snappy, bitchy and meddlesome - has started to annoy Rae. A couple of days after her encounter at the Lotus Room she heard Libby drawl to Sergeant de Troy, "These Immigration people only make all the fuss they do about some people. Asking questions about what boat you're on, such a stupid rule. But not a rule for everyone - they never are. I know a young lady who's not living on any boat right now but do I see Immigration going round asking questions? No. Because she's not the personal friend of anyone important."

Rae has no doubt as to who that 'young lady' is. The tenor of the conversation was on the evils of Immigration Officers but Rae knows that mischief-making lurked beneath the surface. As if getting rid of Lynn would make any difference to Libby and Boss's situation! Charles has made it clear he will never EVER use Boss if Libby goes out with the boat. But, thinks Rae, she still carries on as if everyone will eventually bend to her will - just because she looks the way she does.

Anyway, Rae doesn't have to like Libby anymore, she has far too much to do. Not only does she now have a variety of beaches to go to in Arthur's car but she is also teaching Lynn to drive.

This was Arthur's suggestion. So now they are practicing driving every morning, going to whichever beach they think of that day. Beach then lunch, that is the order of business. Cut lunches from the Frangipani kitchen are OK but….. Rick is looking so weary, he is a sucker for the I'll-give-you-four-hours-at-the-bar-if-you-give-me….. a teeny weeny little lunch somewhere nice with, just for example, a planters punch. So here she is, just swinging her legs and sipping from her glass and lolling by the pool. Rae loves pools. And Lynn loves pools too. There she is swimming, swimming the supercoloured blue pool of the Beach Hotel, her body like a sleek porpoise bloobloobloo blowing out like the sound of the water bubbling through the cleaning system. Walls appear and disappear as she dips and powers away, not racing, just lazily turning the blue water; turning the water in an overarm lazy fashion seeing in memory the sand and blue sea of a Queensland beach, seeing the life-guards in their caps and the movement of waves and how true blue life is when you're happy.

Yes this is the life under a blue beach umbrella, its white plastic fringe like a moving reef of whitecaps, where leaning back and looking up into the sky is like gazing into clear water, finest glass, blue sky so glass-like that when a plane goes over it looks like it is scratching with a diamond on perfect blue pyrex. Happiness like a soft song bubbling, a hum underwater, umm mm mmm.

Rae lolls, head back with a straw connected to her gorgeous drink, just too happy for words ummm mmm mm.

"What's that my dear," murmurs a voice at her shoulder.

Nasty awakening. Rae once felt a tingling attraction to him but now feels a jab of caution and unease. "What do you want?" It is said in what she hopes is her most unpromising tone of voice.

"Who is our water baby in the yellow bikini that I see you around with?"

"What's it to you?"

Max looks at her with that enigmatic smile which before would have seemed slow and sexy but which now seems vaguely menacing. “I also see you around in a little car now. Things at the bar must be looking up.”

“I think you know pretty well which way things at the bar are looking.”

“Mr Hamilton senior is very hopeful to make a lot of money out of it.”

“Really! Well every time I see the old goat he’s always moaning on about how poor he is. But there again,” she sips her drink, “I have also heard him telling the world that his son is involved in big business right here on the island. Funny thing, for a man to be involved in business and suddenly to be doing a runner.”

“Well I think you could say of Anthony Hamilton that he is minding his own business.” Max pulls up a chair and Rae doesn’t like this, she has fallen for talking to him and now he’s getting cosy.

She can’t prevent herself continuing however. “He’ll be in court soon and then it will be everyone’s business.”

“Well I think the ‘everyone’ will be disappointed as he himself was out at the time that the man took himself over the cliff. I was also out as you may recall.”

“I only recall up until about 1 o’clock after which you could have gone anywhere. You’ve got a smudge on your glasses. Give them here.” He wears mirror glasses, walls that guard the eyes and the direction of the gaze like a mafia boss or a pop star and he gives them to her with an intimate smile. But she has an ulterior motive that has nothing to do with renewing any flirtations because as she is handing them back she says, “So there was something happened, if you’re all so keen to establish alibis.”

The flicker of an eye and he has the glasses back in place, his smile back in place as well. “Everyone has something to hide,” is all he says. “Everyone. Some people might get drunk and forget. But things have a habit of coming out.” He looks at her but she is thinking about what she fancies was the dropping of his guard and completely misses any innuendo in what he is saying. She does notice though that he is looking strangely put out and his smile falters for once. When he speaks again it is with a trace of bitterness. “Yes some people manage to hide their past. And have little idea of the consequences of their actions.”

“I have to get back to the Frangipani,” she says, starting to gather her things.

“In your new little car. How interesting that you have a new car. Perhaps you have a new friend.”

"It's Arthur's car," she says shortly.

"Ah yes. Arthur. He has built up a prejudice, won't even let me in his bar. And turning others against me too. You are not so friendly now I see."

"God, that's got nothing to do with Arthur!" she laughs at the very notion. She gets up and rearranges her sarong around her swimsuit. She is a little unsteady she finds, she picks up her beach bag carefully then turns a dismissive smile on him before walking away. But it seems he doesn't wish to be dismissed.

"I'm sorry," he says following after her slightly unco-ordinated movement forward - come on get it together here, "that I couldn't bring you that little present I talked of. For somehow it got mislaid, which has been very distressing to me. Considering the effort I went to get it. It is a souvenir of the nice time we had together."

"I told you before I don't want anything from you," says Rae who is looking round for Lynn but finds she isn't focussing her eyes that well.

"And yet during the time we were together you seemed happy with what you got."

She lets out a sigh "Ah" but it is only because she has spotted Lynn over by the pool shower. "Lynn," she calls moving in that direction, not reacting to what he has said. Again his smile flickers shut for an instant. Then he reaches out and takes her arm.

"But you know you shouldn't act like this, cutting off old friends," he pursues with his most winsome smile. "You should come up to Hamilton's place again. I could show you round more of it this time, and we could have a drink together like before."

She isn't really listening and her glance at him is rather blank and faintly surprised, as if he is talking to the wrong person. "No thanks," she says. "Lynn, are you ready? I have to go."

"Lynn," says Max. "That's a nice name. Pleased to meet you. I think you are a friend of Arthur's aren't you."

Lynn looks uncertainly at him but Rae says, "Come on, don't listen to him or we'll be here all day." She takes Lynn by the arm, "We've got better things to do."

Lynn glances back and thinks she sees an expression of frustrated fury on Max's face but it changes so quickly into a look of total indifference that she may have been mistaken - perhaps it is after all only a facial tic.

Lucas sits nervously on his motorbike. He has driven out to find Mr Panday senior, father of the dead man. The centre of the island is a plateau where various colonial companies once experimented with palm plantations, sugar cane, bananas, nutmeg groves and so on. Two decaying distilleries are a reminder of the failure of sugar to thrive commercially on the island but there are still some spice packing sheds which provide employment, plus a few other enterprises, and the result is a patchwork of hamlets and individual cabins connected by diabolical rutted dirt roads.

Lucas has had some difficulty finding the address. It is a concrete house on short piles which is only partially completed. It has square holes but no windows, an oblong hole but no door. It is roofed in second hand corrugated iron vividly rusted and Lucas notices that there are substantial gaps between the roofing iron and the concrete walls. Not a comfortable house during the hurricane season he thinks. Now he has to go in and interview the father and he is not yet skilled in such things. The training he received on entering the police force was designed to make him useful when directing traffic, when involved in crowd control and receiving lost property plus of course apprehending villains under proper direction. The more advanced forms of policing, such as interviews, are done by the CID, not his role at all normally. But here goes, he thinks. Wearing his uniform gives him courage: a police officer is a police officer. And he knows what he wants to know.

Getting in the house is another hurdle, the steps being constructed roughly out of odd rocks and bits of cast-off wood. Lucas has no way of knocking because there is only a sort of torn curtain over the doorway, so he calls out, "Hello in the house there!"

There is the creak of furniture and footsteps; a man leans against the wall inside looking down. He is fat and of Indian appearance, his singlet is stained and sweaty. He wears khaki shorts that droop beneath the curve of his stomach. "Yo," he replies in a rather hostile manner. A surly-looking man all round but that could be sorrow, thinks Lucas charitably.

"Mr Sonny Panday? I'm Constable Frankland," Lucas introduces himself, "assistant to the coroner. The coroner has sent me to speak to the bereaved about the death of Selwyn Panday. I'm sorry to come at such a time of grief but the coroner wants me to find out about any health problems your son had."

"He have no health problems," says Panday senior shortly.

"Well can I come in and get a family history?" Lucas asks politely. The man hesitates and then shrugs at him to come in.

The inside of the house is as one would expect from its outside appearance. Two rough internal walls are in place to the height of the external walls but there is no ceiling. Lengths of wire spring out here and there showing that someone at some time had pretensions towards electricity. To one side a folding table with a gas campstove on it indicates the extent of the kitchen. There is a broken-down sofa covered with bits of clothing and one straight-backed wooden chair also covered with scrunched up clothing, washing perhaps. A very thin dark-skinned woman comes round one of the walls to look at him, accompanied by several children. "Have a seat," says the man.

Lucas looks cautiously at the couch which he does not fancy. Its vinyl covering is cracked, torn and gaping in several places and it has a dark greasy stained look that bodes no good for his clean uniform. He has decided to stand when the man, as if divining his difficulty, picks up all the clothing on the chair and throws them on the floor, "Sit," he commands.

The woman gives a disapproving chirrup but says nothing.

Lucas sits. He clears his throat. He is not sure what the sensibilities are here to the dead man. Before he can say anything however the man says to the woman, "Don' just stand there, go down Nelson and get us a couple of beers now." The woman doesn't move. "Tell him we have the coroner in the house. I will pay him sure thing on Friday." With that the woman turns silently and goes out and the children, without her protection, immediately move their lower bodies behind the wall as far as possible while still looking on.

"Do you know anything about your son's unfortunate death at all?"

"That is a bad man he was working for."

"Bad. In what way?"

"Known bad. He was known. You police, you know about that man and yet he free to walk the streets."

"Mr Hamilton?"

"No no no," Mr Panday shakes his body irritably. "That Max de Troy. That is a bad man. But that Hamilton, maybe he is bad too. I don't know about him. I hear things but I think well, they have allsorts in this world and if your white folks will pay for such things then what can you say if a man is game enough to set up such a business and make some money. He make some money well and good, that is fine and he employ my son, fine. But when he employ that Max de Troy then you think maybe he is not such a good man himself, unless it is pure ignorance. And that Sergeant, his brother, giving the man credibility, that is not a thing that should be allowed either. My son go to work for Hamilton. He was a good son, give his old dad some money for a beer and them, that is a good son for you. But now he is dead and it is because after going to work for Mr Hamilton, that Max is employed there too. That should never have been allowed." He rocks his body and looks round impatiently. "Where is that woman? Hey" he gestures at the oldest child, "go see where she is, what is keeping she. No," he continues bitterly, "it should not be allowed and what is to happen to the money owing now he dead? I hear they going to pay it all to the widow but that is not right. That money, some should go to the widow, but there is money owed right here which have nothing to do with his wages. And why they are waiting to pay it? I tell you something going on there and it's so the widow get the lot. They in each other pockets there. Coming up with some conspiracy. That money should be shared out right."

"There's a problem about the payment of the wages owing?"

"Wages and other things. A problem for me, oh yes. The widow having little talks with Max de Troy about those lies they telling, and me who got plenty chillen to look after and feed."

The woman comes back in silently with two small bottles of beer. She is accompanied by two other women, one middle-aged, one younger. "Pour the officer a beer why don't you," says the man fretfully. "Why you bring over all the family?"

"No no," says Lucas to the woman as she makes to take off the top. "I'm on duty."

Mr Panday rearranges himself as if honour at any rate is satisfied.

"Was Selwyn sick at all?" ventures Lucas.

"What you mean by that?" asks the man as if Lucas has said something darkly suspicious.

"Well was he in good health when you saw him last?"

"Of course he was in good health," says Panday. "A young man like that, why would he not be in good health?"

"No reason," says Lucas. "I am just covering all the possibilities."

"He did not throw himself over the wall, if that is what you mean. He was not sick in the head no way. He have a good head on his shoulder and he told me he was going places, Papa I going places. Does that sound like a man who sick? No that Max is spreading all sort of bad rumours, don't listen to that man, that man liard."

"Right," says Lucas politely. "What about in the rest of the family, any medical conditions? Any sort of sickness in the family at all?" There is a rearranging of arms among the women.

"What you mean in the family?" says Panday. "Well I sick as you see. I am not out working like I once was, no, because the doctor is telling me I will be a dead man."

"Sick," mutters the older woman. "You no more sick than me donkey."

"What sort of sickness is it you have?" asks Lucas.

"Drink," interjects the older woman. "Drink and more drink."

The man glowers at her for a minute and then clutches a slab of his chest. "Here. This is what is wrong. Twice, I go to the doctor all dizzy and he look at me blood pressure and tell me I am a sick man. Twice."

"Heart?" suggests Lucas.

The women, including the woman who Lucas imagines to be the present Mrs Panday, all laugh. The man gives off an angry sound and makes to get out of the sofa shaking his fist at her.

"There," says the older woman. "The police officer is on duty and he is taking notes. Now you watch this, police officer man, because I coming to help me daughter and I will not be hit about the head by this drunk while a police officer is present. We going down the road now and taking the chillen and their clothes and what belong to her."

Mrs Panday at that gathers the remaining children. She makes a swoop on the bundle on the floor beside Lucas, just as Panday leaps to his feet roaring and cursing.

"Hey hey," says Lucas getting up and standing between them.

"What, look they taking all me things, look."

"They not all you things," says the older woman. "You don't own nothing, all here is my own including the chair the Constable sitting on, which out of politeness to himself I will be leaving for now. This poor woman done try leave before but have been put in fear of her life. He threatens to kill she if she walk over that doorstep."

"Don't you go interfering between a man and his wife. Hey, you going to let them steal all me things?"

"I'm just going to prevent any violence," says Lucas.

"Violence, this is not violence, this is between a man and his wife. A man can do what he likes in his own home."

"No he may not, that is why I am here. Your son was in Mr Hamilton's home….."

"What, and you think violence was done?" The man instantly stops his fury to look intently at Lucas.

"Death is always violent. When a man is found at the bottom of a cliff. That is what I am here to discover. If you can help me at all."

All of the women have stopped. They are holding various possessions but their faces all turn towards Lucas, their curiosity preventing them making good their escape. Lucas sits down cautiously as does Panday.

"Is there any other heart conditions in your family? Your father still alive, brothers and so on?"

"Oh yes, they all healthy as anything, all working flat out with money to spare. No time for sick relatives though. That is what comes of being healthy, never a thought for the likes of me."

"That man not your father." The older woman turn to Lucas. "That father of his not his real father, everyone know it, his mother own it and his father own it. That is not his real father. And that rich Mr Panday, only his half brother you'll find."

"What happened to your real father?" asks Lucas turning back to Mr Panday.

The man laughs dismissively. "One day they come up with a test and then you know for sure. Some say he one thing, some say another. When Selwyn come in the world how do I know I'm his father, how do I know hey? Only the woman know for sure and not even then sometime. Selwyn could have been Pier Bart's kid, he was hanging around alright and she plenty interested in that bastard but she said it was mine."

"You think Selwyn was your son?"

"I acknowledge him. Anyway she ran out on me in the end."

"With this Pier fellow?"

"No, that man drop dead. Just like that. One day living, next day dead. No she found some other fellow, plenty money and all, left me for the money."

"Left you on account of the drink you mean," says the older women. "Like this one is."

"Oh she'll be back." The man in his previous agitations has come into possession of the two bottles of beer and he now takes the top off one. "Who else going to put up with her? You see officer, all this riot and she'll be back by the end of the week. Always making to leave with the most fuss possible, crying attempted murder or some other thing, and end of the week she is back again. No point you getting involved. She and her mother and that sister of hers, they all fall out by Friday for sure. Screams and murder down the other end of the road. I thump her one side of the face one week and then her mother thumping her on the other the next, what a life hey." He lifts the bottle to his lips and drinks deeply.

Home we go, thinks Rae hazily. But watch it now. She has had a bit to drink but Lynn is OK. Home they go, a bit jerky on the clutch, mind now. But she doesn't really care how Lynn goes because the walls of the road are like landscape from a cartoon and it is hard to concentrate after two lovely luscious lollopy juicy-full planters. Hello, here we are home again jogetty jog. Ah yes, coffee I suppose, does she want coffee - that might take this lovely squiffy veil from her brain. No she won't have coffee, she will lie on the bed with her feet up for a minute..... What a bullshit artist that man is, swaggering away, talking to the waiters, smiling here and there and inviting me up to Anthony Hamilton's house as if he owned it. Up to the house again, what does he mean 'again'? He must have heard we were all up there at the fort looking down. Of course there is a certain morbid temptation to go inside, stand where the dead man stood, all that. But if it comes with Max it's too dangerous, that slight edge of ice that fringes any pool that Max is the centre of. It was exciting at the time but.....

He is a powerful man. Presence, the way he walks and that way he smiles, yes he is powerful alright. Dancing with him when he put his hand in the middle of her back guiding her, and then as the music slows and the lights dim, moving his hand down to the curve of her buttock. Stop that, but she doesn't really want him to. Moving to the beat with his hips up close to hers and rubbing, she could feel him hard and his hand back under her buttock. Stop that, stop. But he is pulling her up against him, they are alone somewhere, dancing alone and she can feel his erect penis against her and his hand under her dress moving up and down on the soft skin of her thigh. Stop.

He has a mirror on his ceiling, she almost gasps with shock.

His mouth and lips are down on her breast and neck and here she is come out of the night with all her wetness on her like a furry wet ball pressing down like a baby's head, watering the crevice where his hand is, inside her panties, his finger and thumb like the tentacles of the sea urchin softly touching her wetness and he is taking off her clothes piece by piece like in a show, off they come as he murmurs "Lovely." Off with the stockings unrolled one by one, off with the dress and only her panties left, pulling them off at last and holding her legs apart murmuring "Lovely" and touching her there with his fingers and his tongue and his breath. And then quickly taking off his own clothes until there he is with his great purpleblack penis kneeling between her legs - and something like lava is starting to roll, the mouth of the anemone crazily sucking at water. He is naked and black, she is amazed how black he is with his hand on her white breast, he is a black hand on her white breast where the sun never tanned and his black mouth is open with a red tongue like the wounded vitals of an oyster, his mouth like oyster flesh sucking the shell the hard shell as his fingers probe into the soft fringed interior until he jackknifes above her - she feels him jam into her with a great rush like someone stoppering a bottle before the foam escapes "Oh god!" And she is numb, held there like a fish spitted on a knife while he guts her in clean loops of movement, rhythmically driving down and down and down into the belly of the fish, pulling back on all those shearing guts, all those mucus tendrils, sucking it out suck and suck and suck and suck the sound of it. The sound the sound and his laboured breathing and she feeling nothing.

Jesus. She opens her eyes.

What an awful dream. "I'm drinking too much," she thinks as she scrambles off the bed and goes to make coffee. "It's going to have to stop."

Thank god she has got rid of the man if that is the sort of wet dream she's going to have. His black hands on my white skin. It's all so real and when Rick comes in for a rest in the late-afternoon she follows him into the bedroom. "Oh no," he wheezes, "you know I can't. Not now, in the middle of the day, not with the bar still open. Anyway you said you'd go and help."

She holds herself in angrily, it's always like this with Rick of late. No I can't, I'm too tired, not in the middle of the day, not in the middle of the night, not in the early morning because there is always work to be done. What sort of life is it where you can't have sex. Here she is married to a man – that should mean you get sex. Or what is the point of the deal?

She goes down and helps in the bar, which is busy that evening. Boss is in as usual. And Libby is there sashaying up and helloing, dressed in a new rather outrageous orange dress.

For some reason Libby seems to want to speak confidentially with Rae but Rae is flat out because there is quite a crowd. Eventually Libby catches her in a quiet moment while she is leaning on the bar. Libby sits down opposite her and starts eating peanuts languidly and telling her things that seem at first casual but are also strangely in tune with the events of the day. They include things that any other person would have whispered but when Libby lowers her voice it is only to give her words more force and clarity. Libby always talks as if she is on one of those edgy filmsets where people snap their words with perfect diction, filling up any spaces with their hands. Her topic is the eroticism of black men on white women.

"Of course," says Libby, and everything she says begins with 'of course', as if all of human wisdom has been vouchsafed to her. "Of course it's a great turn on." The pale woman's body, the black skin of the man and the hands that travels that luminous landscape. The huge black man with his enormous black erection looming over the victim-like pale body below him on a white gleaming sheet, and then the black hands slowly travelling the body, with one black hand like a symphony opening and then with both black hands. Libby describes it in voluble succinct detail, and in course of time after the whole erotic experience has been gone through it ends with this great big man entering this thin white space with his hard heavy huge blackness. "Yes yes of course it's a turn on. That's why I don't go to the beach any more. I'm returning my skin to creamy purity," she looks off distantly. Like a virgin in the wind, her Irish hair blowing and the freckles of her face blue as the haze on the hills. "We've been conned by all this stuff about being brown. We need to be as pale as a melon sorbet, we need to return our skin to the feel and colour of apple flesh. We need to get back into our skins, our skins are white, we need to emphasise that whiteness and keep out of the sun, treat it as if it were an enemy." She flutters vaguely at the sky.

Rae is rather disgusted with Libby's erotic descriptions, it sounds like something out of one of Randal's magazines. It is a fly-on-the-wall commentary, an external description all about appearances and nothing about how the woman feels, as if it is all being described so as to rouse male spectators. All that superfluity of fluid is like Randall peering at his awful photos and going on about juices. She replies in a disengaged voice, "But I thought that was all over, I thought you were back with Boss."

"Over!" says Libby with a little trill. "It's all rules and regulations isn't it. I have to look as if I'm with the boat, there are some very unpleasant men around, government men. Suddenly it seems they don't want us here, which is such nonsense. We're the source of half the income on this island but someone is coming round and checking on people, asking where do you live, where are you getting your income from, how can you afford that car….."

"You have a car!"

"As if it's any business of theirs. As if it's any business of anybody. It's all political of course, the Federation is cutting right across the - what's that word for it, when countries have the final say in their own affairs? And Maurice says it's all got out of hand and the Immigration people are a law unto themselves and he won't have it, he's going to make sure that heads roll and soon. But until that happens, I have to be a bit careful. I certainly don't want to be frog-marched on to a plane because of my friends. You know, if it was anyone else they wouldn't bother but that's how to get at a political foe, send in Immigration Officials." She spits the words out like a curse.

"So it's not over?"

Libby does dainty things with her hands. "It's in abeyance. Anyway he's away at a conference. I have other fish to fry but of course he doesn't know that. When he comes back," she flicks back her hair, "I shall be pale from pining for him, thin from fretting for him," she laughs. "Men are such fools. But you should follow my example and stay out of the sun. Look," she reaches out to Rae's face, "it starts around the eyes. Keep indoors, think of the purity of your skin."

"Bugger my purity," says Rae. "I wouldn't give up the pleasure of lying in the sun for the ugly bastard you're going out with, I can tell you."

"He has a huge erection," says Libby doubling over her hand into a fist, "as thick as my arm and as long as this," she indicates a spot several inches above her wrist. "And he stays hard for hours, through orgasm after orgasm. I have to almost beg him to finish but once he's out of me I want him in again; once he lies there exhausted with his hand between my legs gently feeling me as he pants, gently rubbing me as he breathes, I want him back. I can't explain the lust of it. Do you know he's hardly ever flaccid. I'll get the oil and start to massage him and by the time I'm half way down his belly he's erect again and then I get on top of him and he lies there making little um noises while I work away on top and when I get off he's asleep with his erection sitting upright in the bed. I don't know when his poor tool gets any rest because then in the morning there it is again."

"I suppose it must go down sometime," says Rae. "He couldn't meet heads of state or go to the premiers' conference with that sticking out in front all the time."

"Oh I'm not talking about him!" Libby laughs. "I thought you were talking about someone else! The Premier, he's as ordinary an old root as you could ever hope to meet with. No no, as I said, I have other amusements." She lights a cigarette with much blowing out of smoke and laughs, as if the thought of the important personage being in the same league is exquisitely amusing. Suddenly she fishes her compact out, an indication that she is about to go. "Darling," she says applying her bright red flamboyant lipstick, "you should come with me one evening. I'm off to the most delightful little cocktail venue. You're wasting away here, I never see you having any fun. What about it, go out and make a night of it?"

"I'll see," says Rae non-committally.

Libby leaves with a patting of the air, working her sinuous way up the bar. Rae then thinks it might be a good time to go to the Ladies, as no-one seems about to finish their drinks in a hurry. There is a small lavatory attached to the bar but it has been used recently and stinks. She decides to go to the shower block a couple of minutes away.

Outside in the carpark, near the gate, she sees Libby waiting and Rae has nearly reached the toilet block when a car pulls in. Rae assumes she is waiting for Michael's taxi but it is a white car that stops beside her. To her surprise, Max gets out, good god she's not going out with him is she? But he goes round to open the front seat passenger door and she can see there are other people in the car. A man is sitting in the middle of the bench seat at the front and when Libby gets in she first kisses him and then reaches back apparently to shake hands with some people behind. Rae is curious and slips down the side of the toilet block so that she is near the road. The car goes past slowly and at that very minute someone switches the inside light on. A middle-aged white couple, well-heeled by the look of them, sit in the back, one is holding a piece of paper and looking at it. Good clothes and Rae notices for the first time, with rather a surprise, that compared to the couple's understated elegance, Libby's dress is rather tarty, a stagey sort of dress, flounced off the shoulder and flashing cleavage, not at all the soigneed elegance of the other woman. Not really like Libby's usual taste in clothes either. They turn right into the beach road.

Lucas is sitting at the kitchen table looking through the notes he intends to type up. On the way back from interviewing Mr Panday senior, he called on Mr Bobby Panday, Selwyn Panday's businessman uncle. Bobby Panday is known to abhor mixed relationships and was more offended by Selwyn Panday's liaison with a coloured woman than by anything else that the young man ever did. The interview Lucas had with him was short: he had no interest in the young man's death, he had cast him off, he refused to acknowledge there was any relationship between himself and the dead man. The morality on the island was a terrible thing and he intended to stand at the next election, before the whole place went to the dogs. That was all he had to say.

Lucas doesn't have a clear idea yet where he is going but the more he gets to know about the case the better. He now has the pathologist's report to read and also the book Dr Woodrow thinks he might find useful on coroner's courts and forensic medicine. At this point Randall strolls in with some rustling paper bags and for a minute Lucas doesn't register what he is doing. Randall has been shopping and is putting away groceries into bug-proof containers. Lucas stares. "What's that?"

"I have been getting in a few things," says Randall trying to find a tin big enough to put spaghetti in and giving up and putting it in the unused bread bin.

"You are going to cook?" Lucas is astounded.

"Yes," says Randall. "I've got some books out of the library and I thought I would try a bit of cooking. Look," he opens a rather soiled library book. "This is going to be my first triumph. Spaghetti and meatballs." He starts clattering about the kitchen.

Now here's a thing, thinks Lucas. This table is never used from one month's end to the next and I set up my typewriter on it and the next thing Randall is getting domestic. Lucas takes his papers and typewriter off to his bedroom. However the unaccustomed activity in the kitchen draws him inexorably back. “Ah-ah-ah what are you doing?”

“I’m putting in the spaghetti.”

“No man, that water has to be boiling.”

“It is boiling.”

“That water is not boiling, that is just a few bubbles. It must seethe before you put in your spaghetti. Man, I’m thinking you’ve never even boiled water before and here you are making complex cuisine.”

Later when the two of them, after much arguing, have managed to put together possibly the first meal ever produced in that kitchen and Lucas has cleaned up, he sits down in a lounge chair with the coroner’s book. To his surprise and concern, Randall shows no sign of going out. I hope he is not having his friends over to look at vice, thinks Lucas. Randall however has got out a book himself, clearly another library book by its shiny cover so therefore, knowing the local library collection, not pornographic. After a while Lucas looks over and sees that the title of the book is ‘Tropical Fish’.

“What’s Libby up to?” Rae asks Karlo later when she has a moment.

“That woman is poison. Leave her strictly alone. She’ll be on a plane out of here any day now and not a moment too soon.” He looks across at his friend Boss. “She’s ruining that man.”

“She’s hanging around with Max de Troy.”

“Two poisoned chalices to steer clear of.”

“Max came up to me while Lynn and I were at the Beach Hotel today and invited me up to Anthony Hamilton’s house. And then later Libby asked me if I wanted to go out with her for a night on the town. And two minutes later I see her getting in a fancy car with Max.” She furrows her brow.

“And you’re asking me if they’re connected? Well I can’t say. Libby is a great disappointment to me. I used to admire the woman but now I think she’s common trash. And if you want to be seen in that light, by all means start hanging around with her.”

“Oh don’t worry about that. I don’t like her any more. Ever since I heard her trying to shop Lynn to Sergeant de Troy for some immigration thing.”

“Oh lor,” says Karlo. “Did she do that? What a nasty bitch of a woman. We’ve got to get Lynn back on Tom’s boat.”

"Whenever Tom stops drinking."

"The place is falling apart," says Karlo. "Look at us all. This used to be a lovely little bar. Everyone with their own favourite table, everyone coming in as you would into your own lounge room, cheers all round. It's why I've never thought of moving on, it felt like home. And now there are all these bad undercurrents. What's to be done?"

Rae doesn't know. Except, she has in mind a diversion. "Lynn's getting quite good at driving up and down the road to the beaches so we were thinking of going further afield. Everyone says you're the one to give us directions. Apparently there's a really amazing bay at the bottom of the island but I can't quite work out why it's so amazing but everyone says we have to go there."

"Ha," shouts Karlo with laughter. "Yes indeedy. Horseshoe Bay. Well I will not only give you directions, I shall come with you. It's ages since I went down there and it is definitely a place not to be missed. What better time than the present. We will go tomorrow."

It will mean an early start explains Karlo, so the next morning she drags herself up at what seems like the crack of dawn and goes into the kitchen to make coffee. She looks out and sees Lynn trotting up the steps from the marina. God, here is she thinking this is early but clearly Lynn has been up even earlier.

"I've seen Karlo," she says as she bounces in, "he's just having breakfast. He thinks we should leave as soon as possible so as not to be driving in the heat of the day. He thinks it will take us maybe three hours because of going slowly and the roads being bad."

"Three hours!" says Rae. "I didn't know it was so far!"

"Apparently down there the roads are only tracks."

"Well then I'd better drive when the going gets rough."

"Yes I think you'd better," agrees Lynn happily. "And Arthur asked what we were taking for lunch and I didn't know if we had anything in the fridge so he's organising some sandwiches for us. Isn't he nice!"

Yes he is nice. For the first time Rae wonders if Arthur isn't just a little too attentive and if Lynn isn't just a little bit too happy whenever he does something for her. But that is ridiculous, not even Lynn could be that young and silly. Especially as Rae has divined that Jim is also interested and with his aristocratic relations, now there is a sensible connection.

Meanwhile Lynn is bouncing around. A picnic. A picnic, this is fun, and the bug has infected the Frangipani when they get there, a picnic, an outing to far flung regions, half the bar is prepared to come too but what with the paraphernalia - towels, a cooler, books and sunhats and swimwear it is going to require another car or perhaps a fleet of cars and Michael, the huge and phlegmatic taxi driver who has taken the Frangipani as his patch, quickly disabuses everyone. No way is he taking his valuable vehicle down there and what is more Arthur is mad to let his car go to such a place. "Potholes," says Michael, "deep as swimming pools. Runoffs that cut ravines through the road between going and coming back. Corrugation like you've never seen that make your false teeth jangle in your mouth, and ladies now, all I can say is that stiff corsetry is required or breasts is bouncing around and everyone getting black and blue!" His elaborations are enough to dampen the enthusiasm of the bar and so the three of them set off alone.

"All pikers!" says Karlo. "Nothing the matter with the road so long as you take it slowly."

They drive the other way out of town, not towards the Beach Hotel but towards the airport. Cabins dot the coastal plain and gardens are fringed by banana palms. The beaches here are pebble, though that isn't stopping innumerable small boys from swarming between land and sea like amphibians. After a few miles the road turns away from the coast and runs inland. "That's Arrow Bay and the swamp down there," says Karlo pointing.

"I'm going there tomorrow with Arthur and his sister," says Lynn.

Rae looks at her again. Maybe she should talk to her about going about with Arthur so much and how it will start to look.

"They say it's for sale," says Karlo. "One minute I heard they've made it into a bird sanctuary and the next minute they're calling for tenders to put a great resort in there. What sort of a bird sanctuary is it going to be when you let in a whole parcel of cowboys with concrete!"

"So what's in there?" says Rae.

"Nothing's in there. Nothing but birds. And swamp."

"Doesn't sound like much of a place for a resort."

"Well there's a lot of people interested. Including Hamilton senior. Apparently, he's putting up a swag of money and so are others who are planning to go in with him."

"That bastard," says Rae. "That's Rick's sweat and blood he's using. For a bloody swamp."

They now turn off the airport road. Once off the main road, they are soon travelling over what is little more than a pair of ruts. Rae takes over the driving and they move slowly ahead past infrequent cabins through increasingly thick rainforest. "It's impassable in heavy rains," says Karlo. "But various government men come through here the rest of the time and that keeps it open. There's a transmitting station at the far end of the island for the post office and then there's others taking the odd look around, coast guards and excise and what have you. Been someone through recently."

Very recently, they discover, as a tree has fallen across the track and been chainsawed through in the last few hours as evidenced by piles of new sawdust. "Lucky for us. Let's hope another one doesn't go over before we get back!"

After slow progress, almost two hours after they leave the airport road they eventually reach their destination, a beautiful calm inlet with a white shining crescent of sand. The water close to shore is shallow and a limpid aqua blue. Out near the narrow entrance to the inlet the water is deep and dark. "Look at that," cracks Karlo in astonishment, "we plough along for hours without seeing a soul or a sign of civilisation and when we get here it's like a bloody resort, wall to wall with people."

It's an exaggeration. A four wheel drive vehicle with a Cable and Wireless logo is parked under the shade of some trees. Out in the deeper water a yacht is moored. The entire population of the bay, including themselves, amounts to no more than ten but Karlo has been expecting it to be deserted so he laughs in his chuckly ironic way, "Packed to the gunnels," he says.

Two men are sitting under a tree on the beach having a drink. They both wear khaki shorts, khaki shirts, hats and kneesocks. One gets up and waves at them. He is a small dark-haired white man with a protruding bristly chin and pale blue eyes.

"Bloody hell," says Rae. "It's Randall." It is her neighbour with the appalling friends and interests. Although he is always very respectful and polite to her, even admiring, she finds if difficult to talk normally to a man who spends his leisure hours minutely examining photographs of women's genitalia.

She lets Karlo do the introductions. "You'd never guess he lived next door to you," he says to Lynn. "You never see him because they keep his nose pretty well to the grindstone. And who's your offsider?"

"This is Merville. He is a cousin in some degree of Arthur's," says Randall.

Karlo laughs, "Everyone's related. I remember Arthur saying he had a relative in Cable and Wireless."

"We're only related by marriage," drawls Merville.

"I heard that this particular relative can spit amazing distances," continues Karlo. "A world spitting champion, that's not you is it? Oh it is you."

Merville is a laconic youth, tall and well built in his early twenties, and for answer he takes a piece of a date into his mouth and with deliberation shoots it out in a small bullet of saliva. It so happens that it lands near Rae who has wandered away to wave at heads on the deck of the yacht. The sudden plip of something landing at her feet makes her jump, as much as the sudden exclamations of acclaim. She hasn't been listening and for a moment doesn't realise what's happened. She sees everyone looking at the young coloured man and that he is grinning somewhat sheepishly as he wipes his mouth. The penny drops. He has spat at her! How disgusting. That is what you get for mixing with purveyors of pornography and she will go right over there and tell him off for his lack of manners. Quite right my dear, put them in their place, you don't spit at a white lady, if you let them get away with it this time….. It is a long way, could you imagine a man could spit that far and he is standing there rather alarmed as she walks purposefully towards him and my god he is a good looking fellow. She comes right up close to him until she is looking up in his face and she has forgotten already about telling him off, instead she is looking straight at his mouth only a few inches from her own and she thinks he will back off being that close and he doesn't. "So how did you do that?" she wants to know.

Randall cracks a big laugh out of his jaw. "Because he practices all hours of the day and night, that's why. If he'd give as much attention to his studies as he does to spitting, playing his guitar and chasing women, he'd be a technician already."

Rae smiles an enigmatic smile, "I think you should always practice what you're good at," she says.

Yes a handsome womanchaser, she thinks as she turns away. I hope you notice me in my loose shirt and my hair long and blowing free. She adjusts her sarong. Yes they're all pretty light skinned in Arthur's family, she thinks; his hands round my waist would hardly be browner than mine, that's an islander who sits in the shade.

"I'll show you if you like," he has come up behind her.

"OK," she says looking over her shoulder at him.

There follows a pleasant ten minutes expelling bodily fluids with a man the colour of honey wood, putting fragments of date into their mouths and rolling them in balls. He is of course the winner. His cheeks contract as he curls his tongue - he has a tongue long like an anteater and it unrolls with reptilian zest – Phuh. He spits and then recurls it back into his mouth as if he is sucking back prey trapped in its sticky warmth. Like entering a cave, thinks Rae, that mouth. Subterranean. And what would you do in that cave of shining moisture, warm and full of tongue, like an eager dog pant pant pant Shlurp. "I'm really no good at this," she laughs and covers her mouth as she wipes away the dribble.

After ten minutes Randall is ready to go. They still have some rough track to get over before they get to the transmitter. "Might see you on the way back," he says.

Out in the bay the yacht has responded to waves from the shore and a tender is puttering towards them. "It's the Rita. They're coming ashore," says Karlo. "Have you met them?" he asks Lynn. "You may not have; they've been off on a four week charter. They must be about due back in. Maybe they'll take us out to the mouth, save us having to hack through to it."

"What's there?"

"A giant snail."

"Oh yes," says Lynn.

"A giant pink snail."

She looks at him askance. He is teasing her as they all do.

The rubber dingy comes in to shore; it has on board a couple of very brown Americans in swimwear and a deckhand in shorts and a T-shirt. "Hey Rae, hey Karlo," calls the deckhand. "What are you doing here?"

Karlo does introductions. "This is Lynn, this here is Matey."

"I saw you at the bar just before I left," says Matey recognising her and grinning with pleasure. He introduces them to the two charterers.

"I told these young ladies I knew of a secluded beach we could go to, and blow me, if there isn't a cast of thousands," complains Karlo taking off his battered straw hat in mock exasperation.

"Yes, our thoughts, when we saw all of you," laughs the woman charterer.

"We want to go out to the snail," says Karlo to Matey. "You wouldn't like to run us out would you old son?"

"Sure.' He looks at the Americans who say, "No we've been, we'll just walk on the beach." The three pile into the tender with Matey and zip away in a roar and shudder of speed.

"So how goes the charter? You've been away a few weeks," shouts Rae.

"Back tomorrow," Matey calls back. "It's been excellent, they're a real couple of cards those two, laugh a minute. You'd never guess it but they're in their seventies. They used to work for MGM doing musicals and they can sing and play and act their way through practically every movie you've ever heard of. And the stories they tell. The really rude stories! Skip says if they don't write a book about it he's going to! Seems wrong somehow to take wages when it's been such fun. Look at those two saps on board, hard at it."

They all wave to grinning faces on board who look up from scrubbing, "Hoy" they shout but Matey is past them. "Ha Ha," he laughs. "I get out of it for a bit."

"Not hit any reefs I hope," shouts Karlo.

"Hush there, or you can walk back," sings the young man.

Just then there is a shriek from Lynn who has just seen….. A giant pink thing. "What is it, what is that?"

Matey powers the boat round in a circle until it comes in under the foot of a towering structure as high as a two storey house. What can you say? It is a gigantic pink snail at the entrance to a beautiful lagoon in the middle of nowhere.

"But what, how, what on earth is it? How did it get here?"

"It was built for some film and they just left it," says Matey.

"How could they just leave it?"

"Well that's the film world for you apparently."

"The Premier doesn't mind, I think the Government was thinking of having a theme park here, a purple ant and a large aqua beetle. It wouldn't worry them that someone left rubbish in their backyard, so long as they can't themselves personally see it," says Karlo.

"It's amazing!" says Lynn. "Can we walk up to it?"

The path is easy to follow and a few minutes later they come up to the snail. There is nothing inside, it is a facade and Lynn is disappointed, "It should have windows and doors and different rooms and then I'd come and live here," she says.

"You wouldn't want to live in a pink snail," says Rae.

"Yes I would."

"What, all alone out here!"

"Oh but I'm sure friends would come and visit me."

Rae thinks, I hope she doesn't mean Arthur, she's not thinking of setting up in a snail with Arthur. I must speak to her privately about her romantic proclivities.

They never do get to picnic alone on a deserted beach. Naturally on the way back they stop off at the Rita and are invited to lunch. The two charterers come back after their walk and Karlo tells them about Lynn's wish to live in the pink snail.

"Yes," says the man "we've been talking about it. No seriously. Where else in the world can you get to live in a tropical bay as beautiful as this in a pink snail?"

"Of course the snail would be rather big for just the two of us," says the woman, "so we were wondering about turning it into a hotel."

"Have our guests come in by yacht," says the man. "We thought we'd call it Snail Away."

"Red Snails in the Sunset."

"We snailed on the sloop John B….." The boat is soon singing snail songs lustily.

"You know, Matey's got an incredibly good voice," says the woman. "What a pity he's on the run, otherwise I'd take him back to New York and introduce him to an agent."

"What," says the husband, "and have him give up all this? We worked seven days a week for most of our lives to be able to afford holidays like this. And he has it already, all for free."

"Are you on the run?" asks Lynn.

"Nothing exciting," says Matey. He is a young American who is dodging the draft and working his way around the various charter grounds making sure never to touch American soil. He is one of thousands who have abandoned their homes and their careers and are resignedly waiting for their exile to end.

"So how did you take up song writing?" asks Rae of the Americans.

"Well," says the man, "all I ever wanted to do was marry a woman with lots of money and I thought where do I find such a woman? In the movies or on the stage or singing in swanky clubs and making records, that's where. So how do I meet her, obviously I write the songs. Then I met Betty who also wanted to marry a man with lots of money and we teamed up and wrote some hits and the rest is history."

"He married me for my money, and I married him for his. Ooh look at this lobster quiche! George you shouldn't cook us all these rich things, will our waistlines ever return to normal? Matey caught it this morning you know, it's so fresh..... But we had to go ashore while it was being cooked, they scream."

"No they just click."

"That's like screaming to me."

The charterers have no objection to eating it though, along with a bottle of chilled German wine. Karlo, who doesn't care for shellfish but is fond of anything alcoholic, soon starts a story, which the habitués of the Frangipani have all heard before, involving as it does someone very close to his heart. "Her name is Yvonne. Isn't that an amazingly classy name! And this is an amazing story. It could be made into a film. In fact if it was, Yvonne could play herself, she's still got what it takes."

It seems Yvonne left the islands some years before and followed the usual route of dreams to London. However she always intended of coming back one day, with a rich husband in tow. But neither work, nor love nor life ran smoothly and her pursuit of happiness and wealth was constantly shipwrecked by circumstance. Karlo embroiders her trials and tribulations with a wealth of colour.

"And I was thinking this was going to be a romantic comedy!" exclaims Betty after a while.

"Too much real life if you ask me," says Skip. "If it's going to be a film, it needs a lot more laughs."

"But how does it end?" asks Lynn.

"Of course it will end romantically. Because eventually she comes back here and opens a classy bar which does very well. And I'm thinking the ending will have an older man, an older man who's travelled and has a knowledge of the world, who comes along and marries her. Don't you think?"

"No," says Betty. "If you're going to get Cary Grant, you need him right from the start. You can't have him coming in at the end."

"I wasn't thinking of Cary Grant," says Karlo with a sigh. "I was thinking of someone a bit more….."

"Crumpled?" suggests Matey.

Everyone laughs. "What does Yvonne think?"

“Poor deluded woman, she thinks she’s perfectly alright as she is. But you’ll never have a happy ending with an attitude like that!”

Chapter 8

He is expected to set an example of superhuman activity to the rest

Lucas has been frantically busy and had been looking forward to Saturday as a time when he could catch up and get all his material in order before going on duty. The coroner's court will meet in four weeks' time and already his investigations are throwing out new strands that need to be woven into the whole.

He has not as yet managed to contact the deceased man's widow as she has gone to stay with her sister up the islands. However, while ascertaining this from the neighbours, he found that once due regard had been paid to the conventions and all expressions of regret and sorrow dispensed with, the neighbours were willing, no, eager, to tell him many things of a surprising nature. He sighs. More complications, more scandal. Now he will have to regularise the process by taking statements from a great many witnesses - the whole thing is going to be very time consuming.

He sits at the table with his files. In one of them are the photos of the body but he doesn't need to look at those again. His initial reaction to such graphic pictures is to feel confronted at the messiness of it all. If the wretched fellow did commit suicide (and Dr Woodrow has instructed him to keep an open mind on this), it is just such a thing as a man like that would do. Leave people behind to clean up the mess. Though nobody, as Lucas reflects, dies that neatly where police work is involved. Some of them are not to blame. He's known fishermen who have kept their boats as neat as a pin and yet have gone over the side during a storm and there they are, rotting on some beach and not a pretty sight, half eaten and disordered.

Women are tidier. You don't see them drink themselves to death on some vacant ground among the rubbish and with shit in their pants. Women have more dignity. If they are going to destroy themselves they'll do it neatly with poison or put their heads in a gas oven where there is hardly any cleaning up to be done.

However this is the first body he's ever seen where there is a suggestion of foul play. Everyone else seems to find it intensely exciting but to him foul play is even more depressing than suicide. Murder is not like in the novels. The body refuses to stay neatly arranged in the drawing room. It has a riotous habit of spreading for extraordinary distances, blood spurting, smashed brains, little bits here and there. And it means a lot of work. For instance, it certainly makes reading the pathologist's examination a complex and speculative business. There are several comments on the condition of the heart for instance and Lucas needs a few quiet hours to himself so he can read the report again and try and come to some understanding of the issues involved. From what he can gather at first reading, several ribs have been crushed into the heart and yet there is something there that isn't right, some clot that is not the usual result of such injury and that is why Woodrow wants Lucas to investigate the family and the past medical histories of everyone.

He has finished talking to the immediate family. The last member he saw was the mother yesterday and she seemed no more affected by the young man's death than anyone else he has so far interviewed.

She appeared to be a delicate woman. Lucas has spent much of his life going in and out of the houses of female relatives and he knows a delicate woman when he sees one. Usually it means there is a surgical operation in the wind, something that women whisper about to each other. In the meantime such a woman will sit on a sofa and engage in fancy needlework and not have a thing to do about the house.

The ex-Mrs Panday was from Port Sophia originally and came out of that melting pot of races that makes it difficult at a glance to sort out a person's predominate racial characteristics. Certainly she could pass as an Indian but she could also perhaps pass as Spanish. She is now Mrs Bhola and lives in a large plantation-type house down at Cape Cloud. She dresses elegantly in modern clothes and Lucas could not see a trace of any Indian influence in the nice middle-class furnishings of her house. Her husband has some family in England and there were several souvenirs of trips there; clearly they were fairly well off with a good lifestyle. Mrs Bhola sighed when he asked about her son. "Got on the wrong track, in with the wrong crowd and now look what's happened," she complained. "No-one was surprised, not one bit."

"Do you think he committed suicide?"

"Oh no, why should he do such a thing? He probably fell off the cliff by accident."

"How could that happen? Did he have a drinking problem perhaps?"

"Oh yes, he have plenty such problems. Like his father Sonny. Drinking problem, ganja problem, every sort of problem. Fighting. You name it. Drink and fighting both. But he would not have jumped on purpose, I know that."

"The coroner is trying to find out about possible hereditary diseases. Is there anything in your family you can think of?"

"What you mean like warts? My father and uncle had warts on their faces. I've been worried all my life I'd end up with those but not so far touch wood."

"Anything else? Are your father and mother still alive?"

"My father died of complications - he went into hospital for an operation and died of an infection I think. It was a long time ago. My mother is living still but she is bad with arthritis, all her hands are bent over like this, she can barely put on her clothes. That's hereditary, her mother was the same."

"Do you know of any hereditary conditions on Selwyn's father's side?"

"Well," she reflected. "Sonny Panday is an alcoholic and that seems to have passed on to Selwyn."

Lucas took a breath. He didn't like to put propositions to people who might very well be insulted by them. Yet in this instance he knew he had to, even though the interview might be immediately terminated by Mrs Bhola in an outraged fury. "Was Sonny Panday Selwyn's father?"

"Oh yes. Why do you ask?" Mrs Bhola wasn't outraged, only curious.

"I've seen Mr Panday and he mentioned another man you were interested in at the same time, Pierre Bart."

"I'm surprised he's spreading rumours now. I heard he was trying to get money out of Hamilton. I don't know why Hamilton would pay him anything if Selwyn wasn't any kin of his."

"He didn't say that Selwyn was not his son. Quite the opposite. But it came up in conversation and I just wondered."

"Yes I wondered too at the time. But I'm pretty sure that it was Sonny, otherwise I wouldn't have married him. Pierre was still alive then you know".

"Would Pierre have married you, if it had been his child?"

"Oh no, he was married already. But he was a good man, I was very fond of him. It was tragic that he died so young."

"Do you know what he died of?"

"No-one knows. It was just one of those things I suppose."

Lucas started on another tack. "Do you know why Sonny would expect money from Hamilton?"

"Somebody, I forget who, said that there was some other business between Mr Hamilton and Selwyn. I don't know what it was but there was money involved apparently and Sonny reckons he has some share in it. But even if he has no right to it, he will still try and get it. He was always trying to get money out of me, even after I had been married to Harry for years. I never gave any to him. If you give once to Sonny then you become that bottomless treasure chest - he will never take your word for it that the money box is empty. Eventually when he got nothing from me he gave up. But then years later he took up the boy instead, thought he'd get something that way I suppose. I barely recognised him at the funeral, he used to be such a good looking man. Like Selwyn. They both traded on their looks."

Lucas has to type up the notes from that visit but he doesn't have much time because he has to be on duty at 5 pm. The Sergeant is organising all his time and tonight he is required in the Louisaville district to help keep order at a party in the Exhibition Ground. Not his district at all but there is the Sergeant renting him out - that is the sort of thing he has to put up with and he is fairly sure all this activity has something to do with his new duties.

Sergeant de Troy at first laughed at him for being made the coroner's assistant; he thought it a great joke and it reinforced his poor opinion of Lucas. But since then the Sergeant has been told that in a couple of weeks Constable Frankland would be flying down to Port Sophia where he would be spending a few days doing a crash course in forensic medicine.

"How come," said the Sergeant, "that you are getting to go on a nice little holiday like that? When you hardly start in the police force and it have plenty other men whose turn it is for a junket ahead of you."

"These other men," said Lucas, "they didn't put their name forward for coroner's assistant perhaps."

"No and why should they? Extra duties, no extra pay, and dead bodies on top of it all. Only a greenhorn would sign up for such a thing. And now you are getting a nice little trip staying in a hotel no doubt."

"I'm staying at the police barracks. It's going to be hard work....."

"Oh don't give me that," cried the Sergeant savagely. "I hear about all these conferences, everyone having a good time with girls and them, and rum, all you could drink. And all coming home saying they have one set of thing achieved, as if anyone believe a word of it. What are you going to learn there that you can't learn here on the job? Complete waste of time and completely wasted on a junior officer."

The Sergeant, having once become sour about Lucas's new duties, had started wanting to know what he was doing and who he was seeing, demanding in fact that Lucas account for his time even when it was his own. Lucas refused to tell him anything. "All I am doing is for the coroner's eyes and no-one else's," he said and that naturally made things worse. The Sergeant thereafter found a great deal of extra work to engage him in.

And yet here he is with a few precious free hours and instead of quiet where he can concentrate, the whole house seems to be buzzing with activity. It's like a railway station, everyone coming and going. Arthur has a day off and is therefore comatose in his hammock but this does not add to the peace. Instead any number of people arrive whose sole purpose seems to be to try and wake him up - Arthur Arthur wake up. And Arthur will rouse himself just enough to encourage the person before falling back to sleep again the moment their attention gets distracted. There is Daphne for instance who arrived some time ago and tried to wake him in her gentle ineffective way and has now got swooped up into Randall's orbit. And what is Randall doing? At the weekend he is either out on call or lolling about in bed like Arthur. If he has the day off he's usually been out the night before celebrating and as a result doesn't even stir until evening. But here he is today at home and fully dressed wearing his working boots and knee length socks and clomping noisily around in the middle of the day. And, even more disastrous for Lucas's plans for an hour or so of concentration, Randall wants to share the table.

“God Randall, can’t you ever do anything quietly?” Lucas exclaims, because Randall is putting together a fish tank and explaining to all and sundry that there is a lot of money to be made in tropical fish, as he fiddles with spanners and bits of metal and small heavy things which seems to be constantly falling on the floor.

And now here is Karlo - on his way to tell Rae that there is a rumour that Libby has been deported - impelled to stop and break the news to Arthur first. Karlo has such a loud voice that it soon attracts Rae from next door, yes it is thought that Libby has been sent off by plane early this morning, seen with a suitcase accompanied by a man in a dark suit and Boss nowhere to be seen.

Oh no, Lucas thinks as the descriptions continue, now he will never get anything done, more scandal, more rumour - if only he could just have a quiet hour, just one that’s all he asks. And now, after all this, here is Lynn coming in after Karlo has given up on Arthur and here she is trying to rouse him again, Arthur Arthur wake up. The whole world has gone mad.

Arthur can vaguely hear the surrounding voices but he allows them to drift in and out in a comfortable jumble of parrot fish, deportations and typewriter tappings.

“Arthur.” A voice has called him, a voice he knows. It is insistent. “Arthur!” the voice is very close to his left ear and he turns his head, forcing open his eyes. Lynn has hold of the edge of his hammock and is looking into his face, “You’re not even ready!” she says.

Ready for what, click click, yes there is something. “Remind me Songbird,” he says.

“We’re going to the swamp. And there is a message from your sister through Daphne, look. She’s been trying to wake you. She says Sheila…..”

“She’s going with Michael in the taxi to the entrance and she’ll meet you there at 3,” says Daphne coming over.

“At 3 sharp,” Lynn leans provocatively forward while lifting the edge of the hammock but he hangs on Ahh and comes back over the edge at her, grabbing her round the waist, trying to pull her into the hammock. She shrieks and resists and suddenly in opening his eyes he sees the faces of everyone turning to look with interest. He quickly lets go. Yes, he mustn’t do things like that, it will look as if..... Damn, it's alright with Jim or Matey but no, he mustn't wrestle with Lynn or else it will look as if.....

"OK," he says raising himself and putting his feet on the floor.

"Yes," says Daphne, "and there's a second part to the message. You have to pick up Erica".

"Oh no!" he tips back into the hammock, clutching his head and wails, "not Erica. Oh no no no!" It was to have been a pleasant little trip to the swamp and now it is going to be a nightmare.

"Who's Erica?" asks Lynn.

"She's a friend of Sheila's," says Daphne. "She's rather big."

"An elephant," says Arthur in disgust.

"It means I have to stay behind," says Daphne.

"Oh no! You go instead of me," cries Lynn.

"Better still, go instead of me!" says Arthur.

"I've been before. I'm quite happy to stay here." Daphne goes over to help Randall - it seems she has become rather interested in fish.

"What are you dressed in, Songbird? Have you got any long pants to wear? I'd wear them if I were you, there are a million insects out there, and a long sleeved shirt, have you got a long sleeved shirt?"

"I'll lend you some," says Rae.

As they go next door Lynn says to Rae, "Do you think Libby has really been deported?"

"I don't know, I would have thought she'd be too clever. If you ask me she's ducked off somewhere, been given a tip-off by her friendly Premier and gone off to Barbados for an elegant week or so at the island's expense. Possibly Boss has gone with her to lend the whole thing credibility."

"Yes, how can they deport her? If she was on Boss's boat?"

"They could've been following her, found her not on the Boss's boat in the middle of the night. And then it's straight to the airport and off. That's what they do, no appeals, not like in some countries. It's over before you know it's coming. And look, you know, you've got to get back on a boat or that could happen to you too. And another thing, you mustn't get too friendly with islanders. These things can have unforeseen consequences. You understand what I mean?"

Lynn says yes but she doesn't. She knows there is a problem about not being on a boat and that is somehow complicated by knowing important islanders. However, she doesn't know any important people. It never enters her head that it is a warning about being seen to get too fond of Arthur.

At quarter to 3, happy in her innocence, she gets in the car with Arthur. She chats to him as they go along about the pink snail, "They've been scolding me for liking it," she complains. "Everyone tells me it's an eyesore."

"But you'd like to live in it with so many children you don't know what to do."

"I'd know what to do," she says. "They could all slide down the bank and jump in the water, like water babies. And I wouldn't whip them all soundly or anything, I'd just let them go to bed when they felt like it."

"That sounds like a nice childhood," he smiles.

"Did you have a nice childhood?" she asks.

"Oh yes, most of it," he says. "Though we did live in a bit of a shoe. How about you?"

"Well," she says, "my parents were always quietly at war. But I spent all my holidays at my grandmother's. That was lovely. Then my grandmother died, about 5 years ago, and after that it was awful. We all went to live in England and my parents split up and I was sent to boarding school. But I suppose by the time you're a teenager you're not a child any more and you just have to bear your grief and get on with it."

"Yes," he says sombrely. At that moment they drive up beside a typical small cabin. "Here we are," he says. "She won't be ready, not even partly ready. We'll have to wait. And wait."

He sounds his horn and an arm waves through the window. "Just coming now," carols a voice. Several older men detach themselves from chairs and wander over, "How's your auntie?" And general gossip. After about half an hour a vision emerges from the house and Lynn feels rather than hears Arthur's response, a general slump of his body and an oomph of distress. For her own part Lynn is amazed, "I thought we were going sloshing about in a swamp!"

"But who's going to tell her?" mutters Arthur. "Erica. Hello."

Erica is a tall statuesque young woman with dark skin and a classic hourglass figure like a viola - no, more ample, like a cello. She seems strapped into place by the tightest binding because she is barely making any progress towards them, constricted as she is by a straining gleaming orange and yellow satin sheath and substantial gold-coloured high heeled shoes. From under a sort of turban of red and gold silk a mass of black curly hair is piled in frizzy plenitude. Clearly Erica is amusing, you can see it in the reaction of the old men who fall back chuckling as she shrieks and halloes her way towards the car. "Arthur Arthur hello, hello hello, who's this, oh girl could you," as Lynn sees that it is intended that Erica ride in the front. "Oh Arthur! This the car, surely not! I would have thought Sheila give you a nicer car. You take it back and get something else, you make her get you something elegant. This thing go around without a roof and fuzz up your head. It have a roof! Oh be a doll and close this thing." She turns to Lynn, "Where from, England? Australia! That's nice and is Arthur showing you around the island? Arthur, you must let me know when you're taking the visitors around. He really doesn't know the places you know. Did he take you to the Sapphire Room, to the Blue Lagoon, but I'm sure you went to the Lotus Room? Well at least he took you there. Yes man, I'm feeling good. This is nice. We can go. I expect Sheila will be late, she's always late so don't rush. Yes," she settles herself. "This is good now. HULLLOOO MR RICHARDS. That's Mr Richards. When I tell you that man can drink, he's an alcoholic, he'll be dead before you know it. His liver must be cured by now. Do you see how pale he looks? He can hardly walk you know but he's down to get his bottle of rum in the parlour every day. Ah, you know it is the white rum. I don't think you get so bad on the red rum. It still got some goodness but the white rum is pure poison. Nothing but alcohol. He doesn't eat a thing. Nobody do see him eating. You see how he's thin and magga. Now that is the sign of a true alcoholic, when they don't eat."

"I thought it was the sign of a model," says Arthur.

"HOOOHOOOHOOO I'll tell Sheila you said that. But she eats, course she does, I've seen her eat. And I eat," she turns to him with her broad white teeth. "I eat anything and everything but then I'm not a model, too big in the bust and the hips." She turns to Lynn, "It's the fault of that skinny English girl, Twiggy, otherwise big women would be getting rich and famous too. But then," she turns back to Arthur, "imagine this white man who living along the Beach approach me, offering me money to model. So I ask him what he want me to model. I thought it might be leisure wear or gowns. You know, I could really see myself walking up and down in these gowns, looking nice and sharp, but you know all this is stupidness and this man want me for a photo or painting I don't remember which one it is but with no clothes! Naked as a jay bird, this must be a mad man. Well I give it to him good. Well my voice got so loud that everyone could hear how I fix him up. So what do you think happen? What do you think happen then?"

"What?"

"Well let me tell you the story. Mary-Jane did it. Mary-Jane model for a white man and got $500."

"Five hundred local?"

"Yes local, what you think she would get? For five hundred US I would do it myself!"

"Still seems like a fair amount of money."

"Naked," she chews the word disgustedly, "naked like a jaybird. Yes I suppose that's the money they get for being in the nude but I know I wouldn't do that for all the tea in China."

"You just said you'd do it for five hundred US."

"Yes, but you know they'll never pay that!"

Arthur wonders, as they drive, why Sheila has chosen to impose Erica on him. Surely this huge vivacious feast in the front seat is not her idea of an ideal companion for a country outing. He suddenly remembers the serried ranks of faces turned to look when he put his arms round the kid's waist a while ago. Yes, his sister would have turned to look too and he knows she would have disapproved. The slight pause when she discovered that Lynn was coming was enough. Now however there is no danger of anything untoward happening, Erica has taken centre stage. Arthur glances in the mirror and there is Lynn drinking her in with delight; what a funny kid she is.

Erica is continuing at full throttle, "And you know Mary-Jane all of a sudden have a set of money. Think about it, no-one knows how that coming by but all of a sudden she could buy this and buy that. Imagine, she's starting driving lessons. I don't know what she going to drive, she must be going to drive fowls because I don't know where this car for her to drive coming from. But you know she have some old sweet man somewhere and you know that scandal bound to come out soon."

Erica is an uncomfortable passenger due to her habit of constantly throwing her arms around and lurching to and fro from Arthur to Lynn as she feels the thrust of her narrative demands. As she has long arms, long hair and as her long legs are thrust sideways because of her high heels, Arthur finds he is constantly coming into contact with some bit of her as he reaches for the gears. Damn Sheila. But Erica is entertainment for the kid who, after fifteen minutes of lively speculation on the antics of his family, is laughing uproariously. But Arthur's laughter is not unsullied; he knows how difficult Erica is to cope with in other moods. He turns off the airport road.

"Arthur" she shrieks, "where the hell you going? You taking the wrong road, what you come down here, good god, where in heaven's name we going?"

"To the swamp. Didn't Sheila tell you?"

"She told me we were going to look at some land, she never told me about this old dirt road, a set of dust all over me. And why you stopping now? Look at the awful place."

"Haven't you ever been here before? I thought you said you knew all the attractions on the island. This is where everyone comes to watch the ibis."

"You joking. All my good clothes and you bringing me in a place like this. Don't tell me stupid tourists does dress up and come here to see these birds. I think you have this whole place wrong. This place look too creepy for me. Look, Sheila not here, let us get out of this damn place, I think you have the direction wrong. Let us go back straight where we come from and find out where we really supposed to be."

It is true that despite the fact it is now nearly four o'clock there is no sign of the others. "They're late," he says. "You said yourself Sheila would be late."

"Let us go back and wait for them on the road. This is no place for a lady like me. What happen, you out of you head bringing me here!"

Arthur obediently sets the car in motion again. "And where is this land, surely not in there, I'm not climbing in there."

"No, we're going in boats to see it," says Arthur

"Oh here they come," says Lynn and Arthur stops.

"Boats," shrieks Erica as Michael's taxi lurches passed them through the ruts. Arthur sets the car into reverse and follows the taxi back to the parking area as Erica clings on to the windscreen and her hair and berates him about his manner of driving.

In the parking area there is a general melding of parties and Erica is too busy for a while greeting Sheila. While Erica's shrieky voice is still employed in admiration and exaggerated arm-waving, Arthur leads the way down a path towards the water. A boy of about 12 is lounging near a line of narrow flat-bottomed punts and Arthur brings out a handful of dollar bills to pay him. "Better hop in," he says to Lynn, "otherwise the way Erica takes up space you'll be swimming beside us."

"I don't think Erica will be very comfortable," says Lynn doubtfully looking at the rather dilapidated boat.

"No I don't think she will," says Arthur dryly. "But then comfort has never been Erica's main concern."

Lynn clambers up to the end of the boat and sits down. In the shirt and the over-long pants she's borrowed from Rae she looks like a young fair-haired boy, no older than the youth collecting the money. She looks around her ready to be pleased. "Where are they now?" sighs Arthur. "Look it's after 4. If she's to look at this island….." He stands fiddling with the pole. Now Lynn is on board he wants to be off.

It isn't easy for their friends, going out for the day with a top fashion model. Aunt Marion doesn't care what she looks like and is pottering down the path, clutching a cushion, a rug and a large handbag. Dale is slightly more formal, in a fancy open-necked shirt. What follows is the spectacle - the two young women advancing on the boats, with Erica coming gingerly in her high heels. She shrieks with dismay when she sees what they are coming to. "You never told me we going in these old boats. Sheila don't tell me we going in these things!"

Sheila is actually dressed quite sensibly by comparison; she has on small heeled canvas boots, brown hot pants and a yellow shirt and a large floppy white straw hat.

"Well how else did you think we were going to get to an island," says Sheila, while looking at the boats with equal disgust.

"I thought you could have organised something better than this," says Erica clearly scandalised that someone so rich as Sheila should be getting into something so humble as an old punt.

"This is all there is, apparently," says Sheila and smiles ruefully.

They are taking two punts; Arthur will pole one and Dale the other. Erica is accommodated in Arthur and Lynn's boat with great difficulty and ends perched in the middle of the boat, her legs folded under her and clinging to the sides. "Are you all comfortable?" cries Dale.

Sheila laughs, "Oh sure," and leans back on the ample form of her aunt who herself is leaning back against her cushion.

"Yes we're comfortable," says Aunt Marion beaming and indeed they do look quite comfortable and Dale poles them off.

"Let me lie back like that," says Erica "Oh lord, we should have a cushion." She looks round to the back of the punt where Lynn is sitting, her arms round her knees. "You know, I should sit back there," she says trying to move.

"Whoooah," says Arthur. "For god's sake you'll upset us into the water."

"I want to go back there," says Erica her voice rising.

"Maybe I could creep forward and you could creep back," says Lynn, ever willing to accommodate other people. But they have already set off and the wobbly rocking of the boat has alarmed Erica who has now angrily resigned herself to sitting where she is, a martyr to her friend's whims.

"Oh Jesus," cries Erica, "be careful," as one of the polings sends drops of swamp water in her direction and rocks them from side to side. She has a white-knuckled hold on both sides of the boat and her high heels are digging into one side. "Why doesn't she take her shoes off?" thinks Arthur exasperated. Sheila's stupid unpractical friends!

Lynn leans forward from her seat in the prow of the punt to soothe her. "I think it's quite shallow," she says. "I bet it's so shallow that we could wade if we tipped over."

"Tip over," Erica's voice goes up yet another notch. "He will be a dead man if this boat tip over. And I ain't walking in no swamp in my good dress!" Lynn doesn't know what to say; she clearly hasn't thought of it in that way and Arthur laughs.

"You better watch it there," Erica's voice is shrill as the boat rocks. "Be careful with what you doing there. I really don't want to get this nasty muck all over my good clothes."

"You've both got no confidence in me," he says as Erica sits looking at him with a jaw-clenched scowl. "I'm not going to capsize the boat, I've done this a hundred times." And it's true, this is one of his favourite places. He follows the line of ropes through the black and rather oily forest of mangroves and suddenly they are through into the Glades.

"Oh," cries Lynn in delight, turning round and kneeling to Erica's alarm. "Oh it's so beautiful!"

To Arthur it is best in the early morning light, like opal, like a delicate pool of precious stone. Now it is late afternoon and the sun is slanting on the water turning it a dense green jade and they poll beside guiding ropelines across this parkland of water, across a wide lagoon, and Arthur thinks, "What a strange boat I row!" There at the prow is a slight pixie figure with curly pale hair looking out entranced over this fairy scene and there amidships a garish satyr who is clutching the sides and asking how much further is it. He polls on in silence and there is no sound but the birds, the buzz of insects and an occasional laugh from the boat in front. He loves this place, not so much now because in an hour the place will be alive with traffic; it is a popular spot especially with lovers. But in the early morning, when in popular parlance there is nothing to see, that is the time he loves to come. To sit quietly either on the island or marooned in a punt in the shade of the mangrove and to watch the rich teeming life of the coastal wetland is one of his greatest pleasures. He rhythmically dips and pulls his pole, gently sending the punt gliding across a timeless, flat, becalmed world of green with Erica going "For heaven's sake, for heaven's sake," at every squeak and break of slow progress. But Arthur gradually falls into a dream, and Lynn too is dreaming, of going on and on forever through glades ever more lovely and remote.

Eventually however, after forty minutes during which Erica constantly consults her watch and sighs and looks tragic, they approach the mouth of the wetlands where a sweep of reef has kept the waters calmly sleeping for aeons. This reef, beyond which they can hear the waves gushing, is the barrier between the great outside world of ocean with its winds and waves and currents and this enclosed inside world where, amongst the sylvan parkland of mangroves, the birds come to roost.

Most of the reef has become, through the force of storms and other geological pressures, a long thin island where palm trees have taken root. It is now proposed by the government that a resort should be developed on the island with, on its seaward side, the ocean and a strip of beach, and on the landward side the wonderful evening view of birds coming into roost.

The island is already a popular picnic spot. Arthur follows the partly submerged bottles and waving handkerchiefs of paper that guide the punts toward a flat place for docking. He ties up next to Dale's boat and Lynn leaps ashore. She holds out her hand to Erica who is, however, reluctant to move while any part of the boat is still rocking and is helped ashore with some difficulty. Nor is her humour enhanced by discovering that she now has to walk in loose sand. "Sheila!" she screams. Still wearing her high-heeled shoes, she scrabbles with difficulty, backside stuck out, up the small rise onto the backbone of the island where the others are now standing. "You never told me you were getting me into this mess," she says indignantly.

Sheila looks surprised; she herself has weathered the journey quite well even though she looks as outlandishly out-of-place as Erica. "But I said we were going on an outing to look at some land. Land is land. You have to walk around on it to see it."

"Land is land," cries Erica. "So why this nasty swampy place you bringing me to? And where is this grand land you going to buy?"

"Here," says Sheila, pointing around her.

"Oh my god," moans Erica, "you have to be mad! What happen, you fall in your cradle when you were small? This is the rubbish you want to buy, a bit of sand down the creek and all this swamp? You definitely have a hole in your head."

Dale says, "No this is it. But there's a consortium that has put in a bid and they're likely to be successful if the Premier can persuade the Parliament to let the deal go through. And who's going to oppose it with the number of jobs it's likely to offer?"

"So what are the plans of this consortium?" asks Sheila.

"Well, a causeway with a road along the coastline here - that'll be a major exercise with building workers, quarries, truck drivers. Then once the road is in, they're planning a fair sized hotel with up to a hundred bedrooms. They have some professors jumping up and down because they say it will disrupt the birds and all the birds will go away but as I understand it there have been all sorts of sweeteners handed out to the politicians so that they won't listen to any of that."

"A hundred bedrooms!" cries Erica. "You mean on this little piece of sand?"

"Well you expand it," says Dale spreading his arms. "Drive in piles, spread it out that way a bit," he indicates the swamp. "Rooms above the water, the tourists love that."

"Well I think you all mad. This whole place is an insect jungle and anyone could get sick with diseases here." She starts slapping herself.

"People have looked into that. They say it's nothing that a good spray everywhere won't fix," says Dale. "You give the swamp a spray with DDT and that takes care of the insect problem. Then the guests could sit on a terrace with drinks in their hands and watch the birds in peace. So what do you think?" he turns to Sheila. "I've put in a counter bid for you. You could take it away from them with all your money. You'd like that with some of the names involved."

"I'm not paying bribes to the likes of our Premier."

"Probably won't need to. In fact, I wouldn't be surprised if the present consortium can't fulfil its promises. So much money is finding itself into certain people's pockets right now that I wonder how some of the players are going to come up with the final capital. Big on ideas but shaky financially."

"I don't know," she muses and walks up and down. "What do you think Arthur?"

Arthur is seated underneath a coconut palm looking back towards the swamp. He is depressed. All he can see is that if this consortium falls through there'll be some other group wild with greed - if not next year, then the year after or in ten years and they won't rest until they've buried the whole place in concrete and killed all the insects and birds and turned it over to fat complaining tourists who'd rather be at home anyway. He turns to look at his sister, "I think you should buy it and then leave it as it is."

Sheila clicks her tongue at him and then laughs. "So you are not thinking of me turning it into a money-making venture for my old age then? Well you're a dead loss. But listen Dale, why do they need a great expensive road along there? We put in a jetty and bring people over from the town by fast motorboat. And we'll just have a bar and restaurant here. People wouldn't want to stay here anyway, when there are much better beaches round the other side. No, it's somewhere that people would want to visit once, sit where Arthur is sitting on a wooden balcony with a few creepers, some flowers, the evening fades and they drink in this lovely scene, then they have their dinner and we ferry them home."

Dale shrugs, "The government's not popular at all at all and they want to go into the next election promising jobs. The way you describe it there's nothing in it for them."

"Yes, only because they're a hopeless crowd who don't know how to market paradise. What about tourist attractions? How many people come here to the swamp now? Maybe six punts in an evening. And why? Because people have to drive round, punt for nearly an hour, sit in their boats and watch the birds come in, then punt back trying to find their way in the dark. And how many would come if they could get on a boat in the main harbour and watch in comfort? Dozens. Hundreds. Come to our island for the beaches, the blue sea and the birds. Big picture of an ibis on all the promotional material. An American goes into a travel agent in Cincinatti saying, 'I don't know what the name of the goddam island is but it's the one where you go to see the birds.' The government is unpopular because they're all in business for themselves and getting the dollar bill in their own pockets. What we need on this island are some people with vision."

Erica cuts in at this point. "God have mercy, this is enough to give someone a heart strain, what are we staying here for?" she shrieks over the top of Sheila's speech. And then in disbelief, "Don't tell me you really waiting on these birds to come here?" The way she says it makes the ibis sound like unwelcome intruders with dangerous tendencies.

That's just how they'll turn out, thinks Arthur. Sitting here on a terrace for a while with a drink the tourists will turn to each other, "Have we had enough of These Birds yet, Wilma?" Up they'll get, turn their back and go thankfully into dinner.

He slowly follows the others back to the punts. What a future he foresees, comprising nothing but camera-driven watchers, all impatient for the perfect light and the right focus and then, once it's on film, "Come on, what are we hanging around for?" The tourist has seen it, click, and on to the next thing.

"Let me come in your boat," says Erica to Dale. "That Arthur is too slow for me." Somehow she is accommodated and they can hear her scream, "Look at these things crawling all over the ropes!"

"They're just snails," says Dale.

Pink snails, thinks Arthur as he stops the punt in the centre of an expanse of water. The sun is now behind the western rim of the mountains and everything has turned a pale rose-petal hue streaked with red - the water is like blood leaking and the sky is green verging on blue in a soft and grainy film. The trees that dot the water between the swamp and the reef are now the targets for a seeping chattering mass of white and red birds. Scarlet ibis, as red as the sky, as blood red as the water, are swooping in from their prawn banks. Like apples drawn by a child they clutter the branches, red red red. And scissor birds, white like dabs of paint, are fighting for space in their own separate trees. Fluttering like drifts of confetti they come in by their thousands. White and red among the green of trees and sky. With light fading rapidly, the drifts attach to branches like breath caught and held until there are only fingers of black with their settling burdens against the pearly grey water and the curtain of night pulls down its veil.

Awakening from a dream they notice that Dale's boat is now out of sight. "We'd better go," says Arthur.

Lynn sighs. "I never saw anything so lovely."

"They'll spoil it."

"It may never happen."

"If there's a dollar to be made, they won't be able to help themselves." He punts slowly. "It's the Garden of Eden. But the snake is offering jobs and get rich quick for some politicians. What can you expect?"

"But maybe it will be a change for the best. Everyone will come over the other way to the island to see the birds and you can still come here in this boat and be all alone."

"I don't see why they can't leave it as it is, if it's perfect already."

"Nothing's perfect for ever," says Lynn.

Arthur thinks about that. "I never picked you for a pessimist," he says.

Pauses float between their words as they rock gently forward along the barely visible rope pathway. "I just meant, everything can change," she said. "You can be happy as can be and then someone dies, or someone says you have to leave, and suddenly you're far away from what you love. What I mean is, even if they left it exactly as it is, you might change. You might go off to New York or England and live the rest of your life somewhere else."

There is silence for a while. Then Lynn slaps herself and rummages in her bag. Arthur hears the soft hiss of spray.

"Mosquitoes bothering you?"

"They've started whining round my ear. You want some of this?"

"No I'm alright, they don't like me."

"You're lucky."

"No. It's just how I'm made, not luck."

"If it was me I would think it was luck. I often see people who seem to be lucky and yet they never seem to see it themselves. It seems wasted on them. I think I'd like to be someone else."

"Good god, why?"

"So I could be lucky. I could be Rae for instance, she seems lucky to me. She's got a nice house beside the bay. And she always seems very sure of herself, never at a loss for what to say. I'd love to be confident like that. And she's got Rick. He seems nice, though I don't see him at the house very often because he's always working. I think that would be a nice life, if you had a nice house and a nice man on a tropical island. But she doesn't seem to think she's lucky at all." She sighs. Arthur continues to raise and lower the pole into the mud and says nothing. "If you had the chance to be someone else, who would you be?"

"I'd be the Invisible Man."

"No. Who would you like to be really?"

"It was a sort of serious answer. I'd just like to be who I am but left alone to live my life."

"Is it your sister? She wants you to have a better life I expect."

"I have a life that's just fine. She wants me to go to New York and make myself useful, go to college and study business. She wants me to help her run her empires. My sister is going to be a very rich business woman when she gives up modelling and turns her whole mind to it. But I want to stay where I don't have to be useful. Nature intended me to be ornamental," and he laughs.

"But surely you are useful, at the Frangipani for instance."

"I don't have to be if I don't want to be though. 'Rick,' I can say, 'I'm taking all of Saturday off. First I am going to the swamp with my sister and then I am going to the party at the Fair.' And you see, he can't stop me, I don't even feel guilty. But Sheila, if it wasn't convenient, would raise her eyebrows just a fraction. And there would be just the tiniest pause before she says, 'Oh. Really. You're taking the day off.' In a flat sort of tone. As if, You are going to leave all this work and go to a party! And then how could I go? That's what I mean."

She understands that. There are many subtle and uncomfortable aspects to families.

There is no sound but the loud chirp of the swamp gathering momentum for a while as he polls gently between the pale guide ropes. "How about you Songbird?" He stops polling for a moment, looking round for the moon which should be rising soon. "Apart from Rae, what other person would you want to be and what land would you dream of?"

"I want to be a fair maiden who lived long ago when things were quite quite different," she says. "In an ancient land where they used the old forms of speech like 'thou' and 'thee'. I want a knight to ride up to me on a glistening stallion and hand me the red banner of his undying devotion. To bend his knee and say 'Thou art my one true love.'" She suddenly lets off a peal of merry laughter at herself.

Ahead, out of the gloaming, Sheila calls out, “What are you two doing back there?”

They lower their voices. “But this knight, you’d have to know him wouldn’t you? You couldn’t just have anyone riding up and making declarations. How do you know you would like him?” questions Arthur.

“Yes I suppose. But sometimes you find that you do like someone, just like that.”

“Yes but….. I’m not sure they all turn out to be knights in shining armour. Some of them just turn out quite ordinary like you and me.”

“Yes, but even ordinary people can be quite romantic,” she says. “I was friends with a boy in Australia. Before I left for England he gave me this ring; it’s got my initials twined together, LTM. You can’t see, it’s too dark. Anyway he told me it stood for Lovest Thou Me. He said I wouldn’t get anywhere with the English because they only shook hands and were very cold and reserved. But one day I would meet a Frenchman like Maurice Chevalier or someone and he would kiss my hand and see the ring and ask me what the letters stood for. And then I could say, Lovest Thou Me. And that’s how I’d find my knight at last.” Again she laughs her merry laugh and Arthur poles on, a boat full of slow happiness and something in the dark embroiders snail trails across their eyes so that they can barely see.

In the bar things are not happy. In fact there is an emergency though you wouldn’t know it from the quiet attitude of Rick. Leonard the busboy, who is due on that evening, has had an accident and Clive who was supposed to have gone at 4 has stayed till 7 pm but he has to be at a family party at 7.30, “Sorry Rick, I’m a dead man if I don’t turn up.”

Rick is sitting with his arms heavily on his legs looking at Rae. She is fidgeting. She has taken up smoking again he notices; it is a pose, she is picking up a lot of those sort of affectations. She has a packet in her hand and is playing around with an unlit one in her fingers. “Why don’t you ring Lawrence?”

“How can I ask Lawrence to do a busboy’s duties?”

“Well you do the busboy work and let Lawrence be a barman.” She can’t see the problem, it’s all words.

He sighs and looks away. He feels bad about the way Lawrence was put off, the boss insisted and so Lawrence was out of a job for no reason. “Lawrence is working at the Blue Lagoon,” he says.

“Yes but only casual. A day here, a day there. They’ll be quiet tonight. I bet he won’t be on; you should ring him.”

He doesn’t want to ring Lawrence. “Come on Rae,” he says. “If you just stay till we’ve done with dinners; you know there won’t be much tonight with everyone going to the party; there’ll hardly be a soul in the place after 10.”

“Yes but the party finishes at 12, everyone has to be out by 12. If I stay till 10 then get ready and go I’ll only be there for an hour and it will be over.” The logic of this position is crystal clear to Rae. All her friends are going to this party, it is going to be a great night out and it is going to finish early because of the stupid electricity thing. Who knows, presumably everyone will go on elsewhere but the thing is, everyone drinks together and goes out together but this is a PARTY. “I’ll come back as soon as it’s over. Lots will probably come back; it will be busy then. There’ll be hardly anyone here beforehand, everyone’s going over there early. Oscar’s got buckets full of drink and everything, it’s a real party. I don’t want to miss it. Look I was there when they were planning it. Come on Rick, ring Lawrence.”

He still sits heavily with his hands on his knees while she still stands fidgeting and playing with a cigarette. They look at each other, they look away. “I know what’s going on,” he says.

“What?” Rae spins as if stung. “What? What do you mean, what’s going on?”

His face is dour, he looks at the table then straight at her and says nothing.

“What do you mean by that? Nothing’s going on. What do you mean?”

He is still looking at her, sitting there without moving, while she fidgets furiously about like a mad thing. Then he says expressionlessly, “Go to your bloody party if that’s so much more important to you.”

She stands glaring at him and alternately picking at her nails, the cigarette still unsmoked between her fingers. There is no-one much in the bar, just a few at tables over by the water, subdued talk, occasional laughter. She feels inflamed, as if someone has stirred a pot and brought the dregs and solids to the top. “Well then,” she says angrily, “I will go. If you’re going to be nasty and suspicious. Why should I stay here, there's never any fun here. You're no fun I can tell you. And another thing….."

He gets up at last and moves away behind the bar.

"All the work I do for a few dollars here and a few dollars there….." she pursues him. "I'm just a bloody attachment, dredged up when you need something doing for free. Oh well she can work for nothing, she's only the bloody wife. Well I'm bloody fed up with it," the words are spilling out of her with venom and spleen. He ignores her. "I don't know what you think is going on but I'll bloody tell you, there's nothing bloody going on between us any more. You totally ignore me. For all the good you are, I might as well be on the biggest desert on the moon….." she waves her arms in anger.

"Well go then," he says.

"Yes go, go. Yes I'll go," she sticks the unlit fag in her mouth. "I'm going alright, you can bet on that. I'll be off to somewhere where there's some life."

"Well piss off then," says Rick disgustedly.

Her mouth is narrowed and she is looking around for more invective to throw at him and just at that moment Arthur wanders in. "Sorry," he says casually. "I'm locked out. Lucas must be having one of his anti-crime days and has locked all the doors." He feels in the shelf behind the till and comes up with a key.

"Leonard's broken his toe," says Rae gnawing on a fingernail and not looking at him.

Arthur makes a face of concern, "Poor Leonard, how did that happen?"

Rae makes a gesture of impatience, what does it matter about Leonard? His toe is his own concern; what is her concern is the effect it is suddenly having. "I'm going," she says suddenly, "that's it." She walks out deliberately lighting her cigarette at the entrance and goes on without looking back.

Rick's face is purple with rage. He slumps on the bar and bangs his fist, "Jee-sus."

"What?" says Arthur. "Where's Clive?"

"He had to go to his parent's silver wedding," groans Rick. "And Rae is going to this party. I can't do it on my own, it's bad enough with just the two of us."

"I'll stay," says Arthur.

"No no, I didn't mean….. You shouldn't have come in and seen all this. You go on, I know you're going to the party too."

"I can go later," he says. "It's going till midnight." He puts the key back behind the till and starts collecting glasses. Rick feels intense relief out of all proportion to the actual cause. It isn't likely to be that busy but Rae's desertion feels like a cold knife in his stomach. Although he knows things have been rocky, he always thought that if he asked her to stay she would; if he was in difficulties she would give up whatever else she had on to help him out. What you do for your friends, for your family, what Arthur does so effortlessly with so little fuss. It is clear to him now that Rae will sacrifice nothing for him. If he has any plans for getting out of this hell-hole and making it worthwhile….. She'll shop me to save herself, the cow. He can't put words to the feelings that churn in his chest and make him feel so tight and constricted. He can hardly breathe.

Arthur comes back with his hands full and looks at him. "You're over-doing it boss," he says. "If I were you I'd pull out from under Hamilton senior, let him sink on his backside, he's only going to sell the place anyway. You look terrible."

"I'll pull out all right," says Rick, "just as soon….." Just as soon as I can be sure of a way with the most aggravation. He has had in mind a plan but as he sits there and Arthur flits around cleaning up he realises suddenly it is a small and paltry plan. Now he has a bigger plan, one that will settle all the debts in the world.

There is no official opening time for Oscar's party. Probably from close of business but who knows or cares? The main thing that exercises the minds of the party goers is not the opening time which is a vague amorphous thing, but the closing time which is midnight. "At midnight," the Island Fair organisers have said, "the electricity will be turned off." Oscar has had a hard enough job persuading them to even allow him to go that long so the password is Don't-muck-around. Let's get into it early. All this Rae can gather from the noise level when she arrives and by the fact that Jim, who is behind the bar, hazily waves an arm at her, says "Ah Rae" and falls over.

"Bloody hell," thinks Rae looking around, "the place is packed and I spent all that time arguing with Rick, hours of partying wasted."

Although she is quite prepared to leave Rick in the lurch in their own bar, she is a good sort when it comes to parties and she starts directing punch into glasses with accuracy and speed. "Hello," says Oscar wandering over, "what happened to my right hand man?"

"He's outside spewing," says Rae.

"Good man," says Oscar approvingly. "Just what a Roman would do. I'd avoid the bong that's going round too, it's lethal."

Rae can't see a bong, all she can see is a mass of undifferentiated humanity of all colours and states of inebriation, dancing with loose hipped bravado to a wild band so out of it they are barely able to stand. Eventually the earth's gravity gets the better of them, and they are replaced by another band with a slightly softer approach to reggae. Suddenly she sees Merville floating past in the distance and Rae feels she urgently wants to dance. She looks around. Karlo is standing waiting with his glass, "Karlo, I've been here long enough, it's someone else's turn."

"Fair enough," he says. "I heard Oscar employed two barmen but they only lasted an hour, it must be hell behind there."

"Especially if you haven't had a drink."

"What!" cries Karlo." My dear girl, I'll certainly take over for a bit. That is so sad it bring tears to my eyes. Here, your's shall be the first glass I shall fill."

Rae takes a gulp of her drink and sets off into the press, gazing about her with seeming indifference. She can't see him. Damn damn damn, that's what comes of not being fancy free at any particular point.

"Hello," says a voice behind her.

She turns and he is there. He says, "You remember me? We were over at Horseshoe Bay….."

"I hadn't forgotten," she looks him up and down in the throng where he stands grinning. "World champion saliva hurler."

He laughs. "You're looking lost," he says.

"I'm not lost. I was looking for someone to dance with, but you'll do just perfectly."

"Good," he says and finds a space for her glass on a far ledge and leads her into the midst of the writhing crowd.

Not far away Lynn is dancing. She feels tipsy already though she's only had a couple of drinks. Unfortunately the only refreshment Oscar has thought to provide is the punch. It is punch or nothing and the punch is strong. Lynn keeps looking expectantly for Arthur. After she got back from the trip, she changed into her flour sack dress and was putting on her make-up when Rae came up from the bar cursing and swearing and sucking noisily on a cigarette.

“Come on,” she said urgently, “let’s go or it will be all over. We’ll go with Michael; he says he’s stopping to go to the party himself so we’ll just catch his last run.”

Lynn hesitated because she had rather hoped Arthur might suggest….. But there was no sign of him and Rae was taking no prisoners - before she knew what was happening she was being rushed down the road and into Michael’s taxi with the latecomers from the Frangipani and she had to put on her make-up squashed up in the back, which might explain the rather wistful expression of her eyeliner.

She has been dancing with Karlo who has repeated Rae’s strictures about getting on a boat soon or she will find herself in difficulties with officialdom. Karlo is now pretty certain that Libby has been deported but no-one will say for sure and there is still no sign of Boss. After Karlo goes off to get a drink she stands watching other people dance, especially the locals. Among the yachties, some do silly western dancing like versions of the twist but others have picked up rock steady, using that lazy side-to-side hip movement as if the pelvis is double-jointed. She has seen Boss dance like that; with him it is entirely intuitive and imitative, his slumbers among rum have rubbed some of the rhythm off on him. She hopes very much that Boss will be found and come to the party. But the person she is really looking for is Arthur although she can’t see him anywhere.

Lynn has never been to any event so loud and vivid and energetic as this marquee on this night; she feels as if she is groping like a clumsy crab in her attempts to dance; her attempts to move her hips are, she is aware, self-conscious and stiff. She wishes she could learn this way of dancing so that when Arthur does eventually come he will dance with her like that. Now there is a slow number and she is dancing with Michael. He has her in a waltz hold and they are doing something very much like a waltz only there is more of a lilt to it, a slightly hip-centred lift to it on the turning. Michael is a big man and, having affixed her to his bosom like a large soft brooch, is walking through it with assurance. “I’m getting the hang of it,” she thinks. At the end of the tune Lynn claps enthusiastically. Yes she is getting the hang of it. She enjoyed that, she is enjoying everything apart from the fact she still can’t see Arthur. Surely he has come by now. Where can he be? She is looking round as the band prepares for their next number and she is half aware of someone at her side. “Yo

Michael," says someone and Michael says cautiously, "Well, you here?" in an eyebrow-raising tone of voice.

"Thought I might look in," says the man with a certain bravado and Lynn realises it is Max whom Rae no longer likes. She knows Arthur also doesn't like this man but for the moment she isn't really taking much notice. She is wondering what the band is going to play next; she doesn't really mind if it is another slow one because she likes being waltzed around like an incompetent broom.

"Well I might have a dance," says Max and Lynn is only vaguely aware that he is looking at her. "What about it young lady?" he says.

"What?" she says, suddenly waking up surprised.

"Michael, do you mind?"

Michael slightly shrugs his shoulder and says, "I'm going to pick up some passengers now, some very lovely lady that is a big model and has many friends coming to this dance," and he moves off. Max's face sets for a moment and then with an effort turns to Lynn who feels herself powerless to do anything other than dance with him. The etiquette is, she knows, that you dance with anyone who asks you; her mother has told her that, it is well known. Even with a man who seems to be nobody's friend. So what can she do, and anyway it is her nature not to enquire too rigorously into motives. Especially as she is rather drunk. The band starts up and her hand is seized, "Hey come on little lady I'll show you how to dance like the islanders dance it," and he pulls her towards him. It is not the dancerly and formal embrace of Michael, this is much more intimate and singeing. Lynn looks around for a moment almost in panic; her only thought is what if Arthur comes and sees her locked in the arms of this man he doesn't like. She tries to move off a little. "No no," says Max who is smiling into her face, "these slow numbers you must dance close up. You see it's a hip movement. Opposites. I move my hips around in this direction, and you move your hips in that direction. Now the top part of your body you move away like this." He shows her.

Lynn is polite, she doesn't really like to have her body so close to a man she doesn't know very well but he certainly seems to know how to dance. As she looks to the side, because she finds she doesn't want to look into his face with its broad knowing smile, she sees Rae dancing not far away with a man who looks familiar. "There's Rae," she says. "I'd lost her."

"Ah well Rae," he says shortly, as if he has had enough of Rae and he pulls her in even closer against him. He holds her and sways with her to the music. She is suddenly aware of his body, his hard genital area pushing and grinding into her stomach, like someone pointing and prodding her with an unpleasant stick. It isn't an erotic feeling at all; in fact she is embarrassed for him that he should be hard like this. She understands there is nothing that men can do about it but she has never danced with a man who seems to be so blatantly unembarrassed by his condition before. She would have expected if a man was unfortunate enough to have it happen while he was dancing, that he would attempt to conceal it by holding his body back where she couldn't feel it. Instead he almost seems to be doing it on purpose, she can't imagine why. She is relieved when the dance is over. "Thank you," she says and moves to go away.

"No no," he says. He doesn't let go of her hands.

She doesn't know what to do. "Um I have to go and find someone," she says.

"One more," he says firmly and fortunately the next one is fast and rhythmic. He is a good dancer, she can see that. "You swishing your hips too much," he says and put his hands on both her hips. "Rock steady." She attempts to do what he says. "Put your hands on my shoulders," he says. She can see many other couples dancing like that so she does as she is told but she doesn't like it though she smiles to cover her discomfort. To her intense relief it is a short dance and the band announces a break.

"Thank you," she says again politely and she turns to walk away.

He still holds her hand, "You'll be wanting to go outside for a breath of air," he murmurs.

"No," she says lying, "I have to see Rae about something." She sees Rae tantalisingly close and makes a break after her. The sudden movement breaks his grip but she is afraid he is following in her wake. She bounds off in the direction Rae has taken but when she catches up she sees that she is in very close communion with a young West Indian youth and clearly doesn't want to be disturbed. She glances behind and assures herself that Max isn't in fact following her. What a relief. Now she can go outside, and, yes she does want to get a little air.

The night outside is warm and loud like any tropical night but compared to inside it is cool and peaceful. Many people are walking in the night, smoking and laughing and she can hear the murmurings of lovers. Still no sign of Arthur. She does however find Jim or he finds her "YooooOOOOOOOhooooo Lynnie," a body is sprawled near the entrance.

"Jim," she crouches down next to him. "What are you doing down here?"

"Well," he says considering, "I was up there before but then it seemed more fun down here. The only problem would be," he waves a finger, "is if I get sick. I was sick way over there somewhere," he points vaguely. "It's easier finding a place to be sick when you're up there. Have you thought of that? That must be the reason we got up off all fours and evolved. But apart from that, apart from that, it's very nice down here. Are you having a good time?"

"Yes sort of," she says.

"Sort of!" says Jim with sudden energy. "Sort of! Me and Oscar, or should that be Oscar and I, we did not lay on this party so you could sort of have a nice time. That is an insult. Help me up. If this is only a Sort Of affair, I will have to take a hand again. Oh damn." He gives up the struggle to get to his feet.

"It was just this man, I don't think Arthur likes him. Anyway he insisted on dancing really close and I….."

"You mean Max I suppose. Arthur does not like him but will not divulge why. However he is involved with that awful Hamilton chappie which is reason enough. He was after Rae I suppose."

"No. I don't think so. Rae doesn't like him either. She is dancing with Arthur's cousin."

"And what of Arthur?"

"I don't know where he is. I haven't seen him." She tries to say it lightly as if she hasn't spent all evening looking for him. "I know he's coming….."

"I should jolly well hope he's coming….. Oh god though, I must find Oscar and have Max ejected tastefully because if Arthur sees the awful Max here he's likely to turn round and go home."

The thought of that happening fills Lynn with such despair that she immediately leaves Jim lying there and rushes through the pavilion and out the other side. No sign of Oscar or Arthur. In her search through the sea of faces she doesn't spy Max either. Hadn't he said to Michael – yes, he said he was only staying a while. She feels relief; Arthur might still come. Unless he's gone already; unless he saw her dancing with Max and went. She puts her hand to her mouth and feels as if a sob might break forth. It is after 11 o'clock, he must be here by now surely, if he is coming. Why doesn't he come? He was very quiet driving back from the swamp. It wasn't something she said was it? She tries to remember their conversation but all she can think of is the medieval knights in armour. Maybe he thinks her a bit mad to be talking about such things in a tropical swamp. She threads the dark outside the pavilion looking among the many laughing chatting groups that have come out for air. The band is about to start again; it is probably going to be the last bracket and she can see them going back on stage through an open door. People are drifting inside. The last dance, well not exactly, an hour of last dance but it seems somehow deeply urgent. Suddenly she sees Arthur silhouetted. He is standing at a door looking in. She rushes up behind him and touches his arm. He jumps and spins and looks at her in a strange way. Her heart sinks, he has seen her dancing with Max. "Jim wants to see you, he's round the other side and can't get up," she says shyly.

"Is he sick?" asks Arthur.

"No," she says. "Not at the moment."

Arthur smiles in the old way and her heart goes light again.

The Frangipani had been busier than expected and Arthur didn't get away until after 10. He then went to shower and change and all the time he was thinking about her, her in the boat, the way she looked at him with the moon lighting her face as he poled for home. It was a god-send he thought, being held up at the bar, not being at the party, not being where she was and maybe he shouldn't go at all to be safe. But then that wasn't a possibility either. No, he would have to go. Because his sister would be there with her friends and she would expect him to pay them attention. Whoever his sister presented, he would be required to talk to and dance with and that would at least serve as a distraction; he must be distracted. If things went on as they were going, who knows what might happen. He was determined not to think about what might happen.

He arrives at the pavilion just as everyone is streaming back in and he talks to a couple of people, no, no-one has seen his sister. That is a problem. Everyone else is here of course. Such a small island, where he knows everyone and everyone knows him; it is exactly the situation where he has to be careful or else….. Everyone would know in seconds if he…... He wonders whether he should go back to the gate and wait - his sister will probably come with Michael and yes, Michael has gone off somewhere to pick someone up - that must be her.

He is about to turn and put this plan into operation when there is this soft touch from behind, shooting through him like an electric charge and here he is caught once more in the net.

He goes with Lynn who has taken him by the hand; he is a man without volition and she leads him round the outside to where Jim has now staggered to his feet and is leaning and swaying against a wall.

"You managed to get up!" says Lynn.

"Arthur," he cries, "old son, old friend, you see before you a sad….." he fumbles for words..... "shell of a man. Evil spirits beware the evil spirits, don't drink the punch. Arthur. Arthur. We didn't buy enough lemonade and Oscar was pouring rum by the gallon and grenadine and I said, softly softly good Oscar, more liquids. For the ladies. Help the ladies. Help." He has started to slip down the wall. Arthur puts a hand under him and helps him back up. "Ah," continues Jim, "now there is something partic..... particular I had to say. Lynn Lynn, what did I have to tell him? Something about dancing."

Lynn looks at him with alarm. Oh god no, don't tell him about Max, she shakes her head.

No," says Jim, "There is something to do with dancing that I have to tell you. No where are you taking me? It's hot and crowded in there; I was in there before and it was awful."

"But they've nearly finished, if we don't go in now I won't get to dance at all." Arthur sees that if they could all go in, all three, that would solve it - him and Jim and Lynn.

"We can dance out here," says Jim and starts to jerk around in time to the music.

"Have you been dancing?" Arthur asks him.

"I have attempted…. with a lady I asked….. That's it," cries Jim. "Yes, I remember what I had to….." He stabs his finger in Lynn's direction, "She had to dance with some bugger, because I bet her mother told her to. No no, you might not know this Arthur old son but when a young lady who has been well brought up is asked to dance, she has to say yes. Did you know that? Well all I can say is that all those girls in there who told me to piss off were just rude and ill-couth. The bitches. Just wait till I talk to all their mothers."

Arthur is laughing. Jim says, "You don't believe me. Well ask Lynn to dance, go on ask her to dance, she won't be able to say no to you."

"I think it's OK to say no nowadays, isn't it?" says Arthur.

"Well ask her," says Jim drunkenly putting his arm round his friend's neck. "You'll see."

"Would you like to dance?" says Arthur with good-humoured resignation.

"Oh yes," says Lynn.

"Told you, told you," says Jim. "And then she ends up with some fellow interfering with her on the dance floor."

Arthur feels a jolt. All his carefully maintained detachment disappears in a flash, "What!"

"It was nothing," she says. Nothing. She is desperate for the discussion to end. "Come on," she says, "now you've asked me," and leads him away and inside, away from Jim who might remember to tell him who it was.

They are in a crowd, a crowd that presses in on all sides so that she has difficulty keeping him with her. They are dancing apart looking at each other and she is smiling, it's alright, it was nothing. The music goes on forever and then ends. WHA wha Wha wha wha, someone is speaking into a boomy mike and suddenly the music is slow as slow. Pressed in on all sides, Arthur puts his hand round her waist which of course he is entitled to do when dancing, his face is near hers and his mouth near her ear. "So what happened?"

"Nothing," she says. "Some man was showing me how to dance and I didn't like it that's all."

"What?"

"Well, he said he had to put his hips round that way and I had to put my hips round this way....." and she shows him and his hand tightens around her waist.

"That's for couples," he says.

"I thought so, and I didn't know how to get away. He held me so tight." Arthur moves his other hand to her waist and is holding her so tight the warmth of his skin where they touch sends hot sparks along all her surfaces. She feels her nipples swell forward and her whole body flush and hum and vibrate so that she can barely keep her insides from leaking out, skin to skin. "And then I thought he was going to kiss me." That is a bit she has just made up because he is nuzzling her cheek. Her arms are round his neck and their hips are locked and she can feel him. He is hard too, hard against her in the slow sway of pelvis and the singing of his breath through his nostrils and now because of the feel of him she is almost unbearably excited, as her body moves ever closer in, as if she can drink him into herself wherever their skin collides. She longs for a touching where everything peels off and there is more skin. She needs much more skin, and if he will only kiss her because her lips are as full for him as stuffed pink snails and as she moves her face from his shoulder to face him, he has to kiss her or she will kiss him and he will lift her up into all this heat, how very hot it is in waves against his chest, what a yearning heat and sticky longing.....

"Arthur," cries Erica accusingly. "Arthur, you were supposed to come and pick me up. I've been waiting all night."

"What?" says Arthur, not letting go of Lynn.

Erica is looming over him with one hand on his shoulder. "Look the band about to finish and me without a dance..... Excuse me doll but I have to have a dance with this man."

"What?" says Lynn, not letting go of Arthur.

Sheila appears behind Erica. "Where have you been Arthur?"

"What?" says Arthur.

"I told you to come by before you came here. Didn't I?"

"No," says Arthur.

"Lynn Lynn, there you are Lynn." It is Tom. He drops to his knees in front of her, "Lynn please come away with me."

Lynn feels as if she had strayed up to the gates of paradise, only to find everyone she has ever known bent on turning her back. Because here is Jim, swaying and grinning horribly.

"Say you will, say you will," says Tom, "or I'm lost."

She is aware of clinging to Arthur with all her might as Jim, stumbling and laughing, explains. "Tom thought his charter started here. Charles just saw him and said, 'What the hell are you still doing here?' He found out he has to pick them up way up the islands - he'll have to sail day and night. And he doesn't even have a crew." This last point is the killer. Jim wipes his eyes, "He wants you to go as cook, and me as mate, and he wants us to leave now."

Right now.

Chapter 9

It's all predestinated

There's no time to say goodbyes, no time for any of that. Everything must be done with such expedition that Lynn is suddenly on board with the shreds of unsaid things hanging around her like torn clothing. She can still hear Rae's cry of fury, "A month! A month sailing the islands of the Carribean, I could just die of envy. They should have asked me, Tom should have taken me, oh how lucky you are!"

To be told you are lucky doesn't necessarily make you feel lucky. I understand that now. Seen through Rae's eyes I was off on the sort of big adventure that most people could only dream of - off on an exotic tantalising voyage of pleasure - a voyage of exquisite sights and unlimited potentialities. The shush and slap of water beneath the keel, the azure sea like unending rippled planes of opal and turquoise stone - jewels in which islands broke like peacock feathered hats, reefs which glittered beneath white caps like the shoulders of sequined women and beaches seducing like soft white sheets awaiting endless soft bodies stretched gleaming with coconut oil in abandonment to the goldsheen god of sun. A life where the entire cast wore diamante girdles and Indian silver and ate grapes so big and sweet that every mouth was stained purple and puffed with exhausted pleasure.

Well it wasn't like that. It was no pleasure at all setting off into a black howling sea with two wild fellow crewmen both of whom were drunk. But I have found that history is concocted after the fact from lies and selective memories and has nothing to do with reality. It is put together and edited by those who didn't even participate in it but who now propose to sit in judgment on our recollections, culling from our histories what they don't find interesting. They write our biographies and shape the past. All those long comfortable periods when nothing happened, when the world was at peace and we were happy, are too dull to be worth recording. No, the highpoint of our lives, we are told, is that time when we felt most distressed and anxious, when our progress was littered with unpleasant incidents and the whole episode culminated in catastrophe.

Lynn clings to a rail; she is helpless and can do nothing. The night is big and the wind is rising and the land seems very far away very quickly. "What do I do?" Hahaha - don't you worry your pretty head about that. "So I do nothing. I can't even make anything to eat because there isn't anything….. I said there isn't any food." They don't listen. "Why couldn't we wait till first light and pick up stores and go then?" But no. Away away, now we must fly with the moon but the moon is behind the clouds and the clouds are banking up, but still we must flee some demon with wild shouting. Come on Lynn! Because she's not shouting too. What? Come on, we're off on a big adventure! Oh for the open road, Tom pulls wind through his hair and gives a wild hooray. "And our friends are all aboard," he bellows in a deep baritone and Jim joins in, "Every one of them….. pissed as a lord." "Yellow submarine," choruses Tom as he runs belatedly under the bow of a much bigger boat, some rich man's floating mansion still lit up with lights and people leaning over the side to see what it is that is coming out of the dark. "Yeehaw," shrieks Tom. "Bring on the dancing girls you mother fuckers Hahaha," and Jim collapses with laughter holding his stomach weakly. Then Tom, pretending to be business-like so everyone watching will see what sort of tight ship he runs, says, "Here you hold the wheel," to Lynn, "while I put up the mainsail. Jim Jim you useless piece of fruit, put up the mizzen will you."

"Bugger that," says Jim, "I'm only here for the beer."

Lynn thinks, "This is madness," curling inwards like she carries inside her the empty bones of some old land animal, some cold snailshell that lumps up under her heart. Goodbye. Who knows over the weeks ahead what may happen, every day is a different day. Goodbye.

Once the work of getting under sail is completed the animal spirits sink, no longer so full of beans. Now they are full of curses.

"Come on Lynn, do something."

"I don't know what to do." And they are too helpless to show her. The stars wink in a vast expanse of black as they proceed with the creak and slosh and whine of metal and rope and canvas and the whoompf of waves against the wooden hull, a battering sound.

She goes aft and lies down in the little two berth cabin but she is afraid to sleep. Life seems too precious to entrust to these two reckless men who sing of the good ship Venus and pull their skin on abrading ropes and guard rails. Oh skin, with her arm over her eyes, the touch of it, the touch of his, now there is a voyage of pleasure for sure and what is this in comparison, a dream? The heat of his chest and the smell of his sweat close up like toast and the other smells of soap and aftershave and the feel of his cheek against her face but this is only the very very surface part of it. He nibbled her ear. Only very gently, only once, only fleetingly. But it sent a shock through her. And then they turned to dance face to face, her arms draping his shoulders, his hands moving down her back, holding her close and she could feel him, feel every bit spouting warmth strangely and longingly through her whole body. She doesn't know what to do with these memories, the rehearsal of which sends the same sweet yearning coursing through her as if she is without form or boundaries. She feels doors that she has never opened now pushing down demanding that she oil and open them.

But then he turned and was gone. Went into the crowd with his sister, his sister taking him away; never looking back as if it was just a dance they had had, nothing but a dance. Turning from her as if he was glad to be released from it. Abandoning her without another thought. To go off with his sister and Erica and some other girls that Sheila had with her. She saw him vanishing, being introduced to a lovely girl with curly dark hair, an islander, taking her hand, vanishing. Eventually Lynn sleeps, waiting for some kiss to wake her from the apple's poison. But it is only Jim come to crash, "Oh sleeping beauty, time to take the helm."

So she has to get up and go out. She is frightened by what she sees when she comes up beside Tom. There seems to be a rushing and a flapping and a great deal of wind. She knows nothing, I know nothing of all this. I am so ignorant and I wish I were buried somewhere with my head under my wing. The clouds let through only the dimmest light of stars and often while she clings to the wheel Tom goes off to peer at some instrument by torch light.

Suddenly the dawn breaks, one minute there is a sulky light in the east and ten minutes later she can see land on the horizon.

They are lucky with the wind apparently; it blows them before it all Sunday. They take it in turns to sleep. Later in the afternoon, while Tom is asleep, Jim starts Lesson One, sailing for complete idiots, and tells her the names of things she promptly forgets and how to pull ropes for reasons that go straight out of her head. She can see instinctively how things work but asked to theorise her brain goes to wool. "How on earth did you get by with Boss?" says Jim exasperated.

"He never asked me to learn anything," she says. "He would just hand me the wheel and I'd drive it. I don't see why everything's got all these silly names. As for all this stuff about the wind, I would say it's obvious what you're telling me, I don't understand why you have to turn it into something technical." They argue on and then Tom gets up and they continue to bicker. Jim and Tom gang up against her in their solid masculine way as if there is something ultimately rational about the way they see it and if only she could admit how deficient she is the world would be a better place.

"Women," they mutter. "Go and make us a cup of tea," as if that is all she is good for, as if that is the punishment imposed for being of the delicate sex.

The sea continues to roll in a lash of waves and Tom goes down to listen to the radio. He comes back up and says gloomily, "There's a damn hurricane in the offing. At this time of year!"

"I knew that," says Jim.

"You knew it! You didn't bloody well tell me."

"I always assume my skipper knows more than I do. That way we preserve the distinctions of class and command."

"That's a bloody stupid thing to think."

"It's embedded in my aristocratic soul. You wouldn't understand being an American. How can the leader lead if the ranks keep chipping in with ideas? Plus of course there's a certain amount of self-interest, seeing as how my income from Oscar has now dried up. I say to you for instance, 'This is a bloody stupid idea going on this trip with a hurricane looming' and you say, 'Perfectly correct James my old mate, I take on board what you are saying and I have decided on the basis of your recommendation not to continue with this madcap notion.' Then I'm out of a job."

"So when they put the headstone over you, they write 'James Primrose, Employed.'"

"No, just the occupation."

"James Primrose, Ship's Mate, Lost at Sea, went down with his pay slip."

"Well as for that, you know the battle cry of the pirate, 'Come on lads, do you want to live for ever?'"

"Did they say that? I like that."

"Although now it's been changed. To 'Bring on the dancing girls'." Of course.

Of course. Anyway it's only a bloody hurricane, too true, Yeehaw this is more like it, let's kick some ass around here and get this mother sailing, "Sail on….."

"Sail oh-oh-on."

"With hope."

"In your heart."

"And you'll ne….."

"Ver."

"Sail."

"A."

"Lone."

They all combine for the final bellow. "You'll NEV-er Sail Alone." Are there any more words? I think you just keep singing those ones. OK everyone, positions please, once more with feeling.

Night comes again. Everything is black, not even the stars wink any more. Whenever a squall clears, Lynn can just see on the port side that the black sea is fringed with the denser black of an island hulk but there are no lights on any of it. If people live there they are dead asleep, not even a torch or a candle to be seen. No-one even giving birth in a kerosene-lit cabin, no-one huddled over a fire on the stormy shore, nothing that gives any sign of life in all the length of all this land as if they have passed through a time-warp in coming out to sea and left behind the twentieth century for some other place that dreams deep in primeval nature. And then even the land is lost as rain closes in. Occasionally the moon gleams through but lights up emptiness, just sea heaving and gleaming with evil whitecaps; there is nothing but the sound of the mainsail's uneasiness as the wind swoops and rattles around, threatening any moment to swing the boom madly across the deck in an uncontrolled crack. The whole boat is a cacophony of sound with the creak and slosh and whine of metal and rope and canvass.

No-one has eaten and simultaneously every stomach is empty. "There must be something on board," says Jim discontentedly but Tom says nothing. Lynn goes down below to look.

The galley looks as ship-shape as when she lived on board but opening the cupboards Lynn finds a subtle degeneration. Foodstuffs, which previously had been stowed in airtight containers carefully aligned and sea-ready, are now spilled about, some having lost their lids and their contents. Rice, flour and strands of spaghetti jostle each other for the attention of cockroaches and maggots. She makes an inventory. There are eggs. "There's eggs," she calls.

Yes. Eggs. Anything to go with them?

She makes a search and then climbs up to look out the hatch and gives a mouth down.

Why is it," says Jim, "that I feel like almost anything except eggs? Any bread?"

She shakes her head.

"Biscuits?"

"Yes. But they haven't been kept airtight."

"Bloody hell Tom. Any tins of anything?"

"One small tin of butter."

"Great."

"When will we get to where ever we're going?" she asks.

"God knows," says Jim cheerfully. "We don't even know where we are now."

Lynn thinks they are joking, "You don't?"

"Not a clue."

"So we could be lost."

"Oh no, we must be somewhere but there's no way of knowing with this cloud."

Lynn goes back down into the galley. Strangely the thought of being lost is rather comforting because if they don't know where they are, maybe they'll never get to where they're going and everything will be as it was and they can all go home. She gets out all the food that is fit to eat and then starts going through one of the cookbooks. She hasn't gone far when she finds a recipe for griddle cakes, eggs and flour. She has one tin of butter, there is some rather dubious looking milk powder and there is honey in a jar, that will do. The flour is a bit of a worry, it has a fuzz of small webbing as if tiny spiders live in the tin and as she mixes it she finds lumps forming spontaneously, as if the flour hides new life forms, old parasites and sources of pestilence.

"Hoy," calls Jim.

"What?"

"What are you doing down there?"

"Making cakes," she replies.

"Oh," he sounds surprised. "Carry on."

Lumpy or not, she starts cooking them on the stove, three to a frying pan. The sour buttery burning smell constantly alerts her to the difficulty of turning down the cooker low enough and yet moving the cakes on at a reasonable pace. After an hour she has a pile and puts the kettle on to boil while she covers each of the cooling cakes with sloppy butter from the tin and a smear of honey from the jar. "Gosh," says Jim impressed.

"They're lumpy," she says.

"Never fear, I'm very partial to lumps, and who knows if we're lucky the lumps may be hiding small caches of protein. Isn't that right Tom?"

"Nothing wrong with a nice dead weevil."

"Not keen on cockroaches though, bit crunchy."

Lynn goes back down and makes tea, "There's no coffee", she says emerging, "and the milk powder is suspicious as well." They smell their tea carefully, "Oh it's not too bad," says Tom, almost in surprise. "Well here we are," he says happily after they have munched through the pile of drop scones, "scudding along, nothing more to wish for in the world."

"I think we'll throw you overboard," says Jim meditatively.

"That was a good night last night," says Tom.

"Last night?" says Lynn trying to remember why he should think it good.

"I mean the party. What I remember of it."

"Yes," says Lynn, "I was having a really good time until you all came along and spoiled the whole thing by dragging me off."

"Yes," says Jim, "I think I was having a good time too. Why didn't you put your foot down Lynn, you were still fairly sober. If you'd said no rack off we'll go in the morning, we would even as we speak be eating prime rump steak with all the trimmings. The last thing I remember," continues Jim reminiscently, "is that great big woman collaring Arthur. Where on earth did she come from?"

"Erica," says Lynn in a hollow tone.

"Have you seen her before?"

"She's a friend of his sister's."

"What an ugly woman! I hate women like that with their big self-satisfied mouths. Clearly no-one has ever told her how ugly she is. And all those other women that hang around with his sister, where did she get such a pack of ugly broads from?"

"I wouldn't have thought….." Lynn breathes. "I don't think other people think of them as ugly."

"Not that his sister's ugly, but she's got some character traits that don't appeal to me. And did you see Arthur's expression when she arrived and gave him his orders? I would have rushed to his rescue only Tom pinned me to the wall."

"I was trying to stop you falling over," says Tom.

"Quite. But Lynn, you were dancing with him when she yanked him bodily away, why didn't you stop them, go to his rescue."

"I don't know if he wanted to be rescued."

"Now that's where you're wrong. Plain on his face for everyone to see. What Arthur needs is taking in hand."

"Absolutely," says Tom. "He needs to get married. I need to get married too, I need taking in hand. Marry me Lynn," he goes down on his knees. "I need marrying right now."

"Marry him," says Jim mockingly, "and live a life looking over your shoulder to see what he's up to. With every woman that he meets."

"Now now, if you are going to make aspersions I will have no option but to sack you."

"Oh please sack me," says Jim going down on his knees in turn. "Please please."

Lynn is looking at the dark water contemplating a buttery sort of feeling. "Why don't you write to your fiancee, Tom?" she says.

"What would I say?" he says with genuine sadness.

"Write to her about little things." Like froth on the deck. The moon has come out now and soft motes of silver shiver on the metal rails like the visible tingle, the touch of magic where if you hold your breath someone will put his hand in yours. Maybe Tom's fiancee is also feeling sad.

They are all dead tired and they sit there, their minds merging with the grey glaze of water. "Funny sort of thing isn't it, men and women," says Jim, "who ends up with who? You see people cuddling up together one minute in Love. Perfect Love, garlanded in hibiscus flowers, sipping champagne, you know. All taste and scent.

And then the next minute it's as if it has never been. All gone. Well where has it gone that's what I want to know?"

"It's fate," says Tom shortly. "You can't have everyone ending up together all living happily ever after with their one true love. How boring that would be."

"I think that would be delightful," says Lynn.

"No it would be boring. Where's the drama, where's the pathos, where's the fourteen-year-olds committing suicide in a crypt?"

"You're cynical."

"I'm a realist."

"But look at it scientifically," says Jim warming to his theme. "Where does love go, when the woman who loved you doesn't love you any more?"

"She never loved you in the first place," says Tom. "So it didn't go anywhere."

"Well, she looked as if she loved you," Jim ruminates. Tom says nothing and stares out to sea. Jim continues, "If someone can start being in love then there must be a switch that turns it back off. And I think sometimes the switch just gets thrown accidentally, for no reason. Take me for example. My first love was called Rosemary and she had dark curly hair round her head like a cap of leaves and cheeks like small apples and a red mouth. I adored her and we were sure our love was greater than all the loves in the world put together and when I went to University I thought I'd die without her. But in a few weeks I'd forgotten her."

"You forgot her!"

"Never saw her again. I met someone else. Fellow student."

Lynn is horrified, "That's terrible. Just like that. You can't have been in love."

"I was, I swear to you I was."

"And what happened to her? Did she just stop loving you too?"

"Well she must have done. Someone told me she's married now with two children."

"Maybe she still loves you and married someone else because….."

"On the rebound? No, it was a couple of years later."

"Maybe a couple of years isn't so long. When you're in love."

"Are you joking! It's an age. It's an aeon, it's a lifetime when you're in love. A day is long enough when you're in love, two years is inconceivable. In two years from today the person we are now will be changed, we will be some other person entirely."

"But if you really loved someone….. How could it be possible….?"

"Lynn the romantic."

"No I reckon she's right," says Tom. "I'm very suspicious about this Rosemary business. For a start it's rather extraordinary that you know so much about this old flame. I bet she gave you the flick, not up to scratch. Yes, forget about her burning for you with a hopeless passion that never died - wearing black for remembrance - not a bit of it. I see her wearing red with a flounce. Jim Who, she cries. Oh yes, wonder what happened to old Jim Bluebell."

And so, with teasing and banter they while away the night while the wind blows astern. Tom originally calculated that with a good wind they might be in by midnight and eating hot rotis from a stall, but as the hours go by and the wind drops the calculations change to three o'clock, four o'clock….. And on they sail.

A sort of stupidity like a grey fog settles after they eventually crawl into port at 6.30. Food, after long deprivation, has become an abstract quality, one that is urgently personal. However they now need to turn their minds to the practical matter of what to do next. The charterers are coming on board at 9am, the store opens at 7am and that gives them two hours to buy everything they need for the charter. In the end, because no-one has a better idea, they all go to the store and throw things higgledy-piggledy into a shopping trolley. Lynn has no idea at all what sort of menu she should be planning, only that the charterers will be on board for four weeks, four weeks of something different for lunch, something different for…..

"Just plan for the first two weeks," says Tom. "We can take on fresh supplies and you'll have a better idea of what works." Steak. A large piece of fillet steak, slice it and fry or roast it whole. Mince. Fish, we'll get that as we go along but cans for mornay. Eggs, lots of eggs. Hors d'oevres. Vegetables. Salad. What keeps, what can be frozen. Oil, jam, coffee, butter. Cans cans cans. Frozen peas.

Now they have all the food on board and move to take on diesel and ice and refill the gas while Lynn tries to store everything logically so she can find it easily. There is a lot of food but nothing springs to mind as a menu even for the day ahead. There is no time yet to make breakfast because, despite all this food, there is the onward push of urgency, other things that have to be done. She goes for a shower, maybe ideas will come if she goes back and looks at recipe books.

It is nine o'clock and they move the boat back to their original berth. "Right on time," says Tom. "Prepare to repel boarders."

"You two had better go and have a shower or that will be exactly the situation," says Lynn.

"No no," says Tom, "I have to be here, the skipper greeting his guests."

"Don't you think it might give a bad first impression?"

"We don't smell that much do we?" he noses under his arms. "That's just a manly smell, nothing wrong with that."

"So long as all the charterers are men," she murmurs submissively.

"Um," Tom pulls at his beard. "No maybe you're right. Come on Jim lad, it's only five minutes, now if they come….."

"I'll show them to their cabins and let them unpack. Give them sheets and pillowcases and explain how the head and shower work - I know all that. I've lived here remember." I'll greet and soothe them and pretend I know what I'm doing, she thinks. God help us all, every one.

She waits. No-one comes and nothing happens. People move along the other jetties but no-one makes a move to come up theirs. Lynn sits on the cushions as gracefully as she can, looking decorative. Boss always said, "Look decorative, then whatever goes wrong they won't know it's wrong. If the ship's sinking then lean on the rail in a relaxed manner and indicate how delightful it will be to go for a swim." The sun is beating down. Damn - they haven't put the awning up! She struggles with the heavy canvas and has just got it into position when Tom and Jim come back.

"Where are they?"

"Dunno, haven't arrived."

"What are you putting that up for? We'll be underway as soon as they come."

"It's hot," Lynn is beginning to feel cross.

"Won't take long to take down," Jim says going to help her.

"Well put it up properly then," says Tom and the two men grab it and redo it. Lynn sits down on the still hot seats and feels the boat moving rhythmically under her. Tom is saying….. something about….. Words like fuzz drifting into a block, like a thick blanket.

Much later she wakes up, she is curled up on the seat in a foetal position. Tom is lying on the other seat with a hat over his face and his feet crossed. Jim is stretched out on the deck in the shade, face down with a cushion under his head. There is no-one else. Nothing is happening. She is ravenously hungry; she has to eat or else her very fibre will give way.

She goes down into the galley which is much hotter than on deck; there is no breeze at all. She makes some rounds of sandwiches although she has no idea what the time is. Is this breakfast, or is it lunch? And when the charterers come, what to do for lunch? More sandwiches? Oysters on cracker biscuit? A waldorf salad?

She gets down the recipe books. Yvonne was a good cook. Tom has mentioned the fact a few million times but the boat has limited recipe books and Lynn is not a cook; in fact she doesn't think she can cook at all, if by 'cook' is meant cook for a living so that people will pay for it. As Boss only took day charterers, she's never had to prepare anything complicated because they weren't there to eat; they were there to fish and drink and brag and stand around being masculine; the hunters - look at us and admire. In that sort of atmosphere she just had to be the girl. She brought the men drinks and snacks and then very sweetly said, "What would you like for lunch? We've got lobster or T-bone steak or rump fillet….." She never had to go beyond that. It was always lobster or T-bone and sometimes lobster and T-bone. The tricky thing was not over-cooking the steak. Sometimes the rare wasn't rare enough, and sometimes the well-done still had red spots but they forgave her and the eaters of the lobster would put their fingers in the air and go, "Oh my." But you can't do that every day and anyway, that is just lunch, panic. If only there had been more time she could have consulted Arthur….. But that isn't a comfortable thought to enter on when here she is alone without him and weeks to fill up, empty weeks. She turns the leaves of the recipe books. This is desperate, everything is so complicated and seems to require immense amounts of prior knowledge such as how to make a roue. Isn't a roue an unpleasant sort of man like Max? White sauces seem to be part and parcel of all cooking and there are all sorts of ingredients that she has never thought to get and she isn't sure they have on board. She knows whoever the charterers are, however nice they are to begin with, they'll hate her after one week let alone four. But maybe they won't come; hopefully they won't come and then they can all go home. She shuts up all the recipe books, lifting the batch of them tiredly to put them back on the shelf. She misses. As they crash back on the table a few sheafs of papers fall out. She picks them up. They are written in handwriting she doesn't recognise, not Tom's. They must be Yvonne's. She stares at the pages for a bit and then realises they are some sort of plan, Yvonne had some sort of plan for charters and here it is. Day one, chicken papricash. Chicken, white wine, sour cream (she needs that), paprika, capsicum (she needs that too). She starts to make lists. Day two, prawn and avocado salad. She has prawns, she needs avocados, and for dinner pepper steak, french-fries….. She soon has a list that seems to grow longer and longer, she needs all this stuff. She races out of the galley. "Tom," she says urgently, "I have to get some more things. Look, I found a menu, I need more things, Tom wake up. Tom listen, I have to go back to the store."

"What? What? What time is it?"

"Half past one."

"Jeezus, where are they?"

"Half past one," says Jim also waking. "Now you're sure this is the place?"

"Yes yes. This is the place," he keeps repeating, "this is the place. He said nine. We haven't passed a dateline have we, it is Monday today isn't it? Half past one, are you sure?"

"Tom, give me some money, I have to go and get some new things. Were you listening to what I said? I've found Yvonne's menu. She had a plan, look. It was in one of the recipe books."

"But what if they don't come? I'm going to be done for. I only got some tiny deposit for some reason, they're going to hand over the rest in cash when they get here. Oh Jesus, it's that bloody….. Who's the guy in charge here, Charles's other half? I bet he made a mistake in the bookings. God damn it," he gets up and looks with deliberate fury up the jetty towards the entrance.

"Yes but if they do come….. If they do come you'll want to go straight away, so I have to go now, before they're here….."

"But if they don't come….."

"But if they do," insists Lynn. "Oh for god's sake Tom, give me some money," she wails, seeing her one chance of acquitting herself with honour disappearing.

"Oh well, I'll be bankrupt anyway," he says fatalistically and goes heavily down into the galley. "Here," he says returning, "What's the odd? Here's a blank cheque. Don't spend more than three hundred bucks though, because it will bounce."

The store is now quiet. The morning rush as yachties rummaged to fill their shopping baskets and get off in good time has passed and now in the heat of the day there are only a few islanders apart from herself as far as she can see. However as she is searching through the spice section she is aware of a stir around her and the unmistakable drawl of loud American voices.

"I won't go, if it's going to be like that." It is a flat statement stated in a flat voice, an almost monotone but at a high register that might indicate temporary irritation or on the other hand it might not; it is the kind of voice that pierces a wall of canned grapefruit pieces as if they were mere tissue.

"You can't not go, I signed the damn papers, you know that means they could sue..... You can't not go." The answering voice is ponderous and equally powerful, in a lower register but bulked out with the same apparent simmering irritation.

"Damn right I won't go if there's a niggra on board."

"There won't be, you know what it said in the literature, husband and wife and crew."

"It's the 'and crew' bit. You saw him with your own eyes and I can imagine Moira's face when she realised! Cooped up on board almost like family."

"But Moira's got a coloured maid. Why should she care?"

"That's right, that's why she's gone no doubt. I wouldn't go, I wouldn't have one in the house. The very thought of them touching you, of touching something you eat. I'm always very particular, very particular where I eat and who cooks my food. I always check the kitchen. Always. Imagine how I felt when I went into the kitchen at the hotel and it's just a jungle, I could have been in Africa. Barely a white face among them and at a top hotel! How much are we paying this fellow? Well plenty I can tell you, plenty."

"Plenty. I said we should never have come here. Why couldn't we go to Australia? They're all white in Australia, it's the law."

"No-one goes to Australia. No I want to be here and I want to go on a boat and I want 'husband and wife and crew', with the wife cooking. But then, when I got to the jetty to see Moira and Tex off and there was that man on their boat..... We should have been able to see our boat yesterday and could we? No! They said it's coming from some other island and that's another thing I don't like. If you were going to stay in a hotel you could go and look at it first and if you're going on a boat I would have thought you could do the same.

That's the first thing I asked when we got here - when can we go and inspect. I don't like this idea of just going on board and sailing off like Moira and Tex did, because you can't get off if you don't like it, can you? It stands to reason therefore that they should have been here earlier, so we could inspect."

"Well I don't know Letty. You know Bertram said it was high season and we'd never get anything else. Wait and see. That's all I ask."

"Get more of those crackers Lisa-Marie, otherwise I'll starve."

A younger male voice breaks in, "I thought they were going to feed us. Do you mean to say we're going to eat crackers for weeks?"

"Well you can eat if you don't care who cooks….. It's up to you."

"I'll eat then."

"Well if you get sick don't coming running to me, wanting me to drop what I'm doing, when I told you so."

"You're weird."

"Don't talk to me like that. Jerry, he's not to talk to me like that."

"Don't speak to your mother like that."

"Stepmother," mutters a sulky voice. "And Pop, you tell her to stop talking so loudly, it's embarrassing. Isn't it Lees?"

"Momma dear," says a sweet voice, "its best if we don't talk about Coloured people so loudly when we're in a Coloured store on a Coloured island."

"Well," grumbles the voice lowering only very slightly and then only for a few seconds, "how can I eat anything when I don't know where it's come from, who's touched it on the way, what diseases are lurking around in it?"

"Just drink plenty of rum," says the girl.

"How can she do that?" jeers the younger male. "That's produced right here and the Coloureds have been all over it."

"No, alcohol kills all that, it's the only thing you can be sure of. I have to go and see Bertram, I need to check all this. I'm not saying I'm going at all yet. But let's get out of here, it's giving me the creeps with all this niggra food. And you be sure they add up all that stuff right, don't let them put anything over on you." The voices fade away towards the checkout desk.

"They wouldn't let me even touch their groceries," says the woman on checkout to another with a shrug of her shoulders as Lynn put her own purchases through.

"I heard them talking," says Lynn. "It made me feel so ashamed."

"Lot of them think like that," says the woman matter-of-factly.

"Oh god," says Lynn suddenly overcome with trepidation, "I hope they're not the charterers for our boat."

She rushes back to the boat loaded down with her new purchases but there is no-one on deck. Tom and Jim are backed up in the engine-room with Tom hammering at something. "What are you doing?" she says urgently.

"Ah well," says Jim, "Tom thought, being as there was a quiet moment, that it would be a really good idea to strip down the engine."

"But they'll be here any minute. How are we going to drive out of harbour?"

"Good question. I'm glad you're still paying attention. I'm not quite sure what the answer to it is but Tom has come down with a bad case of the pessimisms and decided they're not coming."

"But they are, I saw them in the store or rather I think it's them. They've gone off to see someone called Bertram and then they're coming here."

"Bertram, that's Charles's offsider up here isn't it? Tom, quit frigging about in there. But how do you know they're ours? There are dozens coming and going."

"Well I don't know for certain, I just had this bad feeling about them. How many are we expecting Tom?"

"Four," says Tom. "Or six. Or two, I forget what Charles told me."

"You're hopeless," says Jim. "How can she get in stores if you don't know how many are coming?"

"Easy," says Tom giving a parting swipe at something with his hammer. "If there are six, you guys eat less."

"I saw four, and they're awful."

"They're all awful," says Tom.

"No they're not," says Lynn. "Most of the ones Boss had were lovely."

"Yes but for a day," says Tom. "Everyone's lovely for a day. I mean for four weeks in an area that's smaller than most of their living rooms, they're awful, everyone agrees. But then so are the crew."

"And the skipper," says Jim.

"Only the skipper comes through with flying colours. That's why he's in charge."

"But these are awful to begin with," says Lynn. "Really awful."

"So why do you think these particular awful people are ours?" says Tom wiping the oil off his hands with a rag.

"Because I gathered they're waiting for a boat which is coming from another island and wasn't here yesterday when they came to check."

"Then it can't be us, we weren't due till today."

"No that's the point, they wanted to check us over, to make sure there were no Coloured people on board."

"Coloured people. Well that's torn it. If they've gone to check with Bertram, they'll have Yvonne down as cook. How much did you just spend? I'm done for, I'm broke."

"Only two hundred dollars. Is Yvonne a West Indian then?" Lynn is surprised.

"No, she's Canadian," says Tom.

"Here they come," says Lynn hollowly. "I can hear her voice."

They go up on deck the better to examine their fate. A group of four are making their way up the jetty commenting on the boats they are passing, their garish holiday clothes making alien splashes against the white glare of sea and boats. The woman in the lead is about forty, with peerless blonde hair and a complexion that is as bland and creamy as a whipped parfait. She is wearing a tuck-in sleeveless blouse and tailored red green and yellow patterned shorts. Her face is expressionless if you subtract the opening and closing of her mouth. She doesn't smile or frown, her mouth simply returns to rest whenever she ceases her stream of generally unfavourable comments about everything she sees. She walks forward in a clipped clacketty way caused by the very high mules she is wearing and, because of the uncertainties of the planking, they progress somewhat slowly. The man walking beside her is much older and much fatter. He is a tall greyhaired man wearing a Hawaiian shirt and white bermudas, white socks and khaki sandshoes. He wears a floppy flowered hat on his head that looks ridiculous, though he has the air of a man at whom it would be dangerous to laugh. He has a bent-forward look, as of someone rather short sighted who is intent on looking closely into matters, especially financial matters. His face is mottled and red, possibly from new sunburn, possibly from a long comfortable association with alcohol. They are accompanied by a girl and a boy in their late teens or early twenties. The girl has curly long ashblonde hair that swings and loops about a plump-cheeked small-nosed sweet-looking doll-like face. She has extravagant lips painted pale pink, eyes made up like an Egyptian goddess and a luxurious body of the sort that is no longer supposed to be fashionable. She wears a white lacy bodice stretched across protuberant unsupported mammaries and very short tight pink floral shorts that ride up in a v-shape from her crotch. She also wears high mules but she wanders forward in a soft bouncy way that makes the cheeks of her buttocks quiver rather alarmingly close to the bottom of her shorts as if edging downward to obtain release. In an opposite and contrary directional thrust, her breasts bounce upwards into the space allowed for cleavage like the surge of thick liquids on the boil. The effect is, that the crewmembers of the various boats along their route who have put up their heads to resent the comments of the older woman find their tart responses frozen on their faces as they inspect the voluptuous flesh weaving past them her wake.

By the side of the younger woman shuffles a tall lanky youth wearing spectacles, his face heavily spotted with acne and wearing a t-shirt and bright red hipster jeans. This is the party that stops next to their boat and looks down at them.

"Hello," says the man pugnaciously.

"Hi," says Tom languidly leaning back on the bench seat, his hands behind his head in a rough approximation of easeful imperviousness.

"You weren't here when we came before."

"When was that?" asks Tom

"Earlier," says the man.

"Moved to get diesel at 7 am, been here all the time since 9 though."

"Well we expected you earlier, been waiting to look you over."

"Here we are," says Tom waving his hands around.

"Humph," says the man. Things were not going too well and he is breathing hard. "We'll come on board and see what we think."

"Sure," says Tom, "but the ladies will have to take their sandals off."

The older woman looks down at her strawberry-painted toenails, "What do you mean?" she glares at him. "They're just sandals. I wear them all over, no-one else has told me to take them off."

"Whites only on board a boat, or bare feet. I would have though that was common knowledge."

"Whites, what does he mean? We're white, what does he take us for?"

"Soles, Lette, he means soles."

"My soles are as white as the rest of me."

"Then take off your sandals, madam," says Tom patiently, "and put your nice white soft soles on my nice unscratched varnish."

"Come on Lette," says the older man who is making to scramble clumsily down.

"Jerry wait, don't just leave me here, these are expensive shoes we're talking about. Look," she takes one off and turns it over. "Fine Italian leather, look at that. Cost plenty. What's wrong with them?"

"Rubber," says Tom taking off one of his own shoes and starting to lose patience. "See these? Cost hardly anything but they've got rubber soles, white rubber soles and it's rubber or nothing on board a boat."

The woman is now blowing out her breath, "I wasn't told, my entire wardrobe….."

"For god sake take them off Momma, why don't you," says the younger woman dropping hers on the jetty and then holding out her hand encouragingly to Jim to help her aboard.

"Hey," says the older woman rounding on her, "less of that. Did you hear that Jerry? I won't have that. I won't have lip from you Lisa-Marie, let's be real clear on that." But she says it without conviction. It is clear from the way her partner ignores this outburst that the young woman has a leeway that the young man does not. In the meantime the young man has got himself on board under his own steam and is staring about muttering "Cool," leaving the older woman all alone and isolated on the jetty. "You, you," she calls to Jim who is distractedly staring at the young woman. She tries to stow her sandals in her little beach bag but the toes peek out, and then with this swinging precariously from her elbow she is brought with difficulty down on to the deck. "Where's the ladder?" she says crossly. "You should have a ladder. Now," she turns back to Tom, "who are your crew?"

Tom waves his hand silently at Jim and Lynn.

"Married couple," says the woman. "It said in the literature married couple, that's why we chose you. This is your daughter right, but where's your wife?"

Tom starts to turn a shade of purple. Tom is a dozen years older than Lynn but is outraged to be thought so old that Lynn is his daughter or that it is impossible that she should be his wife.

"Ah neat," cries the younger woman looking in the aft cabin. "Yea, groovy," says the boy.

"It's very cramped," says the older man, emerging from the front accommodation. "Not at all what we were led to expect. Lette, I can't see a third cabin."

"Let me look. How do you get down there? How did you do that? I can't..... Where are the stairs, these aren't stairs." Lette is transferred into the galley.

"There's one cabin back here, Poppa," calls the young woman.

"Yes but where's the third cabin?" demands the woman who is scrambling up again and goes round to stare into the aft cabin "This is only two, they said there were three."

"Third cabin," says Tom. "Well I suppose they meant in the dining room next to the galley, there are two bunks above there."

"No that's not good enough, for the money we're paying; they said three separate cabins, separate. Me and Jerry will have to walk through there and there's no proper division between it and our cabin. Separate, it says. Jerry show them the description."

The man gets out a sheaf of papers from an envelope he is carrying which includes a roneoed or lightly printed sheet with pictures. Tom looks at it blankly for a full ten or fifteen seconds, beat beat beat. He hands it back, "That's for The Rita," he says. "We're the Golden Dawn. See, there's our name on the side. The Rita is tied up over there on the parallel jetty."

"What," screams the woman. "You mean we've been wasting our time looking round this crummy boat? Why didn't you say?"

Tom shrugs, "How am I supposed to know what our charterers look like. You've got our name, you didn't tell us yours."

"Look sonny," says the man, "time is money. I know, it's one of my business mottoes. Good business practice is to ask, then no-one's time is wasted. You've just wasted fifteen minutes of our valuable time and let me say, we don't appreciate it at all. Not at all."

The woman meanwhile has clambered back off the boat and is putting on her sandals and stamping in them. "Jerry, for god sake, let's go. No good bothering to teach idiots like that anything."

The young woman sighs, "I don't believe we are going, I really don't believe we are going to go sailing at all. I wanted so much to go sailing." She looks at Jim. "We're all staying at the Grand Caribbean," she says and follows after the others.

They stand watching her sway seemingly unconscious up the jetty, her bottom bobbing and the backs of her legs bouncing slightly with her springy walk, like baby bear out at play and not bothered at all who might end up eating her porridge. "Oooahh," says Jim.

Lynn flops down on the padded seat heaving her breath out in relief, "Thank god. Oh thank god, we didn't get them. Thank you, thank you JC."

"It wouldn't have been all bad, perhaps," says Jim still watching the retreating figure.

"You're kidding me!" says Lynn. "They were the most awful people I ever saw. Fancy thinking I was Tom's daughter."

Both immediately remember the mother. "Oh god yes, what an escape."

"But Tom," says Jim. "You must have started mighty early into fatherhood. Might one ask at what age you did beget this lovely young maiden here?"

"Monsters," says Tom.

"Not for us. Saved. The Rita gets them, lucky Rita."

"But what about George?" says Lynn sitting up. "What about Rita's cook, he's West Indian!"

"George! Rita has got George!" says Tom. "What happened to Liz?"

"Too pregnant," says Jim. "Stopped off in Martinique before the last charter and she's going to stay put for a bit."

"I wanted George. Damn. Bloody Skip, he doesn't miss a trick. No offence Lynn but George is the best cook on the boats."

"Well," says Jim, "I don't know. I heard he's let down by his pastry."

"Pastry!"

"Yes, Matey reckons it's just a trifle flaky. And Skip reckons his Hollandaise sauce is a tad too piquant."

"Oh shut up," says Tom crossly.

"When I was on The Rita," says Lynn reminiscing with glee, "the charterers told us they had to run away from the boat and go swimming far off where George couldn't get to them and tempt them with little elegant trifles all day long. We had this lobster quiche for lunch which would have floated away it was so light. You had to stuff it in your mouth really quickly. And while we sat chatting, the whole time he was down in the galley with all these lovely smells making this herb stuffing for rolled roast veal and then suddenly he passes up a batch of muffins….."

"Muffins," sighs Jim.

"Stuffed veal," murmurs Tom.

"Think of Skip and Mate," says Jim. "They'll have to eat it all themselves if the charterers refuse to go with them."

"Maybe they'll insist he's dismissed. If they chuck him maybe we could….."

He realises what he's saying and looks at Lynn apologetically.

"No that's OK. Just give me a ticket and I'll fly back." A surge of hope strikes her.

Tom strikes his head and laughs. "Even if I wanted to give you a ticket out, you've just spent all the cash. So you're with us to the bitter end. Or until I get the bulk of the charter money."

"Damn damn. Here I am," says Lynn dolefully, "admitting I can't cook and can I get out of a job, no. But if George were to come with us I would be honoured to be his assistant. To cut up his carrots and things for him."

"I wonder what they're paying him," yawns Tom. They loll, the water bobs them up and down. "Listen to the postcard I've written to Yvonne. 'First Day of Charter. Went to shop and got milk and cheese and bread. Then Lynn, the cook, found your menu and insisted on rushing back and getting lots of fancy stuff. It's a pity she can't actually cook though. No charterers have turned up. I've spent all the money. An eyelet in the awning needs mending but I'm too tired.' There, not bad. That eyelet will suck her in, she knows it's going to tear before I get round to it. Well suffer baby. Your loving non-husband Tom. I'll post that when I can work up the effort."

Hours drift and they doze at first and then gradually plunge right back down to sleep until the twilight waves its fronds across the sky at them. "Well anyway we're here," says Tom eventually rubbing his eyes, "and we've got lots of food and if they don't come maybe we'll just lie around and eat and have a good time, what do you think?"

“Sounds good to me,” says Jim. “But maybe you should go and see Bertram or call Charles or something. Just being practical for a moment.”

“You're right,” says Tom, not moving.

“Now!” says Jim. “While he's still in the office. It’s nearly six already.”

“Yeah right,” and Tom reluctantly gets up groaning and is crawling slowly up and over the seat when a young woman in a bikini goes by on the jetty. Tom looks at Jim, “What do you think of that?” and suddenly is very smartly leaping up and marching away.

Jim says, “You should have accepted him when he asked you to marry him the first time. You see, he's got a wandering eye, he won’t be faithful to you much longer.”

Lynn only got a fleeting glimpse of the young woman in the evening light, just enough time to notice her self-absorbed expression and rapid intense way of walking. She wonders at Tom going after such a woman but maybe he is just joking. Anyway she only gives it a passing thought. Tom is in charge and while he is in charge, it means the rest of them can relax. She watches the sun going down with the shallow eyes of the unengaged.

Lucas says, “If I am going to do all this overtime, I want evidence that it has been authorised and is going to turn up in my next pay-packet!”

The Sergeant looks at him, “You’ll do the work that needs doing. That is what the job entails.”

“Well first,” says Lucas becoming argumentative, “most of this work does not need doing. And second I know very well you were having a big fight with the pay section about some extra work you did yourself. So if you are going to be getting me to do all this trivial stuff where I can’t properly fulfil my duties as assistant to the coroner, I had better let the higher authorities know the reason I am not able to get on with it.”

The Sergeant breathes hard in anger and then says, “Well if you put that ahead of your duties then go home now. But it will be noted,” he says significantly. It will be noted.

There is not a lot of light remaining when Lucas finally arrives at Anthony Hamilton’s house in Louisaville. If Max de Troy happens to be there it can’t be helped. In any case the Sergeant’s brother has had early intimation of his new role. “So they pick

Constable Frankland," he said with an ironic smile. "Well it certainly will go hard on all the miscreants. Now that Constable Frankland is on the case. Boy, they certainly bringing in the big guns," at which the Sergeant gave out a long laugh.

The door is opened by a person Lucas knows. "Good lord, Lawrence, you here!"

Lawrence looks shamed-faced. "They pay me big money Constable Frankland and I am about to be married, I have to take the work. Since I left the Frangipani I ain't had any steady work. And tips, Constable Frankland. They say when Mr Hamilton returns and he has guests here they're going to give me tips in US dollars. What am I to do?" He spreads his hands and as he does so Max appears in the background.

"Who it is you are chatting to, Lawrence? Ah Constable Frankland, and is this an official visit?" His face takes on a sneer. "Assisting the coroner still. Dr Woodrow needs assisting no doubt, to save him falling into error. Well I would not like to be the cause of Dr Woodrow making ignorant comments in court so naturally we will do everything to assist you." He assists him by leading him to the scene of the 'unhappy accident' and then retiring into the house with Lawrence and shutting the door.

Lucas is now standing where he presumed the dead man stood on the night he plunged to his death. The paving beneath his feet, the tiles on the wall in front, the sculptures of nymphs off to the side are all imported and expensive and speak of the money that has been expended not only on this house but on all of the surrounding houses of the rich. There is wealth here that you can touch. Perhaps it is fortunate for the posterity of the dead man - if he had died at home in his own cabin no one would have given him a second thought. Deaths among the rich are important and demand attention whereas deaths among the poor are pathetic and often sordid. In any case, no one usually cares too much about the deceased person except his immediate family - what people care about is how the death affects them personally.

Professionally, Lucas is required to care about the man in that he must unravel cerebrally the puzzle of how the man died and why. To this end, he tries to put himself in the man's shoes as he stood on this spot. Was he contemplating suicide? Or maybe he was drunk and fell over. Lucas has interviewed the dead man's neighbours and knows that the deceased had gone on a family outing with his father on the day he died and this meant it was highly likely that a fair amount of alcohol was consumed. However no one had suggested that the man was incapable on his return. Had he been drinking since? And what about the other sinister possibility? That he didn't jump, or fall, but was pushed. Lucas has not established the reason for suicide – everyone he has so far interviewed said the man was in good spirits – nor has he established a motive for murder. All he knows is that a body fell through the air on a stormy night and crashed unheard into the car below.

Lucas surveys the site and its surrounds. Hamilton's house is similar to many of the opulent properties in the area. The land slopes quite steeply down to the bay ensuring spectacular views, and the houses are either built into the slope with two or three storeys or else there has been a terrace cut in and constructed to accommodate a one storey building. Anthony Hamilton's house is of the latter sort. The house has nothing but cliff above it and occupies a long narrow block which has concrete retaining walls at the further end. Where Lucas is standing, there is a cliff below dropping to the similar terraced land of Hamilton's neighbour. On his left is the road which turns sharply away in the last of its zigzags and runs on under another cliff. There are six other houses opposite and along that road before it comes to an end.

Where he stands is above the steepest part of the cliff, with a drop below of about 30 feet. There is a band of rock here which bulges out so that looking down from above Lucas can see only part of the neighbour's driveway beneath him. Further along and closer to the road the cliff wall is straight and Lucas can see right to the bottom. Lucas starts to ponder this matter. Now supposing that a man wants to jump off and kill himself and that he can see that this bit is straight and that bit is not, why would he jump from over there when he is bound to bounce off the protruding rock? Why wouldn't he jump from over here where he can see the bottom? The man would have been able to see what he was doing alright due to the habit the rich have of leaving security lights on all night. Why then would he have jumped from the point he did? He could go over wherever he chose because there is only a low wall, less than three feet high, between him and the drop. If he lurched, he might easily have gone over accidentally. Yes, Aunt Marion was certainly right about the lack of a proper safety wall. She wouldn't have liked this house. But then, she wouldn't have liked it anyway, even without the drop below. The ostentatious luxury of the suburb, the late-model cars in all the driveways, the breath of affluence. These unprotected cliff-faces were her excuse to go further up the hill to a less fashionable area where she would feel at home and could form close and intimate relationships with the storekeeper and the neighbours and others on her own social scale.

Lucas walks further along the wall as he continues to ponder the cliff problem. He is aware of an 'ahem' at his elbow and turns to find Lawrence there. "Max has gone," says Lawrence with a big grin. "He told me on no account was I to talk to you and if you asked me a direct question I was to be vague and say as little as possible."

"Why, what do you know?" asks Lucas.

Lawrence spreads his hands, "Absolutely nothing. That's what's so funny. I only started here four days ago. I never saw Mr Hamilton except at the Frangipani so how could I know anything? And in any case Mr Hamilton is away and is not expected back for some time and Max is the only one living here. No-one comes here at the moment."

"No-one comes," says Lucas. "So, no tips. And when is that to change, when is this wealth of US dollars to commence?"

"Well Max is getting a driver - I heard him talking on the phone to some fellow, sounded like from another island. And he is promising this other guy tips too."

"So business must be about to improve then?"

"I think everything is depending on this matter you are looking into. The day I started work here the phone rang and I know it is his brother the Sergeant because I know his voice and as I am going away I hear Max tell him that Mr Hamilton is waiting to find out the way the wind blows and he will come back to give his evidence if it is found to be an open and shut case - the man committed suicide as everyone knows. But that he don't want a scandal and now he is checking out other islands with a view to opening elsewhere. And there is no profit for anyone local if Hamilton goes elsewhere so the Sergeant had better look to his best interests here. I didn't hear any more because I was afraid of being found standing about. Max don't like that in a person."

Lucas thinks about what Lawrence has said. "Do you know what Mr Hamilton's business is?"

"Well I hear it is a club, an adult club, you know what I mean. Indecent carry-ons. My girl don't want me working here but money is money."

"So he may be back in a month for the coroner's court. And then what will happen?"

"I don't know at all," says Lawrence. "Half the house is shut up. The doors are locked. I don't go near the bedrooms or that side of the house. My job is to keep the general living areas clean and well dusted and tend the plants. That's all I'm doing. Money for nothing. Of course when Mr Hamilton comes back I will be given instructions about food to cook. And then I will wait on table too. Serve drinks and wear a uniform. Then I could expect tips. But I don't care one way or the other - I'm getting twice what I was getting at the Frangipani."

"Is that so? It seems too good to be true."

"Yes," says Lawrence doubtfully. "But Max, he's a scary fellow. He is scaring me. He says, you want to gossip about what goes on inside your own house or your cousin's house you go ahead, but if you go gossiping about what's going on inside Mr Hamilton's house you will be waking up with a sore head. If you wake up at all. And he is saying that with a man just dead. He's a scary man. But I'm not ending up like Selwyn Panday. I'm only staying till I have the cost of a bit of furniture saved up."

Lucas looks at him. "You think Selwyn may have talked about something?"

"I don't know," says Lawrence. "But that Max was speaking to me like he was threatening me. And with someone recently dead in this very house. And why would he tell me not to talk to you when I don't know nothing?"

"Well you are here talking to me in plain view and you had better take yourself off smartish in case anyone sees you."

"No-one could see us here. That's the thing about this side of the house. All this on the pool side, you can't see it from any of the other places round here, look around, see. I reckon they built it like this so people could go swimming in the nude."

"My aunt says you can see it just fine from up there, she says you can look right down on it from the fort."

"Is that a fact?" says Lawrence looking up the cliff nervously. "Well they wouldn't be wanting nude swimming with a set of low sorts up there looking on would they?"

Lucas turns his thoughts to other things. "I'm going down below to check where he landed."

Lawrence says quickly. "Well Constable Frankland you know I have told you nothing. And if I am ever found down a cliff I want you to know that I never in my life thought of doing away with myself. That is a fact." He turns to go. "That is a fact," he reiterates stopping to make his point again.

But Lucas is already walking away towards the entrance.

From underneath the wall, the problem reasserts itself. Panday must have struck the rock wall at some point on his way down unless he took a great leap outwards and why would a man expend so much effort if he was merely trying to kill himself? Yet Lucas looks along the line of wall and can see nothing. There must be something there though, he thinks, some microscopic clue; skin, a thread from a coat….. Lucas is looking up trying to ascertain where it would be best to try when a loud unpleasant voice behind him says, "And what the hell do you think you're doing trespassing on my property!" The owner of the voice is a small thick-set man with black shiny hair. He has sharp Indian features and is scowling at him ferociously.

"My apologies." Lucas had in mind that he might have to do some scrambling over the site and has come in plain clothes. He takes out his police identification. "Constable Frankland, assistant to the coroner. I knocked on the door but got no reply."

"Ah," says the man, his attitude changing immediately, as he softly pads forward on expensive loafers. "I was round the other side. I thought you were one of these damn layabout rogues that are always coming up my driveway and pretending they want work. Casing the joint, that's what they're doing. I tell you, if they ever try to get into my house I won't be calling you fellows. I've got my own ways of dealing with them."

"Is that so?" says Lucas politely, thinking to himself how pretentious the man is, with his upper class accent like he has come from some snooty school in England - and him just some local business man no doubt. "Have you had any disturbances of that sort up here?"

"My word yes," says the man. "There are some of the most outrageous criminals on the island coming up this road. And they are all heading for that house up there, that you are looking at. Yes, that's where they end up. But no doubt they don't mind breaking into a few houses en route and roughing up a few residents, I wouldn't put it past them. There was a desperate set moved in when that damn Hamilton rented the house. My God. When they put the house on the market we didn't know what we would get next door, you never do, and you should have seen some of the people who were up there looking it over. Then the new owner rented it to Hamilton and we all thought Jolly Good and look what happens. A white man and the worst of the lot!"

"Tell me what happened on the day of the death."

"Well I told it already to all those policejohnnies who came round but I don't trust them by half. The Sergeant they say is the brother of the man who works up there and how can that be? A Sergeant of police and his brother working in a house of ill repute! And he is telling me 'So the man jumped on your car and did away with himself.' Well I don't know, maybe the man did jump on my car to kill himself which is the kind of unneighbourly thing those bastards living up in that house would do!"

"What did you see?"

"Just what you would see in the police photographs. The gardener found it and when I came out to look, well I ran inside pretty damn smart I can tell you. I called the police and they eventually cleaned up the mess."

"Did he land all in one piece?"

"Oh, what questions you ask! I said, I didn't stop to look."

"I meant, were there things strewn around, coins out of his pocket, things like that?"

"Oh yes, the gardener has been finding things for the last week, they're everywhere you look. One of his shoes was behind that bush over there. And his hammer was found half buried in that bed there. My gardener found it yesterday."

"His hammer?"

"It's not my hammer, it's not my gardener's hammer so it must be his hammer. Some expensive German thing you'd only buy if you had more money than sense. He was a jack-of-all-trades, a maintenance man wasn't he? He must have had his hammer in his pocket."

"He jumped with a hammer in his pocket?"

"No explaining what these chaps will do. He was from a good Indian family then went and got involved with a common island girl, a black skinned woman, black as any you'd see in Africa. It's a terrible shame to see a man go downhill like that. It must be a sort of madness that comes on them, when a man marries beneath himself like that. They say it's love but it's madness believe me. And then out of sheer malice he jumped on my car and lobbed his hammer in the direction of my wife's car - it was parked over there that night - he must have missed it by inches."

"Well thank you very much for your assistance. Oh tell me, were you one of the neighbours who complained of screaming?"

"My wife made me. She woke me up to make me listen to it but I'm such a damn hard sleeper, by the time I'm awake enough - and I don't appreciate it at all, being woken I can tell you - it had stopped and my wife she said it was blood-curdling. She wanted me go outside and investigate. Go out in the middle of the night with people getting murdered out there! That's the job of the police so I rang you people. But then it turns out several other neighbours rang too and a fine to-do there was but nothing was done. If I'd heard it myself I would have gone up there with a gun. But it being my wife, well how did I know she wasn't exaggerating? I would have looked a fool if it was just some horse play in the pool or some such."

"Has your wife heard it since?"

"No. But since then they've had workmen up there and my wife says they've put in double glazing and a great big air conditioning unit. If you ask me, they put in the double glazing on account of the screaming. So now we don't hear anything but the sound of their damn airconditioning unit going all hours."

"I'd like to come back – it's getting too dark now. I want to bring a ladder and climb up and see if the man hit the rock wall on the way down."

"Please yourself. My gardener has got a long ladder. I'm sure he'd help you. The man does little enough of what he's supposed to do but anything that entails standing around and holding ladders will be right up his street."

On the Golden Dawn the time passes almost unnoticed, the twilight deepens, night descends and eyelids barely flutter but Tom does not re-appear. It is hunger eventually that rouses them and leads them to wonder what on earth has happened to him. "Maybe we should go and look for him," says Jim. "I bet he's found out he got the date wrong. I bet he's got the date wrong and we've been rushing up here for nothing and now he's hiding so he doesn't have to admit it. He'll have gone off to get drunk and pretend it wasn't his fault. I bet he's been having a few drinks the bastard. Come on, I've had enough of sitting around."

They wander up the jetty and follow the lights and sound of voices until they find a bar. "There he is the bastard, look at him. It's always first things first with Tom. I bet he hasn't even talked to

Bertram or Charles!" Tom is sitting at a small table with the woman in the bikini. "Ahoy skipper, remember us, the ones waiting for you back on board, getting thirstier and hungrier….. Waiting and waiting. I take it you're buying!"

Tom does not look the slightest bit conscience-stricken by his desertion and says, "Ah, I wondered what had happened to you two. Meet Sandra. Sandra's currently working on a boat called the Tit-bit and you should both be very grateful for the tight happy ship I run."

"It is not a happy ship,' says Jim. 'We have been waiting for hours and not the hint of a beer….."

"Sit down, sit down," says Tom expansively. "Beers is it?" and he gets them both drinks.

"So tell us, it's tomorrow isn't it - you got it wrong. Or the day after. Or next week."

Or never, prays Lynn. Please tell me it's never.

"No it was today," says Tom. "Or it was supposed to be but they're held up, lost their equipment in Miami or something."

"What equipment? Who the hell are we getting?"

"Three or four dozen Korean cameramen."

Getaway.

"No truly. Good isn't it. Because they're very small, we can fit 'em all in the aft cabin."

"So when are they coming?"

"Who knows. When they get their baggage back. Tomorrow, the next day. So my poor friends, you're just going to have to hang around on full pay while we wait patiently for them, Yee-hay!" He holds up a cheque in front of them and waves it slowly, "Money. Bertram has given me a proper deposit because I said we're not hanging around on the off-chance they turn up. So we are free to take off for the whole evening and who knows what adventures we may have."

"Where are we going to eat?" asks Lynn, "We've got so much food now I feel I should cook something on board."

"Blow that," says Tom. "You've done such a good job persuading us you can't cook that no way am I going to try any of it before I have to. Just joking. Now Sandra here is a real cook, she's got certificates and everything. But in any case, if we're going to be cooped up with each other on this boat for weeks, let's make the most of a night off and take in the sights, have a top meal and get some dancing in. Hey, the first thing to do after we get into our glad rags is to wander round to the Rita. I've heard they haven't gone yet surprise surprise. Let's just happen by real friendly-like and invite them out."

"Has anyone told you about the Rita?" Tom asks Lynn later as they are walking towards the boat in question.

"No, what?" says Lynn.

"They call it the Reefa because they have a habit of hitting the odd reef."

"Hitting reefs, what do you mean?"

"Here's a reef, here's the Rita, and smack. The two come together with monotonous regularity."

"Twice," says Jim.

"Twice then, but if I hit a reef even once I don't think I'd be wanting to do it again. Hello Rita," he calls out.

"Friends!" cries Matey.

"You need all you can get, from what I've seen", says Tom adding in a whisper, "Charterers on?"

"How do you know about them?" says Matey.

"Seen 'em. Had 'em on board. Had 'em storm off when they found out it was the wrong boat."

"What," says Matey coming closer, "you want them! Hey I'll go and tell Skip, I'm sure it can be arranged."

"Are you joking," says Tom. "I pointed them in your direction. I made sure they knew exactly how to get to you."

"Then you're no friend of ours. How dare you show your face here?"

"Heeheehee, what's happening? Are they going to forfeit their deposit."

"They're threatening to take Bertram and Charles to court and Skip to court and everyone to court for false pretences and every other thing under the sun. They're back at the hotel after pointing out that Skip is by no means married to George and that was not what was promised. Breach of contract and all, they'll be ringing lawyers right now according to the old guy. But I tell you what, they've about as much chance of getting a deposit back out of old Charles as they have of being nominated for the Nobel Peace Prize. Anyway I don't care either way because I reckon the daughter is a bit of alright. So what are you guys doing, all dressed up?"

"Going out for a drink. Want to come?"

"Might do. Might do. Where are you thinking of going?"

"I've heard the Grand Caribbean is rather a nice watering hole."

"So I've heard too," says Matey. "In fact I have heard that there's a dinner dance there tonight."

"Is that a fact. Well what luck!" They all agree.

The Grand Caribbean smells and looks and feels like an expensive bonbon. A creamy pale pink exterior gives way to a soft and glistening nougat filling. White alabaster figures of vaguely Grecian origin are grouped here and there and flowers of exquisite scent and texture spray down from white sconces. Underfoot the strawberry-piped marble shines in a glimmer of rose lighting, and pink cane lounge settings are strewn with deep maroon puffed leather cushions. The Grand Caribbean is made of money, so much money you can taste it.

Lynn looks at herself in the posh pink-framed mirrors. "I should look like money too," she thinks. "Why don't I?" Because she doesn't, she looks more like a cheap trinket even though here she is wearing the pretty pink dress which Arthur told her to keep. It has a label, an Italian designer label that even Lynn has heard of, a designer who is Big, Expensive and Exclusive. And she's got pretty pink sandals which she bought to go with it.

"I don't understand," she says to Skip. "How come I'm here dressed in pink and she's here dressed in pink, and I'm sitting at the bar and no-one is taking any notice of me at all? Look at the label, go on look, this is an expensive dress," she leans forward and twists so the back of the dress is towards him.

"It's a lovely dress," says Skip comfortingly, making no move to look at the proffered label.

"Just needs to be on a different body," says Jim.

"Hey come now," says Skip uneasily. "That was mighty uncalled for."

"I wasn't being rude," says Jim, looking affectionately at his companion. "Nothing wrong with Lynn, but there's something wrong with that dress. I don't know why you keep wearing it. It's like something off a sugar plum fairy."

Lynn sighs. "Don't you think it's frilly and candysweet and ever so feminine?"

"Yes," says Jim. "So if that's how you want to look, stop complaining about it."

The competition is also wearing pink but it is of quite a different order. Lynn's pink is the pink of baby skin, frou frou pink, little girl pink. The young American woman is in a dress the colour of a hot wet tongue. It is an unguessed-at pink, the inside pink of secret places, a pink that reminds one of snail liquids and the deep beating throb of hidden viscera. Lynn's dress is made to stride the catwalk on a long elegant model wearing white thigh boots and a red beret. It is a day dress playing with the conventions of evening wear, impractical layers of chiffon wafting onto the bus on the way to work. It is funwear, that inbetween clothing that goes straight to the back of the wardrobe and ends up abandoned on a Caribbean island when its novelty wears off in Milan and London.

Lisa-Marie's dress on the contrary has no such frivolous purpose. It is made for expensive wraps in expensive vestibules, it is made to slink through dim doorways into the very heart of desire. It is a strapless dress of a ruffled shiny material which is caked to her body like layers of frosting, with a bodice that encloses her breasts like flan round a jelly. She shimmies to the rocksteady beat of the band and her breasts bob and heave in the centre of the confection in rhythmical counterpoint. Every eye is riveted.

"What's the betting they fall out?" says Jim.

"It's been my experience," says Skip, "that women are always a lot more carefully tied in than you'd think, especially when they've got fathers lurking on the sidelines. I'd be very surprised if anything untoward happened."

"Amazing engineering feat," says Jim.

"You get what you pay for," says Skip drinking his drink. "Like a yacht. How often does a yacht sink? Come on, how often does a yacht sink?"

"Usually only once."

"No, what I'm saying is, a yacht is not designed to sink at all. It's designed to float. And so float it does because that's what the punters have paid money for. Now if your average hundred thousand dollar yacht fell over in some ripple, how long do you think the market in yachts would continue? Not even your average stupid yachtsman would buy it if it was going to sink, however pretty it looked."

"Even if it had leather upholstery?"

"Even if it had leather upholstery and a candystriped awning and a huge crimson spinnaker. Now my point is," Skip lowers his voice, "it's the same with ladies' superstructures. If they pay out the dollars they don't expect a sudden capsize, see what I mean."

There is a pause and they drink their drinks. "That was very philosophical," says Jim.

"You think so?" says Skip.

"Very deep. My word. Any more?"

"No, that's it," says Skip. "But we need some more benzine. Tony, over here. What are you having Lynn? Rum and cokes all round I think."

They drink their drinks and survey the scene. The crew of the two boats met up here and had dinner together, except for George. "No he wouldn't come to a place like this," says Skip. "He knows he wouldn't have a good time here, that's just how things are." After dinner, Matey peeled off the moment he got an eyeful of Lisa Marie and has joined the throng of hopefuls. Skip leans more comfortably on the bar and looks over to where the parents are the centre of a large group of rowdy older yanks. "God, look at the piss those two are sinking! They'll drink me out of house and home."

"But think of the compensations," says Jim looking at Lisa-Marie. "Just the crew and your Texan Princess there. But you're taken, that leaves George and Matey to vie over the honours."

"George!" says Skip.

"It's not beyond the bounds of possibility. Why shouldn't he try his hand? You've got to remember that all together on a yacht, day in day out, familiarity may make him look a lot whiter. And you have to remember that although George may not be god's gift to women….."

"He's an ugly bastard," muses Skip.

"Yes but it's funny what effect a man who makes muffins can have on the female sex. I've often noticed in my travels through this world that the man who is able to stick his head out of a hatch and say 'Who's for muffin?' is never short of female company. It's the domestic virtues, or something."

"He's got all those. In fact, I didn't twig what they were going on about at first. I thought they were questioning his cooking credentials, even though the man did two years as an apprenticed chef. Two years. I mean he didn't finish, he hasn't got the piece of paper but for heaven's sake how many cooks on the boats here have any qualifications at all?"

"I haven't, and I can't cook either," says Lynn.

"Exactly. You'd be lucky to find a ship's cook who can. But George can."

"But even so. I expect you're tempted to make alternative arrangements, especially….." Jim's eyes wander over to the Americans.

"Alternative arrangements, what do you mean alternative arrangements?"

"Oh you know," says Jim drinking his drink. "Find him a berth on some other yacht till things settle down. Till this lot go back to where they've come from. It must have entered your head it's going to be very difficult. Very difficult indeed. Horrible. Hell in fact. That is if they go at all and you don't end up in some expensive litigation. It must be a great temptation to take on this girl from the Tit-bit."

"What girl?"

"The one over there that Tom is fixed to like superglue. Apparently she's done a Cordon Blue course but she doesn't see eye to eye with the Tit-bit's lecherous old skipper. She's looking for a berth. But your loyalty to George of course….." Jim drinks his drink.

"Of course," says Skip.

"Drink up. Another round," calls Jim.

"The trouble with George," says Skip becoming confidential some time later, "is he's so hard to contain. He's enthusiastic, which is good. Yes don't get me wrong, it's good. But he does make it difficult to get anywhere. The charterers come on board and all they want to do is relax, get away from all the hassles of life on shore, get out to sea and go fishing and swimming and dive on unchartered reefs far from other human kind. But George, all he thinks about is food. We'll be swinging down the Grenadines with all sails set and George will be wanting us to stop at this island or that island because he needs something or other and we have these big fights about our itinerary….. The whole thing stops being about the best reefs and the best snorkelling and becomes instead about ingredients he has to have. I ask you. He's telling the charterers 'You wait till we get to this island. I'll cook you this so-and-so fish in this so-and-so sauce and you will never have tasted anything so good'. Suddenly the whole trip is about nothing but eating."

"Sad," says Jim. "Terrible," says Jim having thought it over even more. "He must be a great trial to you."

"Yes and before you know where you are we're having to make diversions to every fish market, every vegetable market, every bloody place he can get fresh fat pork or particular herbs or spices. I mean, then we have to hang around because your average charterer is always wanting to go and explore. Explore, I ask you. What's to explore? Smelly markets with lots of flies. And then if he gets something a bit out of the ordinary, suddenly it's a huge production, and the charterers get all excited and start dressing for dinner and you end up with your clothes getting too tight and everyone lying around too full to move."

"Your patience in putting up with him will be rewarded in heaven," says Jim shaking his head in sympathy. "But," he says drinking his drink, "he could come with us if you like. Lynn's feeling nervous so we don't mind taking on an extra. As a favour."

"You're a good man, Jim lad."

"Yes," says Jim.

"An honest man. A generous man."

"I wish Tom could hear you say such things about my character. And where is Tom? Oh there he is, I must just go and speak to him."

Skip meanwhile has turned his attention to other matters. "Isn't nature wonderful?" he says to Lynn. "There is a young woman," indicating the Texan princess, "looking for a man, and there," with an expansive vague wave of his arm, "are some men looking for a woman. And when the men have all lined up, once they have joined the queue and she's looked them over she will make her choice. Like lyre birds. The lady lyre bird just propels herself forward with minimal energy and all the gentlemen lyre birds start dancing like mad things and displaying and preening and squabbling. You see, there'll be tears before bedtime."

"And what about you, Skip, not joining in? Not a red-blooded male like these others?"

"Married," says Skip.

"Ah."

"Married," says Skip, "to a woman who doesn't understand me, who doesn't understand the very ordinary and necessary sexual drive of the male animal. Married to a woman with a terrible temper and a fearsome right hook."

"Mmm."

"If I was to stray she's not the sort of woman to forgive and forget. No sirree, she is like one of those women with the terrible heads, all snakes spitting and swords spouting blood. But she's a lovely girl. Have you seen?" he feels for his wallet. "I have a picture of her, damn," he is scattering things and gives up.

On the dance floor, the lacquered softly-wobbling blonde is doing a slow fancy jive with a small ugly man. "John Havermore the Third," says Skip.

"He's got a face like a ferret," says Lynn.

"He's got a bank full of money," says Skip. "He owns the Evangelica. You know, that big tart of a ship. He's got ten crew working for him and he's the meanest bastard you'll ever meet. If he comes over here and offers you a drink don't accept because he'll order French champagne in a fit of apparent bonhomie but when you stagger up to go home, you'll discover it somehow all ended up on your tab."

"Why does she want to dance with such an ugly man?" wonders Lynn. A woman like that who has her pick, who has all the available single men stalking slowly straight legged around the edge of the pack, sniffing the air, looking for an opportunity.

"Women seem to find him attractive enough. Though he's a friend of that ponce Anthony Hamilton. Oh bloody hell, talk of the devil."

Anthony Hamilton has had a fair amount to drink and he is a man who tends to turn extremely ugly when this happens. He had been on the point of talking his friend John into a sizeable stake in the consortium with his father, and it would have been a much needed influx of cash and credit, essential almost. But then just when it seemed, over a nice dinner, that Havermore would commit himself, this wretched young woman starts bouncing her boobs in his face. He can't see it himself. If Havermore wants a well-fleshed woman well Anthony can get him one - he can provide him with any number, black, white or any colour of the rainbow. But this one isn't even a certainty. Every man in the place is making a fool of himself over her and yet there are women to be had by the bucket-load for the right amount of cash and no aggravation in the taking. Why, when you can buy what you need, would you suddenly be like a dog on heat over a girl who will make her own mind up about where her favours go? So humiliating.

So he has given up on his project for now and is staggering in the direction of the bar. He is having some difficulty staying upright but hey ho here are some familiar faces. Skip who owns one of the bigger boats, handsome sort of wife too as he recalls. Is that the wife in the pink dress? No, not tall enough. And far too young. She looks a bit familiar though, he's definitely seen her before. Hasn't Max pointed her out? Why would he do that unless she is a possible player? Not really the usual sort of woman Max goes for. Bit dangerous when they're that young. Though Max's choices can be dangerous on any level. Fancy getting in such a fury about the last one - no woman is worth that amount of trouble. He needs to get rid of Max at some future point; he doesn't appreciate his employees getting out of control. That operation will have to be wound up once the inquest is over. No, what he wants is something like this hotel. Once they get hold of the swamp this is the sort of thing he is aiming for. Very select and expensive, especially if Havermore will come in with them. Yes and then he will give up on the other line. This is the kind of future he wants for himself. "Hello," he calls having reached his objective.

The operating guidelines among yachties for the approach of Anthony Hamilton is to drift off quickly in the other direction but unfortunately Jim has reappeared with Tom and Sandra without noticing what is in the offing. He is in the process of introducing Sandra to Skip, and thus everyone is distracted when Anthony suddenly appears in their midst. "Shipmates, well met," he is feeling amiable all of a sudden, thinking of future hotels like this and the life it will be, managing such a place. Full of grateful customers. He pulls himself sideways onto the seat beside Lynn. She isn't bad at all. He'll see how he goes so he gives her his most winning smile. "I don't know if we've been introduced," he holds up his hand like a flipper and takes hers. "Anthony. Like a drink?" He gestures imperiously to the barman down the bar.

"I've seen you before," she says.

"Ah really," he shouts enthusiastically, "and where was that?"

"In the Frangipani."

He drums his fingers on his lanky knee. "The old Frangipani. That dump, hahaha," he shouts. "What was a nice girl like you doing in a place like that?"

"Living in the marina," she says. "I like it there."

"Gone to the dogs," he continues as if addressing a public meeting, being drunker than he thought and having to concentrate so as not to slur his words. "Total hellhole. Needs a thorough going over, new management. Hopeless bloody shower there at the moment," he nods to himself while she looks at him uneasily. "Anyway," he says rousing himself with a lurch and draping his arm around her shoulder, "what brings you here?" She leans back in alarm and he nearly falls off his stool onto the floor. He re-rights himself into an upright position holding firmly onto the bar. "Damn chairs," he says, "never make them properly. That's the trouble with this place, nothing is straight. Have you noticed that, they can't make a straight chair. No-one in these islands has a clue. I mean the bloody West Indians of course, no aspersions on anyone here. Ah barman and what are you all drinking?" He looks generously around him.

It seems that no-one is needing a refill at that moment.

"Come on, drink up. Better still, come and have a dance."

"No thank you." Lynn has learned from experience and now has no compunction in refusing. But her refusal has no effect at all as having got the thought in his head he has grabbed her by the arm and is dragging her by main force onto the floor. "Aark God," she splutters but he is singing the words to the song and to him she is just a parcel that he is moving from one place to the other. The momentum of his sudden lurch towards the dance floor propels her into the middle and suddenly she is there beside Lisa-Marie. "Hello," says the golden girl, "you were on that boat this afternoon."

"Yes," says Lynn.

"I've been admiring your dress. I saw it a couple of years ago in Vogue."

"It's the only one I've got," says Lynn.

"Yes there's no room on those boats. I'm going to have to work out what I can do without."

"So you're actually going."

"I'm definitely going. That's why I came down here. Even if I have to go alone." Then she turns away back to her partner who has moved in as a slow number starts.

"You know her?" says Anthony, who has now also grabbed her in an unwelcome embrace.

"Yes," says Lynn, though as she doesn't feel like talking to him she doesn't elaborate.

"She's very nice, I'm sure," says Anthony. "That's my friend John she's dancing with. He's very rich. I can introduce you to him if you like. I introduce him to a lot of nice girls."

Lynn doesn't say anything. She isn't enjoying this experience and she thinks the shortest way to stop it is to keep quiet. They stumble around in an approximation of a slow waltz, with Anthony's leering face close to her own.

"So, living on the marina. Oh dear me, there's a loose woman works there you know. Quite a reputation she's got though she doesn't know it, hahaha. Yes, what a little scene that was and I must say I was angry losing that, might get in the wrong hands. I'm the one that has to think of these things."

Lynn doesn't know what he is talking about and says nothing.

"But, always looking for a new pal, more the merrier I say, spice of life, variety. You must come to my house."

"I've heard of your house," says Lynn coldly.

"I bet you have," he says smiling knowingly.

"I heard somebody died at your house."

"Oh that," he laughs. "Just some native throwing himself off a cliff, they're always doing it apparently. No, come to my house, you can earn big money there."

"I don't need a job. When I'm not on charter, I work for Boss."

"No no not Boss, that alcoholic. He won't get much more work, he's on his beam end. That boat would have been sold from under him by now only a certain person was keeping the hounds at bay and now she's gone he's lost his safety blanket." He pauses to sing along loudly and off key to the song the band is playing. "Yes those old men hanging about the waterfront," he continues returning to the subject, "all a bit sodden. We had a bit of a problem with one of the Coloureds that works at the Frangipani. They should never have got involved, they don't know what they're doing. All that rum has taken its toll."

Lynn stops dancing, "You're talking about Arthur. I'm a friend of Arthur's too." And she thinks, the last time I was dancing, slow dancing like this Arthur was holding me not you, you horrible drunken….. murderer.

"A friend of Arthur's!" He laughs disbelievingly. "No I can't believe it. You look as if you'd have more class than that!"

"Excuse me," says Lynn and walks away without looking back. "Thanks a lot for saving me from that creep," she says to Jim back at the bar. "At least I know I can rely on you to rescue me in an emergency."

"Not with him, he gets ugly at the drop of a hat. If anyone had butted in there would have been a fight and look, you had a little dance and you're none the worse for wear."

"You're all horrible. I'm going back to the boat." She picks up her bag and makes her way towards the foyer. She hears a hullo behind her but ignores it thinking it might be Hamilton again. However when she stops to look for a taxi, Skip staggers up behind her and leans on her shoulder. "I'll come too. Need to have one of us that's fresh. Bloody hell, had too much, there'll be the devil to pay tomorrow. Don't seem to be able to take it like I used to."

Back at the marina the moon is full. Lynn has to help Skip out of the taxi where he has dozed off. "Look at that," says Skip once roused and again supported by her shoulder. "Look at that moon. My wife will be looking at that moon, she loves moons."

"She'll have been tucked up in bed long ago."

"No she has difficulty sleeping, the kiddy keeps kicking her. This is my last charter, cancelling the others, can't keep on doing 'em while the lady is off fending for herself in her condition, not right is it? It's not right. Who knows what might happen if I'm not there, an alligator might eat it, she's having the baby underwater you know. Funny idea if you ask me but that's what she wrote me. It's being alone, makes women come up with things like that. They don't think it through, not logical like us. There are so many dangerous things in this world, constantly after you. There's a big storm coming."

"Is there?"

"It's going to be rough for days, longer even. It'll keep them down below though, rough weather, it keeps the charterers subdued."

"Well at least you know the worst about yours," says Lynn. "We haven't a clue what ours are going to be like."

"Worse," says Skip "They're always worse than you could ever imagine." He comes to the railing beside his boat and eases himself off her shoulder and on to it.

"But your last ones were nice," says Lynn.

"Ah yes, but then we were expecting them to be hell. That's how it happens you see. We were expecting a couple of complaining geriatrics….." he staggers trying to get his leg over the wire rail. On the other side he turns to face her, hanging from a stay. "It's never what it seems. And everyone tells you such bullshit. Charles, Bertram, all such crap-artists, everyone is always bullshitting everyone else. What were we talking about tonight? Some more bullshitting going on….. God I've got a pain in the gut….. Some bloody thing they were trying to get me to agree to. I've got to go and lie down." With care he creeps across the deck and disappears.

Lynn stands for a while looking at the moon, feeling totally miserable, empty and abandoned.

Chapter 10

Strike nothing, and stir nothing, but lash everything

Lynn is falling. Plummeting downwards. She was on a winding mountain road in Arthur's car and the brakes failed and it all got out of control and now she is falling, falling into a great abyss, screaming, and thinking, oh let this be only a dream.

Thank God, it is only a dream. Her eyes are suddenly open and here she is safe in the real world. She has been woken by a sort of 'Hoy' from the jetty. It's barely daylight and the sky is sea-grey and pearly.

She puts her head up but for a moment all she can see are slabs of dark and pale white water, shadows like wolves on the snow, but as she blinks and clears her dreams she sees there are four people standing on the jetty with a pile of luggage. "Hello," she says.

All four bow. "Herro," says one of the men and, removing his shoes, steps down on to the deck. He is holding a piece of paper. "Tomu Robeesan," he reads carefully.

She stares at him. "Oh Tom," light breaking. "Tom," she calls down the main hatch. Silence. She goes down to the eating area. All the berths are empty except one with a curtain across. A body is scrunched up behind it in a heap, but it is Jim, dead to the world and no sign of Tom. "Jim," she says shaking him vigorously, "Jim, where's Tom? The charterers are here. Wake up."

"Umumum mumble." He is useless.

She goes back up, "He's gone out to get something apparently," she lies bravely. "Won't you come on board. I'll show you where everything is. My name is Lynn."

So that's how Lynn gets to greet Mr and Mrs Tanaka and their interpreter and cameraman. At first she feels quite helpless as Tom never bothered to share any real information with her or Jim about their charterers. She wonders if he knows or cares who he's getting. That they might be truly foreign with only limited English never entered her head.

The four charterers carefully remove their shoes and all stand on the deck nodding their heads in a disconcerting way and smiling. Lynn doesn't know what to do with their smiles. What do they want her to do? The interpreter is by no means fluent in English. However she manages to organise everything with his help, showing them the accommodation and providing towels and linen. That done they go back to bowing and smiling. With a sudden surge of inspiration, she asks them if they would like breakfast. This is translated and there is a slight hesitancy. She thinks, "They've had breakfast on the plane," and is at a loss what else to suggest. However one of the men, who is introduced very formally and reverentially by the man who speaks English as Mr Tanaka, suddenly gives her to understand that breakfast (or bray-uk-fass as he calls it) will be acceptable. With relief she escapes into the galley. She makes them fresh coffee and scrambled eggs and crispy bacon and toast while they put away their things and then she carries it all up on deck where the morning is now bright and morninglike but when she calls them to eat they look in a strange way at the plates that she puts down on the fold-out table and Mr Tanaka makes noises like a cockerel examining a ploughed field. Oh dear, she thinks, maybe this is against their religion or something. The interpreter has meanwhile taken up the forks and knives and seems to be explaining something. Lynn has made some breakfast for herself and goes down and gets it. She then sits down near the hatch and starts to eat. She is instantly aware as she does so that the interpreter has stopped talking and that the eyes of all the charterers are on her. Maybe they have to say grace or something, she thinks. Or maybe I'm not allowed to start until they do. She has a forkful of egg and is in the process of biting into one of the slices of buttered toast. She puts it down and waits. Mr Tanaka is looking closely at her right hand where she holds the fork American fashion and picks up his own in the same crooked position and dips his fork into the egg and transfers it with great care to his lips. He smiles. He takes the toast with his other hand as she has done and takes a bite. He smiles again. Lynn instantly sees that the whole of the meal is strange, not only in the way it is prepared but in the way it has to be eaten. She re-positions her fork in the other hand and picks up the knife. She cuts the bacon which falls into crispy shards. She positions one of the shards with a little egg on the back of her fork and carries it to her mouth. Apart from the interpreter who appears to have some familiarity with western customs, the other three are clearly at sea. Their hands travel like sleepwalkers over their plates. Egg and bacon falls in untidy scatterings as they try to emulate her actions. She takes pity on them and picking up a large piece of bacon in her fingers, she puts it in her mouth and crunches on it. Instantly bacon is dispatched. She licks her fingers. They lick their fingers. She picks up piece of toast and uses it as a shovel to ladle the scrambled egg on. Heads go down, egg and toast and bacon disappear. Lips are licked. Mr Tanaka reaches for his cup of percolated coffee and delicately sips. He sighs. "Aah," he says and nods at her encouragingly, "Ver-ray good-onay!" The whole party nods enthusiastically.

By 8.30 there is still no sign of Tom, and Lynn is running out of things to smile at. So she feels intense relief when she sees him sauntering up the jetty looking pleased with himself and perky. He has clearly had a good night. "Hello hello," he greets and shakes hands all round. "All well? Had breakfast? Good good. We just have to wait for one more person and we can be off."

"We do?" says Lynn.

"Didn't Jim tell you?" murmurs Tom. "We've scored George."

"You're joking."

"You don't mind."

"Of course not. But how did you….? Skip will never forgive you if you've….."

"No no, Skip agreed. He's taking Sandra and she's pleased because she doesn't want to stay on the Tit-bit any more, some problem there. She's going up there now. I hope George is amenable but he'll be much better off with us." He hums pleasantly to himself. "Of course we'll be a bit over-crewed but we can fit in easily enough. George gets first choice of wherever he wants to sleep once the others are tucked in. They're only small these Chinese, they'll probably all fit in the aft cabin."

"Shush Tom, they speak English."

"Do they? Getaway. Anyway how are you Lynn old thing, have a good night last night? That's the ticket. Where's Jim?"

"Dead to the world, can't wake him. I've no idea when he came home and crashed but it was definitely after a good night by the look of him."

"Oh well, not to worry, we'll get the boat out between the two of us and there'll be old George to help as well."

"There's that girl, the one you were..... She looks upset." The girl is coming up the jetty walking fast with a set face and clutching a holdall and another bag.

"Ah Sandra, getting settled in?"

"No I'm not getting settled in!" She is breathing fast. "I got there ten minutes ago just as the American charterers were getting on board so I moved forward quickly in order to greet them and reassure them but the skipper - Skip did you say his name was? - didn't seem to know what I was talking about! He said George was below making breakfast and they didn't need a cook and then he turned his back on me. Just like that. And I've left the Tit-bit and had my say about how they've treated me so I can't go back there." She stands on the jetty clearly saying by her body language, 'You got me into this, you get me out!'

Tom is thunderstruck. "Why he said..... Didn't he Lynn, you were there last night, he said....." He gets up and says "Excuse me" to the charterers then runs off along the jetty in the direction of the Rita. As he disappears, the girl steps over the railing and dumps her bags on the deck and sits down among them all, with a stubborn ugly look on her face. Lynn feels this terrible premonition forming. She goes down the main hatch and shakes Jim unmercifully. "Wake up."

"What?" he stares at her, red eyed.

"Something bad is happening. There's a woman on board called Sandra. Tom's been arranging something with Skip and it hasn't happened."

"It didn't," Jim concentrates. "No George is coming here not Sandra. Sandra is going on the Rita."

"No she's not. Skip's not having it this morning. He was drunk last night. I think he realised you'd pulled something on him but he couldn't remember what. Now he's telling her he doesn't know anything about it and in the meantime she's left her boat. You've got to stop Tom because whatever happens I just know it's going to be bad."

For a minute Jim looks like he might rouse himself but then says, "Oh bugger it! It's always like this," and puts his head down.

"No Jim, wake up, take some responsibility."

"I can't," he murmurs into the bunk. "I can't."

Lynn goes back up on deck and gnaws her fingers. The charterers lift their eyebrows and look at her quizzically as they talk among themselves – it's impossible for Lynn to know if they sense something is up. Clearly Sandra is also being talked of but Sandra has no time for that; she has her own ferocious agenda which has turned her mouth into discontented and bitter contortions.

Sandra is a tall tanned girl with straight brown hair sun-streaked with gold. She is wearing white sandshoes, pale green shorts and a darker green sleeveless top. She is bra-less and her nipples nudge the cotton, making nipple shapes when she sits up. But she is currently hunched over pulling at bits of her hair with her top offcentre exposing one of her shoulders. She has skin with the burnish of expensive plastic, exposed arms and legs at all sorts of angles. All of this the charterers are observing because there is no gainsaying, she is a strikingly attractive girl - even though Lynn feels there is something off-centre about the whole of her.

Tom is coming back up the jetty. He is coming slowly with his head down no longer looking perky and his hands are thrust in his short-pockets making them sag off his hips. He is getting a pot-belly - there is the hint of a curve between his shorts and shirt. He walks the walk of defeated flesh. What is he going to do?

What he does is exactly what Lynn was worried he would do. He takes Sandra with them. Not that Lynn knows anything to Sandra's discredit, but there is something about the timing of the whole thing that spells disaster. The charterers are looking uneasy and it is clear there is going to be a scene. So Tom takes the easy way out and then makes necessity into a virtue. The drums of the apocalypse beat in the clear blue sky and they are sailing away straight towards it. They leave with all speed and Lynn is the crew; it becomes clear that Sandra's duties do not include anything to do with sailing. Tom, who has failed in a savage bid to rouse Jim, is now loudly pretending to make the best of it but Lynn feels as if all the pores of her perception are open and working overtime. It isn't helped when the cameraman gets out a movie camera and starts taking pictures of them.

"What the hell's he doing?" asks Tom.

"He's the cameraman," says Lynn.

"I was told they were all cameramen. Not that I care, just so long as they don't get in the way," says Tom bad-humouredly. Once they were underway he says, “So what’s with the camera work, are we going to be on TV or something?”

Lynn has found out the story. “Mr Tanaka has a company in Nippong…..”

“I thought they were Korean.”

“They’re from somewhere called Nippong.”

“It must be a city, like Hong Kong.”

“Anyway, Mr Tanaka has been sick, I’m not sure what with. And he’s been told to take a long holiday. Mr Yamada is the interpreter. And Mr Fukuda I think his name is, is the cameraman, who is going to make a record of their adventures and it is going to be printed in one of Mr Tanaka’s papers. There’s a writer too but something’s happened to him en route so Mr Yamada is going to do the writing I think.”

“I’m never going to be able to remember those names. Why do they all sound the same? Don’t they have Christian names?”

“I think Mr Tanaka and Mr Yamada are both called Sam. Only they put it after the surname. Mr Fukudu is called Kenji.”

“And what about her?”

“Well I don’t know, she just bows and smiles when I look at her; she hasn’t said anything yet. She’s the wife of Mr Tanaka but no-one has introduced her by name.”

“So how have you arranged them? Him and her up the front and the other two in the aft cabin?”

“No. Mr Tanaka has chosen the aft cabin and Mr Yamada is to have the fore cabin. It seems that Mr Fukuda is not very important. He has been told to sleep in one of the bunks in the main cabin.”

“We can’t have that, not now we’ve got four crew.”

“Mr Tanaka decided it. He decides everything it seems and people do as he says.”

“Damn, well if they booked for five….. I suppose they can do what they like. When are we going to get something to eat? I didn’t get any breakfast. Go and ask Sandra what she’s going to do for lunch. Now she’s cook.”

When Jim rises some hours later and is sheepishly introduced to the charterers, Lynn also pointedly introduces him to Sandra. “It may not be so bad,” he says aside to Lynn. “She’s done some fancy course and while you’re helping her cook you can pick up hints.”

“I’m not helping her cook,” says Lynn. Sandra has made it clear that she is to reign supreme and Lynn is only allotted the tasks which are beneath her, such as washing up, clearing away, serving and other such menial work. "And she doesn't think much about the things I've bought, not nearly enough of this and that. How can she 'create' meals with such woeful ingredients?"

"Oh Lynn I'm sorry. Tom, yes I know, he's a stupid clunkhead. Look what he's got himself into."

"I thought it was you. You were organising it."

"No no it was Tom. He left me to soften Skip up. Then pow, Tom would produce the goods."

"In more ways than one."

"Well that was foreseeable. I told you before you should have accepted him when he proposed. That would have kept him on the straight and narrow for a while at any rate. Anyway look, it's only for four weeks, that's not a lifetime. And as for the cooking, at least we've got a proper…. I mean, the chinks'll love cordon blue. Some of those places have had the French running them already, no that's Vietnam not….. Where are they from? But they're bound to like a nice bit of French cooking. I'm looking forward to it myself, no offence or anything."

Sandra meanwhile is sitting on deck and looking progressively more and more green and it soon becomes clear that Lynn will have to do lunch herself. She has some French loaves from yesterday and these she crisps in the oven before she cuts them into long lengths, removing a little of the inside soft part. Then she stuffs them with salad, lobster and makes up some fresh mayonnaise with eggs, olive oil, wine vinegar and mustard the way Boss has shown her. By this time they have been at sea for some hours and the charterers are finding their sea legs. Mrs Tanaka has changed out of her travelling outfit into flowered shorts and a tailored blouse and her husband has changed into a pair of white shorts, a casual shirt - substantially unbuttoned - and a nautical hat. Mr Fukuda is in a Hawaiian shirt and shorts but it seems that no-one cares what he wears. Mr Yamada however has maintained formality in neat trousers and neat short-sleeved shirt. This seems to be the subject of some jocular exhortations to change into something more informal but clearly Mr Yamada is determined to maintain a certain official air. So with the exception of Sandra who is languishing, they all sit down to lunch with good appetites. Mr Yamada doesn't understand 'lobster' although he asks very carefully – lob-u-sta - and goes through his dictionary but after opening their rolls and tentatively sampling the red meat Mrs Tanaka identifies it, "Oh ah so!" They start eating with enthusiasm, picking out the long shreds of sea food and letting the morsels wash down their throats followed by a stream of beer, their faces alight with pleasure. Lynn thinks, two meals down and only four weeks to go - so far she hasn't made any mistakes.

Lucas is poring over his notes, trying to think things through to their rational conclusion. His ponderings are interrupted by the clatter of elegant mules.

"Sheila, I thought you'd gone. What brings you to our humble home?" he says surprised.

"That brother of mine. He won't come and visit me so I have no option - where is he? Slung out in the hammock I suppose."

"Of course," Lucas starts to pack his papers away.

"Tantie wants to know how the investigations are going."

"The Sergeant has been trying to make sure that they don't go anywhere but I have stood up and told him I intend to carry on with it. I think that my days are numbered."

"Now, you'd wonder why the Sergeant would be wanting to stop you!"

"Yes you would wonder, wouldn't you? Considering he thinks I'm pretty useless anyway. But maybe there's something so obvious about it all that even someone as dense as me is not going to miss it. He is hell bent on obstruction."

"Yes but what would you expect? From that family."

"Well I must be off. Wake Arthur up. He wastes too much time altogether. I wish I had that much time to waste."

Arthur however is not asleep. He is gazing out with a rather wistful and sad expression but smiles when he sees his sister. "How you going, Sis? Film finished?"

"For now. I'll be glad when the whole thing is over. Another few days in Martinique in about a month and that's it." She climbs into the hammock beside him. "We were at the Lotus House and Frank the director has somehow come by all these beautiful girls who have to walk here and there as if, in these worlds I inhabit, there exists no-one without perfect bodies."

"But that's true, isn't it Sis?"

"Anyway Frank is going 'Helpers, Helpers. Where are my Helpers!' because they don't get paid, they do it for the glory apparently."

"Ah I see. No it is a very different world from yours."

"And he's such a nancy boy, Frank, flapping his arms, it all looks so amateurish. I hope I did the right thing in agreeing to do this film. I'll die if it's so terrible everyone laughs."

"They won't laugh at you, though. You'll look as cool and distant as ever."

"Is that how you think I look?"

"Oh yes. A very haughty model of a model."

"But you don't really think I'm cool and distant."

"Course not. You're just my sister," and he gives her a hug. "There's Lucas off again. He's the one who has become cool and distant. No gossip. Poor Tantie."

Sheila rolls out of the hammock, "Now Arthur, get up. I want to speak to you face to face. Up up. This is serious. Right." She gets him sitting in a chair opposite her as she fidgets with her bracelets and jewellery. "You know all I want now is for you and Tantie and all the people I care for to be happy. It's the only reason I work as I do. You may think I love being a model but I don't."

"Is that so?" says Arthur smiling ironically.

"The money, I do it for the money. Modelling is the only occupation that will help me to fulfil my dream of revenge. Dr Woodrow told me way back that living well is the best revenge. And he's right. You see I'm here. And Max is here. And who is it that people come rushing to see? Who is it that people suck up to? Who is it that the local paper follows around every moment of the day, trumpeting Our Famous Daughter, Our Own Girl At The Top? And where is Max? He's nowhere, he's a nobody, he's nothing but some low-down fellow that everyone is suspicious of now. It's a better revenge than if I'd got a gun and shot him. So now I'm going to live the best life I can. One day I'm going to live here with my family. You're my family. You and Tantie. All I want is for you to be happy." She gets up and starts walking up and down twisting her hands while Arthur watches her in surprise. "I don't want you to be hurt. I don't want you to fall in love and be hurt because you chose the wrong person."

Arthur sighs as the reason for her serious talk suddenly becomes clear to him. What is the point anyway? Lynn is far off, sailing away into adventures, Jim by her side. Jim who is the one everyone will think the right choice anyway. She'll never think of him. If she has ever been attracted to him that will fade. She'll meet new people….. But anyway, there is no point in telling his sister all this. She can only be allowed to run his life so far; at some point she has to let him go, let him make his own mistakes. As she has made hers. He gives a non-committal reply, "You'll fall in love with someone soon yourself. There's no guarantee that any of us will fall in love with the right person."

"But some people are wrong, not from who they are but from the situation. You know what I'm talking about."

"Do I?" says Arthur. "What about this English rock musician you're going out with?"

"That's nothing," says Sheila impatiently. "You're corrupting the argument. I'm talking about the marrying sort of love here."

"It seems to me that we all fall in love with who we fall in love with, and there's nothing any of us can do about it."

"That's where you're wrong. For a start, if you stay away from the wrong sort of people, don't get so friendly with them, don't have them round you all the time, calling in, passing the time with you, then you'll never have the call to fall in love with one of them."

"That's true," says Arthur. "But unfortunately for that argument, I never was able to make friends by rote. Maybe it's something you learn on the show-business circuit. I like people or not. I can't help who I like."

"But you liked Susie. Susie. The girl I introduced you to at the party."

"Did I?"

"You must remember her….. At the party out at the Fair."

"Was she one of your model friends?"

She sighs. "No, she's not a model. You don't remember her?"

"Not particularly, though I remember Erica all too well."

"Forget Erica," she says impatiently. "That was a mistake. My how a body changes. Who would imagine she'd turn out as she has?" She sits down and sighs, "So Susie made no impression."

He just looks at her. He remembers some vaguely repulsive woman who was thrust at him; he hasn't a clue what she looked like. They dragged him out of an embrace he never intended to get into but by then it was too late. The deed was done. He understands what his sister is trying to do and he doesn't blame her for it; she wants to screen out the bad times that will probably lie ahead, rejection, abandonment of hope, bitterness. But it's all too late. For all her wealth and fame she is powerless to stop what has now irrevocably begun.

Towards evening the Golden Dawn comes into anchor in a pleasant deserted bay and Tom breaks out the rum and coke and puts more beer on ice. Sandra takes up her station in the galley. No she doesn't want any help, this is her domain. She lost her green pallor as the boat entered the calmer waters of the bay and she has now become nervous about the food and the lack of some ingredients. They can all hear her twittering and cursing down below but the charterers are all keen to swim and soon everyone is splashing lazily about in the warm clear water. Mrs Tanaka changes into a bright red-dotted bikini and proves to be a surprisingly adept swimmer. Not that she takes centre stage: this is taken by her husband who has discovered it is fun to drink a rum and coke and then leap feet first overboard. Drinks, swims, drinks; it gets dark but they feel relaxed and smells of cooking are emanating from below. Tom goes down to the engine room to get more cokes to put on ice and comes up grinning, "We're having that fillet of beef only of course it's now fillet of boeuf or something, with a crust, and julienne vegetables and some sort of swank dessert." They have more drinks.

"Ah," says Mr Tanaka contentedly and gives some pronouncement.

"Very nice day," says the interpreter. "Now he wants dinner."

Mrs Tanaka says something and the charterers all laugh. "His wife," says the interpreter, "she says he always thinks of his stomach."

"Shouldn't be much longer," says Tom and goes down to get peanuts and crisps. "Dinner is at eight," he reports. "And there's no need to dress." His expression shows that he at least has no intention of dressing for dinner but the charterers think they might have a shower, so one by one they file down and Lynn explains to them how to take short showers in the head and hands them towels. As she does this it strikes Lynn that the beef has been in for quite some time, much longer than for Yvonne's recipe. She longs to say something but sees by Sandra's expression that it might not be in order. "Presumably it cooks slower in pastry," she thinks. "I'll ask about it later." She notices there are large quantities of spice and other bottles strewn around in a not-very-shipshape fashion but then Sandra is a proper cook and probably won't cook like the ships' cooks Lynn has watched, where every ingredient is taken out and the container promptly put away again. And being a proper cook, she is of course properly harassed, especially by the stream of bodies pressing past her. “Oh dear oh dear how can I do this if everyone is always getting in the way?” her voice going up a notch. Like a whine. But Lynn represses that thought; after all she hardly knows Sandra and she is a friend of Tom’s.

Time goes on and everyone has had a shower and a third or even fourth drink. They eat peanuts and crisps and look at the starry sky and the sea and get mellow. And slightly restless. All that is needed to make the evening perfect is a good feed. Eventually about half past eight Tom goes down and comes back up, not looking quite so cheery. “Ah well,” he says, “it’s her first time using this oven. The pastry won’t brown, I don’t think she’s had it hot enough although she said she was working off the temperature gauge but that thing’s not much good; either it’s hot in there or it’s not”

At quarter past nine, when goodwill has practically vanished, the meal appears. The plates are beautifully set out, a slice of the boeuf whatever, with vegetables arranged just so. The charterers look at it appreciatively. But unfortunately it isn’t very good. The fillet is overcooked and has practically fallen apart so it is a bit like stew in consistency. The juices have run into the pastry which no doubt they were supposed to do but it has turned what was supposed to be crust into the consistency of boiled dumpling, quite a tasty boiled dumpling but puddingy nevertheless. The vegetables are soft and watery. The whole meal is like something you’d get in a transport cafe. Jim eats it stolidly. “Hmm,” he says, “just like school din-dins.”

Sandra joins them on deck laughing and drinking some wine and phewing over the heat in the galley, seemingly totally oblivious to the general disappointment. Mr Tanaka eats some of it and then says something to his wife who sighs a soft assent; she herself hasn’t eaten more than the first forkful. Mr Fukuda and Mr Yamada, evidently with relief, give up the moment their boss lays down his fork. Tom looks way way over the moonlit islands and Lynn gathers up the plates as unobtrusively as she can.

However it is impossible to disguise the amount of food that is being returned and Sandra, on seeing this, cries, “Terrible beef, where on earth did you get it, Lynn? You must know nothing about buying meat. I’d go right back and throw it in their faces. Look how it’s fallen apart.”

“It was fillet steak,” says Lynn.

“Whatever sort of beef it was,” cries Sandra, “it’s a scandal that they’d sell it.” She continues to eat hers. “I don’t know, the stuff they have down here is just terrible - they cheat you wherever you go - I've never come across such dreadful meat."

Dessert. Well the dessert wouldn't set. It's some sort of mousse that sits soft and runny in the ice box until they are ready to sail the next day when they throw it overboard. So that is dinner and clearly the charter party is looking to Mr Tanaka, who says something to Mr Yamada with a sigh.

The interpreter stands up. "May I use the stove?" he asks politely after a slight bow.

"I wouldn't, it's hell to use," cries Sandra. "You'll never get the hang of it. I've just spent hours and I think I know what the problem is but it's the worst stove I've ever seen."

Lynn goes down with him and clears away the debris Sandra has left into the cupboards. The interpreter comes out of the fore-cabin with some packets. "You brought food!" exclaims Lynn.

"Well, we eat different so yes I bring some things." He puts on a big pan of water. "Do you have potato?" Lynn brings some out and he shaves them up into very thin slices and puts them in the pan. Gradually he adds other ingredients, pastes and noodles and an hour later there is a soup which the charterers slurp out of bowls. "Oh dear it looks horrible," says Sandra. Lynn and Tom and Jim all eat it; it is salty but OK.

Lynn and Jim sleep on the benches in the galley area because Sandra has decreed that she and Tom shall sleep on deck, not that Lynn minds as the wind is freshening and there is the possibility of rain.

Lynn whispers over to Jim, "I told you I had a bad feeling about her."

"Oh come now," says Jim, "that was a one off. Bit over-ambitious making that when you don't know the stove."

"Well," says Lynn and says no more. She lies in the dark and thinks, This is a terrible trip, it is going to continue a terrible trip, nothing will redeem it.

Breakfast. Despite their late night the charterers are up at crack of dawn taking pictures. The sky has a strange orange look to it. "That looks ominous," says Jim but Lynn thinks everything looks stormy and threatening anyway.

Tom wants to leave early to get to a safe harbour up the coast but Sandra says, "Oh no Tom, we must have breakfast first." Tom says, "You can cook it as we go. That's the glory of a boat, you can travel and cook and do all sorts of things all at the same time,' but

Sandra says, 'No I don't think so, not a nice breakfast, not with everything flying in all directions and swaying here and there. I think we should have a nice sit down breakfast."

So they all go for a swim while she makes breakfast. Time goes on and the wind is rising, bits of cloud stream above them in quick darts. Mr Tanaka gets on the deck and says something moving his body from side to side and holding his stomach like a little child; it makes his wife put her hand over her mouth and peal out a laugh. Eventually however breakfast is served.

Sandra has made something called menamen, or that's what it sounds like. It is a Turkish version of scrambled eggs with tomatoes and red peppers in it.

"How does she get the eggs to coagulate like this," says Jim. He paddles his fork in the pink liquid draining around the curds.

"Just eat it and shut up," says Tom shortly.

"Eat the evidence you mean. Poor old Turks is all I can say. Fancy being Turkish and having to eat something that looks like this for breakfast. Oh god she's put chilli powder or something in it; I can't eat this."

"Bloody hell, if all you're going to do is to sit there complaining let's get the boat under way," says Tom in a disgusted voice.

"Yes sir, if I can drag my emaciated body, my poor starving body up to the anchor chain. Oh oh, how am I going to have the energy."

"Toast," carols Sandra from the hatch.

"I wondered who you were cremating down there but now I see….. it's toast. No thanks."

"Well," says Sandra coming on deck and radiantly taking to a plate of the pinkish mixture, "it's like the black hole of Calcutta down there. Already, even at this hour." She eats with enthusiasm. "Um, of course I had to spice it up, Asians like things spicy, isn't that so Mr Sam."

The charterers blink. Mrs Tanaka says nothing and sits with her plate virtually untouched. Mr Tanaka had eaten determinedly for two or three forkfuls and then stopped, spreading his arms and saying something that clearly shows he's beaten. Sandra however eats her eggs and crunches eagerly on the hard scraped toast, eyes down to her food, "My I'm hungry," and she finishes hers off. An empty plate, quite an achievement. Everyone else sits there in silence. It is clear that this feat has awoken some bitterness in the charterers and Mr Tanaka plonks down his plate and says something, indicating it with both hands.

"What, not hungry?" says Sandra. "Well I forgot, of course you probably don't have breakfast where you come from. Such a waste though. Maybe I can save it and make sandwiches for lunch."

Lynn gets up and collects the plates quickly, hoping Mr Yamada won't translate the last remark. She goes down into the galley and tips out the food while a conference is going on among the charterers. She starts to clean up in the galley which is a mess. She is standing near the hatch when Tom comes back from the front of the boat where Jim is winching up the anchor, so she hears Mr Yamada clear his throat.

"Mr Tom, Mr Tanaka want to know," he says politely, "why the food so bad."

Tom runs his hand through his hair and through his beard. "Jesus," is all he says and then starts pulling with all his might on the mainsail.

Lynn ducks her head so she can't see or hear any more; she feels desperately embarrassed. She starts to hum. Conversation is obviously taking place so she hums louder and scrubs and scrapes harder; she's never seen such a coating as Sandra appears to be able to give to every surface just from being there. Suddenly Jim appears down the hatch and crashes backwards onto the seat next to the galley. "Bloody hell!"

Lynn keeps humming.

"I've just been sacked."

She stops humming. "What did you do?"

"Dunno."

"You must have done something."

"Just said what was on my mind about the Sandra situation."

"I thought you wanted to give her a chance."

"Yes but only because I thought at first she was good looking. Nobody looks that great any more when you're hungry. You know," he says judiciously, "if you were to feed me I might think you were a bit of alright."

Before she can respond appropriately, Mr Fukuda comes down, and then Mr Yamada. And then Mr and Mrs Tanaka descend until everyone but Tom and Sandra are sitting below. "What's going on?" says Lynn.

Mr Yamada says, "Mr Tanaka is not happy. Things are not good."

"No it's not great is it? And a storm is coming," says Jim.

Whereupon Mrs Tanaka leans forwards and touches Lynn's shirt and says something which is translated as, "She want to know if you will give us some egg and meat like on first day, very nice meal, she like it very much."

"What's that?" says Jim.

"I made them breakfast when they first got on, just scrambled eggs and bacon."

"Oh no," says Jim, "and now they think you're going to be making them buttery scrambled eggs and crispy bacon," his mouth works, "and what else? Toast, nice unburned toast, would that be too much."

A scud of rain hits the outside of the boat, "Who's helping him sail?"

"Buggered if I know." He gets up and slides the hatch back to protect the stair well.

"Can he sail it on his own?"

"Oh I hope so or we're liable to sink."

Lynn thinks over the breakfast situation. "I'll make French toast." She beats eggs in a bowl and grates cinnamon into it and then adds a small carton of cream. She slices diagonally several loaves of French bread that would otherwise be going stale and soaks the slices for 30 seconds on each side according to the recipe. She fills the coffee pot with water and ladles in coffee grounds. The boat is obviously going out into rougher water as the inside of the cabin starts to sway and rock and she nearly loses the bowl but Mrs Tanaka appears beside her holding it. She melts butter in the frying pan and when it is hot with a lovely buttery-smoke smell, starts frying the bread slices, a minute on each side and being careful not to burn them. Soon the coffee is percolating and the inside of the cabin takes on a fragrant breakfast aroma. Mrs Tanaka proves herself adept at helping and holds plates for her as she transfers the fried rounds of bread to them. She puts out some maple syrup but finds that the bottle of black stuff that Mr Yamada used last night has also appeared on the table.

Mr Tanaka has clearly never come across maple syrup before. "Map-puh syr-ruh," he repeats and tries a corner of the toast tentatively in a small puddle on his plate. He makes a noise like a cock squawking to its hens, "Mappuh syrruh," he beams. "Veree good-onay." He dunks half his toast in the syrup and the other half in the soy sauce and eats them alternatively, holding forth as he does so to the amusement of his party. Once he has had several pieces of toast, he pats his stomach in satisfaction and bangs his now empty coffee mug comfortably on the table. Crossing his legs and leaning back he looks a bit like a buddha. "Bur-ey-fas." Breakfast. Lynn gathers that it was both different and interesting.

"Jim," says Lynn, "take some up to Tom."

"He threw me out," says Jim. "He told me never to darken his door again." But he climbs up so that his face just appears at the hatch and raising the plate he slowly passes it to and fro in Tom's line of vision. There is a sharp, "You bastards, what are you eating?" And, "Come out here and steer you bastard." Tom shortly after appears in their midst. "And coffee," he moans, "give me coffee. What are you all doing down here?"

Lynn has finished her labours and stands against the bench with her hand on her hip, "They came and asked me to feed them and I didn't have the heart to refuse."

"Who would have thought it would all be such a bloody disaster?" says Tom, head down and eating.

Lynn wants to ask him what he is going to do but feels the weight of her youth and is too diffident to give voice. However the buddha has no such qualms, he prods at Mr Yamada and gives vent to a great many words.

Mr Yamada clears his throat and looks embarrassed. "Not like food of other lady, want this lady," he says. "Mr Tanaka here says this lady make good food, very interesting breakfast, frens toast, his wife is writing it down, the instructions. He will eat frens toast and mappu sirrup when he goes back to Nippon. He says he not pay for other lady, she waste of time, been here one day and already hungry. He want this lady or we make our own food." He smiles placatingly.

Tom sighs and pulls his hair, "What am I going to do? She won't listen. She thinks it's all lack of communication, she's been lecturing me on communication. She says in future she'll find out what they want first and then cook it, rather than just assume that's what they'd like for breakfast. When Jim told her the breakfast was awful it was like saying she was a terrible ugly unlovable person. She said either Jim had to go or she would."

"And you chose her," says Lynn.

"What could I do! Anyway I didn't mean it, everyone is always sacking Jim. The last time he went on charter his skipper sacked him a dozen times a day. You see, I've reinstated him already."

"I need to know about lunch."

"Oh bloody hell," says Tom and goes back up on deck.

In the end the decision doesn't need making. By mid-day they are tacking into a strong breeze with short choppy rolling swell and cloudburst after cloudburst is lashing them with rain and sleet. Tom is making for a sheltered harbour which is only four miles off but it takes them all day to get there. In the meantime Sandra is spreadeagled against the rails dribbling pink sick on the deck.

"Throw up to leeward," shouts Tom but she acts like she couldn't care. "Go and clean that up," he says to Jim.

"No way," says Jim so Tom fires him again and Jim goes off to teach Kenji how to play cribbage.

Tom gets Lynn to take over the wheel while he dips buckets in the sea and swabs around Sandra.

"You're wetting me you bastard," she cries.

"Then throw up to leeward," he shouts back. "You're messing up my deck."

Moan, she goes and turns back once more to clutch the deck and dribble.

Tom is clearly getting incensed. "Did you ever see anything like it!" he says reclaiming the wheel. "She's come over from Europe on a boat, weeks at sea and she still doesn't know the etiquette. What must the charterers think, having crew who get seasick. Look at them, none of them are seasick even though chinks are notorious for getting seasick."

"I'm pretty sure they're Japanese," says Lynn. But Tom isn't listening.

No-one is hungry at lunchtime. Lynn has a lot of mushrooms and puts them on for soup but even that is declined.

At evening they finally round a point and make it into a bay where despite Tom's assurance that it is the most sheltered bay in that area they are rocked all evening by squalls. Sandra retires to the bunk opposite Kenji's in the main cabin area and is not at all pleased to find that everyone gathers downstairs for dinner. "I think the very least you could do is to sit on deck, the sound of you talking is drilling into my head," she complains.

"It's starting to rain," says Tom shortly.

"A bit of rain. How can you be bothered by a bit of rain. And what's that awful music, please turn it down."

Mr Yamada has put on some 'music of our country' and Mr Tanaka is playing cards with Jim and Tom. Everyone has become lively and noisy after a few drinks while Lynn is reheating the soup and making chips in a deep bubbling pan of oil to go with the T-bone steaks.

"Really," croaks Sandra pulling back the curtain, "it's too bad of you all, when you can see how sick I am. You're making no effort to keep the noise down. And the smell of oil, I shall have to go on deck myself, and probably die there after today's….."

But at that point Mr Tanaka slams down a fist of cards triumphantly. "Bloody hell," says Jim, "he's done it again. How does he do that?"

"Is anybody listening to me!" shrieks Sandra.

"Go up on deck, if you want quiet," says Tom irritably.

Jim is dealing cards. "Kenji, you in for a hand? I want you to keep an eye on Mr Tanaka here. He's winning too convincingly." At which Kenji looks alarmed and Sandra closes the curtain and starts to cry in loud grating sobs.

Everyone stops and looks at each other. "Uh," says Mr Tanaka, putting down the hand he has been arranging and slowly looking around at the general paralysis. Then he starts to talk in a deep slow dramatic way, his voice sliding up theatrically at the end of each phrase, one hand raised, an index finger up to the sound of weeping, like a mime artist discovering a great truth of life, and the other hand extending out in dumb show to indicate Tom and the whole company. Somehow it is belly-achingly funny, so much so that waves of merriment wash them in an almost hysterical way - in the middle of which Sandra slams out of her bunk in a fury and goes up on deck.

By the next day Lynn has revised her forecast from 'bad' to 'unbearable'. The Golden Dawn has berths for six charterers, with two each in cabins fore and aft and two curtained alcoves in the main cabin. In addition there are two cushioned benches in the dining area running along the sides which can be used as bunks but crew usually sleep up on deck on the cushioned benches lining either side of the cockpit.

A rollicking night is had by the charterers that night with everyone drinking and playing cards until quite late. Tom goes up on deck a couple of times in an apparent effort to appease Sandra, but when she continues to berate him he chucks two blankets and a pillow up to her and decides to sleep with the rest of the crew in the main cabin. The wind rises. At some point in the night it starts to rain in earnest, hard thudding rain sounding like sleet. Lynn hears it vaguely and then she becomes aware of a figure coming down the galley steps and there is immediately afterwards an altercation which is along the lines of "What are you doing in my bunk?" "It's not your bunk, piss off." "Will you get out of my bunk?" "Stop shaking me - piss off." Tom wakes up. "What the hell is going on? For god's sake shut up or you'll wake the charterers."

"He's in my bunk."

"You don't have a bunk, you're crew. You went on deck so Jim's in that bunk."

"And what am I supposed to do?"

"I don't know what you're supposed to do. Sleep on the floor but for god's sake shut up."

"I am not going to sleep on the floor."

"Then fit yourself down the other end of Lynn's bench, she's small, there must be room for two of you."

"Oh that's great," says Jim, "you bring an extra crew member on and then foist her on Lynn….."

"I don't mind," says Lynn, "if only you would all just shut up."

"I have to put the light on," says Sandra.

"No," says Tom.

"I have to put the light on. I can't see what I'm doing in here."

"I shall pitch you overboard if you put the light on," says Tom. "Now just shut up."

Lynn feels her yanking blankets about her down the other end of the bench and it seems for a moment there will be peace. But there is a bang of flesh on something and a sharp cry followed, after some moments of suspense, by the lights going on. "For god's sake!" explodes Tom.

"I had to put the light on. How can I see what I'm doing with the light off? Look I've banged my head now." And taking no more notice of their curses she proceeds to make her bed in a leisurely way and then goes over and cuts the lights. There is silence, an intense hostile silence. Then Lynn hears Jim roll out of his bunk and pad over to Tom. There is a growl from Tom, "What are you doing?"

"I'm showing you what it's like to be strangled. Tom, if you don't get rid of that woman tomorrow I'm out of here. I'm over the side and you can sail this damn thing by yourself."

"Well go over the side then, I don't care," says Tom.

"OK," says Jim and pads back to his bunk.

"Bloody hell," mutters Tom. And then in another mutter, "And how am I going to get rid of her? Where? This is miles from anywhere. Just cast her adrift, is that your plan?"

"No we sail somewhere where you can off-load her. I'm sure the charterers won't mind."

Silence. "Yes, we not mind," suddenly comes the voice of Kenji who clearly knows a good deal more English than he is given credit for. "Yes, we not understand why she on boat. Please Mr Jim, explain."

"Have you heard of using your dick for brains?" murmurs Jim to Kenji.

"What dick?" There is a muttered consultation followed by a crack of laughter from Kenji.

"Excuse me," says Sandra, "would you mind shutting up. I'm trying to get some sleep here."

But she doesn't sleep well, or so Lynn assumes, for she tosses and turns all night keeping Lynn awake. In the morning the storm has not abated and the wind is fresh and blowing on shore. "We're going to have a hell of a job getting anywhere," says Tom. "If we beat up to the next island there's a hotel and there might be some other boats - someone who can give her a lift back."

"Oh don't worry about me, I'm perfectly happy," says Sandra sarcastically.

"Why don't we Listen With Mother and then we'll find out if anyone's up there," says Jim.

Good thinking.

Listen With Mother is what the yachties call the fifteen minutes twice a day when they can talk to the base station and to each other. Much of the talk is to do with mundane matters, but there is always a certain amount of sub-text which the listeners try to de-code.

"Valient Voyager here. Is the Hildegaard there, over?"

"Andy here, come in you bloody piker, over."

"Hello Andy there, sorry we got held up, one of our charterer's escaped. Anyway thanks for leaving the message, most imposing, how on earth did you manage one so big? Someone must have been straining something terrible, over."

"It's sheer talent, plus a quantity of best curry powder, over."

"We're all very impressed. Our charterers ran out of film taking photos of it. That'll be taking pride of place in their holiday albums back home in Winnipeg. How does that make you feel? Over."

"Very humble. And proud. But mainly, very very humble. Over and out."

"Charles, Tom here, wanting to pass a message to anyone at Long Reef. We're going up there today and we need a lift for a crewmember back down the islands. Over."

"Hello Tom. Bill's up there now, I've just been speaking to him. Bill, are you still there? Can you help out Tom? Over. He's not responding Tom, he must have clocked off. Anyone out there at Long Reef? Over. No response. That's funny, they were all chatting away merrily a minute ago. What have you got there Tom, nothing catching I hope? Over."

Lynn can see Tom biting his lip while Jim's are curving the other way into an ironical smile. "The bastards have been talking about us. I wonder what the code word is?"

"Code word?" queries Lynn.

"Keeps the airwaves clean and free from suits of slander. Probably something like, Look out for a bad bit of weather coming north. Tit-bit had it and Golden Dawn's running through it now. Keep an ear open for a plea for help from Tom's boat and keep your distance, or you could get damaged too."

"Hello Tom, Skip here. Over," comes over the wireless.

"Hello Skip. You bastard. Over," says Tom.

"Bastard yourself," says Skip. "We're having a lovely trip, over."

"Everyone behaving themselves? Over."

"We're trying to get up to Long Reef today too so you'll see for yourself. Over and out."

"Well," says Tom moodily, "let's get going. No point hanging round when we could be somewhere else having fun."

It is a most unpleasant day. The sea is heaving and the rain comes over in squalls making it slow going, moving with the wind on the starboard tack with the sails reefed and the breakers constantly dousing the deck. Sandra leans miserably against a rail. All day they tack and tack again and hardly seem to be gaining ground. "We're going backwards with this sea," says Jim. "We should have stayed where we were."

"Your fault," says Lynn, "you shouldn't have complained so much."

They are all looking bleakly out at the heaving sea. There are islands to be seen through the mist but only vague outlines and they don't seem to get bigger. About four in the afternoon, the cloud clears and the sun emerges for a space and the seas moderate somewhat. Tom decides to put on the engine and they take down most of the sail. "There's where we're going," says Tom, pointing. "Let's hope we get into the channel by nightfall." They can see some boats bobbing far off in surprising calm across a very blue-green sea.

"Why can't we just go straight there?" says Lynn. "Why are we heading in this direction?"

"Because there's a reef in the way and no-one's bothered to chart it," says Jim.

"There's no way through?"

"There probably is," says Tom. "What do you say Jim? You sick of this too?"

"What! Well it's your boat….. but our lives," says Jim. "And we could all die."

"Come on me hearties. Do you want to live for ever? Isn't that the philosophy you were telling me we should live by? Why doesn't someone go up the mast and we'll see if we can find a passage."

"In this sea, you're mad."

"No look, it's much calmer than it was," says Tom, ever the optimist. "Go on Lynn, you go up, it's easy as pie. Just give us a hoy which way and we'll sail through like champions."

He is probably joking but Lynn has been looking out through the mist to the vision where the boats lie at anchor in the sun, as if there is some magic land on the other side of the rainbow where she can have her heart's desire, where bluebirds sing without effort and a warm hand is held out waiting - and it can all be reached without being buffeted constantly by unrelenting wind and seas.

And then Jim laughs, "Yes, go on Lynn, climb up the mast and navigate us through to sunny waters."

Why not? If the boat capsizes at least she can go back; that's what she wants, to go back to the Frangipani. So she sheds her wetweather gear. "OK." she says, "give me a heave up."

Jim's face changes, "No, I was only joking."

But she is motioning him to put his hands into a stirrup and before anyone has time for second thoughts she is on her way. Here I am climbing the mast. It is easier than I would have supposed, you just look up to the next rung and climb on and on until you can't climb any more. She is way up in the air, she gets astride the top spreader and looks down for the first time and then feels fright. Everything seems far away now and shortened, people reduced to small plates where they keep their faces. She sees Kenji with cameras slung around him at the ready. Tom is shouting. "What can you see?"

"There's a channel, blue water this way," she says holding out her arm and pointing.

"This is the maddest thing," she hears Jim say but Tom just goes "Yeeeee-hah" with a wild laugh.

People are moving from side to side below her and Lynn clutches the mast tight and tries not to think about having to get down or where she might end up if they capsize or run aground. Her hair whips about her face and she feels the whistle of the wire stays vibrating through her body. What will it be like running onto a reef at speed? Come on my hearties, do you want to live forever?

The channel she has led them into is narrowing but it is too late now. Her arm points, her directions are taking on a life of their own, starboard in 50 yards, prepare to turn, now port, keep her like that.

"What's the depth," shouts Tom.

"Getting shallower, but blue water ahead, there's a passage beyond. Getting much shallower," she bites her lip as the channel leads them towards water of the very palest.

"How shallow?"

"Really shallow. I can't see how shallow, there's nothing above water but….."

It's too narrow to stop, too late to stop, they have to go on. "Yeeee-hah" goes Tom again; he really doesn't care. At that moment a hundred thousand dollar boat is just plywood to smash around with. Ahead is the start of a blue water channel, fifty yards ahead, forty yards, thirty yards….. The sea is so clear that she has no idea what the depth is, only that it is paper white and the coral spins beneath her and fish dart from their keel as if they might be crushed between it and the rockhard organism below. It is as if their rushing progress and the bounding sea is steering them up some great valley to cast them precipitately on to the cliffs. Below her, small soft humans on the deck are clinging to a vessel that is out of control. Suddenly with the roll of the sea Lynn actually sees some coral exposed only a few yards away to the side and her heart clamps ice-like to the walls of her chest. "We're going to be shipwrecked," she thinks. And then, suddenly, they aren't. "We're through!" she screams in relief.

And that's it. The channel leads them through into the bay, through the magic gate into a glorious land. She is high up above the glistening water and everyone below her is truncated and laughing, looking up and clapping. Ahead she can see the other boats and they are dotted with people who also seem to be cheering and laughing. She takes off her T-shirt and waves it like a flag and bangs her heels against the mast and sings of glory.

Chapter 11

What a huge sulk and pout is there

Lucas has his head down and is writing with huge deliberation in an official-looking notebook. He is bent over his task as if everything depended on it.

An absorbed concentration is a very disconcerting characteristic. One would have thought that such a quality would be highly valuable to any goal-driven corporate enterprise so it is surprising to see, when I look in the newspapers today, that it is hardly ever sought after in job advertisements. Employers instead require exhausting quantities of energy, commitment and enthusiasm - making one wonder what sort of flayed hyperventilating people they attract.

Presumably they don't get people like Lucas. If he were to look in the paper for a job that would suit him, he wouldn't see much at all. Explorer, whale watcher, coroner's assistant..... There aren't many jobs that require the incumbent to maintain a deep still focus and to harbour patience. There are even fewer that require a calm scanning of the horizon rather than frenetic purposeless activity.

Lucas is currently in exploring mode and thus is motionless, expressionless, analytical. Basically, in exploring, the only attribute needed is the capacity to get back again at the end of the trip, preferably with a reasonable description of where you've been. So Lucas is listening intently without comment and writing in his book.

This process seems to have an irritating effect on Mrs Georgiana Panday. The widow is a boisterous-looking large woman who must have been several inches taller than her late husband. Her skin is very black and her teeth are very white and she wears a bright red polka-dotted dress and a red scarf knotted in her frizzy black hair - exactly like a black mammy in a children's book thinks Lucas with disapproval. It is almost as if she is aiming for that sort of stereotype, deliberately setting out to make some sort of ironic statement. The result is, she is not at all the sort of witness that anyone would believe. In fact he doesn't believe her himself.

"So tell me again what happened on the night your husband died."

"I told you," she says in a voice loud with annoyance. "I told you already. Have you got cloth ears? I told you a hundred times. Why don't you read them notes? You got it in them notes already."

"You told me," says Lucas turning back a few pages, "that Selwyn left to go into work at 11 o'clock in the evening, and that you never saw him again."

"That's what I told you."

"Did anyone come round for Selwyn?"

"No, why should they do that?"

"Did Max de Troy come round for Selwyn?"

"Why you asking me that?"

"Because I want to know if Max de Troy came round for Selwyn on the night he died and whether he then left with Max."

"I told you what happen. I told you everything what happen. Why you asking these questions?"

"Because I have been talking to your neighbours."

"What neighbours! Who you been talking to?"

"I have talked to all your neighbours. On both sides of the street. And they tell me a quite different story to the one you are telling me."

"What business is it of theirs? Who are they to be looking into my business and then go telling stories?"

"They all saw Max de Troy."

"Whose business is that? Who do they think they are to be telling you such things?"

"Because they heard and saw things. And you are telling me lies. You have a bad attitude to this whole investigation."

"A bad attitude! I will have whatever attitude I like! I wasn't born here among these ignorant people you know. I have lived in Canada and I have lived in America and I have been in the same room as Martin Luther King and I have heard him talk and I know one thing. I will get no justice from the likes of you in a place like this with everyone so keen to curtsy and bow to the likes of Mr Anthony Hamilton. My Selwyn never had a chance, working for a white man like that."

"That is as may be but the world has been looking out of its window and seeing who passes where and how. And Max de Troy came here in plain view, in the light from your porch. Sometime after 1 o'clock. Selwyn was still in the house at 1 o'clock. And then there was the shouting and screaming."

"Screaming? What screaming?"

"Your neighbours said there was screaming."

"Nobody screamed. Maybe the child screamed," indicating a child of about four or five hanging its arm on the angle of her chair.

"Did you scream on the night Max came here?" Lucas asks the child forthwith and before the woman can move the child answers promptly, "No, it was Daddy." The woman turns instantaneously and fetches a clout against the child's head. The child breaks into high shrieks.

"Stop that," says Lucas standing.

"You lying little….." she screams at the child. "Just wait till I….." and she tries to get in another blow at the child but Lucas grabs her arm. She is a strong woman but Lucas belies his slight build and to her surprise she finds herself handcuffed. "What you doing?" she shrieks.

"I'm arresting you for cruelty to this child. I am going to the phone now to get a car to take you in front of a magistrate and to get the Society to take the child to a doctor. Look, her head's bleeding." A thin trickle of blood runs down the little girl's cheek.

"It's only a little blood, I scratch her with my ring. Hush will you, just a little plaster will fix it." The woman's voice has shrunk, her whole body has shrunk, she looks frankly terrified. "You won't take her from me, she's all I got now my husband is dead, you won't….." her voice is going up the register tearfully like the beginning wail of a siren.

"You are a disgrace to be hitting a child that has just lost its father, hitting it so hard it bleeds," Lucas's disgust is evident in his voice.

The woman starts to weep in great jagged waves that engulfs her. Her chin sinks down onto her ample bosom and huge sobs roll out unchecked over the neighbourhood passages and gardens.

An old woman from next door comes hobbling in so promptly that Lucas suspects she must have been outside the door all along.

“Good God and angels in heaven what have you been doing to the poor woman?”

“I have been stopping her hitting the child. Look, she made it bleed.”

“Get away man, she just lose her husband and strike out, not meaning a thing no doubt.”

“Oh she meant it all right,” says Lucas grimly for the benefit of all the neighbours who, in the intervening seconds, have suddenly crowded the doorway and the windows of the little house. “She tried to hit the child a second time and with full force too. This must be a funny neighbourhood if you allow a big woman like this to hit a little child like that and not call for the Society.”

The child, being now the centre of attention, ceases crying and stands gulping looking around. Her mother however continues to let forth her grief upon the less confident ears of her neighbours, who are now each turning to the other and murmuring. The old woman who has gone to comfort her now draws back and stands unsure. What are they doing here anyway? It is no business of theirs.

Lucas removes the handcuffs. “I will be back soon to talk to you again,” he says to Mrs Panday, “and I hope next time you will tell me the truth about this whole matter.” Her crying continues and if she hears him she gives no sign.

In the evening Lynn and Jim and Skip are once more propping up a bar together. Everybody has been celebrating though really no-one can remember why any more. The hotel is the only building on the island and is exquisitely laid out and very very exclusive. Sitting at the tables are beautiful people in evening dress, the women’s satins gleaming in the dim sophisticated lamplight. Waiters in tailored evening suits move noiselessly. Everything is so restrained that Lynn is suddenly happy she has on a pink frilly dress – she feels like a demented five-year-old. She wants to get off her stool and bounce madly about. “Hey,” she says to the barman, “why isn’t there music? We should have music to dance to.”

The barman grins. “It’s early yet; the yachties don’t usually start tearing the place apart until much later. Then we put on the dance music.”

“Of course,” says Skip, “all these rich people, they’d die of boredom if it wasn’t for the yachts coming by during the season and adding a bit of life.”

"But surely," says Lynn, "they pay through the nose to get away from….." she waves her arms about vaguely.

"Yobs like us?" suggests Jim.

"No no, you've got it wrong," says Skip sagely, though a bit slurred. "What we have here is a desert island. Apart from the hotel, of course. Now where is the last place that anyone would want to end up? No no, wanting to be on a desert island, that's a myth. Nothing could be more boring. I've had charterers who've gone off for the day to a desert island all by themselves and they're back by lunchtime. Nothing to do. Oh well, they don't say that. They talk about the sand flies and the other insects - they come up with new species like voracious ants with heads the size of thumb nails who come in tribes and herd them down the beach and into the water. And then of course that perfect beach is overhung on all sides with machineel trees and so the story goes on - they're pathetically glad to be back on board like the real castaways must have been when they saw a boat."

"But people aren't castaway here; they've got all these activities they can do."

"Yes but there's only 15 chalets, that's 30 people, 40 at most. It's so exclusive there's hardly anyone here and what's the point of doing a perfect bit of water skiing if no-one sees it? You don't count the boy in the boat of course. No, when the yachts are here - out come the guests. And the nice looking ones make sure they loll about somewhere conspicuous where everyone can see their bodies, and the vigorous ones make sure they do a fast pass on the sailboard just as we're coming into port. And then the rest ostentatiously come out with a beach volley ball for a bit of practice, in the hope of course that everyone will pile over the sides of the boats and come and join in with lots of screams and laughing and falling about. Mankind is social. There's only so much lying around with a book you can do before you start wishing you'd gone to Club Med."

"But think about the snorkelling. That's one time when you don't want others around."

"Wrong again. They want to be down there together pointing at things so other people can see them, going "Look at that!" That's what people are like. All calling out, "Watch me!" The guests can go over to the other side of the island anytime, pick a time when there are no yachts around at all, because boats can't anchor round there. But do they? No. The reefs there are completely pristine and deserted. It takes an hour or so and it's a bit of a slog to get over the hill but what's the point if there are no people along to enjoy it with you? So when we cunningly suggested to our lot that they should go over there tomorrow, which would mean of course we'd get a day off, what happens? They tell some hotel guests and so on and so on and now there's a party of eight or a dozen going. With crew and hotel staff to carry the picnic stuff. Who will no doubt jump in for a dip as well. And that's the story now. By tomorrow there will no doubt be hordes more, led on by the exhortations of the ones already going. You watch, we'll have thirty people over there while the reefs here will be completely deserted."

They drink their drinks.

"So, I hardly dare to ask," says Jim, "but how are things on board?"

"Rocky," says Skip and drinks his drink.

"I have a proposition to put to you."

"Oh yes," says Skip warily. "Something like the last one is it, where you take off with George."

"No, no. That was a misunderstanding based on incorrect information, namely that Sandra could cook. I wouldn't have wished her on you knowing what I know now, and you would never have spoken to us again. But that's history. Now the proposition is, that you give Sandra a lift to the next island - anywhere will do so long as she can get back to civilisation and take herself off."

"That may not be as easy you think."

"But you're going up there anyway the day after tomorrow."

"Well so are you."

"No but listen. This is the proposition. Once she's on board you let her cook the meals, give George a bit of a holiday until such time as the charterers ask, no beg, for him to cook for them again."

"Yeee...sss," says Skip thinking it over. "But there's a problem, something you're not telling me and that I have since got off the gossip mills."

"What's that?" asks Jim.

"Tit-Bit signed the girl up and committed themselves to flying her home if she didn't prove satisfactory. Which she didn't. But the skipper of the Tit-Bit is a mean bastard and he thought he'd save himself the price of an airfare by making life rough for her. He must have been wild with joy when she hopped off his boat and on to yours. Because Immigration are tightening up, you can't just dump your crew now unless they've got a ticket home, and I bet she doesn't have that much money on her either because the Tit-Bit pays English wages not US dollars."

"Bloody hell," says Jim.

"Exactly. Now she's your problem. And you realise why no-one is rushing to help you out."

They sit and think about it in despondent silence. "Oh well, what's the point in worrying?" says Lynn. "Let's start getting restless so that they put some music on."

They dance half the night away but the problem is still there when they start ferrying the charterers back in the early morning. Tom has disappeared and no-one has seen Sandra all evening. Lynn bounces cheerfully below decks to make everyone a nightcap. She switches on the light and stands in the hatch looking up saying, "OK, what would everyone like? Cocoa?"

"Cocoa?" goes up the shout of disgust. Whisky is the consensus. Then suddenly the light goes out while Lynn has her head in the cupboard. "Oh," says Lynn. "What happened? Damn, didn't Tom run the generators tonight?"

Jim looks down. "Check the switch."

Lynn puts out her hand and finds it and pushes it down. The light comes on. "How did that happen? It somehow switched itself off. Anyway, whisky for everyone." She turns and there is Sandra in a t-shirt making for the switch again which she switches off. "Excuse me, it's two in the morning. Please tell all those people to be quiet, some of us are trying to sleep."

Jim is down the hatch in a moment and has it back on again.

"Leave it Jim," says Lynn pacifyingly. "I can find things without it."

"Why should you? This is not her boat, it's the charterers'. Don't you understand that Sandra? They chartered the boat. This is their boat. They can make as much damn noise as they like. They can switch the light on any time they feel the need. They own the space for the duration - we're only servants."

Sandra turns furiously, "A servant! Of those sort of people! I certainly am not. Now if you don't mind I need my sleep," and she reaches for the switch again. But Jim has put himself between her and the switch and when her efforts at pushing against him and dragging him fail, she gives him a resounding slap on the cheek. Jim ducks down, has her over his shoulder, up the stairs with some banging of heads and heave, she is overboard. It takes no more than a few frantic seconds and Lynn isn't quite sure how it happened but there is Sandra gasping and giving strangled shrieks in the water.

Only Kenji and Mr Yamada are on deck and both of them are rather under the weather. Mr Tanaka puts his head out of the aft hatch and is obviously asking who has jumped in and as the reply is somewhat vague he turns to Lynn and grins, "Mid-u-night swim-mu," and nods his head encouragingly. Lynn feels her smile somewhat frozen and doesn't know what to do and just at that moment Tom appears on the beach waving for the tender. Jim gets in and drives over to him while Sandra crawls back over the side and down the stairs, making yelping sounds as she goes. She is shivering uncontrollably although the night isn't cold. "Assault," she is choking between her teeth. "I'll get the police."

Lynn hears herself saying. "You hit him," she says. "If they lock anyone up, it'll be you." Oh god, she can't bear this any more, her buoyant mood has completely evaporated. She simply can't bear it. She changes out of her pink dress and puts on her bikini and takes up a whisky bottle and some glasses up which she silently hands to Mr Tanaka.

"Ah," he says looking at her costume. "Midu-night swim-mu."

Tom and Jim haven't come back on board; the boat is pulled up on the beach but there is no sign of them. "Yes," she says and lets herself down into the water for a midnight swim. Into the calm clean water that shines so bravely under a black tropical sky.

Lucas calls on Dr Woodrow at his home behind the surgery. The doctor is in shirt-sleeves and in the process of opening a bottle of wine. "Ah Constable Frankland!" he booms. "My wife and I thought we would indulge. Will you have a glass? Go on, forget about duty. A coroner's assistant is required to drink wine with his boss."

"Well alright," concedes Lucas, "but only a very small glass." He is handed a glass about a third full with red liquid and looks at it somewhat dubiously.

"Not used to wine?" asks Dr Woodrow. "No why should you be? It's a taste I acquired overseas."

Dr Woodrow is a big man who lives in a big house with a big wife and his personality is in keeping with his size. He is well travelled, with sophisticated tastes and a large library of books that crawl everywhere down the overcrowded walls and spill from every surface. It is noted in Fort John that Dr Woodrow might have practised anywhere he liked but chose to return to his home island of St Claire just before Independence, a decision that seemed to most islanders perverse at a time when the holy grail was to be found in London, and the streets of Toronto were known to be paved with gold. Furthermore, despite the hardness of the times, Dr Woodrow shows no signs of going away, even though everyone reckons he is an excellent doctor and a seriously upright sort of man - neither of these two qualities being thought to add to one's advancement on the island.

Lucas sips the liquid, its thick acid taste reminding him of blackberries and the woods of England. "So how are you getting along now?" says Dr Woodrow.

"I'm going tomorrow to Port Sophia for a few days so I thought I'd come and let you know what I've gathered so far."

"Yes, I heard you were going on a training course the Chief has organised. They have a much more sophisticated coroner's office down there, full-time magistrate with a law degree, not an amateur justice of the peace like me. I expect you will learn a great deal that will be useful."

"Mmm," Lucas is noncommittal as he has private information about the training course that he is not at liberty to share with anyone.

"So who have you seen?"

"I've seen the father, the mother, the uncle. The neighbours of the widow, the widow, the neighbours of Hamilton. I have not pursued the matter of possible illnesses with the widow as other matters came up which meant that the interview had to be suspended. I will see her again soon. There is a great deal of business coming out which is more to do with police work than medical matters."

"So what are the police doing about this new information?"

"I am sharing this information only with the Chief Constable at the moment. It is up to him what is done with it."

"Quite. So what medical matters are there that might interest me?"

"There is something possible in his paternity and I wonder if you could check and find out more about a Pier or Pierre Bart. I don't know how the surname is spelled. He's a man that must have died about 20 years ago and very suddenly. I don't know who would have been his doctor or what would have been done after his death."

"What of Panday's health? Did you learn anything?"

“Everyone I talked to said he was in good mental health, no one would consider the least chance that he committed suicide. If anything was untoward, any aggravation at work or any pressure put on him, he seems to have had the character of one who would brazen it out. He was known to the police.”

“He had a police record?”

“Yes and no. He was alleged to have been involved in a burglary at his uncle’s shop. He was never charged.”

“And who would have run that investigation?”

Lucas hesitates a moment. “Well Sergeant de Troy led that investigation.”

“Ah. Well go on.”

“As for any other illnesses of the dead man, it’s hard to say. His acknowledged father, Sonny Panday, is in his mid forties and probably an alcoholic and it seems that Selwyn himself was known to drink to excess. There is no history of heart conditions on the mother’s side but on the father’s side it is all speculative - Sonny Panday doesn’t know who his own father was.”

“So what else is there?”

“Just the funny way he fell. He landed sideways – exactly 180 degrees sideways. I need to go and investigate the rock wall when I get back from Port Sophia to see if he hit it on the way down. He could possibly have slipped and fallen but I just don’t think he jumped.”

Dr Woodrow goes to a file and takes out the police photographs. He looks at them, pushes his glasses back from his face to peer closely at one, and grunts. Then he puts them back in the file and turns back to the bottle, pours himself a refill and tastes it meditatively. “It will be a sad thing for this island when the Chief Constable retires. I think some of us will have to get off our arses and do something about the matter. But enough of all that. Drink up now, have some more, relax. You are a man who needs to relax more, you are wound up like one of those clockwork-marching soldiers. The future will be here soon enough without getting all tense about it. And whatever happens, happens.”

It is morning on the veranda of their Queensland house, that must explain the fierce light trying to get through the slats. She keeps her eyes shut; she can hear the birds far off, the cockatoos over the cane fields. And there is a scent, a scent of flowers. Her mother always keeps flowers….. Huge bowls with their petals always falling on the floor boards. She can hear water lapping, lap lap splash - it must be the irrigation dam, and only ten minutes away on her bicycle, the sea. Everything is crystal clear and she only has to open her eyes to see it all. Her mother is bringing her lemonade in a chinking glass, freshly squeezed from their own lemons and, it is claimed, their own sugar but that isn't strictly true. It comes out of a bag and it might be their sugar but it might be the Dixon's down the road or the Bertelli's or anyone's really, across the whole wide plain by the sea. Lap lap, the sound of water like the sea and all she has to do is open her eyes and her mother will say, "For heavens sake Lynnette, stop mooning around and come and help." Help. Help, why is she here? This isn't the veranda at all.

She has been sleeping propped on cushions in the main cabin of the Rita. She is wearing her bikini and over the top someone else's t-shirt. For a moment she has no idea where she has come from or how she has got here.

"Hi," says Matey, "I made you a cup of coffee. You look like you've seen a ghost."

She gets up to stretch, her neck is cricked. "Thanks," she says taking the cup.

The main cabin in the Rita is much more luxurious than the one on the Golden Dawn. It is bigger and the portholes make long oblong windows and through these the early morning sun is now shining strongly despite the wooden blinds. "I forgot where I was for a moment," she says to Matey.

"Well it was a bit of a surprise to me too, your being here."

"Things are not great on the Dawn," she says.

"You're lucky. Things are fucking awful here, whoops 'scuse French."

"I was talking to Skip last night. I simply can't stay on the Dawn any longer. I love Jim and I love Tom but….."

"What about me, do you love me? Maybe we could run away together. Would you come with me?"

"Where would we go?"

"We'd run off to an island."

"We're already on an island!"

"I mean a bigger island, a much bigger island, with a big village called London in the middle of it."

"You wouldn't like it. It's not like here."

"That's exactly why I'd like it. Morning Mrs Dwyer," he turns to greet the American. "You're up early. Everything alright? No, of course not, silly of me to ask. No soap. I'll get you some immediately. How about some fresh brewed coffee to perk you up. You would? Good. Lynn - make yourself useful while I find some expensive top-of-the-range soap for Mrs Dwyer."

The American woman stands harsh-faced with inquisitive disapproval and suspicion looking Lynn over. Since the day they strayed onto the Golden Dawn she hasn't seen the woman at close quarters and she wonders if Mrs Dwyer remembers her. She certainly isn't firing any salvos as yet, even though a few moments before she was speaking her mind quite plainly on the matter of the inadequate soap supply. She looks curiously adrift and shipwrecked at this early hour, the skin which with makeup appears so flawless now seems in the harsh morning light to be faintly runnelled like eroded mud-flats and her blue eyes, probably through being cushioned on a sea of white towelling, look faded and drained. Lynn feels herself observing the woman in a dreamy disconnected way as if still drugged with sleep; she is aware that her unexplained appearance on the boat at this early hour is being seen by the other woman as an indication of something irregular but she really doesn't care. "I was taking an early morning swim," Lynn explains, "and Matey lured me on board with the offer of some freshly brewed coffee." There that will do, even though her swimsuit isn't wet. "Black?"

Mrs Dwyer shudders. "I have it with no milk, yes."

"Sugar?"

"Don't touch the stuff. Makes you fat."

"Funny," says Lynn struck by the confluence of topics and carried away into being chatty. "I was dreaming this morning just as I woke, about my father's sugar plantation in Queensland. I woke up sure that I was lying on the veranda. I even heard the birds, but of course they're not the same birds at all. As soon as I started paying attention they sounded nothing like them." She hands the woman a cup.

"A sugar plantation," says Mrs Dwyer bending her face over to inhale the coffee aroma and then sitting down with the cup between her hands at the galley table. "That would be like a chocolate factory. How could anyone bear it? You'd get so fat."

"No, no-one was fat. It was too hot to get fat I think. We all put on weight when we got to London. We were all as thin as sticks in Australia."

"We should have gone to Australia for our vacation, I told Jerry we should have. So," says the woman after a pause as she sips and looks Lynn over, "your parents had a plantation. That's very down home. Where I come from people used to have plantations. Not now of course, not individuals. It's all companies. Shares. We've got shares in sugar of course but I guess it's not the same. Lot of money in the stuff; don't eat it myself. Your parents sold out I suppose. You'd get a good price for a plantation these days." She has red nails which look rather obscene in the absence of lipstick and other distractions. She is taking a cigarette out of a packet with blood red talons and sticking it shakily into her parched mud mouth, all the while fidgeting through her pockets. "What have I done with my lighter? I'll just die if I left it at the hotel. Someone will have pocketed for sure. Can't trust a soul….."

"There's a lighter on the bench," says Lynn going for it.

"Oh well. Would you look at that, that's the one I lost yesterday. I swore to Jerry someone had stolen it. It's solid gold and look it was there all along, I must have put it down."

"I expect the other one will turn up," says Lynn.

"I expect you're right honey. This holiday is sure turning into a voyage of surprises." She manages to light the cigarette and blows smoke out as if nicotine has come to save the world. "So what did you all do in London? After a sugar plantation it must have been really something, ending up in London."

"My mother's an interior designer. She does mansions and stuff. My father works in the city."

"Mansions," Mrs Dwyer turns her blue eyes in their huge ruff of white towelling full on her. "What mansions?"

"Rich people. People with titles. She goes in and turfs out their old suits of armour and paints everything Chinese red. And scatters geometric crocheted cushions around and goes to sale rooms with their money to get them a Braque or a Picasso print for the walls."

"Well I'm blowed," says Mrs Dwyer. "Where do they put the armour?"

Lynn likes the irrelevancy of the question; it is turning the conversation into a balloon that can blow anywhere, just how she feels at that moment. "In the attic I expect. Until it comes into fashion again. People like that don't throw stuff out, they just put it in the attic. My mother says you wouldn't believe what those old attics can hold; she says there are attics the size of huge apartments and all full of hundreds of years of junk. She tells them to throw it all out. My mother hates all that old stuff."

"We're moving to London in August," says Mrs Dwyer. "Jerry's organised an apartment. I think I'd rather like it if it had suits of armour in it. I shall certainly demand they're moved back if someone's put them in an attic. Are these people aristocrats then?"

"I suppose so, it's hard to tell. Sometimes I think people get titles just for having money."

"Yes, I've heard that," says Mrs Dwyer with satisfaction. "So did you meet any in London?"

"People with titles? Yes there were some at school. But I've met more here than I knew in London."

"What here? In the Caribbean? Really." the woman studies her cup and doesn't acknowledge Matey's cheery re-entry with assurances as to vast quantities of soap. "We've heard they're hard to get to know. People like that. Stuck up."

"Some of them aren't very nice but then some are lovely."

"Have you been to any of these mansions in England?"

"My best friend at school lived in a huge place. I stayed with her once. You got tired just walking from one end of the house to the other."

"There's all the etiquette isn't there, so I've heard." Mrs Dwyer is looking at Lynn with such an expression of intensity and concern that Lynn, who is usually too diffident to get cunning ideas, suddenly finds that she is being clever and duplicitous almost without effort.

"Oh yes," she says breezily, "those awful formal dinners. I used to be terrified of all those knives and forks and glasses – because if I picked up the wrong one there was always someone who sniggered. And all the other stuff of course, things to say and not to say, how to dress for this and that event."

"And they really bother about that sort of thing?" says Mrs Dwyer with shrill consternation.

"Oh yes. But only," she says with consummate haste, "in those sorts of circles. Of course when you go over I expect you'll just mix with other Americans."

"Oh no," says Mrs Dwyer suddenly angry and nervous, "we're going over in an official capacity, as part of a trade delegation. Diplomatic level. Everyone will be inviting us."

"Ah yes," says Lynn.

Mrs Dwyer leans over, pointing at the drawer, "Hand up some knives and forks and show me how they go," she says.

"Me!" says Lynn. "Oh no, I'm hopeless at it. You need to get someone like Sandra to show you. I'd only be guessing."

"Sandra?" says Mrs Dwyer.

"She's been the cook on our boat. She went to cordon bleu school but she can't actually cook very well at all, despite all that money being spent on her. If you ask me it's her upbringing. Having servants. You never have to do anything for yourself."

"And she's over on your boat?"

"Well actually, she's looking for another job."

"Do you think she would work for me?"

"Work for you?" Lynn frames a look of surprise as if such an idea is the farthest thing from her mind. "Well I don't know. The fact is, you've already got the best cook in the Caribbean. You won't like her cooking, I promise you. We've tried it till we can't bear it any more."

"No, not that job. It seems George does have talent in that direction. At least as far as his muffins go. No I was thinking more of a social secretary."

Lynn is aware that Matey is looking intently at her and she lets her hands flutter in what she hopes is a surprised and negative way. "I really couldn't say whether she would or not. You'd have to ask her."

"And ask her I will, the moment I've freshened up." Mrs Dwyer gathers her expensive white towelling robe around her and strides off to have her shower.

Matey sits down opposite her. "This is a fine way to repay our hospitality."

Lynn looks at Matey with wide-eyed innocence and then has to laugh. "But it probably won't come to anything."

Matey however is thinking. "Oh well it might be alright; it would probably be a secretary's job to run little messages, like find her the soap for instance. I'll talk to Skip, get him to plant some ideas about the sort of thing Sandra could do about the boat….. If you can make her think it's her own idea, Mrs Dwyer is really quite easy to manage. Hmmm."

"Hmmm," says Lynn.

It turns into a beautiful day. The bay is flat calm and windless, the boats hang like mobiles connected by invisible threads from a crystal sky on a field of clear aqua glass. Nothing in nature moves. There have been a lot of excited tenders ferrying passengers to shore early on, but by ten o'clock all the charterers have gone off to the other side of the island and lassitude adds to the other perfections of the day. What time will they be back? Those remaining make calculations, a whole morning, maybe an afternoon as well. Who can guess at the vagaries of the charterer even when provided with a complete lunch and an army of navvies to carry iceboxes of drinks and other consumables? There is always going to be someone who will spoil it and get a headache. Yes, always some bitch with a headache. Under their limp awnings the boat crews allow themselves a moment of resentment before sinking into total lethargy. If only they were rich enough for such a life, a life lived like this on their own account: what glory! Turning the pages of their paperbacks eventually becomes too much and the last eyelid left alive slides reptilian-like over hazy bleary salty eyes and only the cry of the birds remain.

The woman in a floral dress is saying….. Who is the woman? It isn't her mother, no her mother is right there at the tea table. She is waiting for the tea to draw no doubt - any moment she will pick up the elegant green and orange art-deco teapot. So they all sit straight-backed waiting too and the woman is saying, "You have to watch the blacks. Be sure and nail everything down or as sure as eggs is eggs every last thing'll disappear into the night. And as for all those Italians and other wogs coming in and taking over, they should ship them all back, the government had no right to go letting them into the country. Did you see in the paper how the ships are coming in with them and turning round to go and pick up more, it's not right. You mark my word." Her stumpy red finger taps the lacquered Chinese table. "No good will come of employing all these wogs and blacks. Colin and Sheree have got a black woman straight out of a humpy to help in the house. How can Sheree let her touch the baby? That I can't understand. If it's only washing clothes and cleaning the house I can see it but I went to visit and the woman had little Jeffrey in her arms wrapped in a towel, his hair all wet. She'd been bathing him, touching him. Can you imagine that! And there's worse I could tell you too," she looks at me.

Mother says, "Go down the garden and play, Lynnette, I'll bring you out a piece of cake when the tea is drawn."

Lynn is furious. She is going to miss her chance to show off; her cup of tea held carefully and sipped, her piece of buttery lemony cake carefully cut up with a cake fork on her plate. Now this awful woman is spoiling it all; she leaves muttering, "Horrid woman. Horrid horrid woman."

Horrid horrid woman. Lynn opens her eyes to the cry of a savage and relentless bird howling from the shore and eventually turning her head sees that it is Sandra. It takes a while to sink in. "Sandra is waving at us and shouting," she says aloud. "Tom." The words fall in to a deep hole. "Jim." No response. "I will not go," she says to herself because she has no goodwill left. But the bird keeps sawing at the silence and eventually she kicks Jim.

"What."

"Come for a walk," she whispers.

"No, wanna stay here."

"Sandra is dancing up and down on the shore and wants to come aboard. Someone else will notice her eventually. Let's take the tender and leave her to come aboard on her own."

"Don't want her on board."

"I think it will only be to get her things."

Jim is awake, "What do you know?"

"Come for a walk."

They walk across the island, by a path that leads up and round by the headland and ducks and weaves among twining vegetation and flowers. Jim is in a buoyant mood that utterly precludes any introspection about his own behaviour; all he can see is that an obstacle to perfect enjoyment is about to be removed and he is gloriously happy. He yodels, cracks bird cries and tries swinging from creepers, with mixed results. He laughs when he falls down and dances in and out of what shade there is, waving an old straw hat and acting like a ten year old. When they reach the highpoint, at the headland, they sit down to admire the sea sparkle about them on all sides.

"What's she going to say when she finds out Sandra is from Hampstead and is no more aristocracy than you or I!" he exclaims.

"I thought you were aristocracy," says Lynn.

"Yes but not born to it," says Jim. "I only had it thrust upon me because all of the blue bloods stopped breathing for one reason or another. Cousin of a cousin, that sort of thing. I went to a very ordinary school, nothing posh at all, and all I know of knives and forks is that the moment someone's said grace you grab them and start thrusting food in as fast as you can."

"Mrs Dwyer may never find out. Why should she? Sandra is exactly the kind of person who would think herself perfectly capable of explaining the English to a woman like Mrs Dwyer. And whatever she learns will give her confidence so it doesn't really matter what it is."

"You're so clever," says Jim. 'Or maybe you're just lucky. Sometimes it's hard to tell them apart. I don't think life is ever going to get the better of you. In the end you'll suddenly see a way and off you'll go, taking us down a whole new channel that no-one knew was there. That's why I always want to be your friend, because when you come through whooping and waving your shirt I can say to everyone, There! I knew all along that she'd know what to do!"

She laughs, "Well that's fine coming from you. It was your throwing Sandra overboard that made it all so awful. I wasn't coming back you know."

"Yes, well, now I see that in future all I have to do is make an awful situation even worse and you'll find a way to solve the whole thing!" He puts his arms round her shoulders and hugs her to him. "You wouldn't really have gone would you?"

"Yes I would; I would have got someone to take me back down the islands."

"You'd have missed the big adventure."

"I don't think it's so very fabulous. This sailing business. Most of the time you just get to be wet and uncomfortable."

"No but it can be magic. Travelling under your own sail, think of the romance of it, not beholden to anyone or anything except the winds and the seas. Everything shipshape and not a penny to pay, just the miles to unravel behind you and every new landfall is some new adventure, every map is a page of choices. If we weren't tied to this cruise we could set our sails for Africa. Doesn't that fill you with excitement?"

"How could we sail for Africa? No-one's got any money."

"I mean we could sail for Africa, there's no technical reason we couldn't."

"I thought there were technical reasons why your boat couldn't. And that's why you're here, to get money to fix it!"

"Don't be so literal Lynn! You spoil romance when you get literal. Come on, let's go and see what adventures the charterers have got up to on their deserted beach, all two dozen of them."

They start down the track which descends steeply to the bay below. "Uh-oh," says Jim. "Some of them will have difficulty getting back up here! It won't be long before this will be a proper road with little jeeps ferrying tourists so that they don't have to walk anywhere. There'll be great fat Americans bulging out of vehicles with their legs blobby with lard and under-use. Yuck, how I hate the way the world is going. Soon every inch of it will be carved into a landscape where rich people can flop. You can hear it already in the way the Americans say, "Walk. Walk. Who me? Why should I walk? Who's in charge of this place? Fancy making a person walk. Walk!" like a vulture croaking. I'll rip you open with my talons and turn your underbelly into a four lane highway."

"You could be wrong," says Lynn. "Maybe people will come on holiday to do nothing else but walk in future - get away from their desks and walk and walk till every part of the globe is crisscrossed with walking tracks and walking-boot shops. These boots were made for walking and that's just what they'll do….." They dance singing down to the beach below.

On the beach a neat pile of iceboxes is stacked in the shade and a woman lies not far off, contentedly reading. She is in her mid forties and is preposterously got up in a teased hairstyle like a carefully contrived thatch. She wears a well-engineered bikini containing mountainous breasts which, as well as their obvious erotic function, also operate as a book rest. To complete the ensemble she sports red-rimmed sunglasses and wiggles red-painted toenails and is obviously pleased to see company because she hallos and hails them over.

"Everyone's on the reef," she says in a croaky voice that sounds as if her vocal chords have spent a lot of time in contact with chain-smoked filtertips and a succession of pleasant fruity cocktails. She is one of those loud comic blondes that always have a man somewhere nearby keeping watch and sure enough one appears out of the sea and starts to flipper clumsily up the beach.

"I wonder what he's doing coming back now," says the woman without moving, and turning back to them continues to enumerate the many and favourite snacks they have indulged in for lunch. A stocky man of about fifty comes up beside her with a scowl.

“The reef is crawling with Japs,” he says. He picks up a ferocious looking speargun that lies near the woman.

“What you going to catch, honey?” she asks.

“I’m going to get me some Jap.”

“No honey, live and let live.”

“Live and let live,” he explodes. “They should have thought about that before Guadal Canal.” The only good Jap is a dead Jap as far as he is concerned.

Lynn becomes quite concerned, “You can’t do that, they’re our charterers.”

The woman says, “Don’t you worry about him, honey, he won’t do it, he’s all talk.”

The man goes bright red and gives her such a look of hate. “Oh won’t I just, you just watch me!” and starts to stompflipper clumsily back towards the water with his speargun.

She calls after him, “Well go right ahead and do it honey and when they electrocute you for murder or whatever they do down here I’m telling you without a word of a lie I’m selling the business…..”

He stops as if shot and turns back, “Over my dead body,” he hisses.

“I said I’m selling the business over your dead body and the house…..”

“The house! What would you want to sell the house for?”

“I’m telling you, I’ll move to New Jersey to be near my sister. So what do you say to that?”

“You won’t get a cent of it…..” he screams doing a flatfoot shuffling dance in the sand.

“Well doll, I’ve already got most of it as you and the accountant and the tax man very well know, so if you want to go and murder someone just go right ahead - I’m just telling you what I’m going to do afterwards that’s all.” And she settles herself back comfortably with her book propped on her breasts and starts telling them what an extremely pleasant peaceful time she has been having and how glad she is to have someone to talk to, while her other half stands there glaring at her and breathing ferociously through his nostrils until he eventually realises that she has stopped taking any notice of him and turns and clumps angrily away.

Lynn and Jim find some spare flippers and snorkels and are soon lying in lightdancing water like a huge plastic glowing pillow into which they press their faces. Lynn again feels the touch of nostalgia which has been pursuing her all day. She lived her youth near where the Great Barrier Reef shimmered under the surface around the islands off the coast and she spent many weekends just like this, face down wallowing in light, blowing like a whale through her snorkel and waving her feet at the water to pilot herself through a magic kingdom.

Yes this is magic indeed, some gentle state where hours disappear and ears and eyes and skin become acclimatised to another world, free from worrisome earthbound care. At some point she realises the pinking of the light means that the sun is now poised in its westward arc and for a moment she rebels against the thought but, putting up her head, she sees that most of the charterers are now on shore and milling for the return journey. Jim's head is also above water and when he sees her he points to the land questioningly and she nods. They steer leisurely for the beach.

By the time they are ready to depart, most of the charterers are on the move back towards the boats. Some of the last to depart are their own charterers because Kenji is required to take various shots of Mr Tanaka with a large fish on a speargun.

She greets Mr Yamada. "Where is Mrs Tanaka?" she asks.

He points up the hill, "Already going back. Just now," he says.

"We'll catch her up," says Lynn.

They crawl up the hill after the throng who make slow progress too, being all somewhat soft in the bone after long immersion. At the top they come across a strange sight. Mrs Tanaka is sitting with the large blonde woman, who has produced a folder of photographs of her house and family. Together they are smiling and nodding. Of the Japanese-hating husband there is no sign.

"Isn't that strange?" Lynn is saying later that evening after recounting the incident to the bar. "Earlier I thought he was going to murder our charterers and then later there are the two wives, chatting together."

"No, that's what always happens," says Skip. "Once you get to know a person they no longer seem as yellow or as coloured or as whatever as you thought. Take George. When I took him on he was a black West Indian. Now he's just George. I keep forgetting. It was a shock getting someone like Mrs Dwyer on board. Suddenly you find you're sticking up for a sort of difference in George that you'd forgotten he had."

The next morning is brilliantly sunny but the weather forecast is for change. Mr Tanaka has some obsession about spearguns and fish and after a fruitless morning of Kenji trailing him through the water without result, they get some dead fish from the hotel for Mr Tanaka to shoot at.

The Rita departs mid-morning with Sandra draped languidly on its deck. She doesn't wave. Tom has been struggling over a postcard to Yvonne which fails entirely to mention Sandra and dwells at some length on the chicken dish Lynn cooked the night before which turned out rather well in the end despite them not being able to work out what 'Cc' in the list of ingredients meant. Once he has finished this labour and has organised postage for it at the hotel, Tom is restless. By lunch time it has started to blow and Tom gets even more irritable; it's time to stop messing about, it is time to go. They sail away.

For a year and a day, Lynn sings to herself. To the land where the gumtree grows. Yes, there's no technical reason why the Golden Dawn couldn't sail and sail till they put down their anchor in a bay amid the rhythmic beating of waves and the cries of children in that higher register that indicates the beaches of her youth. If she could only get back there once more, back to a time when she would run full tilt towards the water, not knowing the meaning of stop. Oh to be a child again, with its head under water seeing the wavy army leggy look of other children from below. Giving herself up to the ocean, leaving the land and rounding the cliffs, meeting the current breast-high, arms up, eyes shut. The surge and lash of it. What joy it was then. Where has all that gone?

It soon becomes obvious that Tom's bad humour and restlessness is more than pure crabbiness; it is in fact the first symptoms of flu. Within a day he is struggling to function as he streams sweat and his voice croaks and his eyes and nose run profusely. Jim goes next and suddenly Lynn finds that she and the charterers are sailing the boat.

Mr Tanaka is in his element. However, every time he pulls a rope the moment has to be captured by Kenji on film, and because this seems to slow the process considerably, Lynn decides that Mr Tanaka should take over from herself as captain. He will steer the boat and she and Kenji will be the deckhands. Mr Tanaka likes this very much and sits cross legged behind the wheel with his hat on very straight, looking hugely responsible.

"He look like ship captain, ney?" says Mr Yamada.

"Yee-ess," says Lynn diplomatically.

Mrs Tanaka picks up her slight hesitancy. Not like ship captain? Why not? she wants to know.

His hat is on too straight. Hats are not worn straight on yachts, captains wear their hats any old way. This is translated and a mirror is brought. After much effort during which almost no thought is given to the progress of the yacht, the hat finds its rightful position, tilted slightly to the right on Mr Tanaka's head. When eventually everyone is satisfied with this important and strenuous activity, Mr Tanaka smiles the lackadaisical smile of a yacht's captain and Kenji takes the picture.

Lucas has been to Port Sophia and been secretly inducted as an Immigration officer. He has been issued with a hand gun and given various instructions and now flies back to Fort John through one of the bucketing storms which have unseasonably been lashing the islands over the past week. As the plane rears from side to side he feels the revolver under his arm while being jolted in his seat. It is a strange journey, racked by fear and yet with this symbol of power strapped to him that almost makes him feel invincible. The warring elements come to no conclusion however; he lands back still alive but shaken in St Claire.

The first thing he does on his return is to go and see Mrs Panday. She has been sick, or so it has been reported to him. Constable Frankland thinks the illness is a rather convenient thing to have happened but he has no intention of releasing the pressure that he has been keeping her under. A distant relation of his lives in her street and it is her report channelled through his aunt that prompts him to insist on an interview that Thursday. "Well Mrs Panday, I am reluctant to force an interview on a sick woman but I have been told that when your husband's wages and other moneys are paid out to you at the end of the month, you intend to pack up forthwith and take the child and go up the islands to where your family lives. If this is the case, I want to speak to you now."

The fight has not entirely gone out of Mrs Panday even though her attitude to Lucas is no longer high handed and belligerent. "My lord, if these people had nothing to gossip about they'd lie on their backs and foam like dogs in a madness. Yes, if you must know, when I get what's legally mine from his employer - and I think it a poor employer what must wait for the regular payday when the man is dead - when I get what is rightfully belonging to the widow, I am getting the dust of this place off my feet quicksmart."

"I can keep you here unless you tell me everything that happened that night. I can stop you leaving."

"What - and leave a widow and orphan in a den of vipers? Where everyone's talking and gossiping and making rumour and making stories up and telling this one and that one that the Society has come when it never has and why should it? Look at the child, the picture of health playing out there. Isn't she well fed, doesn't she have shoes on her feet and a pretty little dress on, unlike some of these other brats. And one rule for the rich and one for the poor as usual too. That Anthony Hamilton, he just had his say to the police and then disappeared and do you know where he is? Could you find him to talk to? No. Now that is a suspicious thing. But the police are not worried at all. The white man has told us what he knows. Why is it that they believe him while you are here day and night harassing me and making me out to be some monster in the neighbourhood?"

"What happened on the night Selwyn died?" Lucas repeats patiently.

"Max de Troy came round, about business between him and Selwyn."

"What was it about?"

"I don't know. I take no notice of business things, that was for Selwyn to take care of."

"But there was an argument and shouting. You must have heard."

"No I don't hear no argument or shouting and I don't hear no screaming."

"This is hard to believe Mrs Panday, because your neighbours heard it perfectly."

"My neighbours will make things up, any bad thing about me and my poor dead husband. Don't you believe nothing that sort of person tells you."

"They said they heard Max shouting, "Where is it? What you done with it you thieving rat?" As if Selwyn had stolen something. And there was the sound of furniture tumbling over and thumping and banging and shouting and finally screaming."

"They make up things, that is all rubbish. Max and Selwyn were having a quiet game of cards before they go to work. Then Max help Selwyn to fix the table, the leg come off the table while they were playing their cards so they went looking for a hammer, and that hammer, that is Max's hammer what he lend Selwyn before and when they can't find it there was some shouting but they find it eventually and then they get some nails and bang the leg back on. But Selwyn bang his finger with the hammer in the meantime, maybe he have a glass or two, after all he was not expecting to be wanted at that hour. So he scream. There, that is the honest truth. That is all that happen. Without a word of a lie."

"So your husband screamed."

"Yes. Now I remember, he scream."

"So why did you hit the child when she said her daddy screamed."

Mrs Panday spreads her hands. "I am a poor widow and there you are asking questions of a child. You have no right to go asking my daughter such a thing, a child doesn't know anything. How can I stop you? Well I can't hit you because then I end up in jail so I slap the child and somehow my ring make her bleed. Now I am the subject of bad stories all over this neighbourhood."

"Are you scared of Max de Troy?"

Mrs Panday looks at him with her red eyes. "Max de Troy is vermin and everyone knows it. Wherever he goes creeping around is all filth with a set of crows pecking at the bodies and bigger crows pecking at the first crows and everywhere corruption and slime. I'll take my money and go up the islands and you could try and stop me but I'll never tell you more than I'm telling you now so you are wasting all your time and my own."

"Hmm," says Lucas. "And what about the hammer?"

Mrs Panday stares at him.

"He died with the hammer on him. In his pocket. Why would that be if it belonged to Max de Troy?"

Mrs Panday moves uneasily. Then she starts to breathe roughly. "I am too sick to be pestered like this with questions," she says.

The weather is dismal for the next couple of days with high seas, strong winds and scudding rain. They ride the bucking tail of cyclones. And then when it clears, as they put into an unfrequented bay, the transmission breaks and they are stranded for a whole day while Jim and Tom, both swearing and profaning at the top of their croaky voices, attempt to fix it. Lynn gets all the charterers into the tender and takes them as far away as she feels safe, in order to get them out of earshot. They are castaways, she tells Mr Yamada. The charterers are thrilled. They are diving on a reef that is nothing special in terms of the reef life when Kenji, who is the best swimmer, finds a wreck in deeper water to one side. It is still quite near the surface, about twenty feet down and just in Mr Tanaka's range of comfort, so the charterers spend a very happy and productive day fossicking about on it. It appears to be a local schooner, probably having come to grief within the last 50 years but from the way the charterers act it might just as easily have been a Spanish galleon full of doubloons. They find a metal anchor heavily encrusted and sunk into the sand. Mrs Tanaka finds a bit of pottery which is reburied so that Mr Tanaka can find it on film. They all have a lot of fun and are all so exhausted that Jim and Tom's simmering bad temper isn't noticed by them at all.

The day after, when the transmission is fixed and they are ready to sail on, Lynn wakes feeling hazy and strange. Her head has a peculiar buzzing in it and she has difficulty focussing. She feels, as she makes breakfast, as if she is moving in slow motion. Tom has more or less recovered and now takes charge. They sail off into a stiff breeze and Lynn finds she is having difficulty adjusting to the ship's movements. She has no appetite for breakfast or lunch either and by mid-afternoon has started to shiver uncontrollably. Mrs Tanaka is the first to notice and starts dosing her on white pills of some description. She loses the whole of the next day - she remembers nothing of it at all. She drags herself into a vaguely upright position the day after and she finds that in the interim Mr Yamada has taken over cooking duties and everyone has been eating Japanese. "Oh that's nice," she says, thinking the charterers must have liked a change from her cooking, back to something more traditional and familiar.

"How well-mannered they are," she thinks. "They'd probably prefer to continue to eat Japanese but they're too polite to say so." After all, what can she cook but simple western food? She stuffs and roasts two chickens for dinner with baked vegetables, peas, gravy and bread sauce. It is the only sort of food she can do, cutting out all complexity to reduce the risk of getting it wrong, where every task requires concentration, where streaming eyes and nose and a throat like a rasped board make it difficult to function. Alone, struggling in the galley she sings, "I wanna go home, I wanna go home, Oh how I wanna go home."

Not England. She doesn't want to go back there. She wants to go back to the Frangipanni. She wants to giggle and chatter with Rae and romp down to Boss's boat early in the morning and tip him out unceremoniously onto the deck ignoring his cries for mercy and his hangover. It is a mystery to her why she is here, in this hot galley, cooking when she can't cook, sailing when she can't sail, singing when she can't sing. "Rinn," says Mr Tanaka, which is as near as he can come to her name, "Rinn alway happy," he indicates, "alway sing." Why bother disabusing him? She just smiles and acquiesces.

"Rinn," says Mr Tanaka, indicating he wants more roast chicken. "Very good-onay. Shiken. Rose shiken." He pronounces these newly acquired English words carefully and rubs his stomach in anticipation. They pick the bones clean between them all.

Very polite. So polite that Mr Tanaka makes no move to suggest that Mr Yamada should do any more cooking. So still feeling like death, she continues with Yvonne's menus, following her instructions for chips which are deep fried twice in oil to make them crispy. And she fries fish gently in butter and spices, or dips them quickly in a boiling chillied broth or wraps them in parcels and oven-bakes them. She fries steaks with pepper, mushrooms and garlic or makes kebabs with fresh pineapple and bacon. Salads she makes with whatever she can find on the islands and dresses them with a simple french dressing or mayonnaise. She makes paella with seafood. Pepper pot of pork. Creole chicken. She deepfries plantain rings and serves them with spicy mince - that is the most adventurous of her offerings and it seems to go down alright as nothing is left. She bakes local bananas in the oven, makes pancakes and wraps up the bananas with molasses, cream and brandy.

Getting from one day to the next is her only concern. Everything physical seems so very difficult. She is aware that the charterers eat everything and make appreciative noises. But she always thinks it is just part of the politeness and reserve of the Japanese. So when it is finally brought home to her that it is not politeness but that she is actually a success, she is so surprised she doesn't really believe it. The charterers are eating the simple dishes she makes as if they come from the kitchens of the Ritz. She has noticed Mrs Tanaka is watching her and writing down everything that she cooks and how she does it but she thought that this was just an amusement, basic life at sea, how the party survive even the cooking, that sort of thing. But one day Mr Yamada tells her that the recipes will be published in one of Mr Tanaka's magazines. She is amazed and isn't sure what she thinks about these basic recipes being held up to the Japanese as something worth following. She tells Tom he ought to say something to them but he just laughs.

Well here's a turn up for the books, he writes to Yvonne. It seems that Lynn's version of your recipes (by the way we worked out Cc was coconut cream) are going to become famous.

"Yes, nothing wrong with the grub on this boat," says Jim. "I've always noticed that when people protest they can't do something it's because they can do it really well and they just want praise. Come on now, you're really secretly chuffed they're writing down your recipes."

"Well they're Yvonne's really," she says. "They're so easy to follow. It's she who should get the kudos."

"Ah well Yvonne. What a woman she was," says Jim. "Good looking, elegant, fantastic cook. If I'd known Tom was going to throw her away like that I would have made my move." He looks at Tom's face. "And then," he adds, "he blew it with you too. If he'd kept on asking you to marry him he'd have worn you down eventually, wouldn't he?"

Lynn just laughs at his fantasy but it makes her feel sad. Why is the only person who has ever asked her to marry him doing it in jest, down on his knees again at Jim's suggestion? She doesn't want a man on his knees, she wants an man upright with his arm about her waist and a West Indian rhythm throbbing through and through into the longing of her body.

Chapter 12

The ungraspable phantom of life; and this is the key to it all

It is all nearly finished. Everything eventually nears an end. Either the explorers come home with flags gaily fluttering and crowds gather cheering on the bank or the boat limps in alone under tattered sail to an ominous silence.

Lucas's report is nearly complete. He would have finished it already only the Sergeant has been working him day and night, watching him like a hawk. But even the Sergeant can't stop him having a day off.

The coroner's court is listed for a week on Monday and he wants to get a copy to both Dr Woodrow and the Chief Constable at least a few days beforehand. Lucas finds he has a lot to say although, as he says in his introduction, much of it is supposition. The angle of the body and its position relative to the car is his main concern. He details his minute search of the cliff and his discovery of marks nearly four feet apart. One mark he surmises corresponds to Panday's wrist watch which, although his left arm was left dangling outside the car, was nevertheless smashed. On further examination it was found to have traces of moss and lichen consistent with having hit the side of the cliff. The other mark, about four feet away and parallel to the first mark, has perhaps been left by Panday's left shoe, the one that was found later under a bush. It too has minute traces of lichen on it. Lucas in his commentary asks the question, why would a man jump sideways? Did he perhaps slip and fall? But then he would have hit the rock wall further up and bounced down it, leaving much more definite marks. Panday had leapt out from the top but by half way down he is sideways. How had the man managed that? His natural momentum would make that a manoeuvre as difficult as any carried out by a diver in an Olympic competition.

Panday had extensive injuries due no doubt to the impact, but his left arm was dangling outside and appeared from the position of the body not to have come into much contact with the car. There was bruising to several of his fingernails including his thumb, as documented in the post-mortem. If this hand had hit the cliff it is unlikely that both the left side of his middle and ring finger should be bruised as well as the right side of his thumb. It is possible that some bruising occurred on the cliff and some with the hand slapping against the car when the body hit it, and yet the bruising has a consistency that suggests it occurred all at the same time. The pathologist considered that it was caused before death and Lucas surmises that there was some sort of fight with Max de Troy earlier in the evening and the bruising to the hand occurred at that point.

Up until a few days ago, Lucas had managed to keep all his discoveries under wraps. He told the Sergeant that Dr Woodrow was dissatisfied with the amount of time he was giving to it and had complained to the Chief Constable that not enough was being done. This seemed to fill the Sergeant with great satisfaction and therefore, as Lucas knew, the explosion when he eventually found out the extent of his junior constable's insights would be all the greater.

Lucas knew that the moment he interviewed Max, the Sergeant would know all about it and all concealment would be at an end. There was no way of confronting Max without revealing the evidence he had collected. That is why he left Max until last, so that he was as near to having the report complete as was possible before the coroner heard the case. He went up to see Max yesterday morning and by lunch time the Sergeant most particularly required his attendance. The Sergeant, who was purple with fury, had discovered that he was spending a great deal too much time on matters that did not concern him and a great deal too little on his duties. The Sergeant told him he would put in a formal report about this dereliction of duty and it would go on his record. From now on he had better pull up his socks. "You young men, all sticking your noses in as if your elders and betters aren't perfectly capable of solving a matter to everyone's satisfaction. There you go, stirring up things, creating bad blood between Mrs Panday and her husband's employer. Why would you be writing down a load of lies from that woman? She's a recent widow and her mind is gone."

"Well I was only doing my duty as I was required to do by the coroner," Lucas had said to defend himself. "There were things in the police report which weren't correct. Mr de Troy, your brother, told police that he had gone from the Lotus Room about 1 pm and driven Mr Hamilton's car down to the yacht club jetty where he had spent the rest of the night waiting to pick up Mr Hamilton from a party on the boat the Beau Geste. And then when Mr Hamilton left the party, he had taken him to the Beach Hotel and then returned to the house in Louisaville about breakfast time. He never said he went to visit Panday. There's nothing in the report about him visiting Panday or taking Panday off in the car somewhere. That seems to me to be a glaring omission that the coroner will want to know about."

Lucas recalls the shades of menace on Max's face when he put this very point to him, how his lips lost their fullness under his moustache and drew themselves into a straight line and how the whites of his eyes had glittered like steel from a dagger. When Lucas had asked him why he hadn't told the police about going round to the dead man's house on the night in question, he said that he understood police time was valuable and had merely speeded things along. He had probably done a number of things in between the Lotus Room and the jetty. He believed he had also gone to the lavatory at some point. He said that he had gone round to give a message to Panday as there were things that needed to be fixed at the house urgently. After saying this, Max then smiled a dismissive smile at him and signified the interview was at an end. However Lucas made no move to go and knew that he was travelling into the teeth of a hurricane. "This is different to other statements that I have, such as the one from Mrs Panday herself," he said and Max's expression changed to one of increasing threat. "I gather that there was a lot of shouting, a fight of some sort, and that Panday left with you, possibly not of his own accord." Lucas was being disingenuous here; this was gathered not from the statement of the widow but rather from what the neighbours had said. However he felt that a slight fudging was warranted in the circumstances.

"That woman is an incorrigible liar and wasn't even present; she was lying down in the next room the worse for drink as usual and the child not even put to bed for the night - she made the whole thing up," and his moustache took on an ugly appearance above his tight mouth. "And now," said Max," if you'll excuse me I do not choose to answer any more questions. If the coroner wishes to know anything more he will have to ask me himself in court," and that was that.

The Sergeant however was not so restrained or so guarded and harangued Lucas, "All those lies of that woman and you believe them!"

Lucas said, "Oh no you're wrong, I don't believe the woman at all. Not at all. I do believe her neighbours though. There are a lot of people live in that street. And a dull life for many of them, enlivened by your brother beating up Selwyn Panday in full view, because you can't expect them to listen to the whole thing lying down in their beds. No, they must get up and go down the road and look through the window which is why I know that Mrs Panday hasn't told me the half of it."

The Sergeant ground his teeth and muttered under his breath and stomped off to file some papers but an irresistible urge seemed to sweep him and he turned once more to his junior officer. "There are things you don't know about the case. No doubt my brother was over-excited, he do hate a thief. My brother hates a thief above anything. A thief that is employed in a house and then steals something from it – that is the worst sort of crime. My brother was angry no doubt and it is true these things should have been written down at the beginning. But remember that Panday is dead. The theft prey on his mind and then he jump to his death. Why blacken the man's reputation when he's dead? He have a family. He have a wife and little one. He have a father and a mother. How are they going to feel?"

"So he stole something?" This wasn't exactly a surprise to Lucas; from the statements given by the neighbours he gathered some sort of accusation had been made. He tried to keep his voice neutral, suddenly seeing a window of opportunity. It seemed he might be able to get more from the Sergeant than he would ever get from Max. "What was it? Was it ever recovered?" he asked.

"No it was not recovered. The man hid it somewhere but it will turn up no doubt."

"And what was this item?"

"I don't think it helps the case to know what it was."

"Oh I think it does," said Lucas. He hurriedly added, "The coroner will want to know what a man would commit suicide for. Maybe if it was an item of great value and he faced serious consequences then he might jump. But if it were a fork off the table, or a small item, the coroner is going to ask awkward questions."

“I don’t know what it was. Maybe Max didn’t know what it was. Possibly Mr Hamilton told him to go and see Panday to get it back and Max got angry because he wouldn’t give it to him.”

“So you think Mr Hamilton is the key? Dr Woodrow says that he thinks the police have been remiss in not finding out where Hamilton is and getting him back here.”

“Dr Woodrow!” cried the Sergeant. “What would he know about correct police procedures? Why bring Mr Hamilton back - what has he to do with it? He wasn’t even there. He stayed on the Beau Geste till late late and Panday was dead by three o’ clock, as the post-mortem shows. So now he wants to make fools of us, dragging Mr Hamilton back here for nothing.”

“He could say at least what was missing. Clear that up.”

“I expect it was jewellery. That’s the kind of thing a man like Panday would steal, cufflinks or some such.”

“No, it was something big. I know that because of the places Max was looking. He wasn’t looking into little places where cufflinks.....”

“Stop this nonsense,” bellowed the Sergeant. “You are to stop all this do you hear? You have duties right here that you have been neglecting, I want to hear no more of all this.”

Lucas has been typing up the Sergeant’s comments. He wonders where Hamilton is. Max has told the police that Hamilton is in America on business but it is more than likely he is still on the Evangelica. Lucas has asked Charles Hook to keep an ear open for any information about the boat’s whereabouts.

He also knows that he has managed to rattle the Sergeant and if the Sergeant is rattled Max might become rattled and then Max might attempt to contact Hamilton. This eventuality is being planned for and Arthur’s cousin Merville is standing by on a tapped phone.

So far however nothing has happened. He decides to take a break from typing. He changes into his shorts and grabs his bucket and mop. The house has gone to rack and ruin since he has taken up these new duties. There is Randall tromping around the kitchen fiddling with his fish and no doubt Daphne, who is always about the place these days, will be calling soon to look at the latest addition. And there is Arthur mooning around, sighing and lying on his bed, as if there is something on his mind. Something is going wrong down at the bar. Something is going wrong everywhere. Certainly everyone is acting very strangely of late.

He starts to wash the floor on the terrace clucking his tongue. Just look at the state of this place! He hears a breathing outside as someone climbs the steps, someone heavy. Damn - it is Aunt Marion and she will want to gossip about what he is doing, and him bound not to tell a soul until the coroner sees it. However it is a different voice, a voice which says, “Hey you. I want to talk to you” and to his surprise he sees it is Mrs Panday. She stands at the top of the steps breathing with the effort and then heads to a chair where she sits heavily and fans herself.

Both Arthur and Randall appear to be out of earshot which is good as he doesn’t want things being spread back prematurely into the community, especially now Randall is always having intimate talks with Daphne. “Excuse me,” says Lucas. “I am not in uniform. But certainly tell me what you want to tell me.”

Mrs Panday, having found her breath, sets off in a torrent. “That Max de Troy won’t give me my money. I have been out there as the day is come and now he tells me that my husband thieve from him and he won’t pay money to a thief. What proof they have he thieve? They find nothing at our house and now they going to pay me nothing. He is saying that my husband, the father of my child, is a thief and while he work for Mr Hamilton he steal something of great value and he is not paying wages and such to a thief, even if he dead. That is my money,” Mrs Panday’s face is purple with fury. “That money is rightfully mine and I will see them in hell before I let them keep it from me. And then he calling me a liard. Max de Troy accusing me of telling lies.”

“Shush shush cool down,” says Lucas. “You will have everyone in the neighbourhood hearing. What is it that your husband is supposed to have stolen?”

“Never mind that, probably nothing of value at all. They a set of bad people up there and it is likely some crime they were committing. But I’ll tell you what happen on the night he died. I’ll tell you all the story. They think they could trample over me but they have another think coming. I tell you I know everything that was going on up in that house and it was all crime and bad things.”

“Hush hush,” says Lucas because her voice again is veering up the register. “Try and stay calm. So tell me what happened.”

“He was dead before he ever went over that cliff.”

“Ahh.”

“I see him there. I have a key for some duties that I do, and I put the child to bed after he left with Max and go round there after them. And as I reach there, coming up the street, I could hear screaming. Terrible screaming. And I am not one to stand by while they torture my husband so I go in quick quick but then suddenly the screaming stop. And that Mr Hamilton was there, I hear him. I hear him say, 'What's the matter with the man?' And Max say, 'Damn, he fainted'. And that Mr Hamilton say, 'Leave him, he'll come round.' And I hear them go in another room so I went in where my husband sitting there in a chair and he dead I telling you."

"They'd killed him?"

"He stone dead."

"Maybe he'd just fainted."

"No. I went right up to him and put my hand on him and there was no pulse. I work in a hospital one time. I know how to feel a pulse and there was no pulse."

"So what did you do?"

"I left."

"Your husband's dead and you left!"

"I don't know what it is he take from them. I thought Selwyn might have hidden it somewhere and Max hadn't found it. I go back home because I want to go through the whole house and check."

"You left your husband dead there and didn't do anything?"

"Some doctor in the hospital in Port Sophia tell him he have to keep cool or he could go anytime. And he was supposed to take pills and that all the time but he didn't. I was always telling him to take them but he told me to shut up my mouth and not go telling such things or he is out of a job."

"So you left and went back to look in your house. Did you find anything?"

"No I did not. I wish I have it whatever it is. Then I'd get money out of those criminals. But maybe they make all this thing up. If it is not in my house then I think he never did steal anything at all."

"Did you let Max know that you saw your husband?"

"Well I did when he wouldn't let me have my money. I said you give me it or I'll really tell them, I'll tell them the truth. I know what happen. And he tell me if I want to keep my child I wouldn't start telling any more lies. He threaten me, man. If I don't want the child taken away on account of my bad character then I'd better not tell these lies. And then he says, no-one will believe me anyway, that I'm no account and a whore. I'm not having the likes of Max de Troy call me that. How is it my husband end up over the edge of the cliff? If you ask me that Mr Hamilton and Max de Troy lift him and throw him over like a common sack of beans, that's what I believe. I saw him dead in the house and the next day he is dead all over some car and how did he get there if he wasn't thrown. I want justice. And I want my money."

"How can I tell you're not lying again? Mr Hamilton was on that big yacht, the Beau Jeste, at a party."

"He certainly was not," says Mrs Panday. "I heard his voice."

"She's right, he was never there," says a voice. It's Arthur. "Anthony Hamilton was never on the Beau Geste. I can vouch for that."

"Yes he was home that night," says another voice. It's Randall. "And I can vouch for that. Because I was there earlier in the evening, about midnight. There was something up there that shouldn't have been there and I went up to get it. I too had a key because….. Well, no need to go into why. It was very stupid of Anthony Hamilton to leave so many keys with so many people and then say he was somewhere else when he was up there all the time shouting down the phone to some bad connection overseas."

Lucas stands there looking at them all, totally amazed. The keys, the story, and all the endings right here in his own house. "But why did you never tell me this before?"

"I'm hardly going to be putting it about I was up there where I shouldn't have been, sneaking about. And no-one told me it was important. I didn't know that Hamilton was telling people he wasn't there that night," says Randall.

"What on earth were you up there for?"

"A matter of honour. Involving a lady. So I'd rather not have any of this going into those reports you're always typing."

What a different complexion it put on everything. Completely. "Mrs Panday, I want you to come with me and make an official statement."

"Will I get my money?"

"If Hamilton killed your husband, even if he only scared him to death, there'll be more than wages in it for you, I've no doubt."

Mrs Panday's face curves into a grim smile.

"So how are you feeling?" says Jim.

"Better. I've felt like death for so long but now I feel almost normal."

"I thought you were bearing up the best of us all, singing away, until I was in the galley and heard what you were singing, 'Got to get out of this place, if it's the last thing I ever do!' And I must admit that since the start of this charter there have been a few times when my feelings have echoed that sentiment. But we seem to be coming through alright, only a few more days to go and nothing major's gone wrong, apart from war and pestilence of course and no-one minds a bit of that."

"At least the charterers are nice," says Lynn.

"Well you find them so and as a result they find us so," says Jim. "This smiling you do and making the best of things seems a trait that builds goodwill even for those among us who don't feel like smiling quite so much. I don't understand why not one of them has become sick. I think they brought this wog with them. Talk of the devil, here they come back from their fishing expedition and here's Lynn smiling and congratulating, knowing full well that she gets to clean it all."

"Well you could help."

"What, with a smile and a song and pretending I'm really glad to see more bloody fish! No way."

They have been sailing through the Windwards, past islands rising like chips of chocolate against hot early-morning hazes, blown by fortune which is not a wheel as the saying goes, but a yoyo going up and down. Now she is over the flu and no longer has to force herself to do things against the great crying out of her body for peace, cool and darkness - she can at last look around at the beauty of it all. One day like this, so perfect, seems to make up for all the other days when she felt wretched. Yes, the boat seems to be running smoothly. The charterers are always out swimming and fishing, gently gliding through the diamond-cut glassiness, through coral like iridescent seabird's wings, revelling in the clear water, turning and looping like seals and bringing back lobster and fish for Lynn to clean and cook for them.

Today they are anchored in a sheltered bay where a couple of fishing boats are drawn up on the beach and a smattering of cabins climb up the mountain. It is getting on towards evening, after five o'clock, and the sun is slipping down brilliantly towards a volcanic mountain cone, slanting shadows across the deck. A local schooner has just come in and gone out, for an instant breaking into their isolation. It sails away into the sun with its battered paintwork - the shabby passengers waving and she waving back. Now it is nearly lost in a haze but still its shape stands out in profile, its worn creamy sails against the sharp angles of the near-brown island and its wake a trail of sparkling burgundy. The wind is pockmarking the sea into a myriad pyramids, the deep-green texture of crumpled rugs.

They will have raw fish tonight, but it will be Yvonne's recipe. Tom and Jim grimaced when she announced what was for dinner but that is because on the day she was sick Mr Yamada made a Japanese version. According to Tom and Jim the fish was practically still alive and squirming, coated with big lumps of ginger and tasting slimy. However among Yvonne's careful recipes is one for Tahitian rawfish and it is this that Lynn is going to attempt. She has already cut the fish and seafood into strips and it is now soaking in the juice of fresh limes. She has added chopped onion and garlic to the juice. Later she will drain the fish and add to it fresh coconut cream, chopped cucumber and tomato and serve it on saffron rice and there will be a crisp lettuce and other greens in a French dressing. She needs bread; she has been waiting for the charterers to come back with the tender so that she can go into the village and try and get some.

So she is pleased when she hears the putter of the outboard motor and the merry cry of Mr Tanaka, "Ah-hoyee Go-den Dawnu!" The charterers pile eagerly on board to show her their catch and it is some time before she can wrest the rope of the tender. "I have to go and try and find bread," she says.

To her surprise Mr Tanaka and Kenji decide to come with her. Mr Tanaka has up until that point shown no interest in the colourful inner life of the islands - he is completely besotted with fishing on the reefs and it is normally only his wife who accompanies Lynn on these foraging trips to shore. If there is a post office then Kenji too might join the party but only so he can send off and receive films and contact strips. Apart from that, the charterers seem to regard normal island life with a squeamish suspiciousness, as of a debased and rather dangerous spectacle best enjoyed from the fortress of the boat.

Nevertheless she is now having to wait while Mr Tanaka and Kenji get changed and so it is late when they land on a little beach in the pink glow of reflected sun. The sky beyond is storybook light blue but by now the land is an intense darkening green. Houses are scattered along the beach in ones and twos and there is a sort of road, a dirt track that leads along the beach to another cluster of houses. It is towards this cluster that Lynn starts, hoping that there will be a shop. When she gets there she finds to her surprise that although there is a rudimentary small dirt square there is no obvious shop, certainly there are none of the rusting advertising signs that are the usual markers of commercial enterprise.

She stops to take stock and finds that Mr Tanaka and Kenji have come up and are standing very closely behind her. She imagines Kenji is worried about the light going; he is always anxious towards evening in case his boss does anything and he fails to capture it on film in the sudden twilight. Now they are straying into a savage land without roads, and to Lynn's chagrin, without shops. There are a few people standing about, hangers-ons from the recent departure of the island boat but Lynn sees one of the men stagger and concludes they have been drinking so doesn't approach them.

After looking about for a few minutes, Lynn sees a woman inside the doorway of one of the houses and goes over. The woman is sitting on her haunches just inside and holding a naked child. She sees to her surprise that on closer inspection the rather picturesque houses are only one-room shanties with dirt floors and not much furniture. "Hello," she calls.

The woman is very black and shabbily dressed and answers in a deep gutteral salutation.

"I'm looking for somewhere to buy bread," Lynn says. "I'm off the yacht, over there in the bay."

The woman looks at her with blank eyes and doesn't return Lynn's smile; Lynn wonders if she too has been celebrating. But the woman suddenly leans around the doorpost and points towards a house that is further up the hill. She says something that Lynn doesn't catch.

Lynn makes to go up the hill but Kenji touches her arm. She looks round surprised.

"Tanaka San think we all go back," he gesticulates.

"Oh it's alright," she says raising her hand to the sky, "it'll be light for at least another quarter of an hour. Look, the sun's just gone behind the mountain." And she goes forward up the hill, registering as she does so some sounds of consternation behind her. She therefore turns to them and says, "You go back if you like, I'll catch you up."

Clearly this suggestion is not in order either; their brows are furrowed. But she goes forward anyway, thinking it will only be a few minutes and also feeling some resentment that here she is on a mission to find bread and they are wanting to do something else; she doesn't know why they have bothered to come.

At the house pointed to, she finds a thin shiningly-black woman in a bright flowered dress with one child on her hip, another at heel and washing a baby in a metal bath. The house is the same sort of shanty but is surrounded by palms and sand with red flowering creepers twining here and there. In Lynn's eyes it looks charming. She has no doubt that Kenji will want a shot of this though it is now in shadow. "Hello," she smiles at the woman. "Do you sell bread?"

The woman frowns.

Lynn waits. Then the woman shouts a name loudly, Pyah Pyah, and a child of about ten appears. The woman says something to him and he turns to them and opens his hands in a question.

"Bread," says Lynn, "I was told you might sell bread."

He says something to the woman who gets up and puts the wet baby in the boy's arms and sets off up the hill without a word. After a few paces she looks back and Lynn gathers she is supposed to follow.

This time Kenji grabs her hand and says something, not in English, but in an urgent strain of voice. "Wait here for me," she says and again there are undertones like moans between the two men. They follow her up a sandy track in the shadow of darkening palms and trees. Flowers hang low with vivid scents; it is like some rude paradise. The track leads between two houses and there, in a sort of garden between them, is a strange structure with a curved roof. It is half the height of a person and has a small cave-like opening facing them. The woman moves forward towards the structure and as Lynn follows she registers the heat coming off the outside. "It's an oven," she says, delighted at finding a primitive bakery set in a glade among palms and flowers. The woman goes to the opening and comes back with two sticks of bread, one held out in her outstretched black hand towards her and the other held at her side. Lynn takes the first proffered bread stick. It is still warm. She looks questioningly at the second and indicates that she will take both. In dumb show, because by now Lynn realises that the woman speaks only patois, they negotiate the price, 20 cents each, which is quite expensive. But Lynn is charmed at the thought of getting fresh baked bread with the warmth still in it and the crisp crust feel on her skin and she is in no mood to argue, especially as Kenji, rather than wanting to take pictures of the oven, seems to be in a hurry to get her away. Once the transaction is complete they go on back down the track and only when they are near the tender do the men start to talk. Mr Tanaka illustrating his feelings by making fluttering movements with his hand above his heart. For a moment she doesn't realise what he is trying to indicate.

Scared. Mr Tanaka has been scared. She is astonished. "What was he frightened of?" she asks Kenji.

"Very bad place," says Kenji indicating he too has been scared.

Lynn wonders what has spooked them. Probably something she hasn't seen. She is aware that her eyesight isn't very good and that she sometimes misses things in the twilight. Probably one of the men near the pier has done something to make them uneasy and then her disappearing into the jungle would have unnerved them further.

She gets into the tender carefully cradling the crusty bread in a fold of her sarong. Mr Tanaka says something to Kenji and Kenji points at the bread.

"Rinn!" he says. "Take on boat?"

She wonders if it is getting splashed and looks down at it. No, it is safely away from any spray from the engine. She doesn't twig for a while, not till they are back on board. The charterers are not going to eat the bread; they look on it as contaminated. "I've missed something," she says to Jim. "Something happened that I don't understand. Why do they think the bread is dirty? It was just newly baked, out of a woodfired oven. Was it because it still had ash on it? But why should that be dirty, that won't harm them and I dusted it off pretty thoroughly. I can't understand it, they want me to throw it overboard."

"Better do it," says Jim. "They're the boss."

Funnily enough, this is hardest thing of the whole voyage. She thinks of the woman in her flower-bedecked cabin surrounded by a multitude of children. She thinks of her kneading that bread, pounding the dough on a board and shaping it into lengths. She thinks of the bricks eating up the heat of a wood fire and then the ash parting to receive the loaves, the crusts forming and the smell of new baked bread and her 40 cents as she takes the brown crusty loaves, putting the silver coins into the woman's hand whose fingers close over it gratefully. She thinks of the black hands of the woman with its dusting of ash and flour from the bread and the touching of her skin as she hands her the money and the woman smiling. The bread should have tasted sweet but now she must give it a sea burial.

Something she doesn't understand is being cut loose and her heart feels sore within her chest.

Now here they are nearly at the end; this is to be their last night at sea. By nightfall on the following day they will dock in a marina and the charterers will disembark and fly home.

They are entering a bay where they will drop anchor and Lynn is in the galley preparing for the evening meal and Mrs Tanaka is as usual standing by. Tonight they are having fillet of beef but this time no fancy pastry, no fancy name. She will simply sear it quickly then roast it in a hot oven just before it is needed. Twenty minutes is all it will take for medium rare. She has already made the basics of the green peppercorn sauce that will go with it and she will add the cream and brandy to it later. Mr Tanaka is always excited at eating beef now; there is a general satiety with fish - even a good thing gets too much after a while. As for the vegetables, she has found that the charterers prefer theirs undercooked so she is preparing fresh baby carrots and green beans which will be lightly steamed. For the crew she is going to saute cabbage with bacon strips and for Kenji, who has become addicted to tomato ketchup, there will be mounds of creamy mashed potato. She is planning everything in her mind and she is pretty well prepared. She has taken the roll of fillet from under the ice and it is now nearly thawed. She has quickly blanched the cabbage in her big pot, having cut it into quarters, and this she has put to the side. She puts the potatoes into the same boiling water. She will partly cook them now and heat them up later prior to beating them with butter and milk and black pepper and a taste of mustard. She has already made the rum and raisin parfait which is one of the more complicated desserts on the trip.

In her mind she is imagining the final meal, the order she will need to follow to get everything ready at the same time, and thus occupied in this pool of concentration below decks, she is not at first aware of anything untoward. There is the thud of feet on the deck but that is the usual activity prior to putting down the anchor. Jim suddenly shoots past her into the engine room and starts the engine and shoots back without a word. The urge to go up and see the bay into which they are coming is no longer particularly strong in any of them, one beautiful bay looking pretty much like another beautiful bay and Tom has said that this one is nothing spectacular and not even a particularly good anchorage. They are all looking forward to port, to hot showers that you can stand under and stand and stand until the water encases you.

"You've done well, Lynn," Tom had said the night before when they were all settling to sleep. "We all want to get to port for the showers and well, lots of things….."

"Lots and lots of things," agreed Jim.

"Yes but food isn't one of them. In fact after those hamburgers you made for lunch today I'm not even hanging out for junk food. The charterers certainly went big on those burgers too. Fancy that. You can never guess what these Asians are going to like; it's just as well you got in all that ordinary food."

"You do her wrong," says Jim, "I think the food's been extraordinary."

"Yes yes," Tom agrees, "I just meant not getting in packets of chop suey. I don't think that would have worked, not the way old Sam Tanaka was getting stuck into all the spare hamburgers. I've never seen a man who can slide in for seconds as fast as he can."

Lynn can now hear Mr Tanaka up on deck and he seems to have been putting on weight - his footsteps banging on the deck are quite pronounced. Other sounds are pretty well wiped out by the engine running. Vaguely Lynn hears shouting and a splash but when Mr Tanaka gets involved in anything, especially when he has a vassal at hand like Kenji, there is always a lot of shouting. "He's gone in for a swim," thinks Lynn without even wondering why the anchor hasn't yet gone down. She just thinks he will be getting Kenji to take as many photos as possible now the charter is nearly over. The revs in the engine room change as Tom put it into reverse and then the engine suddenly stops. Oh-oh. Lynn doesn't have to hear Tom going "Oh mother fucking hell," to know that the transmission has sheared a second time. "Jim," he shouts at full voice with an edge to it, "Jim get back here. JIM!" Lynn can now hear the humming as of a second engine and realises that the tender is also in use. What on earth is going on? She turns the stove off and makes to go up the ladder but Mr Yamada has got up from writing at the table in the main cabin and has already gone up the first few steps. He is standing there, his head protruding from the hatch, giving exclamations of dismay. Lynn and Mrs Tanaka are behind him, at first too polite to push past but also very concerned to see what is going on. When Tom starts shouting loudly again for Jim with an edge of hysteria and panic in his voice, Lynn put her hand on Mr Yamada's back. "Go up, go up," she says urgently and Mrs Tanaka, who is also pressing forward, says something to him in Japanese. He turns to say something to Mrs Tanaka but suddenly there is a crash and the boat swings violently up to one side. Mr Yamada puts out a hand but is too late to grasp the rim and falls backwards, bouncing off Mrs Tanaka and landing on Lynn. Lynn has a feeling of falling helplessly backwards and the sound of a crack inside her head like a huge fuzzy gong going off right next to her ear. Oh.

She is vaguely aware of lying on the galley floor and of things coming and going, swimming towards her and swimming away. Noises move around her like a record grunting roughly on a turntable. She watches things stretch and condense through a mist of lethargy as time slows right down and stops. There are gaps when instead of moving slowly, people aren't there at all or are there but are doing different things all of a sudden. She knows she has to get up, someone in fact is getting her upright, oh mind my….. She wants to say mind my….. Something hurts. But she is on the deck and wanting to be useful as a great many things seems to be going on and everybody is very busy and then sometimes someone will come over and dab at her head and say in her face, "Lynn how are you?" Or "Rinn, OK?" She can't seem to respond because there is this sharp pain in her head and a dull bruised pain in her stomach so she sits looking at a pale blue oval, a darkening oval into which people's heads loom and murmur. She is aware that people are talking to her but there is an unreality to it all that goes with the darkening light - a splendid light like a soft evening dress of darkgreen silk. But suddenly there are torches and lights that she doesn't like at all - pointed stars that drill at her head. "OK let's go," says a voice and she feels that someone has hold of her and is urging her down. She knows she is getting into a boat and she tries to do everything that people tell her and it is all so immensely hard. She is travelling towards more lights and then they are urging her up another ladder but it is just too high - it is hard to make her body do what everyone wants. In the end she seems to be lifted up and over. "Oh oh oh," she is so sorry. I'm being a nuisance, she wants to say "I'm sorry, I'm sorry." She is being helped into a lighted space which hurts her eyes and people are supporting her and guiding her to a sofa onto which she is lowered. A lot of other people are looking at her, in fact the room seems to be full of people who are looking at her, and a woman who she knows from somewhere - oh yes she's that American – who has been speaking sharply in a very complaining way suddenly stops and says, "Jee-zus."

A man steps forward, he looks vaguely familiar, "She's still bleeding." Lynn sees that he's looking at her head and she puts up her hand; her hair is caked and matted like scurf.

"Oh my," says a soft voice, "what do we do?" A young woman with soft curves has come forward and is holding her hand - of course this is the Texan princess - what's her name? How nice she sounds after all the other harshness and panic. "Doesn't anyone know anything? Momma, you used to be a nurse."

"Sandra, find some bandages," the older woman says sharply and comes up on the other side. She is dressed in a swimsuit and has a towel draped around her shoulders. "It's alright honey," the woman's voice drops some of its sharpness, "I was a nurse in past life. Where is that useless girl?" She turns to look around and then her eyes become distracted and she drops her voice to a horrified whisper, "Oh mercy, it's all those Chinks. Surely he's never going to let them on board too!"

Lynn turns her aching head and sees that Mr and Mrs Tanaka, Mr Yamada and Kenji have come in and that everyone is now looking at them instead of at her. Suddenly a large thick-set man detaches himself from the crowd and Lynn instantly recognises him despite her befuddled state - it is the man from the island resort who hates Japanese and here are….. Oh dear, now what is going to happen? She hopes there won't be fighting; she can't bear to think of Mr Tanaka being abused or Mr Yamada or someone hitting Kenji, and having their holiday ruined on the last day. To her astonishment however the man is smiling and says in his loud voice, "Ken, there you are, how are you?"

Kenji immediately exclaims, "Ah, Mister Champion Fishingman!" and gives a ceremonial bow which brings a crack of laughter from the other man.

"Johnny, this is Ken, the photographer I was telling you about. Hey Ken, did you get good pictures."

"Very good," says Kenji, "You will be star in Nippon, big star." Again he gives a deep bow.

"Where are they?" says the other man greedily.

"Over on boat," Kenji points. "Big problem neh?"

"Hey Johnny," says the man, "what you going to do about all this?"

"Get the girl seen to," says Johnny. "I'll have to talk to Tom and Skip about it."

The next moment, she is sitting in front of a sink with women clucking around her. "Oh for heaven's sake Sandra, get out of the way. You're so clumsy and useless….." Mrs Tanaka silently appears in Sandra's stead and starts handing Mrs Dwyer things. "Yes thank you," Mrs Dwyer says with restrained politeness. Mrs Tanaka says something in Japanese and makes a sewing movement. "Yes I think you're right," says Mrs Dwyer and adds to herself. "I wonder what they've got in First Aid?" Mrs Tanaka produces something from a cabinet as Mrs Dwyer finishes swabbing and hurting Lynn's head. "Oh they've got….. Right," says Mrs Dwyer sounding surprised. "Did you used to be a nurse?"

"Eesha," says Mrs Tanaka pointing at herself, "Doc-utoh."

"Doctor, you were a doctor!"

Mrs Tanaka makes casting movements, "Long time-oh." She makes a narrow space between her thumb and index finger. "Leetah docutoh."

"Little doctor," translates Mrs Dwyer. "Maybe a junior doctor. Long time ago, yes. What should we do here?" she points.

Stitches. They agree on that.

"You do," says Mrs Dwyer.

"No no," says Mrs Tanaka, "you do."

Oh pain pain.

"Very good-oh-nay," murmurs Mrs Tanaka.

"Mmm," says Mrs Dwyer in a pleased voice, "that should hold it. Twenty years," she holds up fingers to Mrs Tanaka and then points at herself. "Twenty year since I was a nurse."

"Ah," Mrs Tanaka sucks in breath. She points at herself and holds up twenty too.

"Now what shall we give her?" Together they rifle through the medicine cabinet. "I guess it's pretty sore," says Mrs Dwyer as they turn back to look with a proprietary sympathy at their patient.

It is sore, it hurts on the outside and on the inside and Lynn longs for some state of oblivion where all her pain will go slipping away.

It is a time of astonishment and consternation at the marina, or rather in Charles Hook's office where for the last couple of days the habitués have congregated to hear the incredible news that is continually breaking around them. "What exactly happened?"

"Well I'm not totally sure of the fine details but as I understand it there was some sort of contretemps on board the Rita, set off by a loose cannon called Sandra. It would appear that while they are at sea Sandra is prone to seasickness and is therefore generally prone. However when coming into calm water Sandra livens up with remarkable rapidity, to an extent that is often inappropriate because the crew are focussing on putting down the anchor. It would appear that she gave a rather peremptory instruction to Matey who retorted with the spirit that we would expect from our Matey and it would then appear that she slapped his face….."

"Slapped his face. What on earth for!"

"I'm just reporting the facts. Only the facts. The next thing is, he threw her overboard."

"Quite right."

"Now this is apparently something that Jim also did when she slapped his face….."

"She slapped Jim's face! What on earth for?"

"Ah well, I do know the answer to that but you are messing up a good story. I'm saying, Matey whacked her overboard and instead of swimming to shore or back to the boat, she lay in the water screaming at the top of her lungs; she went right off, completely hysterical. It seems she's become allergic to being thrown overboard. The crew were therefore distracted from their tasks because Mrs Dwyer came up and started making a fuss and Mr Dwyer came up and started making a fuss with Mrs Dwyer and then all the little Dwyers joined in and in the meantime the anchor dragged, no-one taking proper notice and a reef that shouldn't have been there was there and the Rita ended up on it."

"Oh no, not again."

"Well come on, it's only the third time and it sounds like there were extenuating circumstances in this instance. Anyway I got a call about four but I couldn't raise anyone at first until the Evangelica answered and said they'd be in the same bay about dinnertime."

"Not that prick….."

"Oh poor Skip….."

"However before the Evangelica arrives, the Golden Dawn comes round the headland and sees them there. Matey and George are in the tender trying to pull her off so Jim leaps in their tender and takes a line while Tom stands by with the engine ready. But when he goes into reverse the bloody transmission breaks….."

"Oh ho, not again."

"Yes again. So he suddenly realises he is drifting really quickly on to the other end of the reef and Jim hears him too late and they hit with a crash unlike the Rita who just sort of glided gracefully on. So when the boat hits the reef poor Lynn is knocked unconscious....."

"You're joking! Oh poor thing!"

"Bleeding profusely and clutching her stomach too because it seems several of the charterers fall on her."

"Oh. Oh. Oh."

"The Golden Dawn is holed and taking on water. The Rita is just sitting there. And up comes John Havermore the Third on the Evangelica."

"Who promptly claims salvage."

"No, Tom and Skip aren't that silly! The Golden Dawn has the pump going full bore and is just holding the line, hopefully till morning when Jim's going under to see if he can do some rough patching so they can make it up to port for repairs. The Rita is pulled free after the charterers are all decanted on to Evangelica but her rudder is damaged and they're going to have to hang out there till someone comes up with some parts. It's the last day of the charter for both of them though….."

"So Havermore offers to take the charterers for $1000 a head."

"No. Apparently he's going to take them all for nothing."

"What! The whole lot? A whole day of eating his vittels, drinking his fine wines, mixing with his guests? I'm disappointed in him, this is not the John Havermore we have all come to know and love. Why would he do such a thing?"

"I believe that there is a young lady on board the Rita....."

"I've heard of her! Tits like....."

"But what about Tom's horde of little Japanese people?"

"Havermore's uncle got friendly with one of them apparently. Anyway they're all spending the night on board and he's taking them and all their luggage up to Martinique tomorrow."

"And what, may one venture to ask, happened to the lovely Sandra?"

"Someone should write a book about Sandra. A girl who gets seasick every time she puts to sea, is a terrible cook, throw tantrums at the drop of a hat and slaps men's faces when they won't do as she wants. And coming to a boat near you."

"Not if I see her first!"
"So how's Lynn now?"
"From what I gather she's doing as well as can be expected."

Lynn is sitting out on deck the following afternoon but she is not feeling well. The sharp ache in the top of her head radiates down to her knees and there is also a dull pain in her right side. She has however taken some more pills under the direction of her medical team and finds that she is now fit to look about her. What she sees is surprising.

Mrs Dwyer has taken to Mrs Tanaka. She clearly has not taken to the rest of the Japanese charterers. However somehow or other during the course of the previous evening Mrs Tanaka has ceased to be Chink, Jap, Asian or even foreign. In order to cement her status as an honorary American, Mrs Dwyer is teaching Mrs Tanaka to drink cocktails. They have started with a Derby Daiquiri and Mrs Tanaka is writing down the ingredients. Half a jigger of lime juice, 1 jigger of orange juice, one and a half jiggers light rum, bit of caster sugar and a lot of shaved ice. "Chotto," says Mrs Tanaka to Havermore's bartender indicating with her fingers that she wants a little. Mrs Dwyer has a larger chotto and Mr Tanaka has the rest, which is Mrs Tanaka's idea as no-one is paying any attention to Mr Tanaka at all. Kenji has already photographed him from every angle swanning around the large and palatial decks of the Evangelica but now Kenji is in demand elsewhere and Mr Tanaka has been abandoned. Quite rightly. Mrs Dwyer is clearly of the opinion that any woman who trained as a doctor, especially twenty years ago, must be a pretty smart and unusual woman who has no business deferring so meekly to her husband. However as this can only be expressed in English and Mrs Tanaka understands very little English and Mr Yamada clearly thinks it politic not to translate, Mrs Tanaka is free to encourage her husband to join them in 'cock-utays.'

They have moved on to an El Presidente which is Bacardi, sweet vermouth and bitters and then to a Planters Punch. Mrs Dwyer tells Mrs Tanaka that when they have got through all the West Indian cocktails, she will introduce her to some good old American ones. Mrs Tanaka however seems to be having some trouble already in rendering maraschino cherry into Japanese and Mr Tanaka has a large and expansive smile on his face and is clearly enjoying himself enormously.

In the meantime, everyone waits on Lynn. Lisa-Marie comes very often to see if there is anything she wants, so often in fact that John Havermore, who is devoting himself with some assiduity to the Texan princess, thinks it wise to station one of his crew at Lynn's beck and call. The large blonde lady they met on the beach has also taken up a seat on her other side. Her name is Delia Fromm. "Call me Delia dear," she says but Lynn finds she can't; ladies of Delia's age are always 'Mrs' to her. As Delia is so insistent, she manages to call her nothing at all. In fact she doesn't really feel like talking as it means turning her head which hurts.

Mrs Fromm doesn't seem to mind Lynn's silence, and clearly has a penchant for lolling and chatting, seemingly quite happy to lie in her sun lounger and do nothing but talk and flick idly at a large paperback. She is Havermore's mother's sister and thinks John is wonderful, so much so that she frequently feel the urge to call out and tell him so. She loves his boat, his beach houses, the resort where they stayed in which he has an interest and where they had the most exquisite accommodation and the very best service and such food, the best food that money can buy and plenty of it, all day long with everyone being so attentive and the very best sort of clientele and such nice people visiting the island. Yes it is so nice for Mort to have met someone who knows a lot about underwater photography just at the point he is getting interested in the subject. Of course they probably could have afforded to come down here by themselves but Mort's business has had a couple of set-backs of late and Johnny is so generous; why he is talking to Mort already about maybe running underwater safaris. Mort was a diver in the navy during the war and there is another resort….. She doesn't think it's a secret but Johnny might be about to get involved in another big resort on an island. She can't remember the name of it, but this is going to be a very different sort of venture because the land they are going to buy - well it is some old swamp at the moment but when they're finished, it will be the premier resort of the whole island and during the season there is really no reason why Mort can't leave his own business under a manager and come down to the island to run underwater tours which would be wonderful and Johnny is such a wonderful person for suggesting it and having faith in Mort because some people in her family think her husband is washed up which he certainly is not. And Johnny is such a wonderful business man, with so many strings to his bow. Apparently there's a lot of money to be made from local antiquities, bits of old stone and such things. And as well as that he has a thriving business in property development and hotels and everything first class. The only thing he needs, she says, is a steady wife. He's been so unlucky up to now.

"He seems rather keen on Lisa-Marie," says Mrs Dwyer.

"Yes, he does seem to go a bundle on her alright," says Mrs Fromm. "But sometimes these things come to nothing. I try never to pin my hopes on such outcomes - hearts are so fickle among the young. I thought when you came aboard that your son, the young man over there, was sweet on that girl there, the one that everyone is always shouting at. And that she was sweet on him. But now look, she's hanging off every word that Johnny says and that's always a bad sign. I've noticed that men, when they're trying for something they can't get, will often settle for something they can get."

Mrs Dwyer sits up suddenly with a jerk during this speech and makes a noise like a growl in her throat.

Mrs Fromm continues to minutely watch her nephew. "Yes, I don't know what this other girl would be like, Sandra, is that her name? She seems a flighty sort, though at least she isn't being seasick at the moment. I was told she spent all her time being seasick but there she is, seemingly quite well and calling on the crew to do little things for her as if she were quite at home. Maybe a bigger boat is better for people with seasickness. I've never suffered from it myself."

Mrs Dwyer's lurches to her feet, "Where's Jerry?" she demands. "Excuse me," she says to Mrs Tanaka, "I must find my husband."

"Is there anything I can get for you, Miss?" asks one of the crew appearing at Lynn's side.

"Oh I think we need some more little sandwiches," says Delia. "Why she hardly ate any of the last lot and she has to eat, to get her strength back. Ask Jean-Luc if he has any of those nice pastry cases left, maybe some little chicken fillings, you know. Or if not, how about some of that anchovy toast? That's delicious; that will build her up."

Delia has a large paperback but is not really tempted to read it as so much is going on. Lynn is glad of this because from the first moment she came out on deck she became aware that also on the boat was that awful Anthony Hamilton who said things about Arthur and to whom she has resolved never, ever to speak again. The empty seat beside her feels like an unprotected position that the enemy might swarm over at any moment. And here he is, coming over and starting to leer at her again. However it soon becomes clear that Delia does not like Anthony either. "Now don't you come over asking her questions and bothering her head. She just needs to sit quietly and get her strength up. Talking's not good for her, it will give her a headache. Letty has just gone off I'm sure to get a few more aspirins to soothe her, so don't come and get settled….."

Fortunately Mrs Dwyer hoves back into view at this moment and Anthony is fended off. Mrs Dwyer settles herself back into her chair in a dissatisfied way as if some errand she has set off to accomplish has not met with total success.

"Well I'm glad you're back; that was a close call," says Mrs Fromm. "We nearly got that Tony fellow - can't imagine what Johnny sees in the man. I know he's thick with Johnny on the business side but I've heard that he's been involved in some scandal as well. As I heard it, he accused someone of stealing and threatened to call the police and then the next thing the man jumped over a cliff. Did you hear anything about that? Well what did he steal? I asked him straight out at dinner, what did he steal? But he just said he didn't want to blacken the man's name now he's dead and just to let it rest. How can you let such a thing rest, I ask you. Why is it made into such a mystery? I would think it must have been something very valuable. You wouldn't jump over a cliff for some little thing would you? No, especially not a Coloured. It's not like they feel any shame in going to jail - in fact no-one seems to feel much shame in it these days. Look at all these people who go to jail rather than go to Vietnam and it's quite all right apparently. Well there you are, it's different from the Second World War when it would have been a disgrace but that's how people live these days and I'm sure glad we didn't have sons."

"Yes you were lucky there," says Mrs Dwyer in her harsh monotone. "We were going to take Frankie with us to England but I'd be against it now. I'm not so impressed with English people as I used to be. I think the ones who are supposed to be well-bred can be an underhand bunch and I certainly wouldn't want Frankie to be getting into trouble with any of them."

"Young men can be difficult," says Mrs Fromm.

"Yes," says Letty. "But sometimes Jerry can't be bothered with these things until they happen, but I have warned him." She seems to get some pleasure from this thought and shortly afterwards turns to other matters, "I think we should start on some American cocktails now; there's nothing like an American cocktail. Are you having a Manhattan, Delia?"

"Oh I don't think so," says Delia. "Mort and I have had a few problems that way so we have a pact, no drinks till the dinner hour. He's already had a close call, you know, because of all the business entertaining and that leading on to a little accident, though no-one was much hurt. But he certainly never shirked his responsibilities; he held his head up and went to court with his lawyers and all. He could have used his connections but I'm glad to say it never entered his head, not like that Tony Hamilton over there who is sailing the high seas right now free as a bird with the case not settled and then yesterday out of the blue he tells Johnny he's coming up to Bermuda with us. I said, yes but what about the matter of this dead man? I understood there was to be a court case and he said, 'I've told the Sergeant all I know and I'm talking about a senior man here, the next Chief Constable, and if he is satisfied that I have nothing more to contribute then that's it as far as I'm concerned'. And next he was telling Johnny in a joking sort of way about some junior police officer who's in charge of the investigations for this hearing. As if it was something to be laughed at, a young coloured man in charge of an investigation. I'm sure in this day and age it shouldn't make a dollar's worth of difference who's running an enquiry or what the complexion of his face is. In my view, you have a responsibility to do what's right. Maybe I'll have a little of that cocktail, just so long as Mort doesn't see me. It's not me that has the problem but somehow, between husbands and wives….."

Mrs Fromm's voluble conversation swirls about Lynn. Across the other side of the deck on a cushioned bench sits John Havermore. He still has a face a bit like a weasel but he is dressed in a naval-looking outfit in which he looks relaxed and at ease and perhaps, Lynn admits, he isn't so very repulsive out of doors like this. He's explaining something to Lisa-Marie who sits placidly looking down at what appear to be a set of plans in his lap. On the other side of Havermore, her brows puckered and excitedly making comments, is Sandra. Next to Sandra, and attempting with leech-like persistence to engage her in conversation, is Hamilton. Sandra is ignoring Anthony as much as she can except when Havermore responds to some of his comments, whereupon she switches on for him a look of approval, well done, you have interested the chief. Frankie is leaning over from the back and is looking at Sandra in a baffled way as if some situation that has existed is being denied, as if the princess has been woken with a kiss and then maintains she has never been asleep. Lynn thinks, "There is something very peculiar about Sandra."

She lies there watching them all, like watching a play. She wonders if John Havermore will notice how peculiar Sandra is. Probably not, after all Tom and Jim didn't to start with. But then there is Lisa-Marie, who is a lovely person with her placid sweet manner and her body all voluptuous curves. Even now, as Lisa-Marie gets up to come over to her - "Not eating the sandwiches honey" - she notices that Havermore stops what he is saying and sits transfixed. Maybe while there are Texan princesses loose in the world, men like John Havermore will simply not notice girls like Sandra at all.

But if Sandra notices Havermore's distraction, she doesn't seem put off by it; she merely redoubles her efforts. Lynn wonders why she doesn't settle for Hamilton, after all he is a dark off-centre person too. Lisa-Marie doesn't seem bothered at all by Sandra's efforts to cut her out. She just sits there all lovely in her bountiful body with her nice soft sexy voice. Clearly if she's interested in Havermore it's not for his money. Her father seems just as rich. But she does seem interested in him and what he's telling her. Lynn thinks it might be a plan for the swamp, yes it is the swamp because she sees Lisa-Marie lean forward and point to something, "But what happens to the birds?" Sandra laughs and it is clear from her reply and the movement of her hands that the birds can easily fly somewhere else and..... well, birds! Sandra is laughing and Anthony is laughing and Havermore looks at them laughing and tries on a smile himself. But when he turns back to Lisa-Marie, she is looking at the other two with a look of puzzlement which immediately wipes off his smile so that he just sits there looking thoughtful.

"He'll do anything for her," Lynn realises and for some reason it gives her a thrill. What a powerful thing sexual attraction can be, she thinks. Birds live or die, wars are fought, money is spent like water or not spent at all, all because of a woman. He will die on his knees to do anything she wants. Really he's got quite a nice face, Lynn thinks in surprise. I don't know why I thought it was mean and rat-like before. He's looking at her and she's looking at him and no-one else exists. Lynn sighs. How lucky Lisa-Marie is to be looked at like that. The thought hurts her head so that she orders some more aspirin and dozes gently away in a panadol haze as the port looms closer.

Lynn is thus mid-way between sleep and wakefulness as a launch comes alongside and men in uniforms come aboard; everyone has moved and they are handing things to these men and now they are looking at her. One of them comes over. He is a darkish-skinned official, well fed and in a rather sloppy-looking uniform. "Passeport, mademoiselle," he says.

She opens her mouth and sits up. Passport! She hasn't given a single thought to it since it disappeared some weeks before. "Passport," she cries. "It's on the boat" and then puts her hand to her mouth. Here she is coming to a strange island on a strange boat from which she is going to have to disembark and she has no passport! The enormity! What will they do to her? "Oh no, where's Tom?" she says, getting up to see if the Golden Dawn is in sight. She has no idea what happened to it. Someone said it would follow on after repairs and she looks back the way they have come, but turning suddenly makes her feel dizzy and she clutches at the nearest thing which is the Texan princess who has appeared at her side. "Where's the Golden Dawn, I don't have my passport. I have to get back on my boat," she says.

"Oh lord, hush there," says Lisa-Marie seeing that she is about to burst into tears. "Don't fuss about that. Isn't it in your bag? No. Well don't you worry. No-one cares about your silly old passport. You sit right back down. I'm sure Johnny knows what to do about such little inconveniences. A man with so many hotels must be dealing with folks losing their passports all the time."

Havermore, who has developed a habit of appearing over Lisa-Marie's right shoulder, immediately creases his face into a smile and says, "Sure thing. You just relax back down there, honey."

"So what's the latest?" asks the Frangipani crowd impatiently gathering in Charles's office and bringing their bottles of rum and glasses and coke and limes and whatever with them.

It is difficult to know which parcel of news to unwrap.

"Well the Evangelica has arrived in Martinique. Half the charterers were totally legless as far as I can gather, much fraternizing and mixing of cocktails having been going on all day. As a result some surprising alliances have formed, the end result of which has been people weeping copiously on each other's shoulders at the thought of parting."

"But not with Sandra presumably."

Charles sets out what he knows on that subject, fresh from the horse's mouth through the first mate of the Evangelica, usually an unruffled and amiable individual but one who has started of late to harbour an uncharacteristic bile-laden hatred for Sandra. Therefore what happened next is reported with glee. "The Immigration people questioned Sandra on her intentions and she said in an offhand manner, 'Oh I expect Johnny won't mind if I come up to Bermuda with him' - a suggestion that appears to have taken everyone aback by its sheer effrontery, Havermore in particular, and Havermore is not usually a man at a loss for words. However a certain well-endowed young lady, who seems to have a spell-binding effect on everyone in her vicinity, was engaged at that moment in sashaying off to the lounge where the luggage was stacked and she came to a full stop at this suggestion, which according to all reports was a bit of an engineering nightmare for a body like hers, with its superstructure and all the other bits. Yes, a body like that coming to a sudden halt plays havoc with a red-blooded male and especially in this case when she melded it with a smile and a murmur, 'I'm sure that will be nice for Johnny, won't it Johnny, taking a pretty girl up to Bermuda with you.' And then she turned her back and started her body in forward gear again with all the counterveiling and difficult engineering stresses that that entailed. So Johnny jumped as if he'd been shot and turning to Sandra said, 'No way. Sorry honey, but this is as far as the lift takes you,' and he darted off after the Texan princess and was heard telling her that he surely would like a pretty girl's company on the way to Bermuda, in fact he would like a pretty girl's company through life etcetera etcetera. And after that they went below decks and paid no more attention to anyone, especially Sandra who started wailing and carrying on, 'What's going to happen to me? No-one cares about me,' sort of thing."

"What is the matter with her?"

"Needs spanking if you ask me. Anyway that's enough about her. What followed was so amazing that no one gave her a further thought."

If the previous information had been reported with glee by the first mate, it was nothing to the unbridled almost hysterical joy with which he reported what happened next. Because no-one was allowed to disembark because of irregularities - Lynn had no passport and Sandra had no ticket home - everyone was sitting around having a last cocktail, one more for the road, down the hatch, bottoms up and so on.

“Then the police came alongside and everyone assumed it was to do with the Immigration thing so you could knock them all down with a feather when one of the police officers, a keen young constable not unknown to us here, stepped smartly on board and said, ‘Anthony Edward Hamilton. I have a warrant for your arrest for the murder of Selwyn Panday.’”

Wow! What? Jeezus you’re JOKING!

“Lucas was apparently sent first thing this morning to arrest him once it was learned that the Evangelica was due in port there today.”

“They’ve arrested him for murder!”

“Or manslaughter, I’m a bit hazy on the details. But he’s to be brought back here as soon as extradition has been organised.”

“We live in exciting times.”

The Frangipani crowd settles down to a consideration of this latest blockbuster, which sends a thrill through them all, a good juicy murder trial to add to all the other exciting things that are happening. Eventually the talk turns back to the others involved. “So what happened to Lynn?”

“Constable Frankland has been put in charge of her and will bring her back with him once all the paper work has been done.”

“Who’s paying for her hotel? Should we have a whip round for the airfare too?”

“No, I think it’s been taken care of.”

Mrs Dwyer has had some more conversation with her husband during which she has finally persuaded him that Frankie needs to go back to college straight away. However she thinks that the rest of them can stay on for a while in Martinique in a hotel that Havermore has suggested. Mrs Tanaka tells her that they will pay for Lynn to stay there too, which Mrs Dwyer thinks is another indication of Mrs Tanaka’s superior goodness and generosity. And <u>of course</u> she agrees to a request to look after Lynn; Mrs Dwyer would do anything for Mrs Tanaka.

Havermore says he canvget very good rates for them all and in fact he thinks that he and his aunt and uncle will stay there too while he tries to find out what is happening to Tony and if there is anything he can do. So they have all arrived at a palatial hotel like some scene from a grand colonial history play, where beautiful people wander in beautiful clothes across matchless polished marble.

As Lynn traverses this magnificence steered by a rather unsteady Mrs Dwyer on one side and the Texan princess on the other, a group of these beautiful people turn to look at them. “Some of those Coloureds can really dress up quite nicely when they try; it must be the French influence,” says Mrs Dwyer. “Oh! One of them’s waving!”

She steers Lynn indignantly away while Lisa Marie drops back exclaiming, “Momma, that woman waving, I think I’ve seen her…..” And then they all come to a halt. Because Lynn has just stopped dead. She is staring mouth open at someone coming down the ornate staircase, as if she has seen a ghost and wants to be sure it is real before she reacts.

Arthur.

Yes, he is real. Her first reaction is to run helter skelter to greet him but then when she moves suddenly she feels quite dizzy and she finds she can’t. In any case she doesn’t have to, he has increased his rate of descent in a very rapid manner and is now standing in front of her looking at her bandaged head with concern. He opens his mouth and then shuts it. “Well here you are,” is all he says in the end.

“What are you doing here?” she says, incredibly agitated at the suddenness of his appearance.

“Didn’t Lucas tell you?”

“No, he was too busy arresting people. He never said…..” She trails off, her hands shaking helplessly.

“I came over for a few days - Sheila’s here making a film. Look, she’s waving at you.”

“Oh I didn’t see her. Hello.” Sheila has come up and is smiling down at her. She looks more beautiful, more lusciously exotic, more absolutely expensive and chic than she remembers. Mrs Dwyer is staring at her close up. Good god isn’t she….. Isn’t she that model kicking the white dress out in front of her on the cover of Harpers Bazaar? The model that Time magazine says will be the face of the 70s. Standing right next to her. Well if this isn’t the icing on the cake. Wait till she tells everyone at home about this!

All Lynn thinks of though is Arthur; all she has eyes for is him. And he too seems to have some difficulty moving his thoughts on and introducing new topics. Eventually he says, “There’s someone else you might….. She flew in this morning to meet the Golden Dawn….. Before the shipwreck….. Tom’s friend, Yvonne.”

He moves his hand in the general direction of his sister and her party but doesn't for a moment remove his eyes from her.

So many surprises. She feels she should react. She doesn't know how. She feels breathless, almost in a panic, as if something might be suddenly pulled out from under her and she will be left falling. She wants to clutch something. Nothing to say comes into her head, in this press of people, except, "So you're here on holiday?"

"Well sort of. I'm not working at the bar any longer."

"Did they give you the sack then!" she cries out, her indignation at last compelling some physical action, some movement towards him.

"No they didn't sack me. The bar has been closed. I don't know how long for."

Lynn can't grasp it. The Frangipani closed, when all she wants to do, all she has ever wanted to do for the past month, is get back to it. Get back to everyone as they were, with Arthur there, and all the others. And now, "Closed! Why is it closed?" She is trying to disentangle her thoughts; she has never heard of the Frangipani closing, not even on holidays.

"There's been a very unexpected development. The police have been there, and auditors. It seems....."

Havermore has been standing behind Lisa-Marie but in the last few seconds he has suddenly become deeply interested and comes nearer.

"It seems," says Arthur, "that Rick has done a runner and gone off with all the money. A great deal of money. And they say that Ed Hamilton is bankrupt."

Chapter 13

Retribution, swift vengeance, eternal malice

What a truly wonderful thing a scandal is! Such lessons there are to be learned from it, such morals to be drawn. It is a thing of infinite amusement and limitless conjecture, it leads to any amount of deeply interesting conversation at any number of pleasant social gatherings.

The time I am writing about was certainly one of the most exciting times on the island that anyone could remember. The slow sleepy life seemed only a memory because in the same few days here were not one but two giant scandals. It was better than Carnival, better even than Independence – yes, everyone agreed, they had been getting by on very inferior entertainment.

Two scandals involving white men, one of whom everyone had thought to be an upright member of the community and suddenly, oh pleasure and enjoyment, he was found to be as bad as the other. Nothing is so delightful as to wake up one morning and find one's own small sins barely register on the scale of sins that others have indulged in. Aunt Marion is in heaven because of course she knows the principals, by sight or by reputation, and has a great deal to say to Mustaffa at the store on the matter, which he drinks in as if she is pouring him champagne. Champagne, she tells everyone. Ah yes, what a wonderful feeling to be right in the middle of a good scandal; how a body loves to be washed clean by the thought that although one may have cheated the occasional neighbour over the eggs and maybe eaten a few mangos that were not strictly one's own and got away with an extra yard of dress material when the assistant was distracted, what are these but minute peccadilloes compared to what others have got away with. These small acts are merely evidence that one is careful with money and a good manager. Rick on the other hand stole money - a barefaced thief it seems, yessir - because he stole US $50,000 or more. More, they are now saying - yes and got clean away. “And how did he manage to steal so much? A fortune!” exclaims Mustaffa, entranced. A fortune for some, corrects Aunt Marion, because her own niece would have that much about her as small change but for others, a huge sum. Who could imagine such a sum was there at the Frangipani to steal when Mr Hamilton senior was always moaning that it wasn’t profitable? Something fishy about that. I don’t believe he stole a fraction of that amount. Although they say that old Mr Hamilton is on the rocks because apparently money was going this way and that and any number of politicians are involved. We can guess who they are, yessir. Yessir. And no sympathy for Hamilton senior either. A most unpleasant man making all sorts of accusations about this person and that person. Why her own nephew was accused, slandered no less in front of others, on account of his owning a car and that man contending he couldn’t afford such a thing. Yes that Hamilton accusing him of having his hands in the till - it was said right there in the middle of the bar where all could hear. We’ll be having the law on him over that. Hamilton doesn’t know the half of what Arthur might own but he never got any of it from working at that bar. He got it all legally and accounted for through having a sister who could buy out the likes of Hamilton and barely notice it from the grocery money. Yes a most unpleasant man and she doesn’t blame Rick for running off with what he could get away with after working for a man like that, because on the wages that Hamilton paid - well a body would starve - it would only feed a man who was still single and what if Arthur wanted to marry, what then?

Mustaffa at this point shows an unfortunate tendency to get sidetracked on to a subject a lot less pleasant to Aunt Marion’s feelings. No he has no plans of that nature, she says shortly. Rumours that he is mooning around as if in love are not true at all, not at all. And she will give Daphne an earful if she finds that she has been gossiping.

Everyone is gossiping, “What’s happening man?” Oh that comfortable feeling, a chair, a cool drink and a circle of friends not in a hurry, ready to sit and get to the bottom of it as best they can.

Time slides; everyone sips, sighs and puts the glass back down. What fine times these are to be sure.

The Frangipani moves out of Charles Hook's office and up to Rae's terrace. They come with chairs, ice buckets and other friendly items necessary for admiring the new view. It is a view without the intimacy of the Frangipani or the finger-on-the-pulsiveness of Hook's office but gives instead more of the large picture - boats coming in from far off, boats departing; it is soothing and pleasant. Yes it is surprising how pleasant it is everyone agrees, as they settle down to being relaxed and happy.

Rae is the only one not filled with a general feeling of wellbeing. Often in the course of enthralling speculations she will stop proceedings by bursting into sudden squalls of angry sobbing or ill-considered reckless accusations.

Some days later Lynn comes back from Martinique and she too does not seem particularly joyful. Poor Lynn. Poor poor Lynn. I see her there, sitting mute and miserable. What a poor clueless child - how was it possible for anyone to be so thick? From this distance I feel like shaking her, sore head or not - which shows what a sharp unsentimental old bitch I've turned into. She had no grasp of reality at all. No idea how the adult world worked. She thought that when you fell in love, either you would dance deliriously with your beloved in palm-fringed romantic places until, after a delicious interval of swaying together, you would get into a big white dress, walk down the aisle and live happily ever after. Or, if that didn't happen, then it meant that the person you loved didn't love you and you died tragically of a broken heart That was how things worked in women's magazines and she thought that was how things worked in real life.

So there she sits, bandaged and sad and she is not able to give the assembled crowd much of a report on Arthur's doings in Martinique. Apart from the first day when he told them the shocking news of Rick, she scarcely saw him. He seemed very busy. Very busy. His sister had a lot of things for him to do and he only popped in briefly a couple of times to see her. And he seemed strangely nervous and distracted on those visits, hardly saying anything, not like his usual self at all.

Ah well he's been like that, he was like that before, is the general opinion. Yes something has been bugging old Arthur.

"Don't tell me he didn't know about Rick. I bet he knew," cries Rae. "He knew everything that went on."

"Well if he did," says Karlo reasonably, "he would be stuck between a rock and a hard place. But I don't think he did know. He seemed as shocked as everyone else. And anyway I don't think Rick would jeopardise the whole thing by telling Arthur. When he didn't even tell you, Rae!"

This last comment fans Rae to fever pitch. Fortunately she has someone to tell her wretchedness to, now that Lynn is back. And Lynn seems to enter into her concerns; in fact Lynn at times seems ever more dispirited than Rae. She manifests it by a general cheerless lethargy, but everyone puts this down to the physical ramifications of her late accident.

Things have changed since she sailed away. And it seems nothing will ever be the same again. However at least Boss is back. Apparently his relationship with Libby is over. No other explanations are offered. The world is left to contemplate the vagaries of fate and the fact that in his absence his creditors, cruel money lenders with harsh unfeeling natures, have taken possession of his boat. "They don't seem to understand that the only way they are going to be paid is if they let me take it out on charters." Boss says, "Common sense must prevail," as he squeezes limes for his fourth daiquiri.

Mainly though, talk is about the scandal at the bar.

"Rick went to the airport saying he was going to Barbados to see Hamilton," someone starts, but this is too plain and unadorned for the outraged feelings of Rae who must tell it with its full quotient of treachery.

"He brought all the account books up the hill as if he was going to take them with him. But later when I looked in the wardrobe, there they all were on the top shelf; it was a ploy to put me off the scent because otherwise why would he do that? The slimy rat."

Everyone at the bar believed that Rick had been called away to see Hamilton. Yes they even remembered Rick's face: bloody Hamilton, making him leave the bar understaffed and go to Barbados just like that. Everyone joined in the groans, poor old Arthur left on his own again.

"That bastard Rick acted the whole thing, the big slimebucket. He should get an Oscar for a performance like that. He got me to work while he was away. I never got a cent out of the bloody place and there I was agreeing to work for nothing. And he was saying what I had to do and I'm going yes yes give me a break,

I've done it a thousand times before. And he's cursing Hamilton and I'm cursing Hamilton but it was all play-acting. To fool me! Everything he did was a sham. Taking the books up the hill and when I came in, the suitcase was sitting there. Not a word of anything else. Not a word of goodbye. Just out the door in the morning and that's the last I saw of him." She howls.

Karlo says, "He had a ticket to Barbados. I saw it, he had it on the bar. But they found out that in Port Sophia he had a flight to Miami booked."

"He organised his US visa weeks before," Rae cries between angry sobs. "Can you believe that? He had it all planned. Weeks he'd been planning it, the sewer rat. Coming and going like everything was normal. How could he do that to me?"

So off he went in the early morning and wasn't expected back until the following day but when he didn't return by the last plane the next day, nothing much was thought of it. It was assumed that he would turn up the day after. The early plane and the mid-day plane came and went and he didn't appear. Rae started to get bitter.

"I was doing full shifts. I thought he was just taking me for granted as usual, no phone calls, no apologies. But I didn't think there was anything wrong as such, no more than usual, no more than the lousy way things were usually run around there."

Then Hamilton rang and wanted to speak to Rick. Rae said, "He hasn't got back yet." Hamilton said, "Back from where?" and Rae said in surprise, "Back from Barbados." Where else!

Hamilton said, "From Barbados?"

Rae said, "From going over the books with you."

Pause.

The penny dropped. He'd never been with Hamilton. Even then Rae didn't realise what had happened, she thought he was having a fling somewhere. Her fury was uncontrollable: the bastard, after all I've done..... Off having his end away while I'm slaving here for nothing.

But then there was Hamilton frothing and screaming down the phone. He was going to come right over and make sure Rick and Rae both ended up in jail. That was the first indication that there might be more to it. She went back up to the house to see what clothes he taken and it was then she found the books in the wardrobe. She got them down and had a look inside and it wasn't long before she guessed. It was a huge jolt. Sitting there on the bed and realising, suddenly quite clearly, what he may have done. She didn't know the extent of what Rick had taken but she also knew that no way was she going to let any of it rub off on her, she wasn't involved. She wanted that to be made perfectly clear so she rang the Chief Constable.

Hamilton also must have called the police because the next thing there was Sergeant de Troy looming over her at the bar and asking questions in a very personal and unpleasant manner. Rae was put on her mettle and said she knew nothing, Rick had gone off to see Hamilton about the books and had not come back. And she wasn't having the Sergeant accusing her. How would she know anything? She had no part in the management of the bar as he very well knew; she was working for nothing and Rick hadn't told her anything - he never talked to her about the bar now, he never had time. He was worked half to death. He had probably had a nervous breakdown and was off somewhere in a hospital. Had they checked the hospitals?

Hamilton arrived on the first plane the next morning and added to the menace and the accusations. He had some fancy accountant with him and headed straight for Rick's office. But the same plane also brought some men in neat shirts and thick sunglasses from Port Sophia, a fraud squad called in at the invitation of the Chief Constable to take over the investigation. They were very polite to Rae and as a consequence Rae handed them the account books she had found in the wardrobe. "I wasn't sure what I was going to do with them. I certainly wasn't handing them to Hamilton or to Sergeant de Troy. But the fraud squad, they made no accusations, they seemed to believe what I was saying. The look on Hamilton's face when I went and got them - I thought he was going to snatch them out of my hands. Then telling the police they were his and in the next breath saying they weren't the true account books, that he had those. And then the fraud squad telling him to hand over any other books he had which he wouldn't do, even though they had a warrant, and a very undignified tussle resulting which included our very own Sergeant de Troy. Can you believe it, the police at each other's throats? But our Sergeant cuts a pretty sorry figure beside their police. They acted like the real thing, the way police act in England."

No-one knows exactly what is missing but it is common knowledge that there is no money left. No money for wages, no money to pay the bar's suppliers. The Frangipani found it impossible to keep trading and closed its doors.

"And Hamilton was saying he would get the money back from me, that I would be working till I died to pay him back. And any thing I own, that's his. How can it be his? He's saying it's his because he doesn't pay wages to thieves and he wants it back and he's going to take me to court. Let him try, yes take me to court and I'll tell them what sort of employer he was. All the work I did and was never paid for. He never paid me wages so how can I owe him anything? And making accusations! I'm not having Hamilton saying those things about me; I'll sue him."

At first it was thought that just a few weeks' takings had gone. But later it appeared there was a whole lot of other money missing that seemed to have nothing to do with the bar. "I don't understand the fancy bookwork but Rick made it well worth his while," Karlo says admiringly.

Different figures are thrown into the pot of gossip. These figures increase every day. No-one has a clue how such large sums could be involved but there is a rumour that Ed Hamilton was laundering the money for his son who seemed to have had money about him that couldn't be explained in the ordinary course of business. And there is talk of others being involved too, people who also had unexplained sums of money about their person and who were in some sort of consortium using the marina as collateral; it is all gloriously scandalous.

"And Rick went off with it all in a suitcase."

But there isn't consensus about that. A suitcase packed with hundred dollar bills is a pleasing fantasy but some of the more financially literate among them know of easier ways of moving a mountain of money rather than sweating under the weight of it.

"And who knows where he's gone!" says Karlo. "The FBI are looking for him but he probably had a plan. I wouldn't be surprised if some day I'll walk into a little bar on some tiny Pacific atoll and there he'll be!"

"And you'll go straight and call the police before he can get away," cries Rae passionately.

No way and get old Hamilton's money back for him, give us a break! Rick is one fine chap for separating several unsavoury and obnoxious persons from their illicitly earned cash. The world shifts in its chairs in agreement and Rae weeps.

Poor Rae. This has not been a period of happy discoveries. The solid edifice that gave shape to her activities is gone. Now she is cast adrift and all the pleasant things she has been flirting with of late are dearly bought. Danger laps at her feet in all directions. Dear Mother, Rick has run off and left me. He has stolen a lot of money from his employer and is wanted by Interpol. I have had relations with a black man though he is not so very black, more a honey-colour and sweet tasting as well. Your loving daughter Rae. PS. In your reply could you please allow more than one sentence for the first two disasters and less than six pages on the last. It may interest you to know that this whole experience has made me realise how very few people on the face of the planet live in Sussex. PPS. I think I am in love.

A few days after Lynn's return, Dale comes by looking for Lucas and is invited in to join the gathering. "What a waste that son of mine is, never to be found. What good is a son like that to anyone? And Arthur wasted too, over in Martinique at the beck and call of his sister. She says it's to keep him out of trouble though what trouble he could be in I don't know because it's Rick what have shafted those Hamiltons. Good old Rick - that man is a hero. Arthur had nothing to do with it, how could he? He's just a lowly barman minding his own business. Yes it is a delightful thing such people losing their money and plenty sour and savage some of them are about it I'm telling you. If only they could make someone pay but Rick got clean away and good luck to him! But I had a feeling; I knew that consortium would never last. And Sheila has a chance now they've all fallen in a heap. But who knows what will happen with the election coming and all? The Premier will never get back in. He's such a scandal I wouldn't even vote for him myself, not now there are other people saying they will stand against him. But it will be a pity if they don't do anything at the swamp. Sheila is right as usual; a little restaurant at the edge of the sea so people can come over by boat to see the birds. She's got a good head for business that girl. But what lovely scandal there is all about. And the icing on the cake is Anthony Hamilton arrested for murder hahaha! A man so disliked that only if he'd been taken for sodomy in a public toilet could it give the world greater joy hahaha!"

While Dale is giving full flight to these and other pleasurable thoughts, his sister Marion also comes in, having heard his voice from next door.

"Boy, why you not coming to see me?" she berates him. "I have to come all this way. But where that Lucas now? The very man who know everything that is going on, all these weeks and he never said a word! I'm fed up with him. Imagine my own nephew wouldn't tell me a thing. Oh my god, what have they done with your head?" she cries on seeing Lynn. "Well they have messed up your hair putting in those stitches, you gone bald. I hope it grow back girl! These men all losing theirs. I said to Arthur, Arthur you better get married quick as all that hair on your head will start falling off and that handsomeness will be gone."

"You had better keep him up to the mark there," says Dale. "He's lost his spark of late. Barely looks at a girl."

"Sheila will take care of that."

"I don't know so much. He is taking no notice of all the fine looking women she has about her."

"But Dale, you saw them both, why didn't you come and tell me?"

"For god's sake Marion, I am back this very minute from Martinique, how could I come any earlier? I wanted to find Lucas first and then I'm coming up."

"How is Arthur? How are they both?"

"Sheila has him acting as her 'personal assistant' though he is not looking at all cheerful about it. But what could you expect with the Frangipani closed and no proper occupation. He thinks nothing of this modelling racket and no more do I. You say anything to Sheila, like you got too thin child, something like that, and she reacts like I'm telling her she's lost all her looks. What am I meaning by that - is it the skin - is it beginning to sag? And she's in front of the mirror looking terrified. And I just laugh - she's too darn thin. Her eyes come out of her face like lilies on a deep pool, she's all dark around the eyes but you can't tell her. It amazes me that they pay her so much. I would think the world wants to see a bit more flesh for its money. Now that Erica, she's got the flesh but the only modelling she ever did was standing beside a truck for Mountjoys, purveyors of Ford trucks, and damn fine she looked too."

Discussion now turns to the coroner's court which sat a couple of days previously. Several of those present had squashed in and peered from the back but only Dale had managed a seat. "That son of mine is good for something at any rate. There is not a seat to be had but Lucas was sitting there at the front and I said 'Get up and give your old dad a seat' and he did! So I am comfortably ensconced in a ringside seat and looking around feeling pretty pleased with my position. And then, oh my what a funny thing. Sergeant de Troy don't have a seat but sees me get one and I'm sure he would have shifted Lucas too if he'd thought of it first. But anyway he went up to the front row and told this young chap to move but that young person is not his child you see, that young person's not moving at all at all having queued for hours. And the Sergeant says he is police and is telling him to move on and this person says, 'And what regulation or sub-regulation or by-law is you proposing to use for that?' And the Sergeant is getting very angry as he is not a man to be crossed but then Dr Woodrow come through the door 'All rise' and the Sergeant breathing there like a furnace because he have no official position and he know it as well as anyone, so he must go elsewhere and woe betide that young person - he will be beaten up in a dark alley before long, you see. But as for myself, I am in the best position for hearing and seeing everything and settled in for days with my thermos of cold cordial and my sandwiches for the breaks in proceedings and then, the whole thing was barely an hour long! What kind of court case is that! They should have spun it out, the crowd demanded more entertainment for its effort. And to find that everything I needed to know I could have had from that son of mine! For he has been beavering away in a manner that is remarkable. And the Coroner having access to his report and several signed testimonies - the court clerk went through a set of rigmarole that no-one could make head nor tail of - the only witness called was Lucas who said that Anthony Hamilton and Max de Troy had both been arrested and were to appear for committal at a date to be fixed and that was it. Death in suspicious circumstances, or unlawful death, or some other such legal finding."

"Yes," says Aunt Marion, "they're sure now young Hamilton killed that man. They have evidence. And he told lies, a white man and he told lies. He was there all the time and marks on the body apparently. But what is this that I hear about them being released?"

Others have heard this rumour too and Dale has heard that both have already been granted bail. But where is Lucas? Lucas will know.

"What does that mean, they granted bail?" cries Aunt Marion. "Surely it don't mean they free to walk about; we could all be murdered in our beds."

The crowd at Rae's house sighs with contentment; all the excitement and the edge of danger and still the committal trial as the next festivity to look forward to. And everyone reiterates, "Fancy that Lucas not telling us anything." It is a sad thing when your neighbour/son/nephew/friendly local policeman can't be relied on to pass you the gossip.

And where is Lucas these days? Not still engaged in prosecuting the case? Surely that is left for others in ridiculous gowns with white horsehair on their heads. Where is Lucas?

Lucas is a rising star. He feels himself to be so. The Chief Constable is pleased. The coroner Dr Woodrow is pleased. "Damn fine bit of detective work," says Dr Woodrow. "It was like reading an Agatha Christie novel. And that deposition by Mrs Panday - I don't know what a jury will make of her leaving it so long but there we are, there is evidence and it is not up to us. It fits with the facts and there certainly has been some collusion and lies on the other side as well. I hate an open finding; the world wants to know what happened, society has a right to know what happened. And if in the course of the trial it becomes clear what happened to the deceased, then the world is satisfied - whether anyone goes to jail for it or not. The world would certainly like that Max de Troy in jail for one, but they are slippery customers and they'll get good lawyers."

Yes the sun shines on Constable Frankland from some quarters though he has also, as he knows all too well, earned himself many enemies. However he has no time to bask in the light from one side or consider the danger from the other as he has been instructed by the Chief Constable to immerse himself in his duties as an Immigration Officer now that he is no longer needed as coroner's assistant. If Hamilton is acquitted, the Chief Constable wants him deported straight away. And Lucas is told that while he is gathering evidence for this procedure, he can turn his mind to all the other irregularities taking place in the white community.

Apart from the Chief Constable, the only people who know of Lucas's secret duties are the other two Immigration Officers on the island and they are to give him more training when he is not engaged in police duties.

Both of his fellow officers are large, muscled and grim. The first thing they say to him is that he needs to bulk up, lift some weights in a gym, get himself in trim because it is a rough and tough sort of world he will be moving in. They are a law unto themselves and they know it. "Don't go thinking this is like the police force and you could do anyone favours. You may be required to shop your own grandmother for excise evasion and you will do it too. Don't think this is pleasant work."

Lucas already knows what they mean. They want him to look into Lynn's situation and he knows that anything he does there will be very unpopular. They tell him that the thing to do is to persuade the young lady to leave of her own accord as in the case of Libby. Libby of course had been a different kettle of fish, thinking she could do whatever she liked because she was doing it with the Premier among others while at the same time giving a show for the paying crowd.

Lucas doesn't understand. "Paying, what do you mean? She was working as a whore, charging the Premier?"

"Nothing is free," says one of his brother officers called Leonard. "And as for our Premier, even if she don't charge him directly she is always expecting expensive presents, a car for her use or some other bauble. She was bleeding the man dry and he was putting out his hand in turn to others and now it is likely to be bitten as too many have been laying their folded notes directly into the hands of the leader of the government. But she would not leave at first because she thought we took our orders from the Premier, so we had to disabuse her in the middle of the night with a pair of handcuffs. But when she understood, she went cool and calm to the airport as if it was the thing she had thought of herself."

"It would have been better perhaps to have publicised it," says the other called Wayne, "so that all the white folks coming here to make money out of us will realise we are not here to be milked by such people. But it was considered at the time to be the best course of action in that particular case."

"What about Boss?" says Lucas.

"That big sap. He was just a cover. Pretending she was on his boat - when she was away every night disporting herself, and some pretty low companions she had in her pleasures."

It is clear now to Lucas that things have changed. There is a new mood abroad all around the islands and the Immigration Officers have instructions from the Federation. Every alien who works has to have a work permit. From now on only aliens with businesses that employ a majority of islanders are to be allowed to operate. And as for the boats, there is to be a check on who comes in with the boats, crew are not to engage in money-making activities off their boats and no boat is to employ new non-islander crew except in accordance with rules to be administered by Immigration.

Also there are to be no more aliens living on the islands without visible means of support and none who are known to be living off immoral earnings.

"Which is what will see off Anthony Hamilton when this trial is over," says Leonard. "And if he breaches his bail conditions by carrying on his business, we will have him in jail quick smart. Now we can turn to some of the less urgent cases."

And there they are all around him, no wonder Lucas is absent so much. Jim is being investigated. So is Karlo. Rae's current situation is being looked at. And of course Lynn. And many other Frangipani habituees.

"Lynn is your case. You brought her back here despite you knew that she didn't have a passport. It's up to you to look into her circumstances and see how she is earning a living. If she have her own money sent from somewhere that is alright, but if she is only here to make money and take bread out of the mouths of islanders then you know your duty, we will teach you your duty. It is to send her on her way in the same way that was done to Libby."

Lucas thinks of his days as a carefree constable at the station, going home at lunch time to swab the floor and laugh and talk with Arthur. Fortunately Arthur is still away because Lucas knows in some corner of his mind that his new duties will not be cordially received by his cousin. He knows that he should move swiftly on Lynn before Arthur comes back but the trouble is that Lynn sits there looking so ill and so woebegone that he finds he is not quite brave enough yet for his new tasks.

The Frangipani opens suddenly again - a meeting of creditors has been told there is a potential buyer and that if the marina is to be sold it should be sold as a going concern. Arthur is coming back to manage it; he is due in on the early plane. Rae will be given a temporary work permit to help as she already has the experience and if it is only to be a short term thing then it isn't worth while training someone else. Rae is very happy about the turn in events; at last a proper job with proper money and she goes off to open up the bar again with enthusiasm. The habituees sigh happily and move back to their old watering hole.

Lynn is left alone. Her head is better but her stomach is still sore and there is something else that is wrong with her. She has a depressed wistful look as she lies back on the cushions and stares blankly out to sea.

Marion comes up early, expecting that Arthur will visit his house before starting at the bar. "Did he come yet?" she asks, coming into Rae's house.

"No," says Lynn sadly.

"Ah," says Marion pleased to see that at least he hasn't rushed to see this little girl when he hasn't yet seen his own aunt.

"Will you have a drink?" says Lynn and painfully gets out of her chair.

"Don't worry, Daphne will do it. Go get the drinks now Daphne," she instructs. "You don't look so well."

"I've still got this pain in my stomach."

"Girl you still have a pain after this accident! That is too long. Go and see Dr Woodrow. Leaving it too long could be looking for trouble."

"Yes I should. But when I'm just sitting in a chair I feel alright. It's moving that hurts."

"You can't sit there forever."

"Arthur sat around like that all last month," says Daphne.

"Yes well, enough about that."

"Randall told me he's in love."

"Don't tell me you're talking to that wretch Randall again. What you talking to that man for? I told you never to talk to him. I sending you over here to find out about things from Lucas and instead you want to play fresh with the man."

Daphne blushes. "I saw him in town, when Evelyn and I were having an icecream soda - he was there in the shop and talked to us."

"I hope you didn't sit down with that fellow. If I ever find you with that fellow you will never go into town again. Young innocent coloured girls is only for these white fellows to have one good time with and then they put you right back."

Daphne blushes an even deeper colour. "No we were just there drinking a soda and he was drinking a cola. He said that Arthur was in a bad way and he reckoned he was pining for someone."

"I don't want to hear anything that man have to say. He can't be human; he has books you can't even describe under his bed."

Daphne's mouth is firming. The first looks of rebelliousness are starting to form on her otherwise biddable features while her mother breathes hard and looks ready to burst out of her seat if she hears one more word about Randall. Lynn who has been listening to this conversation with a sinking heart, says, "Maybe he's in love with that girl at the dance."

"Who's that?" exclaims Marion sharply.

"I don't know her name," says Lynn hollowly. "They were dancing together. She's a friend of his sister's."

"Not Erica!"

"No, not Erica."

Marion furrows her brow in concentration. "Well who is this now? I wonder if Erica knows, maybe not. Erica only takes note of what concerns herself. Well Sheila didn't tell me anything about a girl. I must go now. I have to find out who this girl is. Lynn, you better go and see Dr Woodrow. He is the best doctor in town and he will tell you straight as it is what is wrong."

It does seem to Lynn, after they leave, that the stony spaces of her stomach ache more than ever. The day drags by and still Arthur doesn't come. He will be busy of course, so much to do down at the bar. Rae too is absent until late, saying they were swamped and over-run with people, the whole island it seems wanting to come and drink at the site of the latest and biggest scandal. The next day is the same; still no sign of him, yes yes they are very busy still. Lynn feels she has to do something or she will burst and maybe she should go and see a doctor - a person shouldn't have to put up with this much pain. She manages to creep down the road and gets Michael to take her in the taxi. She will worry about climbing back up the hill afterwards.

Dr Woodrow's surgery is a pleasant colonial house hung with creepers. Inside, the waiting room is full of battered cane chairs and old copies of Punch. Dr Woodrow sits behind an enormous desk loaded with a litter of pharmaceutical company promotions; he is dressed in a short-sleeved open-necked shirt and dark green polyester slacks and golfing shoes. He beams at her when she comes in. "Ah, been in the wars!" he says.

She tells him what happened and he asks her questions about how she has felt since and then looks at her head. "Oh well, that's healed quite nicely," he says. "We'll take out those stitches before you leave. And how is the rest of you?"

She tells him about her continuing stomach pain.

"Now then how old are you?" He looks at his notes. "Eighteen in a couple of weeks. And how are your periods to date?"

He is detached and professional but Lynn isn't used to discussing intimate personal subjects. All she knows about periods is that they come every month, make you feel seedy for a while and that you have to wear a bulky pad in a crackling plastic bikini for three or four days till they go away again. This is just a given as far as she is concerned and you put up with it without complaining and try not to get blood on the bedclothes. She never discusses it with anyone really, except in a distant way such as saying she needs to buy some things. She is now being closely questioned about this and about her waterworks and stool and even worse, he is asking her if she has boyfriends, and whether she has relations with her boyfriends - she assumes it's a way of asking about sex.

"Ah well, right," he says, noting things down. "Now take off your clothes and pop up on the couch. I'll get in Nurse Masters. I think we'll have a look around to see what we can find."

He goes out and she is left with this horrified feeling of helplessness; she doesn't want to take her clothes off at all. However a large nurse comes in. "There now take everything off and hop up here," she says laying a clean white sheet on the couch. Lynn obeys miserably. "There," says the woman spreading a second sheet over her.

Doctor Woodrow returns and washes his hands carefully and puts on rubber gloves. He gently palpates her stomach and sides. "Oh", she groans.

"Quite sensitive there?" he says. "Now I'm going to feel inside, just open your legs as wide as you can."

The nurse gently pulls at one knee so that it comes out to the side more and holds her hand, "Nothing to worry about," she says. "Why when you've had as many children as I have, it won't seem like anything at all."

She is tense as a bow though, having no idea what to expect. However in the end nothing happens. Dr Woodrow, having felt between her legs, says, "I think you're too narrow. I don't want to break anything, that's up to your husband or boyfriend to do. Pity. But if the pain continues, I think I'm going to have to get up there by hook or by crook." He takes off the gloves. "Pop your clothes back on," he says, and goes back to his desk to write up his notes.

"I think it's just internal bruising, which will come right of its own accord. However if there is still pain in a week you're to come back and if the pain gets worse or you start getting unexpected blood, you're to come immediately. Apart from that you should just take it easy for a while and not do anything too physical."

His nurse takes out the stitches in her head and she is so relieved that nothing worse is going to happen that she barely minds. In fact in the rush of relief, her stomach feels much better all of a sudden.

At Anthony Hamilton's house, Sandra sits drinking demurely from a tall frosted glass with a straw. Anthony lounges next to her with his arm around her shoulders and a satisfied look on his face, as of a mother who watches her first born take its bottle.

"Very nice," she says.

"House speciality," he says. "Ah! Here come those fellows at last." Max de Troy comes in accompanied by a tall muscular man who wears a white short-sleeved shirt open over his bulging chiselled chest, and snug fitting jeans. "Sandra, meet Max and Vince."

Sandra finds the introduction odd. You don't 'meet' Coloureds, it is enough to be merely told their names. But then Anthony is an American and doesn't seem to know how to treat servants. She nods in acknowledgment, barely lifting her face to them. Max says nothing and is looking rather grim but Vince gives Sandra a nice smile which she ignores studiously. What a cheek! Then to her further astonishment Anthony's houseboy floats up and the two men are offered long glasses of green sparkling liquid with lime slices. Surely they are not going to be invited to sit down!

But Max does so anyway, without even being asked. Anthony really doesn't have a clue. "Not if it's got rum," Max says waving the glasses away dismissively. "This requires a clear head."

"No, it's just juice and soda. Sandra loves it, don't you sweetheart?" Anthony turns teasingly to his companion who he still holds around the shoulders. He smoothes her hair back from her face.

Max looks at Sandra's drink and frowns. "We need to talk of things," he says.

"Well I'm sure Sandra knows that everything that goes on in our pow-wows about the case is top secret, don't you darling?" He plants a kiss on her cheek possessively.

"I have to powder my nose," she says. She finds the whole situation outrageous. She will have to have a serious talk to Anthony about things.

He watches her go. "She really wants to check up on poor Lawrence and make sure he's cooking dinner right. She does love servants, they're like toy soldiers you can order round a battle field. Charming to watch her in action. They must teach them to do it that way at finishing school. Now, you were going to tell me something Max."

Max gestures at Vince who turns and goes into the house. "I've been speaking to this lawyer Trumpeter. You know there's a problem."

"I gathered there was a slight hitch. I was arrested after all!"

"It's more than that. You told the police..... More inconveniently you signed a statement, that you were at a party on board that boat and not even here that night."

"Yes. Why, who's telling any different?"

"Well they've interviewed Arthur who says that between certain hours he could swear to the fact that you weren't there. On that boat."

Anthony laughs in relief. "That piece of shit! I should have had him crushed a long time ago. But who's going to believe him? Come on, no jury is going to believe his word over mine." He takes out a cigarette carefully and lights it, breathing out in another burst of laughter. "Arthur! How would he know?"

"And you said John Havermore would vouch for you."

"Sure he will."

"Well that's the problem. Because there was a conflict, young eager beaver Constable Frankland tracks the owner of the Beau Geste down....."

The smile fades off Anthony's face and he starts to look ugly. "Who allowed that?"

"He's been doing it all off his own bat. He turned into a menace with them extra duties. He goes into Charles Hook's office and somehow gets the boat owner via the ship's radio and the fellow says, yes he did invite you but you didn't turn up."

"Well if that's all, no doubt he was drunk. I shall tell them he was drunk and let them bring him all the way back here at tax-payers' expense to prove otherwise. He wouldn't have seen me come on board no doubt. We don't know each other; he only invited me because I'm a friend of Johnny's."

"The boat owner said Havermore came alright but on his own. And you can't rely on Havermore. When young Frankland put it to him what the chap said and that you weren't at that party, he apparently said he couldn't remember now and one party got to be pretty much like another party down here."

"Oh well," says Anthony taking a deep drag and blowing out smoke. "Johnny'll always look after number one when the chips are down. We'll just have to cloak it in confusion. Was I there or wasn't I? Johnny can't remember, the owner and his wife were partying and don't know me, so....."

"So they bring on Arthur, Jim and Lynn who were all there."

"Oh come on, that riffraff. No-one's going to believe that they were invited!"

"The conversation with the boat owner was heard by half the world and apparently he doesn't come across as the sort of fellow that gets drunk and don't know who's coming on his boat. The boat owner knows that Arthur, brother of the lovely Sheila Harris, came on his boat. What a pleasure it was to meet him! And if the boat owner doesn't know who you are, Arthur sure as hell does. He's the spanner in the works." Max is grimmer than ever.

There is silence. "I see," says Anthony slowly. "We'll have to think about this." There is a frozen pause and then Anthony suddenly leans forward and grabs Max by his jacket. "How could you let this happen?" he screams.

Max disentangles him, "Calm down."

"Calm down," says Anthony breathing hard. "What do I pay you for except to sort out things like this?"

"Well I am sorting them out."

"You are?"

"The girl and Jim are going to be sent packing. They're on a hit list apparently; that's as far as my information goes. Immigration are as keen as mustard to get rid of as many white hangers-on as possible. Two more witnesses on the other side of the Atlantic."

"So what about Arthur?"

"I think he could meet with a little accident."

"Do it now."

"Not that easy. No point in half measures. I think a set of scores could be settled if we do it properly but at the moment he's too visible. We have to get him away from the marina. I'm thinking about it." He shifts his gaze to the sound of footsteps. It is Sandra returning, weaving somewhat unsteadily across the patio tiles. Vince appears after her, watching her tottering steps with a knowing sort of smile.

"Darling," she says to Anthony sitting down, "you've no idea what Lawrence is up to in there; it really beats me why you employ these people."

Hamilton plays with her hair again. "Yes, we want it to be nice today; we've got some very special guests coming any minute. Rich people. Rich sophisticated people."

"I shall look forward to meeting them." She reaches for her drink again.

"Yes they're looking forward to meeting you. And Vince. But when they get here you're going to have to work."

"Work. Oh yes, don't worry about that, I know how to put people at their ease," she says negligently finishing her drink. She laughs suddenly for no apparent reason.

"But I mean work, darling."

She looks at him, swaying slightly in her chair, with eyes like blank mats. "You don't mean cook? It's far too late for that. Lawrence is in there doing things..... If I'd known....."

He puts his hand on the back of her neck and kisses her under the chin, "No no. Vince will show you. They'll be here any minute so Vince, could you....."

Sandra gets up unsteadily looking mystified and is helped into the house by Vince.

Max is looking at him, "What the hell are you doing man? You can't afford..... What if she starts creating?"

"Oh she creates over everything," says Anthony. "She'll soon stop. She'll like it, they all like it eventually. She's doped to the eyeballs and that will help her like it. Ah here they come."

"What are they wanting?"

"Oh they want a bit of carry on. They asked for a bit of violence. Part of the show." He gets up to greet the people who are just getting out of a car and they go into the house together leaving Max sitting alone and contemplating his drink. Max's fingers drum on the table, his expression is not satisfied. Here he is doing his best to extricate them from the last damn contretemps and here is the man tempting fate again with this girl. Sure she can scream the place down and no-one will hear this time, but what is to stop her waltzing out afterwards and down the road to the police station? Hamilton'll be spending all the profits on her silence or calling on Max to do his dirty work in getting rid of her damn quick. He wonders how many people know she is here. The whole scene is getting too complicated. He has to get out while the going is good - he hasn't come back to this island to go putting his neck in a noose for the likes of Anthony Hamilton. No, he has much more important plans. He'll try and organise some way of fixing Arthur quickly; he'll enjoy that. Then his lovely sister won't have anyone to go buying expensive presents for - all that money she makes from her looks and no-one to spend it on and that will settle a few scores too - it is a bitter thing to him how all that turned out.

Yes, that will be one piece of aggravation out of the way and it should make the trial easier. The prosecution doesn't have much evidence apart from the widow and he knows how to fix her. And that girl Lynn to be deported soon..... She's a pretty little thing. Not as pretty as the girl inside, but though Sandra is pretty she is just one of the passing throng. Lynn on the other hand is something more, she stays in a man's mind. Not that he doesn't find Sandra fanciable too and that is another ground of discontent; the fact that he is left outside to cool his heels and wait on the whim of his master, while he might be inside watching with the others. He gently eases the cloth around his groin. He can imagine what is going on inside; in fact if he goes and sits in the lobby he can probably hear some of it but why discommode himself, he knows how it goes. The only wild card here is the girl and he hadn't seen her above a minute to know she is unbalanced and dangerous. And the fact that she doesn't know what is to come….. He hopes that Hamilton is right and she is well drugged. Yes they'll all have taken their seats looking through the two-way mirror at the first room, the dressing room next to the bedroom, and Sandra will have stumbled out of her cubicle in a French maid's costume going, "Oh this is ridiculous! Where is Anthony? I can't wear this, look how short it is," or some such thing. Yes she'll come and look in the mirror with her blank eyes and how sexy she'll look - the French maid tart with black lacy knickers just visible under the high frilly skirt, the high heels impeding her. And then Vince will come out, black sunglasses and thin black silky stretch-pants skintight over his crotch exposing the size of his cock and she'll look at him; everyone would have to look at a sight like that. She'll try not to stare in amazement, no she'll turn back to look in the mirror at this man come to mess with his hair behind her, naked to the waist and those revealing pants.....

The audience will already be feeling themselves or each other going "Oooh look how big and bad he is." And then the play will begin. He'll proposition her admiringly, reach over to touch her and then..... instant erection. Vince is a marvel like that. Say 'Up' to his tool and up his tool will go. It's pretty certain at this point that there'll be a struggle. Anthony says she'll like it but Max doesn't think so. Vince is a black man, very black and beneath her. But that won't stop Vince. Even as he imagines these things and slides his hand up and down through his pocket into his own crotch he hears an outraged yell muffled from inside. No doubt Vince has taken another crack across the face but Vince is used to it, doesn't mind it at all though he keeps the dark glasses on as he is fussy about round the eyes when the woman is struggling. Damn Anthony, what is he thinking of getting in a girl like Sandra who can go right off? But Max turns his imagination to the best bit. He loves that bit where she's struggling or pretending to struggle, because women always play-act, and he's done with the feeling and the fingering and out comes his cock, out through his fly and he rips away the lacy panties and right into her, wham! Skewers her and Sandra will probably holler like a stuck bull at the size of that inside her - even the ones that are aroused and wet can't resist the big moan first.

Women. They pretend they're being raped even when they're leading you on and crying out for it and then afterwards they accuse you out of pure spite. Damn women. Damn the lovely Sheilas of this world - Max looks savage - with their money and their good life and their turning everyone against you so you end up like a criminal even when you were found innocent. He hears another muffled cry. He hopes Vince gives it to her good. Vince is big. He sorts out the women alright.

The watchers will love all the flailing, they'll be moaning and getting themselves in a lather. Yes they love it, that bit of violence, especially the women, they get really high on it. They'll howl how they want him themselves - how black, how luscious, how big, how virile, how hard, how dangerous, how strong, how thrusting, how..... Max leans back and gives himself to his hand and his own erection, hearing her scream, making her scream, her cries becoming more frantic - damn the way he was led on and then the girl fighting him off, well he deserves a bit of pleasure for himself. And then thump thump thump of body on body until aah the release as he rolls off limp and sweating. And if there is blood on his tool, say there is blood down her leg and her weeping and holding herself well it isn't his fault - she could have liked it if she'd wanted to. She does it on purpose, that weeping. And the audience is thrilled. Yes they love that too. But for Max there is no fun in it now, bitter bitter as gall.

Marion has trailed up the hill again at lunch time with Daphne and is displeased, Arthur is still not home. He'll be down at the bar she knows, but is the boy always to be working? She is not a woman who goes into bars but she'll have to call in when she gets back down. She wants to learn from him about his stay in Martinique, about his sister and any and every news available. What kind of family is it when your own kith and kin never come near you?

She is sitting in a chair fanning herself from the climb when Rae goes past; at least Rae gets time off it seems. "Where is that dratted boy? He's never home," she cries in the depth of her discontent. So Rae comes in and sits down with her although Marion was not really intending to converse with Rae as she has heard gossip recently about Rae herself - Rae is another bad influence on the family and she shouldn't encourage her….. But here she is at least willing to sit with a body and she must have news. Rae says that the marina and the Frangipani are as good as sold and Marion is grateful even for that scrap.

"It looks like you'll be out of a job then," she says comfortably. Yes that will send Rae on her way and get Arthur back where she can see him; she definitely needs to start taking an interest. Sheila has sent a letter to her by Dale. Things are serious with Arthur and they must all pull together if there is not to be some repeat of the mistakes made in the past.

"Yes we'll be out of a job, if we live that long," says Rae. "With those murderers out of jail and wandering the streets. That Max de Troy could just wander up here any time and to think....." She puts her hand over her mouth to cover some thought.

"Yes and the committal hearing for the murder a whole month away," agrees Marion scandalised. "But maybe we'll get some questions answered when that happen. Everybody is tight lipped about what went on in Hamilton's house, even Dale. I am sure he knows, you know. He's the man who does know everything. You think it one of these whore houses, girl?"

Rae doesn't know. "I think it was like a high-class bar," she says. "Expensive drinks, expensive people. That's all I can gather. No-one will talk about it."

At this moment the door to Randall's room opens and Randall comes out wearing nothing but daggy khaki shorts. He is unshaven and red-nosed. He really is one of the ugliest men I ever saw, thinks Rae. Who on earth could ever fancy a man like that? "So what are you doing home?" she demands.

"I've got flu," he grumbles and honks into a grimy handkerchief.

"There's a lot of it about," concedes Rae.

"They have none up by us," says Marion coldly. "Daphne, stop twisting and turning. Go home now and put some food on, girl."

For a moment Daphne doesn't react and when she does get up it is by no means with her usual compliance. It seems that times have changed and this does not bode well for future mother-daughter relations.

"Shouldn't she be at school or something?" says Randall who has gone over to the patio wall to watch her go and possibly, it is hard to see, wave at her.

"She nearly sixteen; she has had all the schooling she needs."

"She's such a bright girl, it seems a pity."

Marion is bristling, her face swelling, a storm about to break. But Rae is still on a different agenda. "What goes on at Anthony Hamilton's house?" she asks Randall. "Do you know?"

"Sex," he says as he trails over to the fridge.

"Ha!" cries Marion as if shot. "I thought as much, didn't I say.....?"

"A brothel?" says Rae. "Surely not."

"No, not a brothel," says Randall considering the meaning of the word as he takes the top off a coke, "not strictly a brothel. A theatre. A performance. People come to watch. If they want to do it themselves they have to pay extra and then they go elsewhere as I understand it."

Marion's eyes are popping out. "I know about those places. People taking off their clothes, dancing to music and people watching them do that thing."

"No no, it's not a strip joint," and Randall sits down at the table tapping his bare feet on the tiles. He tells them about the two-way mirrors in the walls and the cantilevered mirrors on the ceiling for good all-round viewing and how people can sit at ease in one room and watch people have sex in another. Most of the time the people on the other side know they are being watched but he has heard that sometimes they don't. "It's all black on white, that's what people want to see, black men having sex with white women and white men having sex with black women. Sometimes just ordinary bedroom sex but sometimes less ordinary, pretend violence perhaps, or even real violence, I don't know. Perversions and kinky stuff so I've been told though I never saw any of that. Sometimes they film them too; there've been a few films around that would surprise you."

"So tell me how you know all this?" says Marion ominously.

"Oh I used to go up and watch." He isn't the least put out by Marion's disapproval. "Customer numero uno. I used to like that sort of thing but only regular performances, where the people knew what it was all about. And then Hamilton asked me one evening if I'd like to make $200. Some guy had let him down so I said I didn't mind. I had to creep in the house like I was a burglar and then this great fat black woman dressed as a maid caught me; she held me down and had her way with me. Look, you can still see the scratches on my back. But it was all pretend. She got to go off with one of the voyeurs - there's real money to be made at that end - but none of them wanted me." He sighs and looks at his coke.

"What are the authorities doing about such a place?" cries Marion scandalised.

"Oh the authorities all go there to watch. I mean half the cabinet. I believe one of the leading lights of St Claire will actually perform himself, if the money is right. I never saw him because he charged too much but apparently he had a bit of a show worked out with Libby, Boss's girlfriend. I heard on the grapevine it was very ordinary. But I won't say who the person was....."

He doesn't have to. Marion's face has set.

"You said not everyone knows they're being watched," says Rae, who for some reason feels short of breath and full of foreboding.

"Yes that's not right. They should pay the woman if all the fee-paying customers get to see her pussy, don't you think? And those hunks of Libby's, once they've taken their trousers down and the world has seen their private parts..... It's a small island. At least they should get paid. And then making a film of it, that's what finally turned me off the place. I don't go up there any more. In fact it's given me a distaste for the whole thing."

"And what about Selwyn Panday?" asks Marion.

"As far as I could see he didn't have anything to do with it, he was just a servant. He let people in and served the drinks in the other room and then went home. I don't know why he would go there specially to jump off a wall in the middle of the night. He wasn't around when I was up there earlier."

"You were up there on the night he died?"

"Yes, but I wouldn't let Lucas put it in his report for the Coroner. I shouldn't have been there. I might have to give evidence at the trial though."

"Why were you up there?" asks Rae.

"Because there was a film there that shouldn't have been made." Randall suddenly picks up his coke and goes back to his bedroom to Marion's disappointment as there is no end of things she needs to know about this terrible scandal - all these goings on that no decent person even knew about and what a terrible thing and only a stone's throw away from her own house - exclaiming and fanning herself in agitation.

Rae is also agitated and starts excitedly walking up and down. Something, a mirror on his ceiling….. She remembers the dream, the dream that is almost as real as if it had been..... She suddenly bolts into Randall's bedroom where she finds he has sunk back onto his untidy bed. She closes the door and stands there against it, shaking.

"Who was on the film?" she asks.

"Why?"

"Who was it?" Randall is fidgeting and not looking at her. She can hardly get it out. "Was it me?"

"Yes"

It is a terrible shock. But Rae now realises she has known it all along. During these last few weeks it has been hanging over her, that lost evening. Dark tentacles of pain and humiliation. The bad tide that has washed her along since that drunken night could only throw her up in some sewer and here she is, collapsed against the door.

Randall continues, "It was really bad. You were obviously drunk or drugged and Max was awful - I mean it wasn't even erotic, it was obscene and that's why I stole it. I don't like obscene stuff with people in it that I know. It gives the porn business a bad name. And another thing, you were laying yourself wide open in more ways than one doing it with a guy like Max....."

Suddenly Max's meaning at the Lotus Room becomes clear. "What did you do with it?"

"I just put it under my arm and walked out. It's a bit of a size, a roll of film, but anyway I got it back here without anyone seeing as far as I know and the next day everyone was going on about Panday's suicide so it's possible no-one has realised it's gone."

"Where is it?"

"Oh now that's a question. I either threw it in the garbage or I threw it up there with the other stuff" - he indicates a shelving unit which is littered with film cans, magazines, books and rubbish of one sort or another.

Rae goes to it and impatiently rifles through, scattering magazines which fall to the floor. "Ooh," says Randall suddenly interested, "Miss October. I'd forgotten about her. What a beauty."

"Is this it?" says Rae. She holds a round flat blue metal can – the only one with no identifying title on it.

"Oh it is there," says Randall. "You can throw it away yourself. I'd steer clear of that Max fellow in future," he says as she leaves the room, "he's bad news."

Rae goes and sits back on the terrace holding the can, her mind distraught and whirling. The moment she returns Marion starts again on her outrage and surprise that such things go on and everyone ignores them and what she is going to do and who she is going to tell - hardly noticing Rae who sits there white and unable to stop shaking, unable to think what to do next.

Into this scene comes Lucas who has been next door looking for Lynn. "Has anyone seen Lynn?" But Marion immediately gives him is a piece of her mind for allowing Anthony Hamilton's business to operate and so close to her own house, close to his own cousin, with that piece of dirt Max de Troy allowed to ride around in taxis with respectable women like Daphne and Rae here.

Lucas looks more and more harassed. "I'm seeking Lynn on official business, I'm here in an official capacity" but this doesn't stop Marion's rising request for an explanation.

Eventually he sighs and shrugs. "Sergeant de Troy is of the opinion that it is not breaking the law and what people watch is their own business."

"And why have you never told me what goes on there before?" says Marion.

"Because I didn't know the whole story about what did go on there until recently. I never bothered my mind over it until there was a dead body connected to it."

"And do you think it nobody else's business?" exclaims Marion

"So long as they are all consenting adults and it doesn't break the law. And Tantie, they will take you to court and sue you for any slander or libel on young Mr Hamilton. These are not your friendly neighbourhood types. They are bad guys with lots of money for lawyers."

Rae can stand it no longer. "How much does a lawyer cost?" she says.

Lucas blinks.

"How much does a lawyer cost? I want a lawyer. Because I was not consenting and that Max de Troy took me up there when I was drunk or drugged and he raped me. I didn't remember..... But now it's all been coming back. Being taken there..... I remembered now trying to hold him off….." (This isn't exactly true or how she remembers it but it is becoming true). "And" - she holds up the can - "it's all here on film, they were paying to see me get raped." She weeps tears out in great sobs, being used like an object to be looked at, being put on film for all to see - she is going to sue them, all of them, the shame and ignominy.

Anthony Hamilton sits on his veranda admiring Sandra, "My, you're a star," he says.

She doesn't look at him. "You didn't tell me about the work," she says, her voice flat and inexpressive.

"I said if you came with me I'd solve all your problems and I have." He puts his arm back round her neck and she doesn't shake it off. He kisses her cheek, "And this could be the start of something big," he breathes. "You were just wonderful. And all those little mannerisms you have – they kept thinking you were going to slap Vince's face and you never did! Not that I'm saying you can't slap Vince's face, he's used to it, he's got an indestructible face so he tells me - hardened by the slap of many a woman and their nails and teeth - it all goes to build character in a man's face....." He releases his arm for a minute and feels expansively in his shirt pocket. "And here's the money, there's lots of money in this game. Two hundred smackeroos. And another fifty as a tip - I tell you, they loved you."

"No," she makes no move to take it.

He looks at her with astonishment. "But I thought that's why you came here. Because the world is so unpleasant to a girl without money. How else did you think you were going to get out of that hole in Martinique?" He holds the money in his hands. "It's American, not the local shit. Look," he holds it out.

"No," she says turning her head from him and sipping her drink. "That's not what I want."

He looks at her, suddenly unsure. "What more do you want?"

"I want revenge." He stares. "You kill people don't you?"

He gives a laugh, humourless and surprised. "Lord no, well not me personally. I know what you're referring to, my supposed killing of that damn servant but in actual fact, no-one seems capable of believing it, he died of natural causes. He just died."

"You must have done something. They said on the boat that he stole something."

"It was something of Max's. A record of one of Max's little escapades went missing. It was obviously Selwyn. He'd tried blackmail before but this time - well the film was a private keepsake for Max, something to remind him of a wonderful night. Even though I must say it wasn't clear how much the lady was enjoying it. But I'm sure she liked it in the end, you're so predictable you creatures, you all like it in the end. Now come on, you loved Vince. Everyone could see at the end how you gasped for it."

"So the film went missing and Max killed him."

"Selwyn definitely took it but he denied it….. And Max is a bit of a tough customer, he wanted that film, maybe he was too taken up with it. Silly really - because in my view that film needed destroying but I couldn't persuade Max, he can be very headstrong when a woman is unco-operative. He wanted his own little revenge, just like you. But in my view it could have misfired….. Max though couldn't see it, he's blind when it comes to women. He's had a pretty sad history there and he gets in such a state; so he was rough with Selwyn but it made no difference, the man kept saying he didn't take it. So Max said he was going to Selwyn's uncle to tell him who really robbed his store. And he held up a hammer and said, 'Look what I found in your house, your uncle will recognise this won't he!' Selwyn just started screaming and screaming and the next thing he keeled over in a faint and we left him and then later when we checked he was dead."

"They say there were bruises."

"Yes but that was just Max getting a bit rough beforehand. He wanted the film and Selwyn wouldn't tell him where he'd hidden it."

"Are you going to tell them in court what really happened?"

"More or less. There's no need to bring the lady into it of course. It's going to be a little tricky explaining how the body got over the cliff but that's what lawyers are there for. It seems we panicked, got rid of it and the incriminating hammer, that sort of thing. The police just assumed it was suicide off their own bat. Actually they were supposed to find the hammer and deduce he jumped out of remorse - but the damn thing went missing. There are so many thieves about. So you see my dear, I don't really kill people. Max is occasionally a bit rough though."

"Well you're going to have to start killing people now, because I want people killed," her face is screwed into a snarl of ugliness. "That is," she suddenly says with a superior sweetness, "unless you want me going and telling the police what you do to people here, which I don't think you would like at this time."

Anthony's face hardens for a moment but he schools his expression and looks at her again with a smile, it is a different sort of smile but still a smile. "Who do you want killed, darling heart?"

"All of them. All of the people who've treated me so badly. I want Tom killed and Jim killed and Matey killed and that awful old woman Mrs Dwyer and that Lisa-Marie who turned Johnny against me so he wouldn't take me to Bermuda. I want them all beaten and killed and their faces broken," she turns savagely on Anthony who holds a smiling mask towards her. "If you won't kill them, I'll go to the police and tell them what you just did to me."

"But darling," he says smoothly, "none of these people are on the island except I believe Jim may fly back any day. And let's face it sweetheart, your tumble in the sack with Vince doesn't equate to a crime to be hung for. With you so obviously liking it. And of course we kept a record of the last bit because the customers like to see a lovely white girl like you liking it with a big thick tight-fit of a man like Vince. That's not to say," he says easily, seeing that she is now starting to cry, "that we can't do some damage to some of these people when they get back. Oh yes we could give them a bit of a drubbing in the dark, perhaps."

"Dead," she shrieks. "Dead. I want them all dead. And that girl Lynn, yes her as well."

"Ah, now Lynn. Lynn. Now I remember something about Lynn."

"Well I want her," she is standing up and walking around, "I want her done to the same as me, yes by Vince," she is half breathing half screaming. “I want him to do that. Why should everyone be nice to her, when she never even has to sleep with anyone.”

“Maybe we can do something there,” says Anthony placatingly. “Will that satisfy you? If Vince gives Lynn a nice time, like you had? Yes, have another drink, go and order Lawrence around some more. I have to go and organise things now. And remember darling, I am organising all this for you. And when Vince comes in, you can tell him exactly what it is you want.” He saunters off and while he is still within range his face is schooled into a pleasant smile. His expression once out of sight is not so amiable however. He finds Max in the office. “I think I know how all our little schemes can be achieved in one go. That girl, Lynn. Well she told me that she’s a friend of Arthur’s. A good friend, I gathered. Now Sandra would like Vince to be Lynn’s friend too. And wouldn’t that galavanize young Arthur, his little bit of fluff being lured away to some remote beach and being given a good time by Vince. I think there should be a scenario there for you. Only do it quickly. I have other things that need attending to urgently after that is done.”

“And what things would those be?” says Max looking at him cautiously.

But Hamilton has already turned away.

Chapter 14

Drawn towards the closing vortex

Lynn has been sitting most of the afternoon in a cafe in town. She doesn't want to go home. Something has changed and she has been trying to work out what, going over everything, sorting through her memory for clues.

Because she really was clueless at that time. She had somehow managed to drift through life up until then unconscious of the sort of issues that concentrate the minds of other people. She just didn't get it. For instance, many years before she had heard her mother say to her grandmother, "You're never letting her go out with them are you?" She thought her mother was referring to her boots, the ones Jimmy, the head stockman, had brought her back from town – silly white plastic things with rhinestones. So the next time she went out mustering with the men she rather expected her grandmother to tell her to put on something more sensible, but nothing was said. So off she rode in her treasured boots, under an endless sky in a huge universe, bivouaking under the stars as Jimmy, or one of the other men, made her tea and damper. It never for one moment entered her head that it was going out alone with the aboriginal stockmen that her mother might have been referring to.

I suppose London should have enlightened her but she was sent to boarding school – a tiny world filled with the daughters of very rich people. By the Sixties it was no-one's ambition to form missionary intentions with regard to Hottentot babies or take up the white woman's burden in any way whatsoever. In fact I can record here that the chief ambition of those well-bred girls was to sleep with as many rock stars as possible. One of her school-mates claimed to have laid Jimi Hendrix and there was argument as to whether he was mainstream. It was a fine distinction, separating as it did the Rolling Stones from the chaff, and it required judgement as to what was enviably individualistic and what was merely sluttish. Lynn, being a slow starter, thought it had something to do with the music.

I can laugh about it now. But there was Lynn, nearly 18, and still with that monumental level of incomprehension about the meaning and motives of others. As I said at the beginning, she was an extraordinarily stupid girl.

She is now sitting in a coffee shop completely unable to account for Arthur's apparent change of attitude. In Martinique he seemed rushed and agonised. And now he is manager of the Frangipani it is the same; he doesn't have time to come and talk to her. Too busy. That is the most charitable explanation. If she goes to the Frangipani though she will know - he will either greet her cheerfully with his broad smile, hello Songbird. Or he will just smile at her blandly, another customer. Getting through the day before he can rush off to whoever it is he's in love with.

Her stomach has started to hurt again and it is late - she has been sitting for hours pretending to read magazines and drinking cups of coffee and the cafe is ready to close. She goes back out onto the road and gets a route taxi to the marina. She can either crawl up all those steps to a lonely house or go into the bar and..... She can't finish the thought. She doesn't have the courage for the second alternative.

It is dark before she arrives at the marina. As she moves slowly in through the gate, she is surprised to be greeted by a total stranger sitting in a car where Michael usually parks. "Ho there, you Lynn?"

She nods.

"Michael have a message, for him to take you out to Jim's house as Jim just reach here now and you not to be found."

"Oh." Suddenly she is cheered.

"But Michael waiting here for you and now have to go to town and not coming back a while. He telling me I could take you out there. Three bucks."

She gratefully takes up the offer. She longs to see Jim, to hear what has happened, to have someone to talk to.

"Is Tom back?" she asks as she gets in.

The man looks blank and shrugs. But Lynn remembers vaguely the face of Yvonne; no, he probable isn't.

The plan is working well. "She won't go with <u>you</u>! She wouldn't get in the car if you were there. She'll know by now that no respectable woman goes anywhere with you in a car, especially at night."

Hamilton never bothered softening unpalatable facts. Max's face set like stone for an instant and then he took out a cigarette and lit it and started playing through scenarios. "Someone rings Michael saying he's Jim and has just got back from up the islands and could he find Lynn and bring her out to his place. Michael collects Lynn and goes to start his car and finds, well people are such jokers, someone has let the air out of his tyres. Michael is heaving and moaning and Vince passes saying, 'Hello Michael, remember me?' And he says, 'I'm going out to my uncle Will Johnston, I'll give her a lift.' And Michael knows nothing of Vince except he has been away all these years and of course he knows Will so....."

"But Michael might know something of Vince."

"No Vince has been keeping a low profile, just driving, nothing else. The only person who knows he works here is Lawrence and I have told him particularly to keep his mouth shut if he knows what's good for him."

"No-one knows what's good for them. No, we get Michael out of the way, send him off to the airport or something. The girl won't know Vince. So Vince gives her a lift. And then what?" asked Anthony.

"Then you go in the bar, pretend you're drunk or whatever and tell all the world...... No, that's not going to work either because who's going to let you into a respectable bar full of white folk?" Max had got a serve back. "We have to find a way of bringing it to Arthur's attention….. Maybe we use Lawrence. It's time he was of use to someone. We make sure Arthur knows that there is some mischief going on and his little friend has been lured into a car with me going to White Fish Beach - that's a place will have some memories for him no doubt. So he takes off after us. And then when he arrives, pow bragadam!"

Anthony sat drawing carefully on his cigarette. "There's a lot of chances of it going wrong."

"Oh well, then we'll get him some other time. There's a lot of dark lanes around here."

But it isn't going wrong. Max is pleased and excited. Vince is driving and there's Lynn in the back seat hugging that big silly bag she carries with her everywhere. Women always have stuff like that littering up the place. And then, as arranged, Vince sees him waiting by the road and offers him a lift. "Just drop me at the road down to the beach," he says of the deserted beach they have chosen. "I'm meeting young Dinny down there with his boat, we're going fishing."

They drive along chatting while Vince asks him questions as if he hasn't seen him in ten, fifteen years - about his family and stuff and then when they get to the turn-off Vince says, "That's a dark road, man, with no moon. I'll run you down there. You don't mind do you miss?"

"No," she says, but she does. Her stomach is hurting again and there is something she doesn't like about this ride. She doesn't at all like being in a car with Max.

They drive down and stop. Now the idea is that it should take place in the car, keeping a girl in a confined space, that prevents injury. Max has long ago learnt the perils of allowing spheres of action to become too spacious. But no sooner do they get to the beach than out she gets. What the hell is she doing! "My stomach hurts," she says in explanation. "I just have to stand up for a while." Damn. Now what? Lynn stands under a tree thinking that when Max gets out she will get back in again. She doesn't want to be in there with the two of them. She has a bad feeling and her stomach nags at her.

The two men look around carefully. The beach is deserted and is surrounded by rain forest - no boats, no other cars that they can see. The beach ends just to the side of them where a long promontory goes out to sea. This is popular during the day with fishermen and there is a further bay too but the likelihood of anyone driving through just then is very small. So they have to either drag her screaming back to the car or do it on the beach and they have to be quick because Arthur will be here soon. That will be good actually, his little white friend naked and spreadeagled on the white sand. Yes, that will be very good and then whack they'll get him from behind while he is contemplating their little tableau.

They make a mistake in both getting out of the car. If Max had got out as if he were actually going to go fishing and Vince had stayed and looked impatient, Lynn would have got back in. But they have forgotten that scenario now, they are only looking ahead and

Max is excited. Hamilton said it was to be Vince but why shouldn't he also have his share? There will be time; if he goes first there will be time. Now they are out of the car this occurs to Max. Lynn stands under the tree fiddling with her bag and the moon comes out at that moment - that is not good; hopefully it will go back behind a cloud. They advance towards her. The plan is obvious, grab her from both sides - Vince will put his hand over her mouth and then they'll hold her, the idea is that Max will hold her but he will have to tell Vince of the change of plan and it is this that is filling his thoughts - he should have looked where he was going.

The plan goes wrong. As they come towards her she realises immediately something is up and at that very moment Max puts his foot under a tree root and trips heavily. Vince leaps at her and grabs her, pulling her round in front while his hand is going for her mouth. But she has something in her hand, something she has pulled from her bag - it is a hairbrush, one of those damn things with a long thin metal handle - and holding it by the brush-end she stabs at Vince's head behind her, quickly stab stab stab and the next thing Vince is down on the sand howling.

Max is up though and coming at her. She drops her bag and runs towards the water. "I've got her," he thinks - at least he doesn't now have to argue with Vince. But she goes straight in. "I've got her all the same," thinks Max as he goes in after her, kicking clear of his sandals and taking the water in a muscular overarm crawl. To his surprise after a few strokes he sees that she is still ahead and swimming strongly but he has no doubt he will catch her - he is a good swimmer, proud of his prowess. They swim stroke for stroke out into the bay but she must exhaust soon he thinks and then he won't bother fucking around, he'll just drown the bitch. A midnight swim, who will know? Yes, that is an even better tableau for Arthur - his little white morsel face down in the water. Ah, she has tired at last, she is ahead and has stopped and he is coming up towards her, reaching for her and he has got her..... But somehow it isn't holding, something is tearing and it somehow doesn't happen. He is being held in some sort of headlock and in some bizarre dream he can hear her counting, "And one, and two, and three....." He is thrashing to come up and she is holding him there, bloody hell he can't do a thing and she is still counting, "And twelve and thirteen and fourteen." The more he thrashes the more he fails to make progress, goddamn water is swimmingly black around him and in his fury he takes a mouthful - it goes up his nose. "I'm drowning, she's drowning me."

And he suddenly feels fear. She is drowning him - how can this happen? This little girl is drowning him and he is helpless.

And all the time she goes on counting, just as they taught her to do for her life-saving medallion. Lynnette Morgan, five foot one, who could never have been a life guard because she is female and because she is too small, is subduing Max de Troy with techniques perfected on the golden beaches of her youth and there is nothing he can do about it.

Lynn comes ashore at the end of the promontory and sits shivering on a rock. She has on a pair of white underpants but the dress she was wearing has been ripped off. She is half naked in a dangerous land and her breath is coming in little sobs. She desperately tries to quieten them because she can hear footsteps. They are coming to get her again - she stumbles up ready to get back into the sea but a voice says, "Lynn?"

"Arthur. Arthur is that you?" she dissolves into his arms and he holds her; she starts shivering uncontrollably and he is shaking and they stand there for a moment holding on with all their might.

"Are you alright?"

"Yes I'm alright. But they…. Max….."

He whispers urgently, "We've got to get out of here. There's a fellow still up there on the sand. Did you hurt him somehow? I hope so."

He wraps her in his shirt and half carries, half leads her to his little car and she clings to him as he drives, feeling the warmth from his body, his sweat, as they drive frantic through the night in desperate fear of pursuers. They get back on the main road. There is traffic now; the sight of people driving here and there doing normal things quietens them for they are both still shaking and they drive at a normal pace back towards the marina. However when they get there the thought of what has happened suddenly rises again and swamps her.

"I think I drowned Max," she gulps.

"I wish you had," says Arthur. "But I fear you didn't. I saw him lying on his back in the water, gasping and moving his arms and legs….."

"Thank god," she says holding an unsteady hand to her mouth.

"No, you would have done the world a favour." He helps her up to his house and wraps a blanket round her. He holds her, they lie on his bed. They just lie there for ages and she stops shivering. "Tell me what happened," he says.

"They attacked me. I didn't do anything to them. I don't know why they suddenly ganged up on me, they only just met after years and years and suddenly they're attacking me together."

"They knew each other. Vince is Hamilton's driver now, has been for the last two or three weeks. The whole thing from beginning to end was a lie. It was a plan to lure you there."

"But why me? What did I ever do to them that made them want to attack me?"

"They didn't want you, they wanted me; they are evil men. Listen. Shhh," he says. He kisses her forehead. And then her cheek. Maybe he will kiss her lips. She looks at him and her lips are ready to be kissed, trembling even, but he seems to gather himself, to remember himself, even his arms slacken from around her to her distress. He lies on his back looking up and she lies on her side looking wonderingly at him.

"Max raped my sister," he says to the ceiling.

"Sheila!"

They look at each other and Lynn's fingers are in her mouth in horror. Arthur takes them out and kisses them and holds them in his hand. "She was always lovely even as a young girl; she was queen of the island when she was fourteen. Every man desired her and she was a laughing happy giddy girl but she was a good girl. Max wanted her. Sometimes she encouraged him. Sometimes she favoured someone else. No doubt it drives a man mad, that sort of flirtatiousness because Max was in his twenties, grown up. Now a young boy glows one day and sulks the next according to how his love treats him and a girl weeps in the night over some slight from a boy and the next day she sparkles like diamonds over some little kiss. But Max had forgotten all that. He wanted my sister and he intended to have her. He asked her if she wanted to go to a party up the coast in his car. All her friends were going by taxi but she thought it would be more queenlike to arrive by car so she went in his car but never arrived. She got home with blood down her leg and no longer a queen. When they arrested Max, he said they stopped at that beach by her invitation and had sex at her invitation and that he could barely keep up she was so insistent and then he produced two friends who said they'd had sex with her the night before and she was painted as a loose woman and he got off. She was devastated. It was all lies and people know it now. Max is a person to be avoided by women."

"I never knew any of this."

"No, because my family never talk about it. Dr Woodrow got up in court and said the injury to my sister could never have been caused if she was sexually experienced but the jury couldn't be sure. Dr Woodrow was a new man here at the time and wasn't known then as he is now and the defence lawyer tells the jury, 'Oh these girls! They're always leading a man on and then when it's over they pretend they never wanted it in the first place. These girls, they all wear the suggestive clothes to lead a man on and they toss their heads to fire a man up and then they turn round and make up stories.'

So there she was, held up as a woman who, even if you could believe what she said, brought it on herself. After the court case she wouldn't eat, she would vomit even looking at food and they took her back to Dr Woodrow. Once he was sure she wasn't pregnant, he said the best medicine for her was leaving the island. He told her to go to Martinique. Aunt Marion somehow managed to raise the fare for her - we didn't have much money in those days and you know some of the family wouldn't put in because they thought it was all Sheila's fault - her own family! Dr Woodrow had a friend in Martinique with a boutique and got her a job working there. He lent her, well gave her, $100. He said buy some clothes, make a life, don't come back until you can piss on all the people here.

When we saw her off on the plane her face was awful to see, as if she was being sent into exile, as if she couldn't understand what she had done wrong. For the first few months, there were brief letters full of misery and then suddenly nothing. Dr Woodrow found out she had left the boutique and we were all so worried and then one day we got a letter with a French stamp; she was in Paris. Some man had come into the boutique and seen her and said he would take her to Paris and make a model of her. Of course we all feared that things had just gone from bad to even worse. But then time went by and she started writing long letters full of strange and exciting things - we couldn't make head nor tale of, it was just a sort of fairy tale. And that Christmas she sent Tantie a cheque for two thousand US dollars and boxes full of expensive presents – and a French fashion magazine with her looking just beautiful. Suddenly she someone to be proud of, someone to show off around the district, our Sheila, the famous Paris model."

They lie again in silence. "But how could she ever get over it?" asks Lynn.

"She couldn't," says Arthur. "But it made her strong. Nothing else could ever be that bad. So she wears bikinis in the snow in Central Park and thinks this is only a little bodily discomfort. She stands for hours while someone fusses with a dress and thinks this guy is an asshole but he's not the worst man I've known. You see."

"Who knows what she would have been without that experience?" continues Arthur after a while. "She would probably be married with three kids living in a two roomed cabin and fretting perhaps, or maybe in a three roomed cabin and happy. Pregnant for the fourth time. Getting fat."

Lynn shakes her head in disbelief.

"Why not? People are happy with quite ordinary lives. Paradise isn't really a place until you have to leave it. Sheila is only gorgeous, thin, beautifully dressed and sophisticated because she was thrown out. If she'd stayed she would have lived the life of an island girl."

Silence again. Looking at each other. Hand in hand. And then he puts his face to hers and put his lips on hers. Lips like the soft warm petals of a flower. He puts both arms round her and kisses her again and she kisses him back, reaching for him, moaning with longing. She thinks she is being allowed to stay in paradise and that her whole body is meant only to be touched like this and kissed like this and her longing is like a shouting on the surface of her skin and all her body is like a tidal wave pushing forward with all its might.

At this point the light goes on and Lucas stands there in the act of unbuttoning his uniform and throwing off his hat. Instead of politely withdrawing, he bangs his hat back on saying, "Blow me. I've looked everywhere and here you are. Lynnette Trudy Morgan. I have a warrant for your arrest. I am to take you in charge and accompany you on the 5.30 am flight to Port Sophia. You are being deported."

Lynn doesn't stop crying and Arthur doesn't stop saying, "Lucas what are you doing, how can you do this? What kind of man are you?" on the brink of tears, beside himself, tearing at his clothes and hair in misery.

"Look knucklehead," says Lucas, "it need not have been like this but right now it's for the best. I've heard that Max and Vince are down at the station filing complaints. She was going to be deported anyway. Do you want her taken in charge by Sergeant de Troy and marched down the station with those two there? Now stop standing around like a useless lump and go next door and find her some clothes." In this way Lucas manages to get her out of Arthur's shirt into a dress, but such a dress; it is a silly frilly pink thing and not at all what Lucas has in mind for a journey. And that is it, no handbag. "Where's your bag?" he asks but she just keeps crying and crying. Bloody hell, she always has that big floppy bag about her and now it isn't to be found. He can't wait any longer, he knows the Sergeant is making out a warrant for her arrest. "Come on," he says. "And Arthur, take us in your car, save me getting Michael and making a spectacle out of the whole thing."

Lucas is fed up with Arthur. What does he mean by complicating things cuddling up to this white girl? It is just as well she is being deported or who knows what further carrying on there would have been. Does Aunt Marion know that her beloved nephew lies on his bed kissing little white girls and then stands around as if the world has come to an end when he is saved from an unfortunate liaison? He hopes Arthur will realise one day what a close shave he's had.

They go down to Arthur's car, with Lucas holding Lynn by the arm and Lynn crying now like her heart will break. Lucas wonders if, given half a chance, she might run away into the bushes, which is the sort of silly thing women do in a state like this. The Sergeant would have her handcuffed. At that thought, Lucas says to Arthur, "I think I had better handcuff her to me, lest the Sergeant pulls a fast one. I've got something up my sleeve the Sergeant doesn't know about but....." He leaves unsaid the subtext. He is not strongly built and the Sergeant is. "Here you are," he says to Lynn as he puts a cuff on her wrist and the other on his own. "Just like you see on TV." But the desperados on TV are handcuffed on both wrists and walk between two big grim-looking police officers - whereas here he is on his own and he will have to keep his wits about him to stay in control.

Control, that is what the battle is about. "Drop us down the road here and don't hang around," says Lucas to Arthur. "There is something ugly on foot and if I am not mistaken Anthony Hamilton is mixed up in it too. Go somewhere where there are people about, go and spend the night with Boss or Tantie. Now come on Lynn, you don't know it yet but this is for your own good."

When he walks into the station he finds Max sitting there talking to the Sergeant, still in wet clothes and not looking the best, his eyes red and vengeful. There is also a thickly built young man he knows from Lawrence to be Max's driver, holding his eyes and weeping. Max and the Sergeant stop and look at them and the atmosphere has a poisonous viciousness to it, especially as the girl gets behind his back and her hysteria goes up a notch.

"Well," says the Sergeant, "you have been at work Constable Frankland. You have brought in a wanted person, wanted for a savage assault on my brother and his friend."

Lucas allows a certain relaxation on his previous resolution of impenetrable gravity by letting out a loud laugh. "Well that would be a sad reflection on the natural order of things when a little slip of a girl starts beating up a man like your brother."

"Never you mind about that," says the Sergeant grimly. "You have done the right thing in bringing her in and turning her over to the authorities. Now you can be on your way."

"I am not turning her over to the authorities, I am the authority. This young lady is to be deported forthwith and I am acting in this instance as an Immigration Officer."

"Don't talk such rubbish. You sign off now and go home, you're not needed here."

"I am not here as a police constable. As I said, I am here as an Immigration Officer and my orders are to keep this young lady in the cells at this station until about 5 am when I shall be setting off with her for the airport."

"Constable Frankland, in the last few weeks you have been taking a great deal on yourself above and beyond what is required and now I am telling you to stop. I am <u>ordering</u> you to go."

"You can't order me to go because my authority is not coming from you."

The Sergeant by now is in the highest state of rage. He thrusts aside the stool he is sitting on which falls on the floor and he advances on Lucas clearly with the intention of taking Lynn bodily from him.

Lucas takes out his gun.

The Sergeant stops as if he has in reality been shot. "Where you getting that gun?"

"It is standard issue to Immigration Officers and I have formed the opinion that you are not listening to me." With his handcuffed hand he reaches into his pocket. "This badge I am now holding is not a police badge. With this badge, if anyone is about to strike the holder in the course of his duties, the holder is within his powers to discharge this weapon. In other words to shoot you dead if you come at me again like that."

There is complete silence. The Sergeant backs slowly up to his desk and he and Max look at Lucas with cold calculating stares. "You think you can hide behind that gun for the rest of your life?" says Max. "I think you'll find you have to sleep sometime."

"I'll sleep well enough when you're in jail," says Lucas.

Max laughs. "You haven't been listening to that girl? She may look like nothing but she's a most notorious woman."

"No I have not been listening to this girl, as this girl has been crying ever since I took her in charge. I have been listening to another woman who has been laying a rape charge against you with the Chief Constable."

"What's this?" asks the Sergeant looking sharply at his brother.

Max stares at Lucas puzzled for a moment and then shrugs his shoulders. Bloody Sandra no doubt, but before explanations are forthcoming, a car pulls up outside.

"Here come the doctor now," says the Sergeant. "We'll listen to what he have to say and then I'll charge the girl. Even if she is deported, we'll make sure that she is never coming back."

Doctor Woodrow comes in wearily; it is about 2 o'clock in the morning. "Hello," he greets Lucas and then looks at Lynn, "What's the problem here?"

"That is our suspected person. Over here is the persons she attack," says the Sergeant.

Dr Woodrow says nothing. He listens to Max's chest, looks in Vince's eyes. "I'll take this fellow with me," he says indicating Vince. "He needs urgent treatment." He comes over to where Lynn is sitting crying on a chair next to Lucas and still joined to him by the handcuffs. "Take those things off," he says. Lucas immediately obeys but keeps his eyes on the Sergeant. "What happened to you little girl?" he says but she can't answer. The doctor goes back to her bag and gets out a syringe.

Lucas says, "She has to be on a plane in four hours, she's being deported."

Dr Woodrow looks astonished. "Why, what happened?"

Lucas says, "She has been working on the island without a permit. There is a crackdown and I have my orders. Even though in the meantime I am told she has been attacked....."

"Rubbish. Rubbish," says the Sergeant cutting across Lucas. "She has indeed been working illegally. This woman has been plying her trade as a woman of the streets spreading vice and disease in the community and now she has turned her hand to robbing men by suggesting that they all go swimming where no-one will see and then blinding them so she could steal their wallets."

The doctor stands stock still and turns to look at the Sergeant as behind him Lucas feels his mouth drop open and his heart race. "Is that right?" is all the doctor says in a rather strained way. "A woman of the streets!"

"Oh I assure you doctor, I have been with her myself and a dose of clap I get from it too. She have the worst reputation and such an innocent face that a man don't suspect nothing and then he turns round and finds the money gone from his wallet, money for his children and his wife and them. No wonder they deporting her."

"You are deporting her for being a prostitute?" the doctor asks Lucas, looking at him with a curious fixity.

"Certainly not," cries Lucas incensed almost beyond bearing at what he has heard. "She has been working for wages on Boss's boat and on the Golden Dawn, that's all. That's why she's being deported."

"Good," says the doctor for no particular reason. "Yes well I must give her something to calm her down." He gives her a shot.

"I'm amazed you would worry yourself over such trash," says the Sergeant.

"It's my job to treat trash, which is why I'm taking this fellow with me even though I believe him to be as big a bit of trash as you and your brother."

Both the Sergeant and Max bristle dangerously and stand up.

"Before you tell me any more lies, I have to say one thing," says the doctor raising his voice and he has a loud and powerful voice. "I have the ear of certain people in this island, not that that amounts to much. But, until the next election when I intend to stand myself, I shall use the ears of those I have respect for, such as the Chief Constable, to tell them what you have just told me about this young woman and then to tell the world the following facts. That this very afternoon I examined this girl and found her an intact virgin. You'd barely get a finger up there let alone a posse of men. So you

Sergeant are a liar. As for your brother, I believe he has been accused of rape by the wife of that fellow who used to manage the Frangipani, the woman I believe having come by a film that was made of the event so I expect he will be in jail before long where he rightly belongs. Now," he says to Vince, "you can come with me, unless you want to go blind."

Vince whines and weeps, "I was just doing Mr Hamilton's orders, just what that Sandra says she wanted," and allows himself to be led away. Out of the spinning silence.

Lynn is now sobbing more quietly and Lucas sits beside her with one hand on her arm and with the other he has hold of his gun under his tunic. He is as tense as a bow string. He sits watching the Sergeant and his brother. The Sergeant and Max have sat back down and are staring at each other as if things have been said that are too surprising to be taken in. For a whole long minute nothing is said. And then the Sergeant leaps to his feet and launches himself at his brother's throat. Max dodges, manages to unlatch himself and flees out of the station. The Sergeant runs after him, inarticulate words howling from him. They can hear scrapping and crunching and shouting going down the road and then silence. Lucas goes to the window. He says nothing. He goes back and sits on the chair next to Lynn. He feels in shock. He sits there for a long time just looking in front of him. He has been forced to take out his gun and point it at a superior officer. Then he has heard that superior officer tell a series of blatant lies - a policeman and lying bare-faced! He can barely believe it, it is the most shocking thing of all. He always knew the Sergeant had a selective approach to law enforcement and he knows that the Chief Constable has suspicions that this stems from a generally corrupt attitude in the force but he himself has never actually caught the Sergeant in blatant illegality before. Suddenly there he is saying Lynn is a thief, a prostitute; all lies but so hard to defend against when made by a man in authority, a police officer. And then the doctor's calm assertion, an assertion that everyone will believe implicitly because he is a man who now has tremendous respect.

What will happen? What will happen to the Sergeant? Can a society really continue to operate with such officials when their corruption has been revealed? Max is finished. Probably the government is finished but if not then it has lost so much credibility that the whole political system will be like a pack of cards just waiting to fall over in the future. To continue on as it is, the system must be in danger of revolution, assassination, terrible turmoil. The enormity of it. And what is to happen to himself? Now he has seen the rotten side of the police force, he has no desire to stay if there are not to be changes. But if there are changes, if things come right, then who knows? For a moment he half persuades himself that he might gain a promotion from the whole thing. Too early to say but he knows that if things do change then he wants to be part of what happens next. He is young he knows, but he has played a part and when a new age dawns he will be there with a good reputation. "But they need to clean up the force." Lynn is looking at him and he realises he's spoken aloud. "Things will change," he says. "We will have respect for law and order and there won't be these white folks getting out their chequebooks saying 'And how much would you like for yourself?' Lock up a few white folks and scare a few more so we are seen not as figures of fun but as a force in our own land. There's too much laughing at us you see; all that laughing is going to stop. The police officers in London, you never see people laugh at them. No they pull you over and ask you most particular questions in that manner they have and you'd never think to crack a smile or put your hand in your pocket."

Her mouth is trapped in some drug that is calming her. He's glad to see she isn't weeping any more and he gets up and starts walking up and down. "Everyone despises the Sergeant. Now everyone will know he is a crook but will anyone do anything about it? There will be new people standing for parliament and who knows who will be our next Premier? But if someone like Dr Woodrow gets elected he would as soon let them promote a man like the Sergeant to Chief Constable as fly to the moon. There will be a new beginning with men like that. Even though we might lose a good doctor to other duties, at least there will be respect and dignity here. And if that happens then there will be other doctors coming from England and America and Canada to practice. This could be such a good place to live if it was run properly; a place to raise families, a place to gather at each other's houses to gossip and play music. But people should lead ordered lives when they are undertaking a public duty. Not screwing around and everyone on with one and all and money from out of the till. What kind of impression does that give? It allows people like Anthony Hamilton to come here and take people for suckers with his sex games and make a lot of money. It turns the black man into a joke, a recreation for the upper classes. Something to look at and point at and whisper about. But there's no respect.

You've got to have respect. That's my resolution. From now on I shall demand respect from the people I deal with, it."

He has been thinking aloud as he paces the floor, his shoulders back, resolving on the new walk he will walk, the new bearing he will have. After a while he looks at her. "Don't go to sleep," he commands in his new tone. Her mind comes back with a jerk and her eyes fill with tears automatically. Oh damn. Lucas gives up on the new manner for now and looks at the clock. It is quarter to four. Michael is booked to arrive in an hour.

He sits back down. "Hey," he says patting her arm. "It's not personal this deportation. I'm taking you back to Port Sophia which is the last place you had legal entry and then they'll work out what to do from then on. Maybe your family can send you the fare."

"I've got the fare in the bank but....." She moves her mouth inarticulately.

"This is just something that is happening. Jim will have to leave too; he's been working at the Expo and on the Golden Dawn. And they are investigating others; Karlo was seen serving drinks at the Lotus Room so they are looking into that. Everyone is being looked at; it is how things are now. You shouldn't have been working. You've got to understand, there are people on this island without a crust of bread to their mouths and we can't have young people swarming in from overseas taking the jobs and no regulation to it at all. Boss is getting up some sort of committee to take to the Government about how much the yachties put back into the economy. Everyone is in ferment but it's too late for you, I had to move quickly. Losing your passport and then not getting a replacement makes it your own fault to some extent, because you have come to official notice. And then, I have to speak personally and maybe out of turn, you may see it one day as the best thing that could happen. I know you are feeling some sorrow just now and how much is the shock of being attacked by Max I don't know. But I suspect some of it is my cousin Arthur who had no right to go taking liberties with you on his bed, because he knows himself that a friendship like that is not a thing that is ever going to work."

Her eyes swim and the tears run silently down her face.

"I have to be cruel to be kind," he says. "It never does work. Now why don't you take up with Jim? He's a nice young man - that would be just been the thing. You and Jim are from the same class, the same background, you have things in common. I think you could live together in England in a nice little brick house on the coast,

Folkstone perhaps, where he can keep his boat. And he'd put on his suit everyday and go up by train to the city and you'd dust the house and plant cottagey things in the garden and there'd be climbing stuff growing up the sides over leadlight latticed windows and inside you'd have a nice navy and grey sofa and two matching chairs and a polished dining table and it would all smell nice like waxpolish. I know that white people can live like that, with a Morris car in the garage. I've been in that sort of house. I had a white friend in England who invited me to his home and his parents were very polite.

"And living with Arthur, everyone would be just as polite and cautious, not bringing out the best cups in case he breaks them. And not quite knowing what to talk about, not wanting to talk about the latest books in case it transpires that he can't read. Or films and plays because they think we don't have such things in the Caribbean and music is a problem because their only copy of Island in the Sun is scratched. Think how you'd feel, year in year out, explaining that he actually went to a normal school and has read Lord of the Rings, loves Van Morrison and has seen Easy Rider thirteen times. You have to be realistic. Love doesn't conquer all, that's a lie. I saw love like that in England, love getting chipped away by little irritations. And then there's the big irritations. How are you going to put up with the name calling? The people who feel outraged enough to explain miscegenation to you in the street, or say appalling things like 'It's his big dick, isn't it? I've heard they've all got one. And that a certain sort of woman finds that irresistible' - looking at you, looking at a certain sort of woman. How would you feel? And what about work? He's not going to be putting on a suit; no he'll put on a uniform and go off to work on the Underground. That's the kind of jobs West Indians have to do. Don't think they would have him in a respectable bar, managing anything like that; that would be unheard of. And you can't count on Sheila; she's inherited the prejudices of my aunt when it comes to mixed marriage. What's all that going to do to him? And you'll have to get a job typing in an office; you'll never live on what he brings in. Oh damn," as the tears turned to streamlets and then to rivers. "One day maybe it will be different," he says. "You have to live in hope. We all have to live in hope."

"My," says Michael looking at them as they climb in the back of his taxi, "there certainly are a few glum faces around tonight." It is still full dark without even a glimmer of light in the east as they bowl along the coast.

"This is a job," says Lucas, "getting up this early."

"I am not getting up this early, because I never even been to bed. I been up all the night ferrying people here and there." They are passing the turnoff to the swamp. "Young Arthur now, his car was commandeered by Boss who have been rushing around on account your young lady, so I brought him here myself in the middle of the night."

"Who? Arthur?" says Lucas. "Here?"

"Yes," says Michael. "He go in there. He don't say why. Nothing in there but swamp. The moon come out fortunately, otherwise what's he going to do? In the dark! Beats me. Boy, he get eaten alive by insects!"

Lucas becomes agitated and concerned. "The boy is mad. I told him to stay with other people. Who knows what all these evil men around are capable of? There'll be murder done before the night is out, I just know it. And what does he do? Goes off in there. All alone. Because he likes to watch the dawn and the birds fly out. I don't know why I bother." He reconsiders. "However now I come to think it through, I think Arthur is the last person on anyone's mind at the moment."

He is the first person on Lynn's however. She hears what Lucas is saying. Arthur has gone off in there to watch the birds - he has given up on her. She continues to stare back in the direction of the swamp for some time, her heart aching with longing and regret.

They arrive at the airport and get out at a corrugated iron hangar where check-in and various other functions take place amid scenes of bustle and confusion. A couple of minibuses have disgorged hotel patrons, most of whom are sensibly dressed for travel. Outside Lynn sees Arthur's car but she knows now that there will be no Arthur, no he isn't coming to say goodbye, it seems there is nothing more to say. However just about everyone else is there, a whole crowd of people from the Frangipani. Rae throws her arms around Lynn's neck and breaks into loud genuine tears. "Hey stop that, stop that," says Lucas "you'll set her off." But it is too late. "Now look at what you've done! The doctor gave her something to calm her down and now you've started her going again."

"How can you do this?" cries Rae.

"Because I'm an officer of the law and this is my duty," says Lucas harassed and reflecting suddenly how hard it is to keep respect for himself and the law when so many people have the wrong attitude to policing. Her friends gather round the weeping figure of Lynn while Lucas tries to fight with the bureaucracy above the pandemonium. "Two tickets," he keeps repeating over the sound of wailing women, "there should be two tickets to Port Sophia. Yes I'm going..... I'm accompanying her to..... OK yes that's right, one return and one single to..... Oh for heaven's sake." It is hard to manage things with any dignity when everything is so inefficient and where so many people are trying to get in on the act of telling him what a terrible thing he is doing, to say nothing of the tourists standing around staring as if the whole thing is a theatrical performance. "No," repeats Lucas, "we have to sit together. For god's sake, what's the point of me accompanying her under arrest if you are putting us in separate seats. You will have to move someone else around. The Chief Constable will be rung if you don't co-operate - you will never be allowed off the ground." Eventually his threats take effect as the time for boarding arrives.

"Now look at you," he turns to the group of people surrounding Lynn. "You say you're her friends but not one of you has brought out any clothes or things for her. Look, she has lost her bag and hasn't even a handkerchief for all the crying she's doing. Should an officer of the law be constantly using his own handkerchief to wipe the face of his prisoner when there are friends of hers who could have rallied round? And the only thing she's wearing is this silly pink thing and they'll be sending her to England in winter for heaven's sake. Did no-one think to bring her a cardigan or something?"

Everyone looks crestfallen but it has been a momentous night of sleepless commotion and by now woe and lamentation are all they are able to contribute. Rae in particular is not to be pacified; she must weep at full bore right up to the door of the plane and reveal all her sorrows. These include the revulsion over that monster Max, the sheer evil of the man and the anguish over Merville, the humiliation, the pain. Yes and then Arthur, not even he was to be relied on, running out of the bar and leaving her there to run it on her own, in the state she was in and after all she had been through! "Don't ever rely on any of these West Indian men, never never trust any of them. How lucky that none of them has started telling you lies, pretending that they love you. Never believe it. It's all lies, lies and more lies. That sweet-talking, those kisses - none of it is true. They just want a trophy to boast to their friends about but then when the least unpleasantness arises, like the family hears about it and starts making a fuss, they just give up and don't come around any more. And in the meantime you've fallen in love. These men here are bastards, bastards, all of them. They wouldn't even know what love is. It's just sex and showing off. I wish I was dead."

Rae weeps of her despair, weeps that her life is now over and only dreariness and exile await her. Poor Rae. All those tears from the terror of being left floating on the margins. Of course all these years later I could, if I wanted, roll out the sort of epilogue that you see during the end credits of films, which tell you what happened to all the people in the story. So you leave the cinema imagining you know which of them lived happily ever after and which didn't. But that's all crap. Even those who were happy for some of the time were unhappy at others. It's more than 30 years ago and some of the people in this story are dead for christ's sake. How happy ever after is that?

The best any of us can hope for is to survive. We are the lucky ones. But back then when we were young it seemed somehow more heroic to be swirled around and sucked under by the momentum of the vortex. Just surviving - that was some dull thing that only happened to old people.

But it's no good telling Rae that. For one thing, she couldn't exist without the drama of the moment. And for another, she knows instinctively that the poignancy of a missed destiny is the Great Shipwreck that makes our lives somehow fabulous and noteworthy. Whereas the strange thing about real life is that when our destiny <u>is</u> fulfilled, we end up living quite prosaic and ordinary existences.

And it's no good telling Lynn anything either. Because Rae has set her off again and she is weeping ever more desperately, as if the torrent of her feelings must flood the world. Sobbing, shuddering and gulping, she is helped on board the plane where a stare of disapproval from the entire plane is fixed on Lucas. Murmurs of hostility comes from incensed passengers as the coloured policeman shunts his blonde-headed prisoner into a window seat. He sits down on the outside as his charge weeps unrestrainedly curled in misery against the window. "She'll have to do up her seatbelt," says the hostess severely and he leans over to do it but a white woman tourist nearby says, "Gasp, take your hands off her" and leans over and does it herself and gives him such a look; despicable black man touching lovely young white girl. Yes he knows that look. "If I've saved Arthur from that look at least I've done something," he thinks.

The plane's propellers start to turn and it taxies down the short runway. Then the whine becomes a howl as it thunders into the dawn sky. As they circle, the light is unfolding by the minute. The plane turns under the lee of the mountain and starts heading back towards Fort John, flying as it does so over the swamp.

"What does that mean?" says a woman behind them to her partner. "Look. Down there, someone's made letters. LTM. ILT. Is it one word or two?" Several passengers are staring down out of their windows.

Lucas looks over Lynn's huddled form. Down in the swamp someone has been rearranging the rope guidepaths. The early morning light makes the water shine white where the six letters appear, three above and three below. "What has that boy been up to?" he says aloud and Lynn stops sobbing. "Look what he's done! He'll be in trouble for that."

"LT Milt," says the man behind. "It'll be an advertisement for something. Probably milk. They spelt it wrong, they spell everything wrong - it's the way they talk."

Lynn is looking down arrested, blotting her eyes.

"LTM. They're your initials," says Lucas suspiciously looking at her. "What has that stupid boy been up to?"

She stares at the letters, her hand on the glass. Suddenly the ring on her finger floats into focus. Her heart seems to stop with a jolt. Her head throbs. Realisation contracts her chest until she can barely breathe - she thinks she might faint as blood throbs rhythmically in her ears. "Lovest Thou Me," she murmurs.

"What the hell is ILT? They're not Arthur's initials?" continues Lucas without hearing her, cross at the thought of all that illegality going on down there and his own cousin responsible.

Yes what is that? ILT? ILT? She puts her other hand to her head and her brow furrows with concentration. For a moment her brain is as blank and as smooth as the water below and it's possible at that moment that some tendril, some thought wave, some extrasensory perception passes between her and an unseen figure far below in the swamp because she doesn't even know where it comes from; it is suddenly with her, warm and huge and enveloping. "I," she draws the letter and then a heart on the window, "I Lovest Thou." She stoops her head to kiss the glass.

In an instant everything has been transformed. Bleak departures are now bound to be followed by homecomings in a storm of rosepetals. The rise of hope removes every grief because once there is love, how can there fail to be happiness for ever? And ever. Hallilujah.

Lucas sees that she has stopped crying and that her face is now lit by a radiant smile. "Oh god, I give up," he says throwing himself backwards and putting down his seat. "I give up. What's the point?" He lies there in total resignation. What more can anyone do? He suddenly realises how tired he is. Give up, give in and let them have each other. Let them learn the hard way, it is too difficult and he is far too tired. So very tired.

The initial disapproval of the plane towards him is nothing to the outrage it feels when Lucas gives up. Never is there less respect for the law or an officer of the law than when he lies back, lets fate take its course and goes to sleep. And never is sympathy for a poor maltreated white girl dissipated so quickly as when she slides sideways and goes to sleep as well, the work of a moment for the two of them after a night of stress and watchfulness. His arm thrown out encloses her frilly pinkness, her head ends up on his shoulder, their two heads of black and blonde curls combine and they sleep together in perfect harmony, their breath goes out and in together, their chests rise and fall as one.

"Good morning everyone, this is your captain speaking....."

No-one pays any attention to this voice breaking in upon such an unbelievable spectacle. The details of the flight are unimportant compared to the traumatic happenings within the body of the plane. Who has allowed such a thing, who is responsible, who must put a stop to it? Passengers strain red eyed in the early morning to glare and mutter, two black-skinned business men turn their heads to bluster, the white tourists gasp aloud in distress, the hostesses go pale and confer, everyone is in turmoil.

"If you look to your right, you will any moment see the sun coming up over one of the largest volcanic mountains in the region....."

But the voice falls on deaf ears; no-one is looking outwards. They are blind to the mountain and to the sun that has just burst forth above it. They are blind to the spike of light which is soaring up like a trumpet's awakening to heaven. Deaf and blind, all of them.

"We are expecting a fairly uneventful passage, however I suggest that you keep your seat belts fastened in case we experience some initial turbulence....."

How can any of us know what will happen in the future? The trials we were expecting may never eventuate. The problems we encounter we may never have foreseen. The traps and hurdles are different for every generation.

"So welcome one and all, to a whole new day."